The Cradle Operation

The Jack Series

Todd LeRoux

Published by Todd LeRoux, 2024.

THE CRADLE OPERATION

First edition. February 27, 2024.

Copyright © 2024 Todd LeRoux.

ISBN: 978-1738317561

Written by Todd LeRoux.

Also by Todd LeRoux

The Jack Series
The Cradle Operation

The Quest
The Beginning

Standalone
The Jinn
The Wanderer
The Quest
The Island

Watch for more at https://www.toddleroux.com/.

For all the men and women who sacrifice so much for our freedom. Thank you. It seems to be so little to show our appreciation.

The Cradle Operation
A novel by
Todd LeRoux.

Chapter 1

†

THE LAKE WAS PERFECT; British Columbia was like a pitcher, an ideal place to bring a young family needing a vacation.

Jack, a young, loving father and husband laughed at his wife as she chased their son Junior around the picnic table. Jack watched as the woman he loved caught and picked up his son. He didn't know how he could love her or his son any more than he did. For Jack, the annual trip to the Okanogan lakes of the western province of Canada was the perfect way for his young family to release the tension of their lives in the city. It was on this lake twelve years ago he had met Betty; he fell in love with and married her. The couple loved the lakes and always came to Okanogan Lake in British Colombia. It allowed him time to unwind from chasing stories, stories the governments of the world wanted to keep quiet. It also gave his lawyer wife time to relax from putting corrupt cops away. Unlike the other trips to the lake, they brought her nephew with them this time. Jack and Betty, his wife, felt terrible for the kid, his father wasn't in the picture, and his mother, Betty's sister, did nothing but screech and scream at the kid all day. Tommy was a bright, intelligent child. He always asked questions and was great with Junior. Tommy laughed as he watched Betty and Junior play chase around the picnic table. Once she had caught the young boy for the second time, Jack decided it would be fun to have a game of catch. As Jack watched his son throw the ball to his cousin, the boys laughed. Jack wondered how it could get any better than this day. It's days like this that he would remember when he was old, he thought. Junior tossed the ball to his dad. Jack caught the ball and then threw it to Tommy.

A tall man sat behind a desk and read what two men found in the house sitting on a tree-lined street in the Canadian city of Toronto. The house belonged to Jack and his wife, Betty; it is where they lived with their son. The men knew what to look for. It didn't take long for the two men to find it.

"We have it, sir; it's only a copy of the story, sir." The tall man with dark brown hair said into an encrypted cell phone. As he looked at his companion, his partner was a short emaciated-looking man with a sharp, bird-like way of looking at everything. On more than one occasion, the taller of the two men had watched as the short one would smile while they killed some reporter or lawyer. These two men have even been sent to kill another country's politicians. They always killed after they had finished asking the questions that needed answers. The taller man always talked to Hollyford, he was the voice of the team, and it was this man Hollyford would give the orders to. When he received the orders, Hollyford would never use a name, hell if you tried to find his or the other man's name, you could search every computer and payroll database in Washington. You would never see these two men.

Simply put, these men did not exist; when the one who took the orders looked over to his partner, he knew that he was working with a man that would have been a serial killer. The taller man wondered how his partner had fallen into the hands of G.W. Hollyford. He wondered if there would be a time when he would be ordered to kill his partner. The tall man wouldn't care. He didn't like his partner anyway.

"Good, get out and burn the place to the ground." Came the sharp order of G.W. Hollyford, the director of the Central Intelligence Agency, who at the time was sitting in Langley, Virginia, holding another encrypted phone. In his other hand was a glass of forty-year-old single malt scotch. Hollyford smiled as he looked at the nude twenty-something call girl who was crying as she fought against the handcuffs binding her to the bed. Her right eye was swelling shut, and she had bite marks on both breasts. Her bottom lip was going to need stitches to close the cut from a vicious punch Hollyford had dealt her when she refused to say she loved his abuse. Looking at the door, Hollyford nodded to the suited man who had opened it and glanced in, confirming the night's entertainment had concluded.

Without a word, the fit man went over to the bed and started to unlock the handcuffs holding the struggling woman to the bed. When he had freed one hand, she lashed out, trying to scratch him. With the viciousness that brought this man to the attention of Hollyford, the suited man smiled as he punched the blond behind her right ear, dropping her into the embrace of unconsciousness.

"Drop the body where she'll be found; that will keep the local cops and Hoover's retards running around in circles," Hollyford told this man as he watched as his personal killer draped the blond call girl over one massive shoulder. Turning, Hollyford grabbed another phone. He only said two words into the handset, then hung it up and leaned back in his chair, smiling. On the other end of the phone in British Columbia, a man wearing ended the call and nodded to his partner; one hour later, Jack and Betty were dead, both shot in the head. The killers placed the loving parents of Jack Junior back on the houseboat they rented for their holiday. The boat had been sailed out to the deepest part of the lake and then sunk with the help of a small pack of explosives. Nothing of the family and the rented houseboat was ever seen again. G.W. Hollyford smiled as he watched the team of killers silently work. The two boys were taken away from the lake unconscious.

Jack Jr had no idea what was going on; he knew whatever it was, it couldn't be good because Tommy was crying. Jack Jr thought it must be bad and cried for his mom. Both boys watched as another man walked over to them. He smiled and then jabbed needles into their legs. Tommy screamed, and Jack Jr tried to scream, but the needle man slapped him. The two boys found themselves in the hands of killers, who took them to a small airport to be spirited away to a center where other men and women waited for them. At first, Jack Jr thought these people would be friendly to him and Tommy. Then a man dressed as a doctor entered his and Tommy's room. Jack Jr liked his doctor at home; he was nice to Jack. He would give Jack a treat when he was good, so Jack thought this man would be nice to him. With the doctor was a lady; this lady wore a long black dress; she was pushing a machine of some kind on a cart with her. He watched as some other men came in the room, and they took Tommy away; then things became bad, real bad.

The doctor and the mean lady hooked Jack Jr to the machine, and with others watching, they started to ask what his name was. Jack Jr knew his name and his mother and father's names. When Jack Jr told the woman and the doctor his name and his mother and father's name, the doctor turned the machine on, and he would scream. It felt like his teeth were going to explode from his mouth. At one point, it hurt so much that Jack Jr messed himself. The mean lady started to scream at him then she slapped him. Jack was strapped down, he wanted to run, but he couldn't move. He didn't understand why they would keep hurting him when he answered their questions. The mean woman called him stupid and a retard. Jack knew this was something terrible people did; he remembered his mommy telling him never to use these names because it was wrong. Then the doctor would ask him the same questions, and when he answered, they would turn the machine on, and Jack Jr would scream. Jack Jr didn't know how long this went on. One day the mean lady came in the room and told him if he didn't smarten up, they were going to turn the machine on and leave it on just to see what would happen.

That was the day Jack was asked what his name was. He couldn't remember.

When the lady in the black dress asked him who his parents were, Jack couldn't remember having any parents. Jack Jr was positive he didn't have a mom or dad. The woman smiled and came over to the bed and smoothed his sweat-covered brow; she took all the pads off his head and chest she told Jack that he was a good boy, and she told him he didn't have a mother or father. The doctor was smiling and nodding to a mirror on one wall. The woman holding him and kissing his brow told him his name was John Smyth, that he had always been John Smyth. She told him he was exceptional and he was in a special school. She told him this school was for only the most remarkable boys, and he had one more test to pass. The doctor told John to sleep and that they would see him in the morning. For some reason, the young boy who not so long ago was Jack Jr didn't want to see the lady go. He held her hand until she bent over and kissed him again; she told him it was all right.

"John, my lovely boy, everything is going to be alright." The woman in the black dress said as she kissed his forehead.

John's head still hurt, and his shoulders ached, so he curled up and tried to remember the lady's face. In the morning, a new man came with another machine, at first. John was scared and tried to hide in a corner; John could see that there were lots of needles on the cart, but he didn't like the needles. However, when the lady came into the room, she showed him that if he answered the questions correctly, the machine would only flash pretty lights; John didn't like the needles. The lady told John she would be there the whole time and kissed John's forehead. The new doctor and John had made a game out of it. For weeks, the man came when the sun started rising and would not leave until it was dark.

The whole time the lady in the black dress sat and watched when it was time for them to go for the night. The lady in the black dress would hold John and tell him he was a good boy and she was proud of him, then she would kiss his head and leave, always locking the door behind her. John started to love the lady who always wore a black dress. He thought she was his mother. John began to wake one hour before the man with the needles would come in just to see her, always her. John couldn't remember his mother or father; he couldn't even remember his own name, his real name. John knew he had come here with another boy, an older boy. That older boy was starting to fade from John's memory, he couldn't remember who the other boy was, and he didn't care as long as he got to spend time with her. Weeks passed, and the only thing John cared about was seeing the lady in the black dress. He stopped caring about the doctor and their game. He didn't even care about the pain the needles caused when the doctor used them.

One day only the lady came into his room without the man and the cart of needles. She told John that some men had snuck into the school, the black dress lady was crying and told John they wanted to hurt her. John wasn't scared of the men. All he could think was he would kill them if they tried to hurt the lady...the lady who saved him. Saved him from what John didn't know. He knew it must have been bad. Nobody was going to hurt her, John didn't know how he would save her, but he was willing to die trying. Taking John by the hand, the lady in the black dress was leading him out of his room when two men stepped around the corner of the hallway. With them was an older boy; John could see the boy holding a large knife in his right hand. The lady John now thought of as his mom handed him a knife. She kissed the top of his head and told him that he was going to have to save her. John nodded and watched the other boy walk down the hall toward the lady. The other boy's shoulders were hunched, and he held his knife out in front of his body. John didn't know what had happened, but one second he was standing in front of the lady he was going to protect, and the next thing John knew was standing over the body of a boy he almost recognized, and his hands were covered in blood. He was holding a knife. The boy's eyes were open, but they didn't see anything; John turned just in time to see the lady in the black dress wave to him, then turn and walk out a door. After that, he never saw the lady again, and he was taken to another building where he started school. In time, John forgot about the lady in the black dress and the boy he killed to save her. John even forgot what the men did to him after the lady in the black dress left.

Chapter 2

WHEN JOHN WAS YOUNGER, he never tried to think of his parents or the past. Back then, all John wanted to do was please his teachers and the director of the orphanage. Now when he tried to remember childhood, his trying to remember would result in an intense point of pain. The pain was so bad it left him blind and curled in a fetal pose for hours. Though John asked many times, he was always told that no information could be found about his mother or father. The director of the orphanage where John grew up often added that he might be the result of a girl getting into trouble with the wrong sort of boy. The director would say that he suspected she was forced to give him up by her family. Though the man who was the head of the school tried to look concerned for the boys at the orphanage. The director could never really pull off the fake concern. It never really came through as genuine concern. It seemed to John to be an act. When John was younger, he wished he could have known his mother. He often wondered what she looked like and if she ever asked about him. The others in the orphanage with him were in the same boat, all the boys had been given up by young unwed mothers, or so they were told.

The only woman John remembered was his cultural teacher. He knew there had been another woman, but for some reason, he couldn't quite bring her face or name to the front of his memory. Instead of a face, he would remember a black dress. His cultural teacher had always treated him friendly along with the others she taught. She taught of other cultures in the world, most of them were old, and at one time, each had led the world in one way or another.

Then she spoke of others, these were newer cultures, and of the men that sought to force their views on the world, most of these men were utopians, men who wanted to remake the world. This perfect world often was drenched in the blood of the helpless and different, his teacher told her class.

Hitler was one of these utopians. It was his quest to bring Germany to the head of the world; he had started the Second World War. Along with his wish to rule the world, it was also his sick desire to end the existence of the Jewish race. It was Hitler's belief the Jews were at fault for Germany being crushed under economic failure. Six million men, women, and children were murdered by that madman and his insane pack of disciples. Another six million were killed because he thought they weren't worth having around.

Along with the Jews, people said to be less than human were placed in gas chambers and acid showers. These people consisted of gypsies and people of African descent. If he had crossed the Atlantic, the North American Natives North Americans would indeed have fallen into the less-than-human category this sick bastard lived by.

Jozef Stalin was another; this madman ordered the killing of twenty-three million of his fellow Russians. Pol Pot killed one point seven million in his own country. Another of these absurd little mad men was Kim IL Sung from North Korea; he has the blood of over one and a half million men, women, and children staining his soul. John's teacher asked one question on the final exam in his senior year. The question was what would cause a human to commit this level of evil that has seen these men into hell for an eternity of torture. Sitting in the classroom, John could remember looking out the window and watching as a cat stalked a small bird, which was intently listening for worms. The bird had no idea it was being hunted until it was too late. John watched as the cat crushed the small bird in its teeth. He received an 'A' on the exam for his answer; John wrote men committed such vast evil because, for some, it was their nature. Like the cat, these men were born with something wrong. In today's modern education system, a teacher or guidance counselor would have seen the symptoms they would have raised concerns about the child. Hitler's actions towards others would have seen him being placed in an institution. We would like to think this would have happened to the others, but some of the best psychotics hide their true nature well.

In the afternoons at the orphanage, John and the others had physical education. This is where their instructors would run them through an obstacle course, screaming at them to get lower or to push harder. John enjoyed this; he could run harder and longer than most of the others. John had to run a course until his time was the same as the instructors had on their sheets. Rarely did John ever have to redo an obstacle course because he failed to meet the time. In most obstacle courses, John beat the time challenge and set new times. In the winter, you had to run with a full pack on through a water-filled ditch; it was deep enough the water was chest high. John then ran the course he was placed on after the water-filled ditch. John ran all the obstacle courses he was placed on. He never failed at one; by the time spring came, he was doing most of the courses in his tee shirt and track shorts. After the physical education was over, John would have to run to the rifle range for target practice. When on the range, John was expected to hit the center of the target while loud music was being played and others were shooting rifles on automatic fire. Through it all, John seemed to thrive; some of his instructors thought he'd grown to like the adversity, the challenge. John knew he was being groomed for the army or some kind of service. He became stronger and stronger as the years went by. While John was in hand-to-hand combat school, he broke another boy's arm. This boy hurt a smaller classmate and had laughed about it during dinner the night before, so John decided he would teach the bully a lesson. That night John didn't see the bully at dinner or any day after that. What John didn't know was the way the arm had broken. The bones would have needed a plate and pins to heal correctly. The bully's arm would have been weak for the rest of his life, which was unacceptable to the people who ran the school. It was decided the bully would be killed and buried in a shallow grave in the Ruby Valley of Montana. By the time he was eighteen and ready to leave the orphanage, John could outrun and outshoot all of his instructors. He had been trained to fight, and as in all things he had been trained to do, he excelled at it. By the time John graduated at nineteen, most of his instructors had feared John in hand-to-hand combat. His speed and what his instructors thought of as a love of violence had, on more than one occasion, put an instructor in the hospital.

The first man John could remember that he really had a bad feeling about was a man named Mike Styles. When John met this man for the first time, he thought of a giant snake he once saw in a film about the jungles of Asia. John couldn't tell when he knew, but the reality was this man only wanted him because he was an orphan was apparent. John had no one to worry over him, and this Mike Styles liked that. John was sure he had it right from the first time he shook Mike's hand at the airport.

"You're going to do good things for me," Mike told John. When John turned and asked what they might be, Mike just smiled and walked away; mistake number one, John thought. On John's twentieth birthday, he was taken out of the orphanage and told he was expendable. Mike Styles told John that he was to do as he was told and to keep his mouth shut if he wanted to live long. Standing in front of Mike, John never said anything. He refused to look away when Mike finished his little intimidating speech. John knew he shouldn't have pushed it, but both he and Mike got into a stare-down contest, and it had been Mike who looked away first. Smiling, John picked his bag up, turned his back on Mike, and climbed into the van waiting for them. Waiting for Mike to get into the van, the driver, a man with the largest set of shoulders John had ever seen, made eye contact with John and arched one eyebrow as if saying you are going to regret that boy. He didn't know why but John thought the driver was probably right, but John thought of Mike as an asshole who needed to be knocked down a few pegs.

Mike told John they were going to relocate to Hong Kong; from there, he would be doing his job, that he would do it well for the sake of America and her Allies. For the first six years, he did what he had been told to do and killed who Mike said the orders told him to kill. Mike and the others who ran his unit showed him orders when he first started with the team. After two years, John didn't want to see the orders. He was told the people he was sent out to kill were a danger to the U.S. and its allies. For John, that was all he needed to hear; none of the people John was to kill had been in China. He had been sent to Russia and South Korea, also to the islands that make up the archipelago of Indonesia. There had been numerous other places where he had left a body or parts of his victim. It had depended on his orders whether the body was of no consequence or whether it would have caused some retaliation. That all changed the day John was sent to kill a family man. This was new for John; the others he had killed were alone in the world or with a group that wouldn't be missed. Once, John killed a man in the custody of the F.B.I. in Japan. The first thing John thought odd about this assignment was this man was someone who would be missed; also, the person was in Hong Kong he never had a job within China. John was told hit target was selling secrets to the Chinese, and because of this, good men and women had been killed. John had never really trusted Mike. When Mike explained to John about his new target, John thought Mike was lying about this target. John never trusted Mike, and this target was far from the norm, so John decided he would do what he had been taught to do.

John followed the unnamed traitor waiting for his chance to kill him. At first, John was just going to wait for the man to enter one of Hong Kong's thousands of unlicensed restaurants. These little restaurants were run outside of a family dwelling and were good places to watch people from. John decided he would slip the man some poison; this poison was derived from the venom of a tiny snail living in the shallow water along the coast of Papua New Ginny. John watched as his target walked from stall to stall in the market, looking at toys and trinkets. John knew from experience most people when trying to act as if they had nothing to hide, never act casual. These people would become obsessive in their casualness. John watched this middle-aged man and thought his actions were that of a man without a care in the world. Before John could act and follow through with his orders, the target met with a beautiful woman about his age and a young boy of about five years old. The target showed the boy a plastic helicopter he had bought. The target laughed as he picked the child up and placed him on his shoulders, then kissed the woman. Then John watched as this would-be traitor ate dinner with his wife and son. After dinner, the happy family walked hand in hand through the open market, stopping only to buy a pair of shoes for the boy. John watched as the child begged for another toy, but his mother shook her head and ushered the pleading child to the shoes. John's unease about this target grew as he watched the man and his family. John knew by the time they left the market the orders were wrong and killing this man was a mistake.

Walking through the crowded streets, John watched as the accused traitor stopped to give a beggar some money. John knew this was not the behavior of a traitor. Nobody risked his life and the lives of his family selling secrets to another unfriendly country would hand some of it over to a beggar, no matter how little it was. John watched as the wife with the son caught a cab. The target turned and started up the steps of the American embassy; John already knew something was wrong with the orders. Standing at the foot of the steps, John watched as Mike Styles walked out of the embassy and was surprised to see the man still alive. Mike was even more surprised to see John standing behind the target, looking up at him. The man turned and saw John standing, looking up the stairs at Mike, holding the door for an Asian man. Turning, the target John had been sent to kill walked to a waiting cab. The target disappeared into the chaotic traffic Hong Kong offered to its thriving populist. The next day, John asked Mike why he had been sent to kill a family man who wasn't doing what the intelligence said he was. Mike sat John down and told him someone in the command had a grievance with this one man and tried to use him and John to rectify his problem. Six years ago, when John came to Mike's unit, he had distrusted Mike Styles, and that distrust had grown into a healthy dislike. Now John thought of Mike as a human slug.

For the next few months, John checked and rechecked all his past targets. He wondered if he'd been used to kill other innocent men and a woman. What he found shocked him; most of the past targets he killed were drug lords. These men were the heads of the most powerful drug Cartels in the Asian and European markets. The one woman he had been sent to kill turned out to be the head of the most powerful weapons trafficking syndicate' in the world. To this syndicate, it didn't matter where or when as long as you had the cash. John remembered the woman had offered him a massive bribe. She told him all he had to was to go back and tell his boss she was dead. When the bribe didn't work, the woman slipped her dress off and offered John sex. John drew the woman into his arms, acted as if he was going to kiss her, then broke her neck and dropped her body on the floor.

Closing the last file he could find, John knew he was being used to erase the competition. The only thing he did not know was how far up the chain of command the corruption went. John didn't know how, but he sure as shit knew Mike was involved, and if he could prove it, John promised himself he would kill the fuck. When John Approached Mike with the information he had gathered and cornered Mike in a washroom with a Kimber.45 under his chin. John learned the whole story. It took a little pressure with the barrel of the .45 under Mike's chin to start the man talking; once he started, John eased up and let Mike off his tiptoes. John always knew Mike was a spineless shit. When Mike began to tell John about who he took his orders from, John stood shocked.

Chapter 3

A MAN NAMED CHOW YANG had started and was the head of the unit here in Hong Kong. John remembered this man, he had met him once, and from the encounter, John came away with the feeling Chow had been pissed off that Mike had introduced them. Mike told John this Chow Yang was using his position in the C.I.A. to kill off the old drug lords and take over their organizations, as well as the world's black-market weapons trade. It wasn't enough to have a slice of the drugs and illegal weapons trade, Mike told John; Chow wanted the whole thing. He was starting with Asia and Europe, and from there, Chow was going to take over South America, killing off the cartels. Once Mike finished his story, John slammed his head into the hot air hand dryer, leaving the human slug unconscious on the bathroom floor. Looking down at Mike, John knew he should kill the slug, but he needed to get out of the building.

John knew he would have to get away. He couldn't go back to his apartment. John didn't need anything there anyway; he could survive with what he had. The one thing John had to do was get off the island of Hong Kong. John had no one he could go to; he knew this Chow Yang would be out to kill him. John knew Chow would have to kill him to keep his actions quiet. John also made an enemy out of Mike. Though he never considered the man his friend, John knew having Mike as an enemy was better. This way, you knew the bastard was going to stab you in the back sooner rather than later. John walked out into the Hong Kong sun and waved to a waiting cab. The driver nodded as John ordered the driver to drop him at the pier.

Standing on Hong Kong's number three pier, John watched as ships were being unloaded. Large overhead cranes hooked large shipping containers and lowered them onto waiting trucks; these would roar off to another unseen part of the pier. Standing in the shadows, John waited until he saw a uniformed man walk down the gangplank of a ship. John knew that some large container ships like this one would sometimes take passengers for a price. This officer informed John his ship didn't take any passengers. The Captain told John it was to do with insurance concerns.

A light steady rain began to fall. John stood under the overhang of a warehouse roof, trying to sit dry and out of the streetlight at the same time; he watched as a man walked along the docks. John knew this man didn't belong on the docks. This stranger jumped and turned twice when one of the cranes banged a container onto a truck a little too hard. When this stranger grew close enough, John knew the stranger was going to try something from the way the man tried to go about killing him almost made John laugh. John thought this could be the oldest ploy in the world of assassination. While watching ships being towed into the port by large tug boats, this man approached John with an unlit cigarette. The would-be killer made a show like he was going to ask John for a light. Now in the new politically correct world of healthy food nuts and non-smokers, this would be bad form, but in Hong Kong, everybody smoked. So this dumb shit thought it would be a good cover to get close. John watched as the would-be killer made a show of slapping pockets and then pulled a knife. The cigarette dropped from the killer's slack lips when he found John pulled a Kimber.45 model 1911. The would-be killer was about to start begging for his life when John shot him through the bridge of his flattened nose.

With all the noise of the cranes loading the shipping containers onto the trucks and men shouting directions, no one paid any attention to the pistol report. Most dismissed the shot as being a truck backfiring. Turning, John walked off into the night's shadows as the pink and grey matter, once housed in this former would-be killer's head, slid down the corrugated metal wall of the building to the ground. The next killer ended with the same type of facial reconstruction. This one had been waiting outside the docks where John had hoped to book passage aboard a ship. As John walked through a hole in the fence surrounding the docks, he caught the glint of a streetlight off a car's windshield. John thought the second would-be killer was even more inept at stealth, but when this dumb bastard got out of the vehicle, the idiot slammed the door. Slamming the door of the car angered John; he thought this guy was used to mugging old ladies. Walking down the street that fronted the docks, John waited until the assassin was twenty feet behind him. He jumped into the hedges lining the sidewalk. John turned in time to drive his pistol into the face of the second killer; pulling the trigger, John stopped any begging before the man had time to think about starting. In the third attempt, the people who wanted John dead used a different tactic instead of using local thugs who didn't know what they were doing. This time they decided to spend some money and hire a professional. John knew he was going to have to leave this megalopolis; he was going to have to try to find his way to a friendlier region of the world.

Walking through the dank alleys of Hong Kong, John realized he hadn't eaten in twelve hours. John remembered a small spot not far from the docks where he could go. Sitting in a plastic chair at a small table, John waited as the woman who cooked out of her house took his order. He could eat and have a bottle of water for a few American cents. Using Cantonese, he learned when he came to China, John asked the woman if she had seen anyone around who looked like him. The small woman told John he was the first big American she had seen in a week.

When she brought him his food, John heard a boot scuff on the damp asphalt then he felt the dart hit him in the leg. John crashed through the small plastic table and ran halfway down the alley before the fast-acting sedative took him to the pavement. When he woke, John knew he was in trouble, not dead, captured. John knew being caught was worse than dying, especially in China. John tried to keep track of the days and the places he was held before he reached his final destination.

John could hear the cries of the other men being held in this prison with him. He saw their faces as they were being dragged out of their cells and taken to the interrogation rooms. He could hear their screams from the tortures and the grunts of exertion from the men asking the questions when they wouldn't get the answers they wanted, or they thought the answer given was a lie. These new inquisitors' of a different religion would apply some kind of new and excruciating degradation. John still felt the hammer his inquisitor used on his feet and hands. He remembered the pain of the bones being broken. John was surprised when his hands and feet were set and wrapped, allowing them to heal, just so they could be broken again, then set and allowed to heal again.

Then a sick little man came into his cell one morning and showed John the knives he was going to use on him. This sick bastard made small incisions on John's chest, placed slivers of wood in the cuts, and then ripped them out of John's body. This lasted for weeks until most of his body was covered by fresh scares. When this little sick bastard was fed up with playing around, he started on John's face. This twisted freak slashed a long ragged cut along John's left jawline. Blood poured from the wound and ran in streams down his body. When this little bastard got close enough and reached up to cut John on the right side of his face. John twisted, caught the freak's hand in his mouth, and bit down with every ounce of force he could muster. The bite removed the little man's index and middle fingers of his right hand. The beating John suffered for the maiming of the little man with the knives went on for hours and was only stopped when an officer ordered it. The guards who gave John the beating dragged him from the interrogation room. Each guard held an arm and a handful of hair as they dragged Johns's battered body through the prison. Once they reached John's cell, both guards held an arm and, with their combined strength, threw him against the wall of his cell, where he finally fell unconscious.

John could still see the face of the man who questioned him. He also remembered the questions that had been asked. The questions had been about numbered bank accounts, always about the accounts. John told these dumb shits he didn't know anything about any accounts, but they just kept at him. He could feel the strikes of the whips as they would hang him by his hands from the ceiling. When John would pass out from the pain, they would wake him with smelling salts then it would start again. When the blood flowed out of the wounds on his back, they would take John and lay him on a table covered with salt. The salt would sear its way into the open wounds left by the whip, then tied to the table. He would lay there as the arches of his feet were struck repeatedly with a bamboo staff. That was on top of the punches that rained down on him at every turn. The fat General who ran this prison came into the integration room. He started to tell John about an article he had read; the General told John some of the North American Indians had a right of passage where they hung themselves by their flesh, the General told John how some other ancient civilizations had something similar, but he likes the Indians version best. The General called his aid in. The little bastard with the knife fetish and missing two fingers was carrying a case full of stainless steel meat hooks. A doctor placed these hooks under John's skin, down both sides of his back and down the back of his legs.

Three men held John up as the hooks were attached to wires that hung from the ceiling. When the last wire was attached, they left John hanging by his flesh. No one stayed to ask any questions. Once John was suspended by his flesh, the men left the room. John could hear them laughing through the roars of his pain. He didn't know how long he was hanging by his flesh before the General came back and asked him about these accounts and their numbers. When John told the General that he didn't know anything, the man became so enraged that he punched John, causing him to gyrate wildly on the wires. Blood dripped in steady rhythms on the floor under his suspended form. For hours the General screamed he wanted the accounts, and John would scream he didn't know about any accounts. The whole time John hung by his flesh, the General's little aid would hit John with his walking stick. The old General stopped the aid and walked up to John; looking into John's eyes, the fat General said.

"I believe you; you do not know anything about the accounts, but we had to be sure." The General Trang of the people's army turned and left. John heard the General tell someone to find out all they could, then throw him away. John was taken down, and the hooks removed from under his flesh. They took John to his cell and dropped him on the floor. Time held no meaning for John, the sky would start to lighten, and the guards would come to unlock his cell and take him to the room. Every day the same questions were asked, and he gave the same answers, day after day, week after week. John didn't know how long this went on for, then one day, a guard opened the door of the integration room, and another guard pushing a cart with a machine on it entered the room. John didn't know why but for some reason, this machine scared him more than the hooks did.

Chapter 4

WHEN THE PRISON DOCTOR hooked the pads to his head, he had a memory of pain and a young boy flash through his head. This young boy seemed to look at John. He watched as the boy cried silent tears. When the man asked his first question, John didn't answer. The guard nodded to the doctor, and the man reached over and switched the machine on. This was the first time John saw a woman on the shore of a lake, her face was bloody, and she was trying to hold onto the small boy John had seen in his memory when another man walked up behind her and shot the woman in the head. He screamed his way into unconsciousness; every time they shocked John, he would see a flash of a woman and a man, though he didn't always see the same woman. After hours of being shocked, the guards took John back to his cell. John was trying to think of who these women could be while he lay in his cell that first night. The guards seemed to tire of beating John every day. Months passed before he and the guards realized it. The wounds to John's body healed; the only thing remaining tender were the ribs where the guards would punch him every night as they threw him into his cell. His feet were still recovering from wounds sustained from the hammer and the bamboo staff used on them. For John, the only thing that mattered was how long he had been held the prison before. They made the mistake of thinking he could not run on his feet.

Each night the same guards would throw John into his cell, and he would let himself go limp and act like he didn't have the strength to defend himself. Then once he heard the two guards leave the cells, John would stretch. John knew his back and legs were taking a lot of punishment from the electroshock treatment. John knew he had to be ready to run when he could. John watched as the seasons changed through the small window set high on the wall of his cell. It had been summer when he had been darted in the alley. John knew he had been in prison for longer than a season. He wasn't sure how long he was moved around before he reached this prison? It was this question he asked himself every night. It was hot and humid; had he been in the hands of the General's men for the winter?

All he could remember was the pain, waves of pain crashing on his own shores of hate and despair. John tried to armor himself against the incessant tides of pain, but the waves would tear down the walls he built every night in his cell. In the times between the beatings, John would lie on the floor of his cell and listen to a river in the distance. In the peace of the night, John would dream of the cool water and how it would feel on his broken and battered body. One night John overheard one of the guards talking about his brother being sent to Tibet. The other guard had said it was good luck; Tibet was not far. The man could get home if anything happened to their mother. Tibet John knew if he could find his way into that country and find a way through the mountains, he might be able to find his way to freedom. It was those 'if's' he knew were going to be the hardest to overcome. John also knew he could die there in the mountains, but he would rather die out there, rather than in his cell, a broken shell of the man he was.

John knew if he could make it to the river, he would be able to make it to Tibet. Once in Tibet, he might find people who would hide him until he finished healing and built his strength back. John knew in the late fifties, the Chinese had invaded Tibet and tried to kill the Dalai Lama. Tibetans still held a deep resentment of the Chinese, the P.L.A., and the leaders of the Chinese government. All he had to do was get his strength back, and he would be able to kill all the men who worked for Yang. John knew that Yang and Mike

Styles had to be behind his being in this place. John waited until he felt his feet and legs could carry him before he made his attempt.

John knew the same two guards would come to take him back to his cell. John realized the men weren't holding onto him as tightly as they once did; both believed John was no longer a threat to them. When they reached his cell, one guard let go of John's shoulder and turned to unlock the cell while the other watched his partner work the lock as he relaxed his grip on John. Sensing this was the time to act, John grabbed the guard holding onto him, spinning around and wrenching the man's head with all his strength. John broke the guard's neck, killing the man instantly. The first guard hearing the sharp gasp and the report of his friend's neck breaking, turned in time to have his head slammed into the bared door of John's cell. The man didn't fall; John was about to repeat the act of slamming the guard's head into the door again when he saw there was no use. A large bolt that protruded from the cell door was holding the guard up. John had used enough force; the bolt had been rammed through the back of the man's skull.

Turning, he could see men staring out of their cells at him. Not one of these poor shattered men held a hand out to beckon him over to help them out of their cells. One by one, the broken men stepped back from their doors, afraid John would unlock them. John was amazed at how few guards were keeping this prison safe. John realized with all the other prisoners too terrified to leave their cells, only a skeleton crew could run the prison at night. He only encountered one other guard as he searched for a way out. This lone guard was sitting at a desk at the only door in the outer wall. The door was easy to find, but it took longer to find the keys that would open the door. The guard he killed at the desk had a large key ring on his belt. John tried ten keys before the eleventh key worked in the door. He almost shouted with elation when he heard a heavy click, and the steel door opened.

Chapter 5

JOHN FELT THE RAIN for the first time; he had no idea how long he had been held in prison. John could feel the rain washing off the dried filth and crusted blood that seemed to be covering his entire body. John waited at the corner of the prison; he listened intently for the river that he had heard in his cell. Standing holding his hands under a branch of a bush growing along the river, John drank mouths full of the rain. He relished the feeling of his strength coming back. Looking around, John knew there was only a finite amount of time before his escape was discovered. Then he would really have to run or hide, and he knew he was still weak. John would love to go to the river and swim in it. John knew as helpless as he was, and with the fast flow of the river, he would most likely drown. So if he were going to run, he would have to be smart about it and use the weather and the night to his advantage. Keeping the river on his left, John turned and started to hike north. The fact they had cut his clothes off him when he had first woken in prison, and he spent the rest of his captivity naked, that he was still without clothing, didn't bother John. He did wish one of the guards he'd killed would have had feet the same size as his, but at least he was out.

Now as John turned to look at the prison, he had been held in from the top of the first hill. John thought it now looked like a great sulking titan, slowly melding with the granite of the mountains around it. As John made his way along the ridge above the river, the rain fell in sheets slashing from the east to the west. John realized how great the rain was when he first stepped through the prison door; the rain was welcome. Now John worried the cold of this hard-driving rain was starting to leach its way into his body. He was afraid it would begin to steal the little reserves he had managed to build up in the little time he had to start the healing process. John stopped suddenly; he could have sworn he heard a whistle. John knew he had made some distance, but how far had he gone before he heard the first sound of a search starting. John was still following the river from the ridge line that ran north of it. Boats, he knew the sounds of the patrol boats; looking around, John found a bush he could climb under and hide. John didn't know how long he could stay under the bush, but the longer he stayed out of the hands of the Chinese, the better off he would be. John knew if he was found, it would mean a death sentence.

Lying under the bush, John could see his feet, and he was shocked at how bad they still looked. Both his feet were swollen and bruised, half of his toenails were just starting to grow back, and his right foot looked as if one or more bones were at one time broken. He knew the prison doctor had set his feet and hands though John didn't think the man cared if he did the job correctly. John was about one hundred meters north of the large river he had heard while he lay in his cell dreaming of the cool water. Hiding under this bush with its natural bowl gave John cover from the searchlight employed by the patrol boats. The only thing he worried about was the amount of water starting to gather with him in the bowl. John could see boats idling up and down the river; John knew what they were searching for, and he watched as they idled up and down the river. Watching as the boats swept the banks of the river with powerful spotlights, someone called out in the night. John watched as the boat raced to the spot where the cry came from, then after some excited chatter, the men with the boats returned to idling up and down the river searching.

One of the spotlights swept over his hiding place. The flash of light caused John to flinch back, and something else happened when he snapped his eyes shut in the bright light of the boat; another more brilliant light exploded in his head. Again he flashed to a woman lying on her back; she was beautiful, John knew her, and she was important to him. He could almost remember her name... almost. Another flash, and this time the pain in his head was so great it caused him to wretch. John's eyes filled with unshed tears, and he felt his stomach turn over and clench again. John forced himself to keep from crying out. He could see the same woman; this time, her beauty had been taken, and her face was contorted in a scream of rage, anguish, and hate. When he looked down at her, John could feel the scream wanting to come out of him. Someone had gutted her; whoever did this used a large knife to cut her from between her breasts to where her pubic hair started. Most of what had been in her abdominal cavity were now on the floor beside her. John could hear a snap, like that of an electrical circuit closing. All at once he was back in his hiding place under the bush, and men with guns were walking toward him. They were looking in all the bushes, trying to find him. John knew they were looking for him. John didn't think he would receive a warm welcome, just the opposite; he thought he might get a bullet from one of those rifles instead of a handshake from the man holding one.

Time to become like a bush, John thought; how the hell was he going to do that. John lay down in the bowl; he tried to sink into the water that gathered with him under the bush, the water was cold, and it caused John to shiver. All he could do was hope whoever came to investigate this bush wouldn't try to crawl in and have a good look. John watched as one of the soldiers walked toward his bush, towards his hiding place.

Chapter 6

HIS FATHER TOLD HIM that he would have to go and do what the Chin wanted.

"If you try to hide, then the army men will come and take our land. Your mother and sister will have to live on handouts while I am in prison." Tran-Ho could still see his mother crying. His sister stood in the doorway of their little hut tears glistened as they rolled down her cheeks and hung on the edge of her jaw, afraid to fall off something so lovely. Tran loved his sister as any good older brother would. It was going to be his duty to see her raised and married to a good man when his father passed out of this life.

One of the soldiers did look into his bush and turned as if to leave, then turning back, the soldier bent down to have a better look under the bush. Well, this is it; he's going to see me under here and will either shoot me on sight or call out and alert the others. Either way, I am fucked, John thought. John couldn't believe his eyes or luck when the kneeling man just winked at him and moved off. Stunned, John lay under the bush; the soldier found him and let him go. Lying under the bush, John listened as the men and boats moved further down the river; John knew he needed rest. His body had suffered a nasty shock. The torture was terrible, but the escape was another thing; using his feet and legs after the months of battering at the hands of the guards then, his escape had sapped most of what little strength he had built up. His heading out in the cold rain and pushing them to run when they were hardly fit to walk from his cell to the interrogation room worsened his condition. John knew if he lay where he was and let his muscles rest, he would stiffen up, then he would hardly be able to move after an hour. Though John just wanted to lay under the bush and rest, John forced himself to start moving. He had to get away, to heal, then get the men who did this to him. John's head began to spin from the adrenalin that his body released when the soldier looked under the bush. For a brief second, John was afraid that he was going to pass out. If that happened, and another soldier came along and looked under his bush, he would be found, and there would be nothing that John could do about it. With all the beatings he had taken, John was surprised his jaw wasn't broken. If his jaw had been broken, that meant that John couldn't eat anything except broth. It would take longer to build his strength back up before he could start to hunt down the bastards who did this to him. It seemed to take a better part of the night before the soldiers moved on and the boats idled further down the river. After leaving the bush he hid under, John chose to head in a North West direction again; this direction would take him away from the soldiers and the river. In his condition, he would be no match for the current of the water, and most likely, he would have drowned if he had tried to swim it; for now, he had a lot to live for. John didn't know when it happened, but sometime during his detention, he decided he would live long enough to kill Mike Styles. Along with that other shit Chow Yang and neither one would die quick.

Chapter 7

TRAN-HO KNEW THE MAN he saw under the bush was the man the officers and the General of this region were looking for. The man under the bush had to be, how many naked six-foot Americans does one find, under bushes along the border between China and Tibet. That a reward of one year's wages had been offered to the man who found him would have been incentive enough for some of the other men to turn this poor soul over to the Chinese. Tran-Ho also knew his family could have used the money, but Tran-Ho was a good man and refused to sell another human for money. The people's army might have his body, but they did not have his mind or soul, and Tran-Ho knew in his heart he did the right thing; it's what his father would've done. Tran could see an officer asking the men as they walked by if they had seen anything. When it came to Tran's turn, he snapped to attention like a good soldier and reported he had not seen any sign of the escapee. The officer nodded and dismissed Tran and turned to the next man. The reports went on like that for another half hour before the officer gave up and stomped off through the mud and into the night. One week left, Tran thought, just one week, then he would go home and see his father and mother. Though he loved his parents, he worried about his sister the most. She was young and had so much of her life left in front of her; Tran couldn't wait until he could take her out to the mountains to show her the different colors the snow caps turned when the setting and rising sun hit them.

Chapter 8

CHOW YANG HAD WORKED in China since the beginning of his career with the C.I.A. He worked hard to build his contacts with the crime families here in China and Russia as well as in other parts of the world. Those who didn't think they needed him went on their way, then one night, they would be visited by a C.I.A. black ops hitman and never seen again. This hitman would, in most cases, be John, a threat to his national security taken care of. Chow had been careful about his operations'. He never sent John to kill anyone who didn't have any assets in the U.S. He could always make something up that would have Washington panting for blood. In time they would get it; happy with his work, the dumb bastards left him alone to build his empire. Now thanks to John, Chow watching as it could fall apart, how could this happen.

An empire is just what he built; drugs are where it all started, then he moved on to trade secrets and industrial espionage. Hell, it all paid well, but nothing paid like dope. Chow had twenty-five bank accounts, all numbered and none with his real name on them. Some of the names he had used were former enemies; still, others had been from Pomes by Poe, and some he just made up. The accounts were in banks all over the world. These banks served customers who wanted nothing to do with any government. Whether hiding the money from the taxman or an angry soon-to-be ex-wife or husband. Chow's most minor bank account was in Switzerland. He called this his mad money; it held one hundred and fifty million U.S. dollars.

Chow knew, in theory, he could lose the whole thing if that bastard John Smyth was, by some miracle, able to get away. The fucker should be dead, but no, John knew too much, and Chow needed to know who the bastard might have told. John's girlfriend didn't know shit, and now she wouldn't be saying shit. Mike had made sure of that; John must have told someone. Chow knew it. He needed to find out who that person was. If he needed to, Chow would tear his way through Asia; he would find out who John had told about what he had found. Chow needed to find this person. They are the biggest threat to his empire; if he had to kill most of the slime that dwelt under his feet, he would, without a second thought.

Chapter 9

JOHN DIDN'T THINK HE could make it through the first night. He found some old canvas and made a pair of crude slippers for his battered feet. When John looked down at his feet, John worried about the damage done to them, and now he was forced to walk on them. He could be damaging the bones or the tendons in them permanently. John remembered an instructor at the orphanage; the man would shout about the care of a soldier's feet being his number one concern behind his weapons. A light as John staggered along, he knew he had seen a small light though the Chinese had invaded Tibet. They forced a score of Chinese to move into this region, hoping by doing this, the rest of the world would see this as part of China; doing this caused just the reverse; it caused the world to demand China pull out of Tibet. Some of these hills still had monks, and these monks took strangers in sometimes. John hoped he wasn't dreaming the light up.

The rain stopped, and he didn't know if it was a good thing. When it was raining, he had been cold, but now that he had started to climb the path leading into the mountains. John realized he was getting colder, and now he shivered uncontrollably. John knew he could be slipping into hypothermia. Leaning against a large pine tree, John looked up into the sky. He was trying to see stars to find the north star or any star he could use to get his bearings. Looking down the path, John found himself staring into a pair of smiling light grey eyes. John would have jumped back if he had the strength, but at that very moment, what was left of his reserves ran dry, and John fell into an old man's arms.

When he woke up, John could hear what sounded like an argument, not that he could understand what the hell was being said, and it sounded as if only one person was arguing. Lying there, he could smell fire, and as he looked around. John watched as a stern-looking old lady waved an accusatory wooden spoon at the smiling old man. John knew it had been this old man who found and rescued him last night. Now the poor old fella was catching hell from the lady of the house. The old man turned around and saw John was awake. Smiling, the old man bowed, and the old woman seemed to be angry with John and the old man. Then she started to shout again. With her voice and the language she spoke, John thought driving a nail into his ear would be less painful. The old man looked at his wife and nodded, and then he went over to the bed, chattering something at John. Smiling, the old man stood and started to pack a large sack. When he had finished, the old man turned to the bed and helped John up and out into the bright daylight while still chattering at him. John knew what he was being told, the lady of the house had told her husband, 'that he was to get him out of there, or he would never be happy again'. And after listening to her voice, hell, John couldn't blame the old guy.

Outside, a young man waited with a cart and a small donkey. They helped John into the wagon and covered him with hides, then set out; at least he wouldn't be forced to use his damaged feet, he thought as sleep retook him. John could hardly believe it when the old man had to wake him to eat something. With the dirt paths that served as roads and the cart having no suspension, John could hardly believe he had fallen asleep. Trying to eat was more challenging than he would have thought. When John tried to open his mouth, he found his face hurt. John remembered the little freak with knives had cut and torn at his flesh with the knives and whittled down sticks, but what happened to his face? Then John remembered biting off the little freak's fingers while he had attacked his face.

When John raised his hand towards his face, the old man gently held John's hand and chattered something at him. John could tell he didn't want him touching his face; he could also tell something was wrong with it by the way the younger of the two would look away when John caught his eye. After they ate, the old fella got John to roll over so he could check his back. The old man was mumbling something and clucking his tongue. The younger man came around the cart, and by the look on his face, John could tell what he saw wasn't good. The old man covered John up again and smiled his toothless smile while he patted John's arm, then went to the front of the cart. John tried to explore his face with his fingers. John found the old man had placed a cloth over the left side of his face and tied it to his pillow so he couldn't pull it off in his sleep.

Chapter 10

TRAN COULDN'T BELIEVE that he had to sit through this film about his duty to the people's army. Even after it was over, he had to go, with another officer, into a room and give his reasons he would not re-enlist for another five years. Tran came from a land of peace, he loved his homeland and believed in peace, but in this room, at this time, Tran was ready to kill the smiling officer sitting behind the desk. Tran had practiced his speech repeatedly, getting prepared for this day.

"Sir, it is for my mother. I need to go, my father is not well, and I'm the only boy, and as the eldest, I must return to my father's farm and take care of my mother and sister. I need to tend the fields, but if my people's army is ever in need of me, I will come back to the home I know here." Tran finished standing at rigid attention, no emotion on his face. However, inside, he hated and detested everything this army stood for. If the leaders of this army thought the rest of the world would do nothing, the Chinese wouldn't think twice about invading other countries in Asia.

"Ah good, very good, I have no doubt about that, corporal. You have been a good soldier and a pleasure to be around." With that Tran-Ho's release papers were signed, and he was dismissed with a handshake. Tran thought it would take him a long time to pack his things, but he realized he had nothing except his uniforms. Therefore, he grabbed his pack and walked out of his barracks for the last time, he hoped. Tran-Ho received permission to catch a ride with an army convoy traveling to a post on the Tibetan border. There Tran would have to find his own way home, which was okay with him.

Tran thought he had spent far too much of his life in the company of the Chinese military.

The dreams were of children and happy times; John could see a lake in his dreams and two people. A man and a woman, the woman he'd seen before, it was when the interrogator first hooked the electroshock machine to him in prison. There was a little boy, and John watched as the woman chased the boy around a picnic table. The man was watching as he opened a picnic basket. John woke to look out from under the blankets. John wondered how he could be dreaming of another person's life. John thought maybe he remembered something from when he was a child. Why would these memories be coming now? Why not when he had been at the orphanage? John knew trying to ask any questions was a waste of time. John felt he needed to do something or say something. When John tried to talk, he found he couldn't form the words, he tried to clear his throat, but for whatever reason, he couldn't get any sound to come out of his mouth saved for a slight croak; he could feel himself sliding into sleep again. So John let the dreams take him to a better place. His dream wasn't something he wanted.

John fought, trying to get back to the happy scene John had been in before he woke up the first time. This time he was at the lake but from his perspective, he was walking backward, and there was a houseboat burning on the water. The flames were reflected in the water giving off the illusion the water was burning with the boat. Then in a flash, it was summer, and a man played catch with a young boy, who in turn through the ball to him, and he threw it back to the man; they were by the lake. It was the most beautiful lake John ever saw. The sun glinted off the small waves lapping at the shore. To the young boy, it looked like the water hid an uncountable number of diamonds just under the surface of the water. A woman knelt down and seemed to pick him up, John felt peace envelop him, he felt completely safe as the woman held him.

"Come on, Jack, time for lunch, then we can go back on the boat." The woman in his dream said to the boy. John dreamed about ham sandwiches and potato chips, plain, the boy liked plain chips, it was the picnic the man unpacked while this woman chased the boy in his other dream. John could smell the lady as she carried the little boy. The scent was her perfume, a lite clean smell. The woman's chestnut brown hair blew in the lite breeze. She sat the little boy at the picnic table. 'SNAP. ' John heard the electrical circuit snap again.

The pain was all-encompassing; it filled his head. It felt like someone was trying to drill a hole between his eyes and through his brain stem at the same time. The pain was so intense it seemed to hold John in its grip, not letting him wake from the dream. Then the dream turned ugly.

The man was face down in the potato chips, and the woman was on the ground trying to hold on to his hand. John knew the little boy was somehow him; this woman was his mother. John was sure of the fact this was his family. How could she be his mother? He knew the director of the orphanage lied to him. The director of the orphanage knew precisely where he and the other boys came from and how they came to be at the center. John never knew his mother or his father. His dream flashed, and a strange man was carrying off the other little boy. Like little Jack, the boy was crying, John could see a large boot kick the woman in the face, but still, she held on to her son. Then John heard a muffled cough; John watched as a neat round hole appeared in the woman's forehead. Someone shot her in the head. John knew she had been shot from his own experience. John also knew she had been his mother, and the dead would have been his father. John knew he had had a family, and someone was responsible for taking his family away from him, for what? John didn't know why his mother and father were murdered, but he was going to find out. John knew he needed to find out, and now he had another reason to live. John silently swore he would find out about his mother and father; he needed to find who murdered his family, and John needed to find the other boy, his brother. John thought about the name Jack. He at one time, had an older brother who could be out in the world somewhere.

Chapter 11

TRAN LOVED THE MOUNTAINS and all they held. His time away only sharpened his love for the snows held in place by the altitude on the highest peak through the summer months. When he was a child, Tran remembered his father talking about taking some white men up to the top of one of the mountains near his home. His father did this when he was young; one time, Tran met a group of men from Britain. These men came to his father and talked about the mountains; one of the men had told Tran his son was about Tran's age. The British man told Tran he would like to bring his son to climb the mountain when he gets older. He asked Tran if he would guide his son when he gets older. Tran remembers his father smiling when he said it would be his honor. However, when the Chinese invaded, all hope for the future stopped. Though Tran had been a little boy when the Chinese came to this part of Tibet, Tran knew things would never be the same, the year was 1969, and Tran was turning six years old. All that was left now was the farm; even then, he dreamed about climbing the mountain with his father. Now Tran's father was too old for that, now Tran would have to climb the mountain without him. Tran hated the Chinese for what they had done to this land. This was meant to be a land of peace. The Chinese invaded and stole from the monks, making some of them hide in fear. Then the Chinese took the sons of Tibet to join their army. People who never wanted to fight were forced to pick up weapons. The next weapon he picked up would be to move the Chinese out of this land forever. Tran made this promise as he looked over the border into Tibet.

Chapter 12

JACK, COULD THIS BE his name? He had been John his whole life; they always called him John at the orphanage. Even that walking piece of trash Mike called him John. When he was in the prison, the men who tortured him called him John. It was getting harder to hold onto what he knew. All his life, good or bad, he had been John Smyth, now for the first time, he didn't know. John knew he was dreaming of his mother and father; they called him Jack, but his whole life, for as long as he could remember, he had been John. The sounds of the older man and the cart changed while he was unconscious. John could tell he was no longer in the cart, moving across the land. He was inside, inside what? The question terrified John for a moment. Was he back in the hands of the Chinese? If he was, where was the old man? Was the old man and his young friend safe?

The kind eyes of an elderly man John never saw before woke him. This man fed him some kind of broth. It was probably the worst-tasting stuff John had ever had the misfortune of having in his mouth. John smiled and nodded in thanks; as John relaxed, the old man looked at his arms and hands. Once satisfied with what he saw, the old monk moved his examination down John's body to his ribs, feeling each rib on both sides of John's body. The kind monk worked his way down to John's legs and feet. Satisfied, the old man smiled and watched as Johns's eyes drooped, then closed. John was surprised when the old man placed the spoon between his lips and fed him some more broth. When the monk was satisfied with the amount, John ate and was sure he would go back to sleep. The old man pushed back the curtain covering the doorway and left the room. 'Room' was that word that shocked John; how did or when did he get to a place with rooms? His last memory was of the cart. How long had he been here, and where was here anyway? He remembered the old man who brought John to his hut. The poor old fella was forced to cart him here or risk the wrath of his wife for the rest of his life. John didn't even know the old man's name or how he could ever thank him for his help.

Chapter 13

HONG KONG, MIKE LOVED this place; it didn't matter what you wanted or when you wanted it, you could find it here. Mike Styles sat in his favorite armchair looking out his living room window at the city's lights; well, to call Hong Kong a city wasn't correct, not really. It was more like an enclave, a small country within a larger one, the same as Vatican City inside of Rome. Though Rome is the capital of Italy, Vatican City is still considered a separate state. If you asked anyone who had been born in Hong Kong, they would tell you that they were from Hong Kong, and some of the older people would say they were Chinese. While the younger generations would say, they were from Hong Kong as if it was a separate country. When he retired from the company, he would have to choose where he would like to live. Mike thought this place would suit him fine if this apartment came in the package, but he didn't think it would. When he retired, what a laugh. If General Trang of the People's Army didn't find John Smyth, then it would be a reasonable probability that he wasn't going to retire. It was more likely he would be retired, in the permanent sense of the word. Mike knew if it came down to it, he would do anything to stay alive. Mike was one thing over all else; he was a coward and would sell his mother to save his life. Mike's motto was 'Never give them a fair fight.'

The cell phone on the side table started to buzz and vibrate; flipping it open, Mike listened, then snapped it shut again. Placing it back on the table, Mike swore under his breath. An aide to the General just told him they had no success finding John. That goddamn Smyth had slipped through the net Trang threw out. Now he was a fish in a vast ocean, a fish; Mike shook his head. John was no fish. Mike knew what had gotten away was the biggest, baddest shark ever built. Mike knew John was a survivor. If anyone could escape and come back to haunt them, John would be the one. After all, he had been in charge of the man's training, hell Mike had been given John when he was a young boy, and he knew him. He had guided his training and education, though John hadn't met Mike until he was eighteen. Mike had been in John's life since his mother and father had been terminated while on a house boating trip in the Canadian province of British Columbia. Mike watched from a hill as the wet work team placed the bodies of Betty and Jack Logan back on the houseboat they had rented, then sunk it in the middle of the lake. John's father was the head of a group of journalists who thought they needed to keep an eye on the darker side of governments. This group had found out about Mike's new training program for a black ops unit. After Mike's team failed to scare Johns fathers' group off the story, it was decided John's father needed to be removed. When Mike found out his target had a son the right age for the program, he convinced his boss the rest of his family needed to disappear. There was no hesitation in the director of the C.I.A., G.W. Hollyford could have cared less for a family not even from America.

Hollyford didn't care for the people of his own country, so he gave the green light to take out the whole Logan family, retrieving the young boy for the Cradle program. John had been with them and another boy, while John's mother and father had only one child; this second boy was John's cousin. As it turned out, John's mother had a sister, and they brought her bastard with them for the trip. Because the boy was older, he was useless to the program. The child development experts and the rest of the shrink squad told Mike to keep the boy alive; they wanted to try and experiment. The shrinks wanted to see if they could use the boy to erase John's moral compass. Mike smiled as he thought about the whole family just disappearing one day, on a large deep lake, in the wilds of Canada. One nosey reporter and one mouthpiece lawyer gone, hell as far as Mike was concerned, he did the world and John a favor.

Chapter 14

SITTING ON THE WOODEN bench outside the last outpost on the border of China and Tibet, one of the soldiers looked at Tran-ho with envy written all over his face; Tran could understand why they all wanted to go home. Still, like so many others and like Tran, these men had to put their time in the military of Tibet's unwanted guests made them.

"So you're going home ... you think." The young officer said with a smirk on his face. In this part of the border, he would be the lone Chinese officer, with no other Chinese officers' only enlisted men. His men would be conscripts from Tibet and the border region of Tibet. These men would speak in their own dialects just to keep him out of the conversations. Tran knew the man was mad at his superiors for this posting; truth be told, he had to have pissed someone off to get this post in the first place. So he now wanted to return the favor.

"I don't think anything; if you wish to check the truths of the paperwork, please do so; I have nothing to hide." With that Tran-Ho sat on the bench and waited. It took a long time before one of the Tibetan conscripts came out of the building and told Tran-Ho that he could go on his way.

"Why didn't the lieutenant come to tell me?" Tran asked.

"Our lieutenant has a bad habit of questioning things he shouldn't, and this is what it got him," The young soldier said as he looked around at the dusty outpost.

"Next, I think he might be guarding a dame on a river somewhere." The man smiled and turned back for the guard shack.

Standing and picking up his pack Tran caught the lieutenant watching him through his office window. Tran just shook his head and turned to walk under the red and white bar one of the enlisted men raised and smiled as if to say welcome home. Tran thanked the man as he passed into the once-free country of Tibet.

Chapter 15

CHOW-YUN KNEW JOHN Smyth couldn't have made it into Tibet. It was impossible. Even that bastard had the guts to pull that off. Not in the shape he was in, he had been in the hands of the Chinese army intelligence and General Trang along with his sick assistant for six months, not a good place to be for an American, especially one with ties to the C.I.A. Chow paid for the bastard to be killed outright, that was to be done when they had John cornered at the docks. The two thugs he hired were less than capable. Then the General's men found John, and they were supposed to use a lethal toxin, some asshole with dreams of making general decided to make a point to get information out of Smyth. Well, look at the shit they were in now, Chow thought. When this is over, he would have to find out who the asshole was and have him killed, slowly. Now his biggest headache was to find John and have him killed. John's death needed to look like he died at the hands of the Chinese six months ago. If he could have that done, he would be able to keep his position in the world drug and weapons trade a secret for a while longer. Chow needed time. Someone once said time was the most precious thing of all.

Once again, the old monk woke John to feed him more fowl-tasting broth. John hadn't been able to keep count of the times this old man woke him to feed him; each time he had, the taste of the broth was horrible. This time it had bits of something John had to chew, and though he was thankful, John didn't know if he could keep his stomach from revolting and heaving everything on the floor. John fought this urge; he thought he was going to lose, but John managed to keep his stomach in check. After John was sure he wasn't going to vomit, he managed a smile of thanks to the old man. This cycle of waking to be fed, then back to sleep seemed to be broken only by an old monk who came in to change the dressings on his feet and wash him.

The first time this had happened, John tried to protest, not too loudly. This man and the other monk had been kind to him, but John thought he could wash. The old monk smiled, handed him the cloth, and watched as he tried and failed. With his kind but forceful way, the old monk took the washcloth and finished the job. John was thankful for the food and the rest, but he still couldn't get over the taste of the broth. John tried to tell the monk how grateful he was, but his voice still failed him when he tried to speak more than a couple of words; soon after, the monk smiled and pulled the curtain closed. John knew the old man was trying to help him, but he still wished he could leave here; John didn't like staying in one place too long; it wasn't for his safety. He feared for it was the lives of these men John didn't want to endanger. John didn't know how he knew Mike and his boss Chow were looking for him, John knew the men needed him dead, and anyone with him would also be killed.

Chapter 16

"SIXTY DAYS, IT HAS been sixty days since we've seen or heard anything of Smyth, and the condition he was in, I doubt he could have made it very far. I think he most likely tried to swim the river and failed, resulting in his drowning; yes, he's dead and stuck under a log, fish bait." Chow-Yun looked at the reflection of the man who spoke to him. To kill this simpering prick would give him the greatest pleasure. Then how would he explain it? He was sure it would be hard to explain away the death of the General in the apartment of the C.I.A. station chief. Well, Chow didn't have to kill him now. He could wait, then have this thing that looked like a human skinned alive later.

"I just wish that we could be sure; I don't like loose ends," Chow answered. The man smiled as if he was talking to a truculent child who needed his years of experience and wisdom.

"Well, you can believe me when I say he is dead; I know men, and Smyth could not have made it to the border. No, he is dead and gone, no longer our problem." Chow turned and smiled at General Trang and offered the old prick a stunning statue of a warrior of the Chin dynasty.

"He is magnificent; I will give him a place of honor in my house." The General said, then turned and left the room. Chow wished he could have filled the statue with thirty pounds of Semtex, then he could have atomized the arrogant old fuck while he raped another of his grandsons. The old bastard was right, it had been two months since John had escaped, and he was questioned for six months before that. God, he hated to admit it, but the old fuck could be right.

Smyth had to be dead, or in such shit shape, he wouldn't make it back to the real world alive. Chows need everything to be tied up, with no loose ends. The thought of what would happen if John wasn't dead caused him to think of what would happen if John managed to make it to a place where he could contact anyone in Langley. Anyone would be all it would take to blow this operation wide open.

Tran caught a ride with a man back to the first village. The tiny village was only twenty miles from the border. Standing in the center of the village, Tran remembered his home; he was becoming excited to see the small village he had grown up in. To see the valley nestled between the mountains with its fertile land and hard-working, kind people who lived and died there. Looking around this small village, Tran could see this village was like so many others in Tibet. Smiling and thanking the man for his kindness, Tran turned and walked out of the dusty village with his eyes firmly set on the mountains to the west. Tran didn't mind the walk; he savored the fresh air of the mountains. Tran made his first camp in the cleft between two enormous rocks.

Sitting in his little camp, he wondered what brought these two giant rocks in line so they would be perfectly placed for his need. Of the amount of soot on them, many others had also been availed to their placement. That night Tran made a small fire; using a small tin pot, Tran heated some rations he had managed to sneak out of the barracks. The Chinese were so paranoid men weren't allowed to have foodstuff in their barracks. The thinking was no food, no desertion. This shows what they knew, more men ran from the people's army than anyone knew, even though it meant a death sentence if caught. But if you were careful and quiet about it, then the officers would look the other way and where he was coming to the end of his time. Tran's commanding officers were happy to do so and let him have some food for the trip home. After he ate his small meal, Tran sat back against one of the rocks and peered up at the stars. Tran still remembered the American he found and let go. Tran remembered his father saying it was every man's right to be free and that no man should be able to claim ownership of another. He smiled as he recalled his father telling him this over one of the meals his mother prepared for their family in their small home.

Tran smiled when he heard the small mountain birds sing the sun over the edge of the mountains. Tran had been so comfortable the night before he never realized he had fallen asleep. He found a small stream flowing out of the rocks at the base of the mountain. The water was from the snow and ice holding the mountains captive, even in the short summer. Tran filled his canteens and then drank from the stream, the water was so cold his teeth stung for a second, and his lips grew numb. Tran knew the way back to his little village. He thought he could do it in about a week if everything went alright. Tran knew it was early in the summer, so Tran wouldn't have to worry about any storms snowing in the passes. Tran knew he was going to have some challenging climbs ahead of him, especially without the right equipment. Tran also knew he was in the best shape of his life, which was the one thing the Chinese army did for you; it kept you lean and muscular.

Chapter 17

JOHN COULD HEAR THE shuffling gate of the old man walking, lying in his bed under the mountain of covers. He listened as the steps came closer to his curtain-covered doorway. As the curtains were pulled back, John realized these steps belonged to a different 'old monk' John decided he liked the other old monk better. This man, even though he had a look of peace and concern on his wrinkled old face, he also had a case full of needles.

"I hope you're here to tailor me a new suit of clothes." John croaked, surprised to hear how weak he still sounded. Holy hell, I must have been damn near dead, he thought. John knew he had been in bad shape; he also knew he wasn't in very good condition yet and wouldn't be for some time. The old monk smiled and smoothed John's brow like a loving old grandfather would do for a sick child. Smiling, the old monk said something that had no meaning to John and inserted the first needle under his skin. Then John felt, well, nothing, the new 'old' monk started to hum some kind of tune, and the tone and cadence helped put John to sleep. When he woke, John found both the old and the 'new' old monks looking down at him. Looking around the small room, John could see the heads of these men nearly touching the ceiling. If their heads came close to the cave ceiling, John knew he would never be able to stand straight up. He also caught sight of his left arm. At least John thought it was his arm. There were needles in the flesh of his hands and along a path running up his arm. John heard of the ability of these needles to heal, but he always thought of the claims as a bit outrageous. Laying in the bed with the needles in his flesh, John knew these hair-thin needles would help heal him. The two old men looked down at him and smiled and nodded in the universal language of 'feel better,' and yeah, he did feel better; John smiled and nodded back to the old monks. This seemed to please the old guys, and they went off smiling. John fell back to sleep and then woke when the monk who placed the needles in his flesh returned to remove the needles. John fell asleep when he tried to count the needles as the old monk removed them from his left arm. John's days blended together, waking for needles, and then to be fed, then retaking the needles. One day the old monk placed his food on a little table at the foot of his bed.

"Ah, the bed and breakfast thing is over," John said. The monk came and helped pull the heavy blankets off him. John was shocked to see how bad his left foot still looked. He knew he'd been with the monks for quite some time; he had no way of telling how long. His system of trying to count the days by the number of times he was fed and then woke up needed to be more accurate. John's foot was now yellow instead of purple. Also, he could see how badly it had been bruised. Either the Chinese or he had broken his big toe and the middle toe; the whole foot seemed to be healing from one deep bruise. It was only after he looked at his foot that John realized he was still as naked as the day he was born. Well, they weren't worried about personal space.

Turning to look at the monk, John saw he was holding up a robe for him. The robe the man held would have fetched a heavy price in the haberdashery shops of New York, London, or Paris. It looked to be handmade with woven wool, which had been dyed the deepest red. The robe was hand-stitched silk, with a mountain scene on the back, and the red of the body was offset by gold silk on the cuffs and the lapels. When John looked at this piece of handcrafted art, he wondered what he ever did to have the right to wear such a thing. When John looked at the elderly monk holding the robe for him, he asked how he could ever find the kind of peace he saw in the man's eyes. John couldn't remember any time that his nurse didn't have a contented smile on his lips; the smile was ever present on the man's face.

Chapter 18

MIKE KNEW THE ONLY course of action he could take for his self-preservation. As far as Mike was concerned, saving his life was the only course that mattered. Mike knew if it came down to it, he would kill his best friend to further his life or to make himself richer. Mike told Chow how John started to research all the orders he had been given from the time of his arrival in Hong Kong to his last order. Mike explained John found out about his past hits. Mike told Chow that John knew about all of the hits. Chow went into a rage; what Mike didn't tell Chow was he had given John all the bank account information for all the accounts. Mike stood and listened to Chow's rage. He wasn't going to tell his boss that right now, John Smyth, the man they most needed to find dead, could be running around with the ability to take billions of dollars from his syndicate. Chow paid General Trang to hunt John down; when Trang's men, with Mike's help, found John, they should have killed him. Instead, Trang thought John had information about Chows' accounts, and the fat General wanted those accounts. Trang should have killed John as soon as he had him in the prison; instead, Trang started to question John. John did him proud. He had taken everything the General and his twisted minions could deal out, then escaped. Well, good for you, Mr. John Smyth, good for you, and it's going to be your sad demise if I ever see your ass again, Mike thought as he smiled at his reflection in the apartment's windows. Mike felt the effect of reflection gave off was more demon rather than demur.

Sitting at the top of the pass, Tran looked back to the valley he'd just climbed out of. The climb was more challenging than he remembered. The difficulty was from a rock slide that occurred sometime while he had been gone. Most likely, the rocks were dragged down the side by an avalanche. Tran was forced to navigate what remained of the trees that at one time lined the lower part of the mountain, drifting off into a valley. Tran smiled; he now knew his skills in the art of climbing hadn't faded. Looking out from the top of the mountain he had just climbed, Tran could see the two passes he would have to surmount to reach his home. Tran couldn't wait to see his parents and, most of all, his sister. Tran wondered what she would look like now. Sitting in a small alpine valley, drinking from his canteen Tran smiled.

The mountains didn't look too far apart; however, Tran knew with the altitude and looking from peak to peak, even the most experienced climbers could be fooled. Often misjudging the distance got climbers into trouble that could and often did take their life. Tran cautioned himself not to get in a hurry. He knew what could happen when one hurried climbing these mountains. Tran had seen it many times when his father and some of the other men from his village would go and rescue professional mountain climbers from the heights. Tran started to go with his father when he was fifteen; Tran's father told him he was old enough to see what the mountain would do if he didn't give the mountain the respect it required. Often his father and the other men of the village would bring back the body wrapped up; other times, the man who came back couldn't breathe right. Tran remembered one who had frozen his feet and hands along with his ears and even his nose and cheeks.

Chow-Yun, the American-born Chinese son of Chow-Yun Senior, switched his identity with a friend with whom he served during the Korean War. His friend, who was Chinese-born and forced to join the army, this friend told Chow – Yun Sr. he would never go back to China. This friend wanted to run to the South and then to America. Chow Yun Sr. and the rest of his unit were caught by heavy artillery. Chow Yun Sr. was the only survivor found after the bombardment was stopped. His friend was killed by the artillery, and lying in the battered field, Yun Sr. remembered his friend's plan of running to the South and then to America; he knew he didn't want to go back to North Korea, to the poverty and squaller that awaited him there. Lying with his legs broken and bleeding beside his friend's dead body, Chow Yun Sr. decided to switch papers before they were found. He could hear the American infantrymen slowly moving to check the bodies of the North Korean men for mines and other booby traps.

When he saw the first white face, Yun Sr. raised his hands and prayed this dirty soldier wouldn't shoot him. To his surprise, the man called for a medic and pulled away his weapon. Yun Sr. could hardly believe it when the Americans rushed him to a hospital and then operated; saving his injured legs, they cared for him. Once he healed enough, the officers at the hospital sent him to a p.o.w camp. Yun Sr. talked to an army Colonel, and he told the Colonel how much he hated it in the North. His talks with the Colonel grew, so he saw the man almost daily. One day as he walked the perimeter of the camp, he watched as the Americans unloaded a captured Chinese officer. This officer was captured in the aftermath of an extended battle. The Americans knew the Chinese were involved in the war effort but had never captured an officer before. Finally, Yun Sr. knew how he was going to be of service. Hurrying to the camp office, Yun asked to see the Colonel, and he was forced to wait, which he was happy to do.

When finally the Colonel walked out of the office, Yun Sr. told the man he was a translator and that he could translate intercepted radio signals. Or the interrogations of this officer, along with others they captured. Yun Sr. proved himself repeatedly. His work helped stop the Chinese from moving more troops into North Korea. For his help in the war effort, Chow-Yun senior had been offered a career working for the Americans in South Korea, which he happily accepted. He never told anyone his real name was Chin-ho-Fat. He knew his family had buried the wrong man, that his mother had cried for him. When he was just a boy, his father once told him some sacrifices needed to be made in life, and that's what he was forced to do; he sacrificed his past. Now he was retired and had a good life with his wife. She was Korean, and even she didn't know his secret. His son worked for the American government though he didn't know what department. All Chow Junior could tell him was it was in the army medical core. He was proud of what he had done, proud of what he had accomplished with his new name. Chow Sr never thought of the consequences for the real Yun family, having a son who was a deserter, then a traitor. He could only guess at the punishment they would have suffered. He pushed it from his mind; he would have to pay for it someday.

When he died, and faced his friend and his family, but his son had a good life and was a good man, thanks to his friend's plan. It was the best plan Yun Sr. could come up with in the little time he had as he lay in the mud of that forgotten field, his lifeblood mixing with the rain of the long-ago day. He had decided that he would not go back to the poverty and squalor of the North; he wanted what his cousins had in the South. Freedom, he didn't have a wife or a child yet, but Yun Sr. someday he would, and he knew that going back to the North was not the answer. He was going to run with his friend, then fate intervened, and he was left with a choice. He never thought about his choice; he just switched identities with Chow Yun and never looked back. Chow Yun Sr. couldn't know his son Chow Yun Jr had become everything he hated. The man who lied and suffered to get to America so his family would have a better life. He was now the father of the man responsible for the pain and degradation drugs brought to the world every day.

Chow-Yun Jr knew what he needed to do. John's body hadn't been found yet. He, like everyone else, was ready to have John buried.

What Chow needed to do was put John Smyth behind him and look toward his future. Chow knew, at best, he only had six months before he had to disappear. Chow knew he might be able to stretch it to eight months if he paid the right people. The only problem with having too many bodies on the payroll was someone always fuck things up for you; no six months, and that's it, Chow thought. He could move to an island somewhere in the south pacific and have everything delivered, including his small private army. Not an army made from the natives, no, Chow wanted men who worked for money, no questions asked, pros, no amateurs wanted, thank-you, six months then it was all his. Chow could keep his drug and arms dealing going from anywhere on the planet, hell once you're as big as he is, it really did become a global market.

Chapter 19

LYING IN BED, JOHN could hardly believe how tired going to the little table and back to bed had made him. He had never needed help before. Now, he needed help to walk ten feet or go to the bathroom. The meal was just as bad as the broth the monk had been feeding him. This time he had some kind of bread to eat with his meal. John had never had bread like this before. The bread was heavy and tasted sweet; along with the bread, the monk brought a bowl of cream. The monk showed John how they dunk the bread into the cream and eat it for dessert.

"You know, I don't know how I'm ever going to repay your kindness," John said as the old monk looked at him and smiled.

"I don't know if you can't understand me or you think I'm just a simple-minded fool blathering at you, but thanks for everything." Once again, the old monk just bowed his way out of the room. Lying on his back, John could hear the two monks gibbering together on the other side of the curtain. John looked at the ceiling of his cave and thought about his plan once he left this place. Listening to the monks, he realized he was damn curious to know what the two old monks talked about on the other side of the curtain. John could remember when one of the monks came in and rolled him over onto his stomach. The old monk then started to hum a tune as he placed his needles into John's flesh. Once the monk was finished with the needles, the monk lit some of the worst-smelling incense, then chanted though John couldn't tell how long the monk stayed or when the monk left. John seemed to drift in and out of sleep, though he wouldn't come fully awake. John would be aware someone was at his bedside chanting. He was even aware of the needles. One of the monks, the one John had started calling Bob, smiled his toothless grin as he helped him into the robe and out of bed.

"There's nothing on the table, so it must be the day that you're going to see if I can walk on my own or if I fall on my face 'eh' Bob?" John asked, more to himself, knowing that he wasn't going to get an answer out of Bob.

"No, no fall on the face, then in bed longer," Bob replied.

"You speak." John started to stammer as he was ushered into a larger room and found twenty monks looking at him. For a moment, John thought he was looking at a large family. John realized even though these men called each other brother, they were all from different parentage. John stood staring at the monks, then around what he thought was a room. It turned out to be a cave, quite a large one by any standard. The walls were painted in different scenes showing a man sitting in other places, surrounded by different people. In the background, you could always see the mountains of Tibet. As John looked at the cave walls, he could tell the mountains were painted at different seasons of the year. John also recognized the figure of the man sitting in the foreground of the paintings as the image of the Tibetan Buddha. Looking at the men of this cave, John knew how bad it would be for them if the Chinese ever found out these men of the mountain had taken him in and healed him. These men of the Buddha would be thrown into prison, where he had been held, and they would be tortured. Then when they finally died, their bodies would be thrown into the mass grave the prison kept in the hills.

"I wish I knew of some way to thank all of you for the kindness you've shown me," John said. He looked at the faces of these devout men. John could see not all of them understood what he was saying, but a few whispered in the ears of others, translating his words. John told them he had been captured by the Chinese and held in a military prison. He was about to say to them about the torture he had suffered. Then John thought they had healed him and washed him. If anyone knew about the torture he suffered, it would be these men.

"I work for the American government, but I was used by an evil man for his own gains. All I want now is to get back to where I can tell someone of this man's evil." John Said as he looked at the sitting men in the main room of the cave.

"You must come with me." A cracked and raspy voice beckoned from behind John. When he turned, John found the voice belonged to a man who could have been one hundred years old if he was a day.

"There is one here. This man can tell you of the cruelty of the Chin; this man doesn't have to speak of the suffering they cause. It is on him daily. You should carry his story with you." John watched the old man lurch and limp his way down a tunnel. Watching this old man walk hurt John, even in his condition. This corridor had curtains hanging in front of doorways. They were the same as his given sanctuary. John wondered if these rooms ever held men who managed to escape from the Chinese as he had. If so, had these others been as close to death as he had before he was found and brought here? Stepping into another room, John could make out a shape sitting in a chair beside a bed in the corner of the room. Looking at the figure, John could tell something was wrong with this person. The old man who led John to this room turned a small oil lamp up and revealed a man; at least, John thought it was a man. One leg and one arm had been amputated. Also, this poor bastard's body was bent, and his face was wrong. It was like half of it had been eaten away.

"What happened to him?" John asked as he looked closer, then, ashamed of his morbid curiosity, looked away. The first thing that jumped out at him about the room, it was neat; it was so neat and tidy that it bordered on the obsessive. The bed was made with military tightness, and the top sheet was folded over the blanket. John would bet the folded sheet measured eight inches exactly. The small keepsakes on the shelves were arranged according to the height of the objects.

"He was questioned by the Chin." The old monk was telling John. "When they couldn't get what they wanted out of him, they started cutting him. General Trang did this, then infection came, and he was thrown out into the wild to die in agony. Friends found him, they brought him to us here, and through the years, we have brought him back to the living, and now he stays here, in peace." John watched as the misshapen face came up and had to look around the room with the one eye the poor man had left. John was surprised when the hazel orb locked on his face, and what John thought was a smile played across the man's lips. John could see the scares on this poor bastard's throat, the old monk explained. The men who tortured this man grew tired of hearing his screams. They had the prison doctor cut his vocal cords so they wouldn't have to listen to his agony. The old monk explained the doctor who did this wasn't good at his job. While he had managed to damage the vocal cords, the operation didn't sever them completely, "So our friend can still whisper." Looking at this poor bastard, John was glad he had gotten the hell out of that prison before they could do this to him. A misshapen hand reached for a small handheld chalkboard and a piece of chalk. One of the monks looked at what the man was writing. Turning, he shrugged to Bob, then to John; he said.

"This message must be for you." John was about to say he didn't speak Tibetan. When the man in the corner of the room was finished writing the message, he turned the board so that John could see the message. To his shock, the message was written in English.

It said, 'My name is Ben Stills; I'm English; if you could, would you get in touch with the embassy and tell them I'm alive and where I am, thank you.' John walked over to Mr. Ben Stills and placed a hand on his shoulder. The man looked up at John, and for a moment, John thought the man was going to cry, but again the smile played at the corners of the man's tortured and battered face.

"I'm going to be here for a while, Ben; I still have a lot to do. When I can leave, I give you my word. I will get in contact with the English government." The head just nodded for a moment. John wanted to ask some questions and then thought it would be rude to do so. Holding the curtain for the monk he now called Bob, John turned and raised his hand to wave and watched as Ben did the same.

"If it's alright, I would like to come for a visit when I'm allowed?" John asked. A horse whisper came from the ruined face of Ben.

"I look forward to it," Ben answered. The whisper was so horse and airy John almost missed it as the curtain fell across the opening to Ben's room. For the first time, Ben allowed hope to burn faintly in his heart. That hope he might see the white cliffs of Dover again and be home. Ben had hopped his wife had found a good man, that she had moved on with her life, then he thought of his mother, he didn't know if she was alive. Ben thought of the way he looked, he didn't want his mother to see him this way, not now.

Chapter 20

HOME ...

STANDING OVERLOOKING the valley of his childhood, Tran could hardly believe that he was hearing the river Brahmaputra. This river had given life to the fields of the family farm. It gave life to the rest of the valley and the family farms in it. He must have been in more of a rush to get home than he knew. When he had camped that first night on the edge of the mountains, Tran thought it would take him a week, maybe longer, to get home. Now five days later, he stood on a ledge overlooking the valley where the village he grew up stood, where his family waited for his return. Tran found the path he had used many times as a young boy playing in the foothills of the mountains surrounding his village.

Tran could not believe how good it felt to be walking down this one path. The sun warmed his face and neck as the birds sang in the trees below. It felt like they were greeting him and asking where he had been for so long. Tran thought of the birds that flew away for the long cold winter. He felt like one of these birds when they get the chance to return for the summer. Tran could smell the wood smoke from the fires in the village homes as it wafted through the forest. Tran knew all the families that lived in this valley. These families had boys his age; he and the other children took long walks to the little school together. Tran could hardly wait to sit at the fire in his father's hut and have his first cup of tea; they would have so many questions. He would answer them one at a time, then go out and find Ling-Tou. Tran hoped she hadn't been married while he was gone. He would take up his courtship of her where they had left off.

Further down the path, the rocks had been covered by moss and dead pine needles. The smell of them as he walked brought back more memories of his childhood. Tran caught his fingers going to the scar on his forehead. When he was ten years old, Tran had played too long in the hills and didn't want to get into trouble, so he decided he would run home. As boys often do, Tran thought he was running as fast as any boy in the world had ever run. All at once Tran slipped on some moss clinging to the path, falling. Tran hit his head on some rocks, causing a large cut on his forehead and knocking him out. Tran's father told him when he didn't come for the evening meal, he and some other men from the village went to search for him. When he was found, they thought Tran was dead. Trans father said he had carried him home with a broken heart. His father told Tran god had him for three days and that his mother wailed so loudly for the whole three days god himself gave Tran back to keep her quiet. Tran laughed to himself and thought how many times he had heard his mother's voice screech at him in the fields. Tran jokingly told his father it would have been nice if god would have kept his hearing before he gave him back. Trans father told him it was not nice to speak like that, but in the same breath, he told Tran he would have given his hearing to have him back. Father and son shared a laugh and would look at each other when Tran's mother was angry at them for lingering in the fields, causing their dinner to grow cold. Standing at the foot of the path, Tran looked out at the valley ahead of him; his life had been spent here. That was until the Chinese decided to invade. For six years, they had left this part of Tibet alone, then, like so many others. The Chinese had to force their will on him and his family, stealing what was not freely given. There had been a dirt path his father and the other men of the village used to get to another village over the south pass. They called it a road, but in reality, it was little more than two dirt ruts running side by side. In some places, the dirt ruts gave way to the flat stone plain of a ridge. It was in these places men built cabins and corals for travelers and their animals to rest at. In other places, it turned into gravel flats. Some of the heartier mountain grasses tried to grow in these places. Some thrived while others, as in life, withered and died. Turning, Tran started to walk to where he remembered his father's house was. He would have called if his family had a telephone, hell his family hadn't even heard of the telephone until the Chinese came. He couldn't have sent a letter, but the Chinese were stopping all types of communication coming into and out of Tibet. They had become increasingly paranoid, and with the growing sentiment around the world that China should leave Tibet, most of the free world knew the Chinese had no right to be in the country. The Chinese were looking for other countries that would support them. At the same time, the Chinese were hunting down and trying to silence any group that pushed any agenda against their claim to the country. If these individuals or groups were found to be on Chinese soil and they considered Tibet their soil. These poor souls would be arrested and, in most cases, never seen or heard from again. Walking down the road that led from the mountain path to his village Tran reached a spot where he remembered his father and some of the village men placed a sign with the name of their village on a post. Tran had waited to see the sign; for him, it was a way of confirming he was indeed home. Standing in one of the dirt ruts, Tran looked for the sign; he could see where the post that once held the sign had been. The post was broken at the ground, and no one ever replaced the post or the sign. Stepping from the rut, Tran started looking in the long grass growing to the side of the road. It didn't take Tran long to find the sign; it was riddled with bullet holes. Standing in the long grass, Tran looked around, a bad feeling creeping into his thoughts.

Mike knew the depths of his rage, and in times like this, he gladly swam in the heated seething waters of it. It wasn't often that Mike got to let his other side out of its cage, but in this instance, he gave into his baser needs. Mike thought about the word needs. He knew at times he truly needed to kill somebody; it was an animal that lived in him. General Trang's assistant made the mistake of being in a single's bar where gay men who liked to dabble in the finer acts of sadism, and masochism, find their partners. For these men, what they practiced was less to do with sex. More times, it was for a pleasure that could kill and often did. By letting himself be picked up by Mr. Mike Styles, Trang's assistant was now in the hands of a monster. Mike had no desire to play the games of this pervert, and if this man had known how Mike felt about his preference, Trang's assistant would have never left the bar with Mike; he would have run to his boss.

Trang's assistant wasn't up to his usual standard of a victim, not since John had bitten the fingers off the pervert's right hand. Having any kind of deformity made him ugly to the rest of the upper clientele of the establishment. Often the little man had to pick up the leftovers at the end of the night. Now Mike wasn't gay, but he knew Trang's assistant was, and Mike needed answers, and he would get them one way or another. Mike could be a cruel and evil bastard, and he enjoyed his cruelty, really enjoyed it. The rumors of this particular assistant of Trangs had been floating around for some time. After watching this pervert at the bar trying to pick up some of the pretty boys and being turned down when they caught sight of his hand, Mike knew them to be true. It was rumored this assistant would use rape to get men to talk and that he would rape young boys just for the fun of it. Mike's way of thinking was that he was doing the world a favor with the course of action he was now undertaking. What was one less pervert in the world, hell Mike thought he could kill all the sick bastards in the bar, and who would miss them, certainly not the police.

The great thing about Hong Kong was, since the Chinese retook control of it, you could get away with murder, really get away with murder. Looking out the window of this apartment, Mike relished the quiet time after a night's hard work. It had taken hours and a course of rituals starting with needles; these needles could be used for the curing of pain and helping the body heal itself. However, in the right hands, they could be used to cause unbearable pain. Most people have a pain threshold, you can take your victim to this threshold, but once you cross that threshold, you delve into the unknown areas of the brain. How the brain will react becomes unknown; with this pain comes the breaking of the mind. At this point, some people can stand any amount of pain. Nothing will bring them back; they become a shell with nothing left inside. All you can do is put a bullet in their skull and move on.

The art was to bring them to the edge and let them teeter on the brink, then pull them back. This could go on for hours, even days, for the more initiated. For Trang's assistant, this wasn't the case. He started to break after the first round, which pissed Mike off. It would have been more fun for Mike if the man had shown some backbone and held out a little. A man who was supposed to be able to torture men into giving up their families. One that was into sadistic acts on men and boys, the coward couldn't handle a little pain himself. At the beginning of the second round, the man started to give Mike some information. Still, it wasn't until the middle of the third round he began to provide Mike with helpful information about what had happened to John. The assistant had talked, and toward the end, the freak whispered, but that was fine with Mike. He had gotten what he needed. When Trang's assistant finally broke, he spoke in bursts. Mike saw this before; most people will answer questions in a rapid-fire staccato burst of speech. However, later during the night, the freak whispered. If Trang's assistant had taken longer and could absorb more than he had, Mike would have enjoyed his time with the little pervert, but in the end, everyone has their limits. When the assistant had reached his limit, Mike could almost hear the pervert's mind break. Mike knew the mind was gone when he took one of the needles and inserted it into the assistant's right eye. Mike stood and watched the man as he gave no reaction to the destruction of his eye; time for the bullet, Mike thought.

The body was gone, and Mike had cleaned up the mess. Of course, he had used drop cloths, and the bleach and ammonia-based cleaners ensured that no d.n.a. was left behind. Fresh as a daisy after his shower, Mike sat in his favorite chair, enjoying a cold beer and looking out at the city; he chuckled as he thought of the advertisement, 'It's Miller time.' Mike now knew for sure Trang had looked for John, and General Trang never found him. At best, the search for John had only covered ten kilometers around the prison, as well as a twenty-kilometer cursory air search. Once they found tracks heading toward the river, the officers in charge reported John tried to swim the river. So, Trang, that old fuck assumed John drowned in the river. Mike knew John was alive. He goddamn well knew it, like he knew the sun would rise from the east in the morning. Picking up the phone, Mike called Chow and reported what he had found out. Mike listened to his Chow breath on the other end of the line. It had taken everything Chow had not to lose his composure and start shouting at Mike. Nodding, Mike ended the call, then turned to look out over the city; this time, he wasn't smiling.

The only thing that could fuck up his timeline was if John Smyth wasn't dead and if John somehow managed to show up somewhere in the world where he didn't have any control. Chow-Yun turned and looked at the unfinished meal on the dining table. There was nothing wrong with the food. The call he had just received from Mike was enough to kill any appetite. He lived in the best places, and the food could be served to any President or Royal family member; no, not eating the food wasn't the chef's fault. He didn't eat because he still had to think of where John Smyth could hurt him. He was going to have to get Mike Styles out of Hong Kong and onto mainland China there; Mike could find out where Smyth ended up. Chow knew that General Trang was sure John Smyth was dead, but he didn't share that hope. After Mike questioned the old General's pervert assistant, Chow had less faith in what the man told him. Chow stood looking at the reflection of the meal sitting on the table. Even in the reflection of the large windows, it still looked delicious. Chow looked back to his reflection in the widow; one man could bring his empire to its knees and him as well. One hundred billion worth of drug money, as well as the profits of his arms sales, one man, and that bastard, had to be John Smyth; it always came back to John. The agency and Mike had built the bastard from childhood, and now their beast was lost in the world with information that could destroy him. There wasn't any handle on John, no way to control him. No friends or family to use against him. Chow looked in the reflection again; he looked scared.

Chapter 21

JOHN STARTED TO COUNT the days; he made a rudimentary calendar with small stones he had found. One day the monk John called Bob and took him out of his room. The old monk walked ahead of him like he was leading John someplace.

They passed what John could only assume were the entrances to prayer rooms; he could hear chanting from some of them, while in others, he saw men sitting on the floor writing on scrolls of some kind. Bob walked over to a large wooden door. The door looked like it was fitted into the stone of the mountain by a master stone mason, looking at the door and then at his silent friend and doctor. For a moment, John wondered if he had reached the end of his stay, but then the smile came to his wizened face; the old man opened the door and stepped outside. Holding the door for John, the old man beckoned him to step out of the doorway. John knew he wasn't going to try and lock him out, so smiling, John stepped out of the door and gasped at the brilliance that seemed to envelop him. Standing on the ledge that seemed to hang out over the world, John reveled in the fresh cool air of the mountain. He looked around and then up and couldn't see the peak of this mountain. At first, John didn't want to get too close to the edge, but as he stood and watched the monk who had taken care of him, John knew nothing would happen to him, not as long as Bob was with him. He didn't know how the old monk would be able to save him if anything did happen. Somehow John knew the old man would. Standing with his toes near the ledge, John looked out over the mountains of Tibet. Standing there, John realized he wasn't seeing the whole mountains; he was looking at the peaks of the mountains. If he were to take a guess, John would have guessed he was seeing the top twenty present of this mountain range. When he looked down, he couldn't see anything. It was all the most brilliant white as if the world had been scrubbed clean, and in its place, nothing but untainted snow remained. John knew in this high redoubt he was above the clouds that follow the valleys. He was seeing the side of the clouds seldom seen by many other than pilots and mountaineers. When you looked at the clouds from the ground, they had shape and definition because of shadows along with variations in the topography, but up here, there are no shadows; it was all a beautiful, brilliant white. Turning, John nodded to Bob, and they went back inside.

"How did you find this place?" John asked. Wondering how long they had looked before this paradise was found. Had these men been to other places and were forced to leave them behind, or had this place been known before?

"It was not I who found this cave, no this place was found long before this life I now enjoy started, and it will be here after I move on to the next," Bob replied as he led John back into the cave. John wanted to ask more questions, but Bob turned and held open another curtain for him to enter. Sitting on a bench was a young boy, his head shaved the same as the older monks. The boy wore the same gold and red rapping as the others, but he seemed to be something special. Bob spoke to the boy in what he thought was Tibetan. The boy stood, walked over to John, placed a hand over his heart, and smiled. Turning boy said something to Bob, then sat Lotus style on the bench again.

"He wonders if you will stay until all your wounds have healed or if your world will call you back early?" Bob asked.

"I don't think I can answer that, and be honest, not that I would lie with the intent to deceive any of you," John answered. He knew the longer he stayed in this high redoubt, the greater the chances that they would be discovered, and if he was found here with these monks, the Chinese would butcher every last one. Once the Chinese were done here, if they thought a nearby village helped these monks, they would go to that village and punish any they perceived as complicit with the monk's actions; also, Ben would be killed outright.

"I am getting worried about the length of time I'm spending here. I worry the Chinese will find me here and punish you for it." John told Bob as they walked back to his room.

"I don't think you need to worry about the Chin. They have long ago given up on finding any more brothers after the news they were stealing and killing like common bandits was told to the world. They ran back behind their wall and are waiting for the day the rest of the world will forget, but thanks to friends we have made in other countries, we can keep the crimes of the Chin in the world news." John thought as long as this place was safe, then he would be foolish to leave there before he was healed.

Chapter 22

TRAN WALKED INTO THE village where he had grown up. He found places where he remembered other homes being, just like the village sign; now, most of the huts were gone or just rotting to nothing. His father's house should have been here; all he could find were some scraps of cloth and a charred board. It was as if nothing had ever been here; turning around, Tran surveyed the fields behind the house and from the growth of the weeds and the lack of care. Tran could tell the fields hadn't seen a plow or hoe in years. Tran had seen some huts further into the valley when he stood looking over his home. Tran thought they would know what had happened and maybe where he could find his family. The first hut he came to was empty and looked like it had been that way for some time. The dirt and dust had collected in the corners and on the tables. Tran could smell the odor of rot. Under the smell of decay, he could smell the faint copper scent of blood. Tran knew that a lot of blood must have been spilled here for the scent to last this long; Tran knew this family, Ling, lived here. Turning from the door of the hut, Tran caught movement in his peripheral vision.

When he turned, Tran could see a man standing in the tree line. The figure waved at him, then turned and pointed up the hill to Tran; it seemed as if the man was trying to keep his presents a secret. Turning in a slow circle, Tran wondered what or who the man could be worried about in the village. Tran hadn't seen anything to warrant a clandestine meeting. Taking one more look around, Tran walked out of the village to where the stranger had pointed. Tran knew the area where he grew up. Tran also knew where the man had indicated was an empty ledge overlooking the village when he left for the Chinese army.

The man who came to the edge of the forest and beckoned Tran to follow him was a man Tran remembered. Buntang was younger than Tran; he was now in his early twenties. Buntang had something to tell Tran, and he said it was important; Tran could tell the man was uncomfortable. Buntang looked at Tran and then at the sky; Tran was shocked when tears filled the young man's eyes. Just before Tran was going to ask why he had called him to this spot, Buntang sighed and then started his story. When the younger man started, he continued until the whole story was finished. The story Buntang told Tran seemed to take the breath out of his chest; his blood seemed to run ice cold. Tran would have never thought of what he was now hearing; it wasn't that he disbelieved the young man. It was that Tran didn't want to believe him. Buntang told him what happened to his family and the village, but it never really sank in until Tran found himself standing back where his father's hut had once been. Tran couldn't remember walking back to where he had grown up. It seemed he had just opened his eyes, and there he was.

Buntang told Tran about the commanding officer of the garrison in this region of Tibet. He told Tran how cruel the man was, and Buntang told Tran the Colonel was a smaller man. What the Colonel lacked in size, he made up for in his sadistic ways. The Colonel's favorite thing to do was to rape young girls. It gave him a sense of power that he was having them before they were married. This Colonel boasted he took what their Tibetan husbands were not man enough to. The Colonel saw his sister on one of his patrols and decided he would be her first, even though she had just turned thirteen.

That night the commander had his men drag Tran's mother and father out of the hut into the rain. This Colonel told Tran's parents and those who stepped out of their houses to see why Tran's mother was screaming. If they interfered, he would instead kill the girl. Buntang didn't want to tell Tran the rest of what happened that night, but after Tran clutched his arm and pleaded, Buntang relented. He sadly told Tran his little sister had gotten hold of the Colonels' knife and had slashed him across the face putting out his left eye. While the man stood screaming, clutching his face, she stabbed and slashed the Colonel in the crotch, ruining his genitals. Screaming in pain and rage, the Colonel ordered Tran's family shot and left in the hut as it was put to the torch.

When the Colonel and the patrol left the village, Buntang and some others went and buried Tran's family. When this Colonel found out the rest of the town had shown Trans sister who maimed him great honor. The Colonel returned a month later with his men and killed everyone who remained in the village, mostly the older people. Together Buntang and some other men placed stones on Tran's family and the graves of the other villagers on the once-empty ledge of the mountain that overlooked their home. Buntang pointed to the mountain Tran's father had climbed when he was a young man. Tran tried to come to grips with what had happened to his family and friends. At the same time, he was forced into the P.L.A. Tran knew Buntang wouldn't lie about what happened, but he still didn't want to believe his family had been murdered in such a way. Tran's father was a respected member of the village, and it showed when Tran found the burial site.

A large pile of interlocking stones marked where the village had interred his family. Prayer's had been written on scraps of brightly colored cloth, red, blue, and yellow. Every time the wind moved these clothes, the prayers written on them were sent to heaven. Tran knew he couldn't add his own prayer to the others. It wouldn't be right, not as long as the hate and rage built in him. He would have to expend justice for his sister, mother, and father. Tran knew his mother would look down from heaven. His mother's wish would be for Tran could leave this country to go someplace where the Chinese had no reach. Turning away from the graves of his family. Tran swore an oath he would return when his hands satisfied his heart's need for vengeance. Standing beside the burial site, Tran looked over the valley he longed to come home to; now, he knew he would never see it again. Tran turned and looked at the granite ramparts he would have to climb to get at the Colonel who murdered his family. Back into the mountains, this time, instead of looking forward to a happy life on his father's farm, Tran knew this would be his last mission. He put all thoughts of a future out of his head. In all reality, Tran knew he would not live to his next birthday, and that would be fine. As long as he died knowing the Colonel and the men responsible were lying dead as well.

Chapter 23

JOHN REMEMBERED A SAYING from his past; he couldn't remember where he heard it or who said it to him; he just remembered the words. 'There nothing more dangerous man than a righteous man quietly seeking vengeance.' John didn't know if he wanted vengeance or if it was justice he wanted. John knew these people who only wanted to live in peace. They needed justice. He also knew the world needed to know what China was doing in this part of the world. John decided to stay with the monks until they said he was strong enough to make his way out of the mountains. He started to walk around the caves that seemed to go far into the mountain. Both his feet were healing, though they still hurt him first thing in the morning. The monk John called Bob and told him his feet would hurt for the rest of his life; John was also told the pain would get worse as he got older. When John wasn't walking around trying to get his strength back, he would visit with Ben Stills. It had taken some time for their conversations to start; Ben would sit and look straight ahead, and sometimes, he would turn his face away, knowing how he looked. John became used to the long silence. He understood why the man hadn't wanted to be the one to start the conversation. Ben had been in this place for so long that he had probably given up hope of ever returning to his family. John did not want to push the older man into any conversation. It was part of the training for most people in secret services of countries around the world. 'If you are caught, then you are on your own unless we have one of theirs, you won't be coming home unless you can get away, and you are obliged to try to escape when the chance arises.' John asked Ben about the prison he had been held in and if he knew the name of the man who had tortured him. Turning seemed to cause Ben pain. It looked painful from what John could see of the man's ruined face, John expected Ben to pick up his little chalkboard, but instead, a horsed, airy whisper came from the man's ruined voice.

"I was picked up outside of the American embassy in Hong Kong; I was on my way to warn the America security people they had a turncoat working for them in the C.I.A. detachment." It seemed to hurt Ben to speak, John filled a small cup with water for him, and after a small sip of the water, Ben went on.

"A group of Chinese men grabbed me in front of an American official; I thought it would be only a short time before my government found out I had been grabbed. I thought they would be working on getting me out. I stumbled on this information decoding telephone calls; I was an analyst." Ben told John.

"So whoever watched you get snatched was probably the one who turned you over to the Chinese, most likely to save his own ass," John said, looking at the floor. He knew that's what had happened in his own case. It only took John a second to think of his next question.

"Hey Ben, have you ever heard of the name Chow Yang?" John asked.

"No, not that I can recall, but then again, so much is gone with the torture and the drugs they used to get information," Ben said.

"Yeah, it does take a toll; how about General Trang? Have you ever heard of him?" John asked as he looked at the floor, amazed Ben could talk at all.

"Him, I know; he was the one who questioned me for weeks, then he was called away. The man he left in charge of my interrogation started using razors on me. Then he would rub filth into my wounds, so the infection would set in. When they thought I would die from the infection, they threw me into a mass grave behind the prison." Ben reached for another drink of water to help him speak. John looked at the floor and realized he was clenching his fist so tight his hands hurt. Ben looked at John's hands for a second, then at the only hand left to him.

"I don't know how long I was in the grave, but I managed to crawl out and into the woods. I kept blacking out; a young man found me and took me to his hut. He cleaned me up and left; I don't know if it was for a few hours or if it had been days. When he came back, I was at death's door. The monks told me I had slipped into what is called death sleep; I thought that was a coma. The next time I woke up, I was here, and the monks were forced to cut the infected areas off of me to keep me from dying. It's been three years since they brought me back from the dead." Ben looked straight ahead as he told his story. John thought Ben would be more emotional about telling of his ordeal. He realized spending three years with these kind, wise men of Buddha had given Ben peace. Maybe that's what saved Ben's sanity as well as his life. John wanted to tell Ben he was going to get back to the world outside these mountains. He would come back for him. Though John wanted to tell Ben he would be back for him, he just couldn't bring himself to. John didn't want to bring hope to Ben. He didn't want the man who had spent years lost to his family, to the world, thinking he was going home soon. John didn't know if he would make it out of Tibet.

Tran knew he would find the man he was looking for at the regional command center. The command center for this region of Tibet was in Ningchi, a small town to the west over the following mountain range. Turning, Tran looked back down at the place he had called home and was, just a short time ago, in such a rush to get to. Now it held only death and pain for him. As he stood beside the grave of his family, Tran promised he would bring pain and death to the man responsible for his family's destruction. Silent tears strained not to fall as Tran turned away from his family's grave. With a shattered heart, Tran started back into the mountains. Tran hoped to find his childhood sweetheart. He was shown her grave. The ones who buried his family knew about their plans for the future, so they buried her family next to his. Gone everything he had planned for was now gone. He was going to find a man, this man killed with no thought, no fear of repercussions. Tran couldn't see any future for himself. He could see his past, and what was to be was all gone for him. Into the mountains again, to hunt, to kill.

From what General Trang's assistant told Mike, they had less than a month before the good General would go to Tibet. The old bastard was going to look around and make sure the people were adequately cowed. Mike knew the General wasn't going to try and make the people happy and productive. He could care less about happy people anywhere. Instead, the General was going there to kill some men from the West. The assistant told Mike a journalism team from the B.B.C. had found and managed to get photographs and video of one of many mass graves dotting the country around the towns where the Chinese set up military garrisons. These journalists were caught gathering information for a news program aired by the B.B.C. This program exposed many atrocities perpetrated by other governments in third-world countries. Now the General could care less about what the rest of the world thought of China. The leaders, on the other hand, were trying to put a good face on the occupation of Tibet. They didn't want the rest of the world to find out about the mass graves filled mainly with the bodies of monks. So the men who governed China sent their meanest dog to do their dirty work, and it helped that the General liked his job. Mike knew while the General was gone, he could get into the man's office, then he might be able to find out where the army lost John. Mike knew from experience the last confirmed location where John was would be the best place to start his search, and that was the prison.

Chapter 24

John couldn't believe how vivid his dreams had become in the last week; it seemed every time he closed his eyes, he would see the lake. He didn't know the lake's name or where it was, but John was becoming convinced it was an actual lake. The man and woman getting killed, John knew they had been his parents, and he longed to remember his childhood. John thought if he could remember anything, the rest would come back to him. John didn't know their names; what was most troubling was he didn't have any feelings a son should have for murdered parents, no anger, no rage. He was shocked every time he saw the woman die. For John, it was like watching one of the news program society glued itself to after dinner. You felt bad for taking someone's life, but no emotional value was put on the loss.

ON THE OTHER HAND, John was bothered by what seemed to be the fact he had a brother out there somewhere. The boy in his dreams was older than he appeared to be. John could always see the other boy's face as they were being carried off. John assumed the other boy in his dream was his brother, and he wondered if this other boy was in the orphanage with him. If he was, John wondered if the other boy managed to be adopted. John heard of other boys being adopted when he was at the orphanage. Still, the boys never returned to the orphanage, was this brother a memory, or was he real?

Chapter 25

TRAN SPENT THE FIRST night truly alone in the world; he had always known his family waited for his return. Even though he had spent ten years in the Chinese special forces, when the Chinese officer had first seen Tran in basic hand-to-hand combat, he had watched as Tran used the skills his uncle taught him as a child. This officer took Tran out of regular basic training and placed him into the special forces. For ten years, Tran knew other Tibetan men who were forced to join the army. Still, he was the only Tibetan in the Zhongguo tezhong budui, so Tran always thought of himself as being alone. Now that he found out what had happened, Tran not only felt alone, he knew he was alone.

The villagers had gathered together and tried to get Tran to stay with them in the mountains. They said they would help him start a farm once again. They feared for Tran, and one of his father's closest friends offered to go with Tran. He thanked the man. This was something he had to do for himself; Tran thanked the people he had known for the first part of his life. Tran told them he was starting a new life, one he didn't want any of them to know of. When they could not keep Tran from leaving, the people of the village put together a pack with food and other things he would need to safely cross the Nyainqentanglha Mountains.

Tran thanked each one of the men who buried his family. He turned and found Ling To's mother standing behind him. Ling's mother held out a small pack with food in it. When Tran looked in the bag, he found Ling's favorite head scarf. Tran hugged the woman. He knew she had lost everything as he had. When the Colonel killed his family, the bastard also killed her daughter and husband. Tran turned to leave this time; he knew he would never be back. Tran wished the people peace and good fortunes, then walked into the mountains. Part of Tran wanted to stay and make a little home by the burial shrine holding his family, but Tran was determined to find the men who killed so many and have justice. Making his first camp on a mountain, Tran found a ledge that formed when a rock slide caused the lower part of the face to break away from the mountain. The giant granite slab fell into a small valley. Tran looked down on the bolder that lay far below. Behind the ledge was a depression in the mountain. You couldn't call it a cave; it wasn't deep enough. Tran thought calling it a depression was more accurate than a cave. That first night Tran watched as meteorites' burned their way across the night sky. He thought of his sister and how she was like one of these bright flashes in the sky. So beautiful in her flash, then gone so soon, looking out over the small valley. Tran promised his sister that if he lived long enough to bring her justice, he would go somewhere where it was possible to forget all about his past. That would only be possible after he killed the Colonel responsible for his family and many others' suffering. Looking up at the stars, Tran watched as three more meteorites burned their way through the night sky. Tran wondered if this was a good sign, if it was a sign that his mother, father, and sister watched over him now. Looking up at the stares, he whispered to his family to look away until he was finished with what must be done. Tran looked down as a tear rolled down his cheek. For the first time since he learned the truth about his family and love, Tran screamed his rage at the night sky.

Chapter 26

WAKING UP ONE MORNING, John dressed and ate with Bob. He followed his regular routine of walking the caves and tunnels that stretched off into the rest of the mountain. Then he went for his daily visit with Ben. After he visited with Ben, John decided it was time to leave this place of healing and harmony. John found he could walk around the cave and its multiple halls without his legs bothering him. John's feet, on the other hand, bothered him when he woke; he was starting to get used to the pain. The monks had been kind to him and had saved his life; John had no doubt of this fact. Ben had become his friend, and he liked to talk to the older man. Before he left, John reassured Ben when he made it out of Tibet, he would make sure he contacted the English government. Then he would come back for him and take him over the mountains himself. Standing on the ledge outside the cave, John turned and said his goodbyes to the monks. He turned and looked at the monk he called Bob and offered his hand. The old monk looked at his offered hand and reached to shake it. John could tell the old man had something to say to him, and when John nodded, the old monk smiled.

"When you walk out of this land, tell your story. You must remember this place is the home of your brothers. You must guard this knowledge, for the Chin will hunt again when you reach the outside world. Son may peace find your heart," the old monk said. John promised he would keep the secrets of this place. John thanked the men who held his body and his mind, then he turned and walked down the worn path. John's feet still hurt, and he could tell he would feel them for the rest of his life. He thought it was better to feel his feet than to have lost them. The monks had packed him a backpack full of food. Ben told John that the monks had found a tent with a sleeping bag; these items had been left on the mountain by some climber who had gotten into trouble and had to make a quick, light descent.

When John thought about it, he had come to the monks with nothing; he had been naked and on death's door. The monks took the time to heal and feed him, then they gave him clothes and a sturdy pair of boots. They even gave him food for the hike out of the mountains and a tent along with other gear. Smiling as he followed the path down the mountain. John was happy to be able to leave the monks of the mountain at the same time. He knew he would miss the quiet men of the cave. John would miss the old monk he called Bob the most. He had never been as close to anyone as he was to Bob. Missing someone for the first time was a new sensation. As John descended the path that led to the cave ledge, he felt a tingle at the base of his skull. Turning, John looked back up at the shelf. He raised his hand and waved to Ben, who had been helped out of the cave by the monks, to see him off. John watched as Ben raised his only hand and saluted.

John didn't realize when it had happened on his hike down the mountain, but he felt an old sensation again, the tingle at the base of his skull. Unlike before this time, he became uncomfortable, just as he had in the past before his time with the monks in the caves. John knew he was being watched by someone, but what were they up to. Not wanting to give the fact he suspected he was being watched, John continued down the mountain. John made it look as if he was weaker than he actually was, trying to draw the other person closer to him. Picking his way around rather than going over some more enormous obstacles. John was able to look back at the way he had just come. He didn't think one of the monks would follow him down the mountain. So if not one of the monks, then who? There was only Ben and himself being helped by the monks of the mountain.

Chapter 27

TRAN WATCHED AS THIS man walked down the path. He knew the monks take refuge in the caves which run deep inside this mountain and other mountains in this along with another area of Tibet. What would an American be doing coming from their cave? Tran wanted to find out? Tran decided to follow this man until he made camp for the night. Then he would wait until the American was asleep, sneak in, and find out who this large American was and why he walked as if he was hurt. Tran thought a man as large as this one would be able to carry his lite pack and tent with ease. As he watched this American, he could see the man took no chances climbing over rocks blocking his path. This American would first try and find a way around them. If no route was availed, then the American would carefully climb over. Tran smiled as he watched John use the rocks as a screen. Doing this allowed John to look back on the way he came. So this man has reason to be careful, Tran thought as he watched John slowly work his way around another obstacle.

John knew he was being followed. He thought he picked up a lone Chinese patrol, then decided that whoever was watching him was more curious than dangerous. If it had been a Chinese patrol, then the man would have run screaming for him to stop and would have forced John to kill him. Instead, the person just watched and kept his distance as well as his concealment. The path grew steeper the lower he went. The more immense boulders obstructed the trail. John began to wonder how the old man, along with his younger friend, managed to get him from the cart up to the cave when he was unconscious. John knew he wasn't what you would call small at six foot two inches and two hundred and thirty-five pounds. John was a fairly big man. Though being in the hands of the Chinese and tortured as he was, John knew most likely he was skin and bones when he was found. Hell, even now, he didn't think he was more than seventy-five. John knew in most western countries, billions of dollars were spent every year as people tried to lose weight. John chuckled as he thought of an advertisement, General Trang's fat camp. Though Trang was a big fat pig, John thought he would help knock the pounds off, then shook his head and chuckled again.

Coming to where the trail flattened out on a high plateau, John decided to make camp for the night. John was growing curious about the man who tailed him; he wanted to see if the man would come to his fire or if he would wait until he was in his tent and then try to find out about him. John didn't know when he had stopped thinking of the one following him as a threat. He just wanted to meet the person who would keep to the treeline making his climb harder just to feed his curiosity. John did not know how he knew it was curiosity keeping the other man watching him. John didn't fear this other person. He started to become curious about his watcher.

Making camp, John heated water to soak strips of cloth to wrap around his aching feet. With his feet looked after, John started to warm a packet of food the monks packed for him. To his surprise, John found they packed some of the broth that brought him back from death's door and some of the tea they always seemed to be brewing along with the broth and tea. John ate some of the dense bread, another staple of the mountain monks. Sitting by his small fire, hunger taken care of, and his feet calming their throbbing, John watched the darkening sky as its herald of the night started its eternal ride through the Tibetan night sky. Smiling at the moon as it rose from the east behind the snow-capped peaks of the high mountains. John had a feeling he would live long enough to see Mike and Chow pay for what they put him through. John watched the moon climb over the tallest peak of the tallest mountain. For the first time, John wondered how it would feel to climb to one of those peaks and stare out at the rest of the world. Then shouted all his rage and pain away, and after it was gone, he could try to find his brother. John remembered the man following him down the mountain. John wondered if his shadow had enough time to decide whether he would come into the camp or if he would watch longer. John guessed he would come in to investigate then he would make up his mind.

John guessed right when he finished eating the broth and bread, along with a cup of tea. John sat in stunned wonder at the night sky the mountains had to offer. He knew of the milky way, the band of stars that give our galaxy its name. By sitting on this high plateau with no source of light other than the moon, John, for the first time in his life, could see what the universe offered. In awe, John climbed into his tent to sleep; he turned and took one last look before he closed the flaps. John was impressed by his tail's willingness to outwait his patience, which told John this person wasn't your ordinary bandit. This man had training and lived in these hills; it was the mans training that peak John's curiosity.

The other on the path had waited what seemed to be a long time before making his way into the camp to find out what he could. John watched from a tiny hole in the side of the tent. The man picked up things and would look at whatever he picked up, then put it back, being careful not to make a sound. It didn't take long for John to decide this wasn't the behavior of a common bandit or one who made his living off the theft of others' belongings. He then went through the backpack with the same care he had gone through John's other belongings. When the Tran had looked through everything in the camp and John's pack, he turned to John's boots. Looking them over, the stranger shook his head and set the boots back down. Tran stiffened, then smiled when John spoke.

"You satisfied that I'm not Chinese?" John asked as he opened the front flap of his tent. To his surprise, this Tibetan man spoke English.

"I knew you were not Chinese from a mile away." He said and smiled. Pointing to the boots, he looked at the tent through which John spoke.

"You need better boots. Your feet hurt bad." John thought he was telling him the boots hurt his feet. Then he realized the man knew how to speak English. He had to have picked it up as he grew up.

"I was in an army prison, and they hurt my feet trying to get information out of me," John told him. Tran nodded, understanding what John said, and watched as John crawled out of the tent. The smaller man, at five foot three inches, Tran was ten inches shorter than John and weighed around one hundred and ten pounds. Looking at Tran, John thought he would not want to have to tackle him. John didn't know how, but the little Tibetan man exuded an inner strength that told of an incredible will to live, John thought as they sat and talked. John could sense Tran was holding something back from the conversation. John realized he was also holding something back. John didn't know why he decided to tell Tran what had happened to him at the hands of the Chinese. He had just met this soft-spoken Tibetan. Somehow, John wanted this man to know there was no chance of him going to the Chinese with any information. It seemed to John he had just started his story of torture and imprisonment when he looked up from staring at his brutalized feet his tale over. Tran sat looking out over the rest of the high valley that stretched below the camp. Tran knew how hard it must have been for this man he had just met to admit he almost broke under the torture dealt to him. Tran looked up into the night sky. Smiling, Tran looked at John and nodded.

Tran didn't pause because he thought John lied. Tran waited because he wanted John's last words to really have meaning. 'I don't think I could have taken another day of the machine; the bastards almost broke me... almost.' Then it was Trans turn to share what had broken his heart. Tran told John of the Chinese Colonel, what he did to his family, and how he had found out. Tran told John he was going to find this man and finish what his sister had started. John sat and shook his head. John believed every word Tran told him; he shook his head because in this country, in these mountains. He found another human who had their family stolen from him. Tran asked John what prison he was held in. When John told him he wasn't sure, but it had to be close to a large river, Tran nodded. John also told Tran that General Trang had been in charge of the interrogations, and he had a mean skinny little bastard for an assistant.

"I know this, General." Tran started. "It is said he and his assistant use boys like girls. I hear this General is coming to Tibet to question some newsmen. They were found by graves the Chinese use to bury the whole village." Tran told John about some of the atrocities he heard about while he was in the forces. Tran told John how the Chinese would go to an area if they found mineral deposits there. The army would move whatever village or town was nearby; if the people protested, the town would disappear with all the people one night. Tran told John how most of the time, this General would go to the town if the people caused a problem.

"You don't know where this General is going to be, do you?" John asked.

"Yes, he will be at the Regional Detention Centre in the town of Ningchi, and this is the command of the Colonel I'm going to kill," Tran told John.

The two men sat on the high plateau and spoke of Tran's family. Tran told John of how the Chinese were forcing boys from Tibet to join the people's army. He didn't tell John he had been placed into the special forces, not yet. John could see Tran was serious about killing this Colonel and decided that trying to talk him out of the killing would be a waste of time. John asked if he and Tran could travel together to accomplish their tasks. When John explained it, Tran thought that it made sense. General Trang would have to go to the detention center to interrogate the prisoners. While there, the Colonel would be licking the General's boots, hoping he'll get transferred back into China. Knowing the rumors of the General, he'll want some company in his bed for the night. The Colonel will wish to oblige him by finding the General what he wants. They could go after the men at the officer's quarters and save some young boy from being raped and brutalized, then killed. As John explained how things would go, Tran could see he stood a better chance of killing his family's butcher. Tran decided to stay with this John, a man who suffered at the hands of this General Trang.

"I know that it's a small tent, but you're welcome to half of it," John said as he crawled back in. Tran thanked him and rolled his blankets into the tent.

The sun was up, and John could smell tea and food cooking over the fire. Bob was right; his feet ached; he sat rubbing each foot, trying to get the stiffness out of them. The damage that had been done at the hands of the sick General hurt now and would for the rest of his life, he had been told. Sitting there rubbing his damaged feet, John thought it was one more reason to kill the old bastard. Sitting by the fire sipping a hot cup of tea, Tran motioned to a plate of food and a cup steaming by the fire.

"When we get the General and that other dog, you should see if you can take their boots," Tran said as John sat down.

"Yeah, I think that this was the only size they had. They fit fine, but they don't have any support left in them, but you know what they say, beggars can't be choosers."

"Who's they?" Tran asked, looking at John.

"It's just a saying; they are everyone. It means if you have nothing and somebody gives you something, then you should take it and be thankful." John explained.

"Only a fool would not take it and be thankful," Tran said as he sipped his tea. John looked over the fire at Tran and nodded.

Chapter 28

IN THE VALLEY, AT THE foot of the mountain, which had been his salvation, John turned and gave another silent thank-you to the monks who lived and hid in its caves and tunnels. Though Ben couldn't hear him, John whispered he would be back to keep his promise to carry him out of the mountains, back to England. John and Tran hiked through the valleys; being in the lowlands walking through the deep green grass of the valley was better and required less strain on John's feet. He knew Tran could move faster if he wanted to, but at some point, while they had hiked down the mountain, Tran had decided that he stood a better chance of getting his revenge with John rather than without him. For this, John was glad though the Tibetan was quiet and, at times, sullen. John had a feeling the smaller man would save his life someday, and after what, Tran came home to find the man had a right to be sullen. John didn't know why he felt the way he did; he had never had a family he could remember. For John, it was shattered and broken dreams where his family existed, if the people in his dreams were his family. The two unlikely travel companions skirted villages and only left the valleys when Tran thought it would be faster to go over the mountain. John's feet hurt all the time; Tran even offered to carry some of the things in John's pack to help lighten it. John would boil strips of cloth, then wrap them around his feet when he and Tran stopped in the afternoon. John knew doing this would help with the pain. However, when they began to walk again, John's feet would start to ache. Just when John thought he was going to slow them down to the point they would miss the General, Tran announced they were on the mountain that would bring them to their quarry. Another day of climbing passed then, and John and Tran sat on the top of a mountain and looked over the town of Ningchi. Tran pointed to a flat cinder block building.

"That is the detention center. That is where the men from the B.B.C. are being held." As Tran pointed buildings out to him, John drew a map of the town. He asked questions, and Tran tried to answer them. Tran had never been to this town. Therefore, he could only pick out the detention center and the officers' quarters. Both John and Tran were forced to guess at the rest of the buildings. For the most part, it was easy. Homes were easy to pick out, and so were the military barracks. The supply depot was at the southern edge of the town, and the last building was the Officer's mess.

"The large building with three floors is where the officers stay." That night the two men sat at a small fire drawing out their plans. John wanted to pull back higher up the mountain, but Tran thought this would be a bad idea. Tran explained the Chinese would be able to see their campfire at night if John and Tran stayed where they were; they had concealment, and they could have a tiny fire during the day. Sitting on the edge of their camp, the two men watched as the town went through a day like other occupied towns and villages in this invaded land. The people walked around the soldiers trying to be invisible. John and Tran watched the comings and goings of officers in the detention center; none stayed any longer than a few minutes.

"The officers must be checking on the prisoners, making sure the guards haven't been rough with any of them," John commented as another officer left the detention center.

"I think the officers of this place have orders; no one is to talk to the B.B.C. men. They were probably told if they did, they would be guarding a pile of yak shit someplace." John said, much to the amusement of Tran, who chuckled.

The sun came over the mountains to the east of them, warming the tent and waking John from another one of his nightmares. Lifting the flap, he looked around their little camp for Tran. John soon realized his companion wasn't there, standing at the cold fire pit; John looked around, wondering where Tran had gone, was his Tibetan travel companion trying to get into the town on his own? If Tran managed to get into the town, would he try to kill the Colonel? If Tran went after the Colonel and killed him, then the General wouldn't come. The miserable old fuck would order the killing of the reporters and return to China. From what Tran said, he wanted both of these men dead. John knew the Colonel was Tran's primary concern. The General had ordered the deaths of so many also angered Tran. Just as John started to put on his boots, Tran walked back into their camp. John saw that the small Tibetan carried a brand-new pair of combat boots. Tran set the boots down in front of John.

"I don't think it's my birthday," John said as he tried on the boots, they fit like they were tailor-made for him.

"I think these will help your feet," Tran said as he pulled out three pairs of wool socks. Holding the socks, John looked at his new friend and thanked him. This was a first. John had never gotten anything before where he wasn't expected to give something in return.

"But I didn't get you a thing." He joked, looking at the socks and the boots on his feet; he laughed when Tran looked at him and said.

"I know you don't have anything; you never left camp." Though Tran could speak English, he didn't have all the subtleties of the language yet. When John asked him how he had gotten the boots and the socks, Tran explained.

"The men who run the Army in this part of Tibet are arrogant. They think once they come into a place, the people bow to them. After a while, they start using the people to do jobs they deem beneath themselves, so they give the job to one of us. Knowing this,

I went to the supply unit and listened to what the men spoke there. After that, I knew they were Tibetan, and when the Chinese officers left, I went to supply Sargent. I told him I was just released from my unit. I told him what the Colonel did to my family. This Sargent told me he had heard the rumors. I also told him of what I had seen in the mountains, so this supply Sargent gave me the boots and socks, and he also gave me this." John turned and found Tran was holding a 9mm Beretta 92 automatic and a box of one hundred rounds for the weapon. The Sergeant in the supply office told Tran when he first started in this unit, he had been ordered to take everything out of the warehouse, then put it back.

The Sergeant said the officers were looking for something. The supply Sergeant said he found it in the back of the building under a heavy box. This Sergeant hid the gun in a hole in a wall and carried the box outside. Then his Commanding Officer grabbed the box and walked away. He has hidden the gun ever since, knowing if he had been found in possession of the weapon, he would have been charged, convicted then thrown in prison. Because it was a Western weapon and not one used by the Chinese military, they would assume he was in contact with a Western spy.

"The Sergeant in the supply office told me the General would be in the town by the end of the week. He said the prisoners have not been touched, the Colonel is under strict orders no one is to touch the English men or ask them any questions." John liked this news; it gave him and Tran time to find where the General would be housed. The extra time will help them get the layout of the other building in town. John knew from his own past operations that to get in, find your target do what needed to be done took planning. You were required to account for every little thing, and once the job was done, you didn't stick around. Going in with a half-assed plan gets you half-assed results, and half-assed results mean you're dead or soon will be. When it came to killing General Trang and this

Colonel, neither John nor Tran was going to let poor planning ruin their justice.

Chapter 29

CHOW STOOD AND WATCHED the traffic below. On the plasma screen was the Director of the C.I.A. The man was a sixty-something balding long, winded, blow-hard. When G.W. Hollyford wanted to feel important, he would start his stories with, 'Back when I ran field agents, they had more respect.' Now he was going on about some foreign sub-committee this or budget that, if the man was in the same room with Chow, he would have to shoot the old bastard, just on principle. The Director called this conference to tell Chow he was going to have to cut his budget. His spending was over the top. That was the way the old bastard had put it. When Chow told him, this area of the world posed more of a threat to the security of the U.S. than the entire Middle East. Chow was told that was not his decision to make, he knew how to play the field, and Chow played it. Chow knew it pissed off the old man when he did.

Thanks to a source Chow had at the Chinese government, he came to have intelligence that confirmed the Chinese sold high-tech circuit boards to terrorist factions. These boards were used to detonate explosives using subsonic sounds. When Chow told the Joint Chiefs of the boards they knew something was up at the C.I.A., the Joint Chiefs told Chow to sit on his hands until they could get someone over to see him personally. The person Chow waited for was now sitting in the corner of Chow's office. Chow told his Director about the boards, and he also told the old man about the dangers of leaving these boards in play. That the boards gave terrorists the ability to detonate any of their bombs with a song, hiding the subsonic sound wave in the music. The old man told

Chow to leave it with him, that he would pass it on to the man in charge of the Middle East desk of the C.I.A. What the Director didn't know was Chow knew the man in charge of the middle east was the old man's son. A man with no experience, a man promoted over others people who had years of service with the agency. G.W. Hollyford gave his son the job, saying he wanted fresh blood at the wheel of the Middle East. When Chow pointed this out, the old man hung up on him. Chow turned from the window; he looked at another man in the room, a person who the Director of the C.I.A. had no idea was on the phone call. If the Director had known this second man was sitting in the office in Hong Kong, the conversation would have gone differently.

This other man was a General. He sat looking at Chow with a look of astonishment on his granite face. The three bright stars on his shoulder gleamed in the Asia sun streaming through the floor-to-ceiling windows. His face was white. The General couldn't believe what he had just heard. The Director of the C.I.A. was willing to risk the safety and the security of the U.S., and her allies, to further the career of his son. A useless man who was a once mediocre analyst is now the head of the Middle East desk. Picking up his cell phone as it buzzed, the General answered the question asked by the Pentagon.

"Yes, sir, Chow was right. The Director is using his position to further his son's career over the security and safety of the U.S., and he needs to be pulled right away. I think you need to tell the president today...Chow has lost men trying to find the boards, and that bastard wants to sit on it until they find their way onto the Middle East desk so his son can disclose it and be the hero." The General listened, and Chow noticed the man sat up and seemed to come to attention while sitting.

"Thank you, Mr. President." Then closed his phone; the General looked at Chow and then told him.

"The man is being fired as we speak, and so is his seed." Standing, the General shook Chow's hand and then left the office. This General couldn't know Chow posed a more significant threat to the U.S. and her allies, with the drugs and weapons making up his empire. Smiling, Chow turned back to the windows of his office. He thought one asshole gone now to find John Smyth and be rid of a second asshole.

He had been at the head of the C.I.A. for twenty-eight years, and he knew when the security service stormed into his office, he'd been set up by Chow. G.W. Hollyford was handcuffed, and with two big security police holding onto him, he was marched through the C.I.A.'s building in Langley, Virginia. People were watching as one of the most hated men in Washington power circles was marched out of the building. To Hollyford's rising shame and rage, some bastard started to clap, he was forced to listen, and others joined in on his shame. Just when he thought it couldn't get any worse, he looked up and watched as his son was escorted to his car. Hollyford always had an intense hatred for Chow, but now it has blossomed. It came close to being insane hatred. If he could've, he would have killed Chow.

Chow heard the stories of the Hollyford family. It had been rumored Hollyford's father had kept him out of Vietnam by getting him into Harvard and then into the C.I.A. Now the old fuck was being tossed out for the first time in days; Chow smiled, one obstacle out of the way. Now if John Smyth didn't turn up, he would tell the home office John had died trying to retrieve the boards. John would get a star on the wall in Langley and die a hero. The next loose end would be General Trang. That fat old pervert was easy; he could be bought for now. Then when Chow was ready, Mike Styles would make sure the General would die of a heart attack nice and clean. The fat old prick probably wouldn't even get an autopsy. The doctor would take one look at the big flabby belly and say he deserved it.

Chapter 29

FOR THE MOST PART, John and Tran spent the week studying the town and the comings and goings of the military personnel. As well as getting to know each other, John and Tran talked about their pasts. They went through different scenarios about the rescue they were going to try and pull off after they accomplished what they came to the town to do. The town was run like most militaries of the world, three eight hours shifts covering one day. After a week of surveillance, the timing of their plan was down and set; the next day, Trang would arrive. The two men sat, ate a light meal, and watched as the stars came out one at a time.

John and Tran watched as the General sat in his car waving to the people forced to line the road and cheer. John watched as Tran seemed to swell with rage. He put his hand on his new friend's shoulder; this small gesture seemed to be what the Tibetan needed to calm him. Tran looked at John and shook his head. John couldn't imagine what his friend was going through, so he patted Tran on the shoulder. The Colonel, responsible for killing Tran's family, was riding in the back seat of the car with General Trang. The two killers smiled and waved to the crowd as the General talked to the Colonel. John knew the men from the B.B.C. were going to be alright for the first night. It was when the General moved them things would get worse for the men. The first thing the General would do is have their feet abused the same as he had done to Johns to keep them from running. John knew once the men arrived at the prison by the river, they would never be seen again.

Chapter 30

BACK AT THEIR CAMP Tran kept busy sharpening short sticks; each was about two and a half long. Tran would test each point he had just created and then place it in the fire. When the point of the stick became hot, Tran would pull it out and check the end to ensure it had hardened the way he wanted. After Tran had twenty of these sticks, he stopped and turned to watch John dismantle the Beretta. Tran watched as John cleaned all the parts, then reassembled the pistol getting ready for tonight. Tran knew John did this for two reasons. The first was to make sure the pistol would work correctly when needed if needed. The second reason was it helped calm John. Neither man spoke; this time was spent quietly so each man to reflect on the path they were about to walk down together. This reflection secured the knowledge what they were about to set in motion was the right thing to do. Not just for themselves but for the men being held in the detention center also.

Sitting around a table in what was called the officer mess, the General was surrounded by other boot-licking underlings, all of who wanted out of Tibet. The Colonel smiled as the General told stories; he knew if you made it too apparent, you wanted out of an area. The General would stick you here longer. It was the fat pervert's way of showing you he controlled your life. So the Colonel was determined to play it cool; he didn't want to give this fat bastard any reason to keep him here in the wastes. He still held a seething hatred for all Tibetans and blamed this country for the physical damage Trans sister inflicted on him. Claiming he was tired, the Colonel excused himself, left the mess, and walked down the street. No one was out after dark. He personally issued orders no civilian was to be out after dark. Also, anyone caught breaking that order might be shot on sight. A Sergeant stood at the end of the alley running behind the Officer's quarters. The Colonel smiled when he saw the man was holding a boy of about eight years old by the arm. The Sargent nodded to the Colonel as he turned the corner. Handing the boy over, the Sergeant turned and walked away. Though he was Chinese and had been in the Army the whole of his adult life, he didn't want to be a part of what would happen to the young boy. Tibetan or not, nobody should go through what this young boy will go through tonight. The only reason he had grabbed the boy was the Colonel told him if he did this, he would put the Sargent's transfer papers back to China.

Looking at the young boy, the Colonel wanted to break his little neck like the others he found in the small villages throughout these mountains. The Monster of the Nyainqentanglha mountains went from raping young girls to killing young boys. The Colonel laughed when they called him the Monster of the Nyainqentanglha mountains. The villagers were right. If he had his way, the Colonel would kill every Tibetan he found. He would love to kill the men in the Army in this town. In his eyes, none of them were human.

Sneaking their way down from the hidden camp, John and Tran made their way into the town of Ningchi. Tran was watching behind them, ready to silence any soldier who might happen to find them as he wandered through the hills on patrol or hunting for small game. John led them through the town. They watched as the Sergeant handed over a young boy and then marched off with a disgusted look on his face. The Sargent knew what was going to happen to this boy if he was handed over to the General. A seasoned Bangkok whore would be shocked at the amount of abuse the General dished out as he tried to slate his twisted sexual urges. John and Tran turned and ran from shadow to shadow until they reached the large building.

The one Tran pointed out had been built to serve as Officer's quarters. Watching the guards, Tran could see this was the same as other places in this land. When it came to security, the Chinese only worried about the upper class.

All the men who stood guard were Chinese; not one Tibetan was heard. On the other hand, John watched as the Colonel walked the boy down the street, holding him by his neck. The boy walked stiff-legged, and the Colonel would squeeze the boy's neck every time the boy tried to slow down. The poor child would whimper from the pain, and the sadistic man would hiss for him to shut up. As the Colonel marched up to the guard standing by the gate, he barked something out. All the other guards left their posts and ran to the Colonel. John looked at Tran and nodded; using the shadows, they hugged the wall and moved around the corner of the building. Tran took one last look, ensuring they hadn't raised any suspicion.

No light lit the back of the three-story building. This was the side that the bedroom windows for the officers were on. The only structure interrupting the flat wall of this side of the building was a fire escape ladder; this was placed on the building as an afterthought. This fire escape was different from the ones most apartment buildings have on the outside of them in America. Those fire escapes came with a platform at each floor, steps between each floor, then a retractable ladder so burglars couldn't climb up from the ground. Instead, this fire escape was nothing more than a steel ladder bolted to the back of the building; it was set dead center of the building. If a fire broke out, all the officers would have to go to one apartment on each floor. Tran was the first up the ladder and turned to make sure John was coming up behind him. Stopping at each floor, Tran made sure the bed was empty, or the man in the bed was sleeping. The beds on the first and second floors were empty. Those men were probably over at the restaurant, still licking the General's boots, trying to be posted back to China.

Looking in the third-floor window, Tran could see a sleeping figure under the bed's covers. When John touched his leg, Tran slid the already open window wide enough so he could climb through. John listened as Tran entered the sleeping man's bedroom without a sound. John had placed his hands on the windowsill, and Tran woke the sleeping man. John watched as the sleeping man came awake and sat up. Starting to shout for help, Tran grabbed the Chinese Officer by his hair, pulled his head back, then drove one of his sharpened sticks up through the man's double chin. Tran's fire-hardened stake drove up through the Officer's soft pallet. The stake punched its way through the Officer's hard pallet, smashed through his sinus cavity, then plowed into the Officer's brain, killing the man instantly. Leaving the stick jutting out of the man's chin, Tran turned to find John standing at the foot of the bed. Both men quietly went through the Officer's quarter. Once they satisfied themselves that the man who was now dead in his bed was the only person in the apartment, they made their way to the kitchen.

Chapter 31

LOOKING INTO THE HALL through a peephole in the door, John waited for a guard to walk past doing his rounds. After ten minutes, John knew all roving patrols of the building had been called off. This was done, probably under the orders of the General; this way, none of the guards would hear anything inappropriate, like the screams of a young child being abused. The sound of boots walking up the wooden stairs caught John's ears. The door at the end of the hall opened. John could hear the sound of a child sniffing, then he listened to the hiss of the Colonel tell the boy to be quiet. Sneaking a look, John could see the Colonel was on the boy's left side and still holding him by the neck. As the Colonel and the boy passed by the quarters of the dead Officer, John reached out, grabbing the Colonel by the hair. John pulled the Monster into the apartment. It all happened so fast that the Colonel didn't have the time to shout out for help. Tran came into the hall of the small apartment as John pulled the Monster into the apartment. The man seemed so surprised he didn't have the time to call out. Not wanting the man to yell before they had him gagged. Tran decided to silence the Monster with a sharp kick to the back of the head, knocking the Colonel out. The young Tibetan boy landed in the apartment because the Colonel never let go of him. Tran tied the man to one of the metal dining chairs using of all things' duct tape', even in Tibet, John thought, amazed.

As the Colonel opened his eyes, he could see the boy sitting at the table eating ice cream. The little animal had it all over his face, like everything in this unforsaken part of the world, it was messy, unorderly. The Colonel could see a Tibetan and a Westerner leaning against the counter of the apartment. The Tibetan didn't worry him; he had been in this wasteland for ten years, and the only one who had any backbone was a young girl, and he killed her and the screaming bitch of a mother. The white man was different; now, that man scared him. Over six feet tall, the Colonel could see by the scar on his face the American was no stranger to pain, yes this man, he could fear. The Colonel watched Tran walk over to the chair and look at him; something was wrong with this Tibetan. He had no fear; it was the slight smile touching the corners of Tran's mouth the Colonel did not like. That and the hard eyes thought the lips had a little smile. Tran's eyes held no light in them; they were flat and hard.

"You don't know me, but you took something very dear from me. You went around this country you and your kind have no right to be in; you raped young girls." Tran said as he bent down so he was looking the Colonel in the eye. The Colonel didn't understand he hadn't raped any girls since that night. That one girl fought back and took his eye, then his manhood. Now, what was left, he could only piss out of. The Colonel knew the men knew this; he also knew they all made jokes about him.

"One girl fought you and took your eye, then took that little thing you had between your legs. Now that you have no balls, do you sit like a girl on the privy, or does it just run down your leg like the dog you are? Do your mother and father know what you are? Do they know how you dishonor their names?" As Tran spoke, the Colonel knew he was in trouble. The Colonel tried to remember how he had gotten into this position. He hurt people, held the power of life and death in this wasteland, and didn't get hurt. Not after the girl had cut him, not after the demon had taken his eye and manhood.

John smiled as he heard Tran taunting the Colonel. After what the man did to his family and others in the village, Tran deserved this bit of retribution before the final act. Taking the boy to the living room, John found a program about tigers and sat the boy on the sofa. John didn't want the young boy to see what Tran was building up to. Walking back into the dining room, John saw that Tran had pulled out another of his sharpened sticks.

"When you get to hell, you are going to be blind; that way, you will never see which demon is riding on your back." Tran then plunged the stake into the Colonel's good eye. Even though John and Tran gagged the Colonel, the man's screams were loud enough to be heard in the hallway. Leaving the man tapped to the chair, with blood and vitreous fluid running down his cheek. Tran used a meat tenderizer to pound a stake into the Colonel's knees. The man's screams grew to the point John thought another officer in another apartment might hear. Tran waited for the blind Colonel's screams to subside before he said his final words to the Monster of the Nyainqentanglha mountains.

"Now you will have to crawl when you get to hell; crawl blind!" Tran whispered in the man's ear. Jack watched as Tran pulled the Colonel's head back, then rammed the stick through the soft pallet and up into the brain the same as he had to the dead Officer in the bedroom. Letting the Colonel's head fall forward, Tran turned and walked into the bedroom. When he returned, Tran brought a blanket to cover the Colonel's body. Tran then tipped the chair back and dragged it on the two rear legs to the bedroom. He didn't do this out of kindness or a feeling of remorse. Tran covered and moved the Colonel's body so the boy would be spared the sight of the corps. John was going to ask his friend if he felt better, but he knew Tran didn't and wouldn't for some time to come. Even though this killing was needed to stop a monster, Tran wasn't the type of man who enjoyed killing, and John knew it. The two men stood in the kitchen of the apartment and let the minutes silently pass. As they stood leaning against the counter, each knew one man was dead.

They waited for the second to make his way to them. All at once Tran and John looked up at each other.

A faint click was heard from down the hall, then the labored breathing from the three flights of stairs the fat General was forced to climb to get to his billet. General Trang could have stayed on the ground floor, but his ego forced the General to believe no one was above him, so he always took the top floor and the best billet. In this case, he was making his way to the Colonel's apartment. The General was strolling down the hall, looking forward to the boy the Colonel told him about being his. General Trang knew the Colonel got him the boy hoping to be posted back to China. What the Colonel didn't know was that Beijing wanted him to be lost in Tibet. Lost and never heard from again, the men who ran China considered the Colonel an embarrassment.

As General Trang walked past the door where John watched him from, John jumped out and grabbed the General. Before the older man knew what was going on, John punched him behind the right ear, knocking the older fat man out. When General Trang regained consciousness, he found he was taped to a metal chair.

Trang's head had been taped, so he couldn't turn to see who was whispering behind him. As he sat and looked forward, he could hear soft whispering behind him; it was American. Trang knew he had heard it before when he visited Chow. He knew different Americans; in Trang's view, Americans were weak; the only strong one he ever met died when the man managed to escape his prison, and he never got Chow's account numbers before John died.

Then the dead man stepped in front of him; it was impossible. It couldn't be this man, please god, not this man, General Trang thought; he was dead. John couldn't be here right now. This couldn't be happening not to him. He was a General. He had the power to do this to people; it wasn't done to him. General Trang was the same as other men who used torture; he feared what he used on others would someday be used on him. Trang knew he was a coward, so to hide what he knew in his heart, he tortured people. John could see by the look on his face the General thought he was dead. John liked the thought of being dead; no one looks for a dead man. The men he worked for were not as easily fooled as this man.

John knew Trang's arrogance was going to be the death of him. John knew to get what he wanted, he would have to lie. This was going to be the easiest part of the operation. People who lie and deceive people for their whole lives are the easiest to deceive; they seem willing to believe almost anything. In the case of the General, this rule was going to be tested. Standing in front of the man who oversaw his torture and, at times, had taken a personal hand in it. John could hardly keep from killing the man outright. This waste of humanity had information he desperately needed, so he could get to the person who aided this gross pedophile in capturing him. When John offered Trang a cool drink of water, John warned the bloated, sweating Trang that if he tried to raise the alarm, he would have no choice but to kill him. Looking at the fat man, John could see relief spread over the degenerate's face.

"Look, General, I'm not going to keep you for very long; if you want to live, then it's easy. You kept and tortured me, leaving me scarred for life, and now all I want is fair compensation; ok, you can understand that, right?" When John stopped speaking, the General thought he could see the light at the end of the tunnel. The man had no illusions, he knew the tunnel was long and it would be challenging, but there was an end. The General couldn't believe his luck when John asked him to recite the number of the Swiss bank account Chow set up for him to receive payments for services rendered. John held a small notebook and a pen; he wrote the numbered account and the code phrase the fat man said would gain him access to the account. John told the General he was going to leave him tied up until the morning when he would be found and released. The General smiled and nodded his head. He knew when this was over, he could get Chow to replace the money and the account. If Chow didn't think this was fair, Trang would threaten the dirty C.I.A. man. He could always call Washington and turn him in; the General knew Chow would pay.

"Now, General, when they let you go, take the newsmen and go back to Beijing. Don't try to change your account or alert Chow. I've got unfinished business with him. If you can do this, I will leave. If not, I think we both know what I will be forced to do." John looked at the General and watched as the man nodded his head.

John was amazed when the sweating General told him how much the account held. Twenty million Euros, Standing over the man who caused him so much pain, John watched as Trang smiled up at him; John smiled. Then, faster than Trang could see, John drove one of Tran's sharpened sticks up through the General's soft pallet. The fire-hardened, sharpened stake destroyed the man's sinus cavity as John's strength forced the stake to punch through the base of the skull and into the fat child molester's brain, killing him instantly. Like Tran, John felt no better for doing this; like any dirty job, it had to be done. John didn't think of the fat General as a human being. To John, killing Trang was the same as stepping on a roach; to some, it would be considered a public service.

Chapter 32

MIKE STOOD LOOKING over the river; he could almost see John trying to swim it. Mike imagined he could hear John panting and splashing, then a gurgle, cough, and then nothing. That is what the Chinese wanted him to believe, but it wasn't John. No, John would have walked into the mountains. The Chinese said this was impossible because his feet had been broken. Mike told them John would have crawled to the mountains if he had to. The Chinese Officer stood shaking his head, telling Mike if John crawled to the mountains, he was dead anyway.

"Your man goes there; he died." The Officer said as he pointed to the mountains.

"Your man goes to the river; he drowned. If he went into the mountains, he would freeze; face it, your man is dead." With that, the Officer spun on his heel and marched back to the waiting Jeep. Mike stood and looked at the river, then he turned and looked at the mountains and smiled. Mike knew John Smyth had limped or crawled into those spires of stone and ice. Mike knew he must have gotten help to survive; he knew John must have found someone to help him. John had never turned up at any of the Chinese-run medical centers. If John had crawled into a town with a medical center, Mike would have heard about the six-foot-three-inch American the Chinese would have killed John on sight. So John must have found some monks or a lone family to help him. Thinking it would have to be monks wasn't a far leap, though the Chinese Army told him and the rest of the world the monks were happily living in their temples. Rumors persisted for years; the followers of the Buddha had fled from the country. Those who stayed live in the mountains to this day, hiding from the Army.

Chow had gotten rid of the old man in Langley. One of the men Chow knew called him; his man confirmed the old man had been escorted out of the building by homeland security and the F.B.I. He said Hollyfords kid was thrown out by C.I.A. security. Chow was smiling at the end of the phone call. Chow's contact told him people were standing in the parking lot and the corridors, applauding as homeland security and the F.B.I., along with the C.I.A. security police, took the bastard out in handcuffs. Nobody has heard if Hollyford is going to be charged with any sort of crime; Hollyford's kid was escorted to his car by the same security. He wasn't even allowed to get his phone or jacket. The useless shit was grabbed coming out of the bathroom and thrown out on his ass, sort of. Chow laughed when his contact told him how it went down. Now, he wouldn't have to worry about the Director. With the information Chow had given the Joint Chiefs and the President, his budget would probably get a boost. But best of all, he would be left alone. With time he could pull off what he had planned.

Chapter 33

LEAVING THE OFFICER'S housing unit, Tran gave the young boy a piggyback ride down the ladder; at the bottom, he asked the boy where he lived. The boy told him where his father's house was. Tran then asked if the boy knew a secret way home. A way the soldiers wouldn't know about, a way any soldier walking around would not see him. The boy told him he had a way home, that he would be alright. The young boy said his mother would be worried, but he would be all right.

As Tran watched the boy run for home, he felt slightly jealous. He could see in the boy a bit of himself at his age; Tran never thought about losing his mother or father at his age. Watching this young boy run home, Tran felt the anger rise in him, knowing he would never be able to run home to his mother or father again. Turning, he found his large and very scared-up friend watching as the boy ran down the path to his home. In a whisper, John told him the boy was going to be all right. They had to make their way to the detention center, where they would find the hostages. Then get the hell out of the town before the General and the Colonel are missed. Turning the corner of the Officer's barracks, John could see all but one of the guards were still enjoying their night off. The one man left behind would be the only one the General would trust, so this man was most likely his personal aid. John tried to grab Tran when he stepped from the shadows. Tran Approached the Sergeant without trying to conceal his movements.

John stood shocked, thinking the man would sound some kind of alarm, then watched as Tran walked up to the sentry smiling. Then

119

before the Sergeant could ask a question, Tran drove the stiffened
fingers of his right hand into the other man's throat crushing the
Sergeant's larynx. As the Sargent grasped his ruined throat, Tran
drove his knee into the wounded man's balls. When the wounded
Sargent doubled over, Tran spiked him in the back of the skull with
one of the sharpened stakes killing the man instantly. John helped
Tran drag the body of General Trangs dead Sargent behind the
Officer's quarters. Once their path was clear, both men ran to the
back of the detention center. Standing at the back of the jail, John
tried to think of a way to get in without the guards' knowing the
detention center was breached. Both John and Tran knew there were
guards in the center.

"I could go back and light the officer's quarters on fire," Tran said.
John thought about it for a minute before shaking his head though
he did have a smile. Just before John was going to suggest they try
to draw out the guards. Both men listened as a guard leaving said
something John couldn't make out. Turning, he looked at Tran, who
translated what was being said.

"This man said he was going to watch the soccer game. He said
the Sergeant gave the Colonel a boy for the sick General. He would
be with his prize all night. Anyway, all the other guards have been
sent home, so there was nobody to write him up for leaving his post."
John watched as the man walked down the road with his rifle slung
over his shoulder. Looking in the window, John could see only one
guard sitting behind a metal desk. He was reading a magazine of
some sort; it didn't take long to tell what kind of magazine it was.
One look at the cover and the girl on it and the material inside
became apparent. Like before, John and Tran waited and counted a
slow five minutes. When no other guard showed himself, they made
their move. Looking in the trash bin, Tran found a discarded plate
and a napkin. Reaching back in the trash bin, he found some rancid
noodles, piled them on the plate, and placed the napkin over them.

Going to the jail door, Tran called out to the guard behind the desk. Speaking in Chinese, Tran told the guard his friend told him to bring food to the jail for him. Smiling, the guard walked over to Tran to accept the food. A look of shock washed over the guard's face when Tran rammed one of his sharpened sticks into the guard's belly. Tran then pulled the stick out and, with all his strength, buried the stick in the man's ear. John went through the guard's pockets and found the keys to the cells in the back of the center. As John hid the body of the guard behind the desk. Tran ran to the cells and explained to the journalists what was happening. When John finished shoving the guard's body into the foot well of the desk, he watched the night beyond the door of the detention center, waiting for another guard to step into the light.

The four men were overjoyed to be rescued. As Tran let the men out of their cell and down the hall that led to the door in front of the center. The youngest of the men stopped at a locked door. Looking at Tran, he asked if they could get some of their stuff. They all agreed only light things could be taken. The men were told they must hurry; anything too heavy would have to be left behind. One of the men grabbed a backpack from the floor of the room. In it, he swept some of the smaller digital cameras, along with all the memory cards, on the table. This was everything that had been found in the four journalists. The Colonel set this table up so General Trang could inspect this material in the morning. Turning, Scott, the B.B.C. cameraman, along with an older man named William, went through a filing cabinet; both men grabbed all their passports. They also found some of their credit cards.

The missing ones were taken by the Colonel. William pointed out that most, not all, but most of their cash was gone. John watched as the B.B.C. men worked without saying a word. Then the six men turned and stepped back into the hall. Tran looked into another room. Turning, he looked at John, smiled, then opened the door wide so his friend could look at the racks of weapons and the ammunition for the rifles and pistols. Grabbing another of the backpacks, the Chinese took off the journalists. John and Tran loaded ammunition into the pack for the light arms pistols they found in the racks, also for one of the Chinese-made QCW-05 each man took just in case.

John looked out the only door the detention center had into the night. He couldn't make out any guards or other people walking in the vicinity. Looking back at Tran, John nodded, then stepped out and immediately to his left so the light from the front office wouldn't silhouette him to anyone looking at the center. John hissed to signal the others as he rounded the corner of the center. John watched as the men from the B.B.C. followed his example; Tran was the last out.

Making their way back to their camp with John in the lead and Tran bringing up the rear, the group of men waited for an alarm to start sounding in the detention center below. John and Tran had packed up their camp before they began to make their way down to the town. Both men knew they wouldn't be staying in this camp when they made it back if they made it back.

John, Tran, along with the four B.B.C. journalists gathered up the packs and started to wipe out any sign they or anyone had ever been here. John knew to hide the signs of a camp was the hardest thing to do. When John was satisfied they had done an excellent job, he started their group into the mountain range to the west of Ningchi. Both John and Tran thought they had been fortunate so far. He knew that would be changing soon. As soon as someone discovers the prisoners have escaped. Then when the Colonel and the General fail to show up when the alarm is sounded, men will be sent to find them. Losing the Journalists and the tapes of the mass graves is bad enough, but to have the commanding Officer and a visiting General killed. Beijing was going to go through the roof.

John watched as the four journalists from the British Broadcasting Corporation made their way into the mountains. The two older men in the group were in their sixties. Tomas was the most senior at sixty-four years old, and William was the second eldest at sixty-two. Jerry was a forty-eight-year-old Welsh producer for their show, and the youngest man of the four was Scott, at thirty-eight years old. His name was a hint to where he hailed from. Scott was from a small island in the Shetland islands of Scotland, and he was in the best shape of the four. Tran caught John's eye, and he could tell by the way the Tibetan shook his head he thought of the four men from the B.B.C., the only one who could make it was the cameraman, Scott. Scott had spent time in the British Army and kept himself in good shape by training for and running in marathons. The three men with him were less energetic than their younger companion. Tomas kept asking if they could stop and rest for a while. The men looked sick as John explained to them what was going on in the town they had just escaped from.

"You can rest if you want." John started. "But right about now, the guards coming on duty have found the dead guard at the center. They now know you have escaped and are forming a search party. Now they aren't too worried because you are in Tibet." John said as he held his arms up and turned, highlighting the majestic mountains. "And they think you are, by now, lost, just out here wandering around. These guards think, at best, you've managed to kill one sleeping guard." John explained.

"Now, when they go to tell the Colonel and find he hasn't been in his room all night, they start to look for him. While that is going on, they send some men to go to the General's room so they can re-establish the chain of command. These men find like the Colonel, the General, hasn't been in his bed all night either. Now things start to become very hectic, and the highest ranking N.C.O. will order the Officer's quarters to be emptied. When the officers start to come out, that N.C.O. will explain what has happened to the highest-ranking Officer, now on the scene. This Officer will take command and do a headcount. When he turns up missing one Officer, he will go to those officers' quarters. When that Officer fails to open the door after repeated commands, the door will be forced open. Because this is the apartment of an officer, only an officer and N.C.O. will enter. This is where the Officer and N.C.O. will find the General, the Colonel, and the missing Officer, all dead." John said as Tran nodded his agreement. They placed the Colonel, and the General's bodies, still duck taped to their chairs, in the bedroom with the dead Officer in his bed. The four B.B.C. journalists stood looking at each other.

"Then your search party becomes a hunting party. When the first reports are sent to the men who run China in Beijing. We are going to have a thousand Chinese soldiers hunting for our asses, but if you need to rest, then have a seat on this rock and have a rest." John said as he patted a flat rock. "But the rest of us are getting the fuck out of Tibet." When John finished explaining what was going on in the town, Tomas turned and looked at his colleagues' then nodded to John and stepped behind Tran to lead the way. Smiling at the morning sky, John headed out into the Tibetan mountains.

Chapter 34

CHOW KNEW MIKE COULD be right when he told him he thought John had made it to the mountains. Chow knew the man could be alive, and if John was still living, then the man was the greatest threat to Chow's plans.

"Mr. Styles, you go and find your creation and kill him, don't come back and tell me you can't find him, and I want proof John Smyth is dead this time," Chow said, looking out the window.

"What kind of proof do you want?" Mike asked, hoping a picture would do. If the man asked for his head, he would laugh and leave.

"Nothing too macabre, a photo will do, and fingerprints from the corps," Chow answered. Nodding, Mike stood and left Chow's office with all the papers he needed to move freely around Tibet.

The news of General Trang's murder came from Tibet through scrambled channels. The C.I.A. monitoring station in the South China Sea picked up the radio message and sent it to be unscrambled in Hong Kong. Within ten minutes of being decoded, Chow knew the whole story. General Trang and a Colonel had been murdered during the night. Others murdered were a Captain and two guards. One of the guards was in the detention center watching the prisoners from the B.B.C. The second guard, who was supposed to be on duty at the detention center, was going to be hung for dereliction of duty. Whoever gained entry to the center and rescued the prisoners also murdered General Trang, along with the commanding Officer of the area, a Colonel. These people also stole weapons with all the rounds housed in the detention center. After the men from the B.B.C. were let out of the cells, they found and took back all the photographic evidence of the mass graves they accumulated during their unescorted hike in Tibet. As soon as Chow finished reading the report, he sent it on to Langley, to the new Director, who he hadn't talked to yet. His next call was to a scrambled satellite phone he gave Mike Styles, who was flying an antique twin-engine DC3.

Mike remembered his grandfather telling him how he flew these planes after world war two. Mike remembered his grandfather telling him how he started his air fright company with planes he bought from the Army and used to fly freight into remote parts of Alaska. Mike remembered the old man telling him the DC3 was one of the toughest planes ever built. By the time Mike learned how to fly, his grandfather had eight of the old sliver planes and was flying fright and food into all parts of Alaska and the Arctic Circle.

Mike's father and grandfather thought Mike would someday take over the business, but on one flight, Mike met some men going to a camp run by a scientist. He had overheard one of the men talking about killing one of the scientists. Mike was told to wait for them on the plane, so Mike did what they wanted and waited fifteen minutes. Later the men returned to the plane, and he flew them back to Anchor. Mike was eighteen when that summer, he joined the Army, Mike was noticed and placed into the black ops program, and he never looked back. Mike never returned to Alaska. Even when his grandfather died, he wasn't there for his father or mother passed away. Mike knew they had died, but he never felt any emotion for their loss. What he missed the most was the money from the sale of his family's air fright company. Most of the money went to keep his mother as she lingered on the edge of death from cancer and Alzheimers. He would have killed her to save the money. Mike still thought the hospital kept his mother alive, so they could milk more of what the company was worth, leaving him with nothing when she finally died.

The droning of the three engines, along with the whistling of the wind, trying to get in through the poor-fitting door was so loud Mike almost missed the warbling ring of the satellite phone Chow had given him. Listening as Chow told him of the killings and the escaped B.B.C. journalists, Mike had to shout to be heard over the plane's noise. Mike shouted that he understood the information Chow told him and that he was changing course. Mike and Chow knew the B.B.C. journalists had a big head start on the search party. What concerned the two was the fact the English men seemed to have help in their escape. Mike feared the help was John, though Mike didn't tell Chow who he thought might be helping the journalists. Mike didn't want to listen to Chow rave about how this was his fault. The sun glinted off the polished aluminum wing as Mike banked the big silver plane and headed over the Tibetan border for the town of Ningchi.

Chapter 35

IT HAD BEEN A WEEK since Tran and John snuck into the town of Ningchi, a week since Tran killed the man who held the Nyainqentanglha mountains in terror. This man also killed his family. While in the town of Ningchi, John had gotten revenge on the man who left him with scars that would forever mark his skin and soul. They had brought the four journalists out of captivity. They all were now trying to escape Tibet through the mountains; both John and Tran kept watch by night. Then hiked through the days, only giving each other four hours of sleep each night. Both men had been vigilant and skirted villages. Though they watched, neither had seen a Chinese patrol. Tran was surprised that they made it a week with the three older men they saved from the Chinese. Tran knew it would be another week before they reached the border with Bhutan. Tran knew even if they had found or managed to steal a car or truck, it would only be a matter of time until the Chinese discovered the group, and they would be forced to fight their way out of Tibet.

Looking out over another valley, Tran remembered the day he stood and looked over the valley of his home as a boy. Now he traveled with a man covered by the scares of a General who was dead. He was also helping his new scared friend get four strangers to safety over the border into Bhutan. Tran had never been to Bhutan, but he did hear of the small country. Some of the officers in the Army said this place was called the happiest place in all of Asia. From there, John said they would go to Nepal and fly out on a chartered flight. Tran had also heard of this Nepal. As Tran looked into the valley, he was going to tell John he would like to go to Nepal and climb the mountains there. Turning, Tran looked at John and then thought he would wait. It would be best if they got the English men out of Tibet first.

"I know it sounds easy, but it's a hell of a long way from here to Bhutan. We're going to have to find some kind of transportation, be it a truck or plane, and steal it." John was saying when they heard the sound of a helicopter's rotor beating its distinct staccato rhythm through the valley. The men watched from their hiding place as the army helicopter flew over them and down the valley; it was going too fast and flying too high to be looking for them or anyone else. The journalists turned and looked at John, hoping for good news.

"Probably carrying orders for the new commander of this region telling him to close off the area," John told them. When John told them the area they were in was going to be shut down, each man looked like they had just heard he was going to have to suffer through a government audit or worse. Each man knew what would happen to them if they were caught again, but none wanted to say it out loud.

As the Captain read his papers, Mike could see John really screwed with the Chinese Army's feeling of superiority in this town.

"I want to know how you got these papers, how you're allowed to be here, who it is, you know." The Captain shouted in Mike's face. Mike knew the man had no real authority over him. The papers that allowed him to be here were signed by a man who sat in the chair of the National Security Minster, the big cheese himself. Looking at the Captain, Mike decided he did not like the man.

"Do I look deaf to you, stupid?" Mike asked and watched as the man's jaw dropped. The man started to speak, but Mike cut him off before he could get the first word out of his mouth.

"Shut up; I was sent here to clean up this mess your laziness and incompetence have brought to our doorstep. I am going to need three of your best men to come with me now." Mike watched as the man tried to think of what had just happened. He wanted to argue with Mike, but the way Mike spoke and the papers Mike held said he was someone of importance. The Captain turned and barked an order at a man, and he ran to another. Before long, three men stood at attention in front of Mike. Of all the men Mike had to choose from, he had chosen these three. These men had a working knowledge of English. At least they had that going for them, Mike thought, as he turned and climbed back into the chopper, waiting for him to land at the regional airport.

Chapter 36

The Hunt

LOOKING OVER ANOTHER small town that seemed to be cropping up along the major rivers in Tibet. John wasn't surprised when he and Tran found an old panel van sitting behind a rundown building being used as an auto parts warehouse. Keeping to the dark shadows as much as possible, John was glad the truck and the building seemed to be abandoned this late at night. With a little more recon, Tran found a way into the building. In no time, they found a new battery that fit the old van and some jerry cans full of gas. Maybe this place wasn't so abandoned, both men thought as John and the other men started to push the old van while Tran steered it down the dark street. Once both men and machine had begun to roll freely down a hill, Tran popped the clutch, and the van coughed its way to life and roared off into the mountains.

Once the sun was up and the van could be clearly seen, the journalists walked around the van and looked over the faded and dented paint. Most of the men agreed the van looked like it had seen better days. But if it got them the hell out of Tibet, then it was a pearl to them. "It's not my Aston Martin, but by George, it will do, eh lads." Tomas, the oldest of the men, joked, putting on his best Winston Churchill impression. The others laughed as Tran drove their stolen old panel van over some of the deepest potholes Tibet had to offer. John sat in the back with the other men and rubbed his feet.

The boots and the socks Tran got for him worked wonders with his feet, but they still ached. The other men watched John as he ministered to his feet. Scott, the cameraman, asked what had happened to him. When John had finished his story, they all thanked him for saving them from the General. William watched John for the last week. He could tell John was in pain while they hiked through the mountains. Sitting here in the back of the van watching John tend to his sacred feet and legs, along with the heavy roped scar running down John's face, William wondered how the man could go on. They all gave Tran a pat on the back for helping to save them also. Tran smiled and nodded to the men and drove on. John found it amazing the older men could fall asleep with the van bouncing and swerving through and around the potholes. The three older men snored softly in the back of the panel truck as it rocked back and forth.

Sitting in the front, John explained to Tran they would most likely run into a roadblock before the night was over. To his credit, Tran nodded and pressed the fuel pedal closer to the rusted floor, trying to coax more speed out of the battered van. John described what they would have to do when the evitable happened. It was one o'clock in the morning when Tran drove up to their first roadblock. Two soldiers were standing in a jeep they used to block the narrow road with. Tran whispered to John, who was at the back door of the van. When he slowed, John opened the door and ran behind the van. When Tran stopped, one of the men approached the driver's side of the rusted panel van holding his rifle pointed at the road. John watched as the second Soldier kept watch on his partner as he walked to the van. John knew Tran had the Beretta held in his right hand and would use it when he made his move.

Raising one of the weapons he and Tran liberated from the People's Army in the town of Ningchi, John used the QCW-05 suppressed automatic rifle. Making sure the selector switch was on single shot, John took aim through the small scope mounted on the weapon and squeezed the trigger. The Corporal standing at the Jeep never heard the shot that killed him. When John squeezed the trigger of his weapon, the bullet propelled by the gases from the ignition of the gunpowder left the barrel at a thousand meters per second. John's target wasn't a thousand meters down the road. The man who John killed was less than fifteen meters away. The bullet hit the Corporal, where the bridge of his nose met his forehead. The subsonic nine milometer projectile blew most of what his head held out the back of his skull, spraying brain matter over the hood of the Jeep. The Chinese private who walked to the driver's door of the van looked up when he heard the cough of the bullet leaving the suppressed weapon John used to kill his comrade. Tran pulled the Beretta out and shot the man once in the groin. The private screamed and doubled over, grabbing at his ruined groin. Tran shot the man once more on the top of his head. The bullet shattered when it encountered the base of the skull, one piece of the bullet cutting its way through the spinal tissue and the other ricocheting around the interior of the brain pan. The second fragment exited through the young man's left eye. In less than three seconds, two men lay dead on the road. The four journalists help put the men in their Jeep and push it off the road. John steered the Jeep down an embankment. The men watched as the Jeep encountered the fast-flowing river and disappeared into the rolling water.

One of the men Mike had picked as part of his team found what looked like an old camp on the mountain in the tree line above the detention center. Mike could see, at one time, there had been a fire pit. Looking through the area, the others found discarded branches and what looked to be firewood. Mike knew this had been John's camp; from here, he could scope out the town and watch the officers come and go. Mike didn't know how. He knew John found out the General was going to be here to pick up the men from the B.B.C. Mike had to give John credit; the prick sat here and planned it out. John knew killing the Colonel and the General would throw this area into a frenzy. John compounded the problem by getting the journalists out. Now Beijing was involved and screaming, standing. Mike waved the men back to the town as his satellite phone rang. Chow wanted to know what the hell was going on; he heard the original report, then all the chatter stopped.

Chow knew the Chinese were trying to keep the fact that General Trang had been killed quiet, but he had heard nothing after the initial report. Mike confirmed it all. John had been in the town and killed the General and the Commanding Officer of the area. Some Captain the Generals personal aid was also found murdered, and the guard on duty in the detention center. The second guard was hung this morning for dereliction of duty; he left his post at the center to watch a soccer game. The four men from the B.B.C. were gone; Mike hesitated for a second, then he sighed and told Chow what he found. Mike told Chow how he knew John had been here and killed the General and the Colonel. Mike also told Chow it would be like John to get the B.B.C. men out. Also, from what he could see at the camp, he didn't think John was alone. When Chow asked Mike if the Chinese knew this, Chow was pleased to find out Mike kept this fact from his Chinese hosts. Mike told him he was hunting for John on the bases he was someone brought in by Beijing. Chow told Mike he would get in touch with their contact and make sure if anyone calls, their contact will confirm that story.

As Chow sat down, he thought about John Smyth being on the loose in the mountains of Tibet, armed and with local help. In the back of his mind, Chow could hear his little voice screaming. It was screaming for him to pick his shit up and get out now. If there is one voice Chow always listens to, it is his inner voice of reason.

Sitting on the floor in the back of the van, John could tell that Tomas, the senior man among the journalists, wanted to ask him something. John could also tell the man was having trouble finding the words. John almost laughed because the man was worried about his feelings. With what he was and what he did in the past, Tomas couldn't know John could remove emotions from the situation.

"Something you wanted to ask me?" John asked as he leaned forward. Almost reading Tomas's body language. Tomas looked at the man who saved his and his friend's lives; he wondered if he should ask the question he thought needed to be answered. Tomas had been asking questions and writing the answers down since he was in junior high school; now, he feared asking this one. The question wasn't what bothered him. It was looking at Johns's eyes. Tomas thought that no light reflected in John's blue eyes.

"If you don't mind," Tomas asked as John made a twirling motion with his hand, meaning, get on with it.

"Those men on the road back there, was it necessary to kill them? Couldn't you have incapacitated them somehow?" John could tell by the look on the cameraman's face he was trying to apologize for Tomas's question. John looked back along the road they were now racing through the night on; he gave the best and the only answer he could

"No." The other men in the back of the van knew by the tone of voice John used it was the only answer they would get. Tomas nodded and decided a follow-up question wouldn't be needed.

Chapter 37

MIKE WAS STANDING IN front of the detention center when the Captain told him one of the roadblocks failed to check in during the night. The Captain was a young, slightly built man with a heavy pockmark face, from what Mike could only assume must have been an excruciating bout of acne. The young Captain informed Mike he had already sent out another jeep to find the men. These men were to ascertain if the men at the roadblock fell asleep and missed their check-in time or if something else something worse had happened.

"Hope for the best, plan for the worse," Mike said to the Captain. Turning, he told the man to have the same three men meet him over at the chopper pad. Mike knew what the men would find when they went to the roadblock. Their comrades would be dead, or they would be gone. From what he knew about John, they would be gone when dealing with John. Gone was as good as dead.

Standing at the door of the Chinese-built chopper, Mike watched as the sky went from blue to grey. He could see the base of the clouds starting to darken. From his own flying experience, Mike knew this was a bad sign. Standing beside him at the chopper, its pilot told Mike if they were not off the ground within the hour, they would not leave. The pilot told Mike this area of the mountains often received storms that form because of the four passes. Mike listened as the older pilot told him of the storms that came down the four passes; these storms would hit where the passes came together. The storms would meld together to become one big storm that would last for days.

The pilot was a fifty-something man with a head of jet-black hair with streaks of grey at the temples and eyes so brown they almost looked black. This pilot told Mike the winds became confused and would start to blow from the four points of the compass, as well as down all at the same time. The pilot went on and told Mike when the military first came to this area, they lost many planes and helicopters from these storms. When the three soldiers arrived at the chopper, Mike ordered the pilot to lift off right away. Turning to the sky one more time, Mike tried to will the storm away. He never prayed to any of the gods the world's religious masses say is the one real god. Mike always watched out for himself, but now when he stood to lose so much, he wondered if he should pick a deity and prey. Mike took one more look at the sky, then climbed into the chopper next to the pilot and pointed up.

Chapter 38

JOHN HELD ONE OF THE barn doors open for Tran to back the van into. Both he and Tran would have liked to have driven on through the day, but the risk of being found on the road was too significant. By now, the men at the roadblock should have missed a call-in; with both men dead, that call-in time was going to go on being ignored. With the check-in missed, the military would have their route and be watching for anyone traveling on the road. Now with the van hidden, the men lay down, trying to sleep. With the escape, the run through the mountains. During the van ride and the run-in with the men at the roadblock, three journalists were fast asleep in minutes. Looking at John and Tran, Scott stood and walked over to where their two rescuers sat, watching the door and the day beyond for signs they had been found.

"I want to apologize to Tomas and the others; they have no idea how it works when you're put into a situation like that. I know you had to do it that way, it was them or us, and I would much rather it be them." John nodded his thanks for the words and motioned for the man to take a seat. Shaking hands with Tran, then John, the cameraman, formally introduced himself as Scott. John looked at the youngest of the four journalists and then at Tran.

"When we get you out of here, go back to the world and tell them everything you've seen here. Tell them the C.I.A. station chief in Hong Kong is a corrupt dirty son of a bitch. Tell the world of the graves and what the Chinese are doing to this country." John said, looking at his scared feet.

"If you can prove it, I'll spill it; there's nothing Tomas likes more than corruption in any kind of clandestine originations," Scott told them as he looked over at his sleeping friends.

"Before we get to the point we have to split up, give me an address where I can send the proof, and you'll get it, remember, it can't be any of your addresses. Or any address of a girlfriend, old or current, will be watched by either the Chinese or the press. The address has to be one the Chinese won't have in their files on any of you." When John was finished, he looked at Tran.

"You know you should go with them. What better witness than one who was forced into an invading army to save his family, only to find out they died at its hands." Looking at his feet, John didn't see Tran slowly shaking his head. Though the Tibetan was smiling, the smile never touched Trans eyes.

"No, with you, I can do more good for the freedom of my country. I have lost my family but not the love of the mountains. No, I will stay here and fight with you until I am killed, or we claim victory and leave together." Tran said as he turned to look out into the day through a small hole in the barn wall. The three men slept in shifts until the light drained from the bruised and tormented sky. Tran told the men it was going to be a stormy night; he told them of how storms in this region of Tibet sometimes raged for days the rivers would swell and swallow the roads.

"Sometimes water comes down the mountain so fast it will bring mud and rock slides covering the roads. If this happens, we will be forced to find a place to wait the storm out." Tran told the men as they left the barn. As he explained about the storms, Tran could see the news they might have to sit and wait until the roads became passable again bothered the journalists. He could understand how the men felt; Tibet was a beautiful place. For these men, it was starting to feel like the whole country was a prison, and that is precisely what the Chinese wanted. They wanted to control the information and images going into and out of Tibet; they were more concerned about what the world saw. The last thing Beijing wanted was for the world to have proof what the U.N. suspected was true.

Chapter 39

THE PILOT WASN'T TOO far off when he evaluated the weather. Mike could not believe how bad it had become in the short time they had been in the air. The aircraft bobbed and weaved in the air. For a moment, all the men in the helicopter held their breath, hoping their chopper wouldn't plummet from the sky. Mike looked over at the pilot and could see the man sweating, his eyes darting over the instrument panel. Mike was just going to ask if there was something wrong when the bucking aircraft shuttered, then the ride became smooth. Sitting in the now stable craft, Mike looked out to make sure they were still in the air; the pilot had a smile on his face.

"Ok, what happened?" Mike asked, wondering what the man had done to make the chopper ride to go from a death-defying roller coaster to a kiddie ride.

"I cannot fly in the wind like that, so I follow the valley away from the storm. We go past where the roadblock was and turn to come back; maybe we will find men on the road. It takes longer, but I can fly faster, and we get there in one piece." The pilot said. Mike knew the pilot was right in taking a different route, but he still had a bad feeling he was going to lose John. Too much rode on his killing, John. Mike needed to find and kill the bastard.

Chow met with his contact in the Chinese government, and it pissed Chow off he was forced to explain the situation to a man on his payroll. When the contact heard the entire story, he nodded his head and told Chow it was up to him to clean up his mess. Chow appeased the man by placing another four million Euros into a bank account he set up for this government stooge in Switzerland. The official thanked him and left without touching his meal. It was all pretense; leaving his meal untouched was a sign of disrespect, just encase he was being watched. It would get back to his superiors; he insulted the American head of the C.I.A. They would laugh and pat him on the back, standing. Chow snapped the cuffs of his jacket, then turned and left the café. Both Chow and the stooge knew he was indeed being watched when the head of internal security for China left without eating or even touching his meal. Chow stood and shot the cuffs of his jacket as a sign of irritation over the petty insult. Chow couldn't wait until he could be finished with all this bullshit. Chow just wanted to find a place where he could run his empire and watch as his wealth grew and grew.

Chapter 40

ONCE AGAIN, TRAN WAS behind the wheel; he seemed to be trying to break any record that might have been set in crossing the mountains in this region of Tibet. The tired ancient van they had stolen screamed as Tran pushed its tired old engine to the red line before he would shift gears. The suspension groaned at every turn, and though Tran seemed not to have a worry in the world. John, on the other hand, was terrified one of the worn and cracked tires would protest the abuse Tran was dealing out and blow under the abuse, causing them to roll over the edge of the dirt road they raced down, crashing them into the swollen and raging river below. When John asked if there was anything behind them that they were running from, Tran smiled and said that nothing was behind them. John laughed when Tran him. He loved to drive fast, was all Tran said, looking a little sheepish as he released the throttle letting the van's speed drop below fifty miles an hour. John turned and smiled as the other men in the back of the van let out a sigh as they felt the van slowing down. Jerry told John when they got out of Tibet, he should get Tran a race car. Jerry said he would put money on Tran winning races, and the other men in the van agreed.

Chapter 41

THE RIDE IN THE CHOPPER was more enjoyable when it wasn't bucking wildly around the sky. Still, with the new route, Mike knew John was getting further and further away from the roadblock and his grasp. Turning to the pilot, he ordered him to fly further into the valley and then turn and come back up the road. Mike told the pilot he wanted to see the whole valley, from the border with Bhutan all the way to the roadblock. Mike knew there were other roadblocks. He also knew the mountains were covered with trails, so a group could get around these roadblocks. Mike hated to think about it if one of the men with John knew the area and could guide him. John could get out of Tibet with the B.B.C. men if John did make it out of Tibet. Mike wanted to hunt John in Tibet, not out in the world on fairer grounds. Mike didn't like the thought of John having a fair shake. If anyone asked Mike if he was afraid of John, he would've laughed. Inside, he was terrified of John; he knew what his creation was capable of.

John knew they couldn't pull up to this roadblock and kill these two as quickly as the first. Tran was waiting for John to tell him what his plan was. He was driving at thirty miles an hour when he saw a small road turn into the forest. Before the men at the roadblock could raise their weapons, Tran turned into the road and started up the mountain. Trans sudden right turn caught John and the others in the back of the van off guard. John and the others in the back slid across the van's cargo space, crashing into each other.

The two Chinese military police jumped into their Jeep and started after the van. What neither of the M.P.s knew was the road ended in two kilometers. It made a hard left-hand turn and just ended. John told Tomas and Scott to get the others out and hide in the trees in front of the van. Both John and Tran could hear the military Jeep screaming up the hill, trying to close the lead the soldiers assumed the van had on them. The soldiers didn't know they were catching the van faster than they could imagine. When the driver of the military Jeep rounded the left-hand turn, he was forced to slam his foot onto the brake peddle to keep from crashing into the back of the parked van.

John set up their ambush and explained to Tran what direction he wanted him to shoot. Tran understood John wanted to catch the Jeep in the crossfire. The crossfire would be set up at a forty-five-degree angle, so he and John shot away from each other. Concealed in the bush on either side of the van, John and Tran watched as the Jeep slid to a stop mere inches from the back of the van. Neither of the Chinese soldiers could come to grips with what just happened before they were dead. John saw the driver's face and recognized the look of terror as the man realized he had just driven into an ambush. The first bullet of Johns three round burst ended the man's shock when it slammed into his forehead. The following two rounds hit the Soldier in the face; neither was needed. Tran had the same result with his target; all three rounds hit his man in the skull, shattering it and sending fragments spraying into the bushes.

When the ambush was complete, Tran moved the Jeep behind a large bush to hide the bodies of the dead men beside it. John was looking at the weapons they found in the Jeep; both men had the type 64 Chinese military police issue automatic pistol and four clips of ammo for each. They also had QCW-05s with two hundred rounds loose and five full clips, the weapon John was enthralled with Tran found in its case under a tarp stowed in the rear of the Jeep. John checked over the brand new AMR-2 anti-material sniper rifle; it fired a 12.7 by 108mm round. The clip for this rifle held five of the missile-like rounds. The barrel was free floating and had doubled baffles to help with the recoil that came with firing a round that large. Tran came over to John and gave him an ammunition box holding one hundred rounds for the AMR-2. John knew this rifle would come in handy soon; he also thought it would take them days to reach the southern border between Tibet and Bhutan. In time they would have to find another mode of transportation. The tired old van they now had wouldn't last much longer, thanks to the roads and the rough ride it was forced to endure. Each man looked at the van and silently prayed the old workhorse would hold out. William walked over to the faded and dented side of the van. William placed his hands on the faded paint, and as if talking to an old friend, he asked.

"Do you think you can hold out a bit longer, just a bit, please?" John walked over and patted the older man's shoulder; he knew William, Tomas, and Jerry were scared, he didn't show it, but John knew how they felt. Tran and Scott stood back and looked at the ground as if to pray. The six men were forced to endure the same pace for days. With Tran behind the wheel of their van, the small group of escapees crawled through the Tibetan mountain valleys. A crawl was what they were down to. The military Jeep had given them the motor oil they required. Tran even went so far as to drain the Jeep's crankcase, so he could use the oil for their own van; Scott and William took the jerry cans on the Jeep and emptied the fuel tank gaining in total seventy-two liters of gas. Even doing this, Tran told John he didn't think the old van had more than a week's worth of life in it. They would sleep in the old van during the day and travel at night, never using the one working headlight to see their way.

One night Jerry laughed as Tomas joked he believed Tran drove using the force. When Jerry tried to explain the force, Tran became more confused. On and on, they went through the inky dark of the Tibetan night. When the moon lit the ground with its ethereal light,

Tran would speed up. Then clouds would conspire to slow them and cover the source of light, and Tran would be forced to slow again. John watched the older men and could see this hardship was taking a toll on them. However, in that oh-so-British stiff-upper-lip fashion, none complained, even on the numerous occasions when they all had to get out and push the van to free it of some snow or mud. All would joke about doing the same for their fathers or mothers back in jolly' ol England when they were but lads. John watched the two oldest men of the group, Tomas and William; he feared one of the men having a heart attack. John tried to tell the two men to take it easy that he, Scott, and Jerry could manage. Tran smiled at John as he listened to Tomas, and William started to tell John they were doing this before he was born. The oldest of the group was expounding on how they had to push one sort of vehicle out of snow or mud while Tran drove through the night.

Chapter 42

MIKE COULD SEE THE border of Bhutan and felt the storm's winds start to slam the aircraft again. The sun began to set, and the pilot said it would be too dangerous to fly at night in this weather. Agreeing, Mike pointed to the chopper pad beside a guard building at the Chinese end of the bridge separating the locked country of Tibet from the free country of Bhutan. Once safely on the ground, Mike looked at the border guards on the Bhutan side of the border. He decided to use them to help him get John and the others back in the chance they made it this far. Walking over to the bridge serving as the no man's land between the two countries, Mike smiled and waved so the men serving Bhutan knew he was friendly. A young man was sent out to meet Mike and to see what his intentions were.

Mike explained to the Bhutanese guard what was going on. Mike lied and told the young guard John and the others with him were wanted dangerous prisoners who escaped prison. The young man asked Mike to stay where he was as he was going to get an officer. Once more, Mike told his story of the dangerous prisoners who escaped and how he thought these men were coming this way.

The Officer assured Mike they would be extra vigilant if the men were caught in Bhutan. The escaped prisoners would be brought to the bridge and turned over to him. Mike thanked the Officer while bowing deeply and walked over the bridge back to Tibet. The Officer watched as Mike walked back to the Tibetan side of the bridge. Something about the Chinese American man the Officer didn't like. The Officer knew Mike was lying to him. If he or his men caught the men running from the Chinese, he would let them go. The Officer didn't like the Chinese; he would have no part in helping them. The Officer told his men at the border to ignore it and pretend the men weren't there if they saw men crossing the border.

Chow heard from Mike; he and his men were at the Bhutan border, waiting for the morning to start searching the road for John and the others. Chow told Mike the two men from the roadblock still haven't been heard from, so it's a safe bet John's on the road and killed them. Before disconnecting the call, Chow took the time to remind Mike how much he personally stood to lose if this all went sideways. Before Mike could answer, Chow ended the call leaving Mike speaking to the static of dead air.

Chapter 43

THE MEN PLACED A TARP Tran had found in the Jeep on the floor of the van so they weren't sleeping on the cold steel of the truck. John could hear the chattering of teeth whenever one of the men fell asleep and relaxed his jaw. John watched at the vapor from the sleeping men plumed, then disappeared into the cold air of the van. The chattering of his teeth would wake whatever man up. Whoever woke would clench his jaw shut, trying not to disturb the others sleeping beside him. The days were getting colder as they gained altitude. On more than one occasion, John had asked Tran if they were still going to be able to make it to Bhutan. For an answer, Tran would smile and say they would, but he did not think the van would. With that answer, the men would sit in the cold van, thinking about hiking out of the country. Scott broke the silence when he told a story of basic training; he joked about the food and the instructors.

"I had this old Sergeant Major." Scott started. "God, the man was a hard ass, but he loved his duty." Smiling, he continued. "He would stand and scream at us when we did our water test. I took my basic in the winter, and they made us jump in the water in the middle of January. The old S.M. screamed it taught us about adversity. This old Sergeant Major I had would stand there and scream that it wasn't cold. If we had not suckled on our mother's tits for so long, we would be real men, and this would be like swimming in a pool. One of the others lads spoke up. He told the Sergeant Major he was a test tube baby and asked if he could be excused from this part of basic for that reason." Scott chuckled as he recalled the memory.

"We all laughed when Jimmy told the Sergeant Major he was a test tube baby, except for the S.M. He stood there looking down at Jimmy. I could have sworn he wanted to wade in and hold Jimmy's head under the water until the bubbles stopped." The men laughed, and it seemed to warm up a little then it was Tomas's turn to tell a story.

"Wading around in the lake in January, humph." Tomas started. "You might think that is what is called adversity. Well, my lad, I'll tell you of adversity, William. Do you remember the summer of eighty-five?" William nodded his head and smiled.

"Now, that was a summer of adversity, let me tell you," Tomas said, pointing to John, Tran, and Jerry. Scott smiled and winked at John, then nodded to Tomas.

"The summer of eighty-five, I was working the international desk. William here was on organized crime. We were working eighteen hours a day trying to get the facts on the stories that landed on our desks straight. Right in the middle of the hottest weeks of the year, the air conditioning gives out in the building. In addition, the bottled water companies have gone on strike, so there were no deliveries. Sixty-five hot, tired, sweating, short-tempered, overly pampered reporters on the international floor, all getting in each other's way. I don't mind saying things were touch and go for a while; you guys think wading through bullets trying to save lives is tough. Man, you should try hanging around with pampered journalists when the pampering stops." Tomas said.

The men in the back of the van laughed when Tomas told his story. Even Tran, who at first thought Tomas was being serious, laughed when John did. Tran knew it must have been a joke when Tomas finished the story. John told the men the sun had set and they should be on their way. Stepping out of the van, Tran looked at the sky and told John it was going to be worse tonight than it was the night before. The other men looked up at the bruised and battered sky. They climbed back in the van and held on as Tran drove out of the stand of trees that sheltered them during the day.

At the same time, John and the others were leaving the shelter of the trees. Mike was standing beside the chopper, telling the pilot he was going to have to fly tonight, like it or not. Mike hated it, but he had a feeling that if he didn't go and look for John, he would lose his creation and the men with him. The pilot knew he couldn't talk his way out of flying this crazy man around; therefore, he started his pre-flight check and was soon in the air. Mike thought his pilot was exaggerating when he told him it would be worse tonight than it was the night before. Mike thought he was exaggerating until the first bolt of lightning struck the mountains to the west of their position. Mike's little voice asked him if he was fucking nuts, and for the first time, Mike thought maybe he was just a little crazy.

Chow was looking at satellite imagery of the storm hovering over the mountains where Mike was hunting for John. By the look of this storm, it would be around for at least a few days. It was going to be the worst storm to hit the region in a hundred years. He thought about calling Mike to give him the news but thought Mike would have gotten it from the Chinese this afternoon before he lifted off. Turning to look out his office windows, Chow swore. To him, it seemed everything was conspiring against his planning; even mother nature was getting in on the act.

Chapter 44

TRAN AND JOHN WATCHED through the cracked windshield of the van as the lightning struck the tops of the mountains. John tried to count how many times the top of the mountain was hit, but the lightning flashed too fast to count. Sometimes two or three bolts would strike at the same time. Turning to Tran, John asked him to get them out of the area fast as he could. Tran knew they didn't want to get caught in a lightning storm, not one like this. Looking straight ahead, Tran concentrated on the narrow dirt road and his driving while coaxing the poor old van over the forty mph mark on the speedometer. Tran tried to drive in the center of the road. He said he wanted to give himself some room to maneuver if something jumped out in front of them. John thought about telling Tran it was a single-track dirt road. There was no middle and no room to maneuver.

Then before John could voice his thought Tran should slow down, he felt a bump, then the soft hum of their worn tires on pavement. Smiling again, Tran pushed the old van faster. The road was forced to follow the contours of the mountain, rounding a curve the road was forced to follow. John and Tran were surprised to find they had driven into a wall of water. For a second, John was sure Tran had left the road and gone under a waterfall. John had never seen it rain so hard in all his life. Tran could feel the back of the van start to hydroplane in the standing water on the road. He took his foot off the throttle and avoided the breaks knowing this would allow the van to settle back to the broken asphalt. At the same time, Tran switched on the windshield wipers. John and Tran found only one wiper worked on this van, and It was on the passenger's side of the van, of course. Leaning over to see out of John's side of the van, Tran watched the edge of the road and brought the van slowly to a halt.

Looking over to John, Tran whispered one of the men in the back must have bad karma for this to happen. Shocked, John looked at his friend and then started to laugh, nodding his head. Tran and John got out and tried to switch the wiper to the driver's side of the van. After some cursing and swearing, both in English and in Tibetan, the wiper was on the driver's side of the van and seemed to be working, for now. Even with the wiper working on the highest setting, it could not keep the windshield free of water, so Tran was forced to slow to twenty miles an hour. Even then, he felt he was at the edge of what could be done safely.

Flying in this kind of weather was dangerous. Mike knew it had to be done; he and the other men didn't like it. John couldn't be allowed to get away, and the men from the B.B.C., if they went back to the world with the photos of the mass graves, well, that would be it. China would be forced by the U.N. and NATO to either pull out of Tibet or face sanctions that would cripple the country financially. That would be the end of Chow's billion-dollar-a-year business and his multimillion-dollar tax-free salary. So Mike couldn't let the pilot turn around, he forced the man to keep flying they had to find John and kill him and the others with him. That one objective kept ringing in Mike's head, 'find John and kill him.' Mike knew he or someone like him would eventually have been sent to kill John someday if John hadn't been killed on a mission. That the day was here so soon didn't make any difference to Mike. What made the difference was if he failed to find and kill John, it would mean his death would not be far off.

Chapter 45

TRAN HAD DRIVEN FOR four hours at thirty miles an hour or slower. At times, he thought he would have to stop and wait out the worst of the rain. The one time he took his eyes off the road to glance at the sky, Tran thought he saw a helicopter bob its way over the trees before a heavy downdraft forced it down again. Watching the road and the sky was too much for him, so Tran told John about the chopper.

"I can not be sure, but it looked like a Z11 to me. Could be some diplomats trying to get home, or." Tran said. Not finishing his thought. He didn't have to; John had known what he was going to say. John had heard of the Z11; it is a copy of the French AS350B helicopter. A cheap little thing, it could seat six. It also shouldn't have been up in this weather. Trying to look out Tran's side of the van without blocking his view of the road. John craned his neck to look up at the tops of the trees crowding the side of the road. He watched as the Z11 popped back up over the treetops and rocked side to side as the pilot fought for control of the aircraft. Just when it seemed the man at the controls of the chopper won his hard-fought victory for control of the aircraft. A blinding light, along with an earth-shattering clap of thunder, slammed the side of the mountain road. John watched the tail of the small chopper shear off and go spinning off into the forest. All the men in the back of the van gave a sharp cry of terror as they thought the van was being shot at by the Chinese. John explained a bolt of lightning had hit very nearby.

Mike watched the trees serge up to meet the chopper, then the sweating, swearing pilot pulled their helicopter from the grip of

155

mother earth back into the air. Looking out of the front windscreen, Mike found an old battered, rust-streaked van driving along the road. The old van trailed a plume of bluish oil smoke behind it. The wind caught the smoke and swirled it into the trees.

Smiling, Mike knew John was in that van. He had him, he would kill John and go back to Hong Kong, and things would be normal again. No more fucking helicopter flights in storms, never again. Just about the time Mike finished promising himself, he would never go up in another storm; something happened. There was an incredible explosion; it sounded like a cannon had been fired inside the cockpit of the chopper, then all at once, he was looking at the side of the mountain, then back at the road, then the trees, and the road again. The chopper was spinning out of control, and alarms were shouting their warnings as the trees groped with green fingers trying to pluck the hapless machine from the sky. At the same time, the pilot screamed they were going down in Mandarin.

John watched as the Z11 was hit by lighting the small chopper and then spun, falling into the trees to the left of the road. Both he and Tran waited to see an explosion; each thought would follow the crash. As Tran stopped the van, John turned and explained to the others what had happened, dispelling their fear.

"An army helicopter has gone down; Tran and I are going to see if there are any survivors. If so, we will make them comfortable, but we must destroy their radio. Don't worry. All choppers now have G.P.S. locators built into them, so if there are any survivors, they'll be found, but not for a couple of days." Turning, John made sure his weapon had a full clip as he shoved three more into his pocket; then he looked at Tran and nodded.

Slowly making their way through the trees, Tran was moving to the right side of the chopper, now lying on its side. John went left, so he walked along the top of the down aircraft. When he and Tran met, they could see the pilot hanging by his harness, still strapped to his seat. The large tree branch protruding from the man's chest told them the pilot was beyond help. John could see one of the soldiers in the back of the chopper moving. He motioned to Tran, indicating the Soldier was trying to get out of his seatbelt. The Soldier looked up and stopped moving when he saw Tran with QCW-5 pointed at him. Tran motioned for him to come out over the pilot, and the Soldier complied and climbed over the dead pilot. Tran had the Soldier kneeling on the ground in front of him. John checked and found the other two soldiers in the rear of the chopper were dead. Both men had been killed by flying metal fragments from the rotor blade.

John could see Mike Styles strapped in the co-pilot seat, smiling. John shot out the windscreen, then reached in and undid Mike's harness. John dragged the unconscious man out to the chopper by the collar of his camouflage jacket. John could tell how Mike's right leg bent above the knee and the left below the knee. Both Mike's legs were broken. Knowing what this man was capable of and what Mike had done to people in the past, John couldn't feel sorry for him. Looking at him, John thought Mike might have broken his shoulder. As he thought about it, he didn't give a damn one way or another. All that mattered to John was he had Mike, one of the men who gave him up to General Trang. Chow was the other one, but for now, he had Mike. Because of this man, John would suffer for the rest of his life.

Chapter 46

THE PAIN IN HIS LEGS was bringing him back to consciousness. When Mike opened his eyes, one of the soldiers was sitting on a log in front of him; another man Mike didn't recognize was standing behind the Soldier with a QCW-5 pointed at him. Mike realized there was another person in the small clearing where the chopper crashed. When Mike turned his head, his worst nightmare came true; John Smyth smiled at him. Mike closed his eyes, hoping he was delirious. John laughed and kicked him on his right thigh, his broken right thigh. Mike started to black out from the pain the kick inflicted. Then a hard slap delivered from John's callused hand forced the fog of unconsciousness back from his mind.

"You're not going to black out on me, you fuck. I've got a couple of questions, and Mike, you will answer in time; feel free to be stubborn if you wish." John Smyth had him, and Mike knew John would get the answers he wanted. Mike knew it was only a matter of time, and John had all the time he needed with this storm. John could take his time, and after what he was put through because of him and Chow, Mike knew John was going to be very diligent in his interrogation. After all, he had been in charge of the man training hell; he had even trained John on ways to get information, ways not covered in the C.I.A. handbook. John had been a good pupil; hell, he had been the best pupil.

John thought he would enjoy getting at Mike, but in reality, he didn't. Standing over the man, John had to stop himself from just outright killing the human slug. He needed answers; also, John wanted to break Chow, to take what Chow didn't deserve. John hoped Tran understood what he was about to do, going to the chopper while Mike lay conscious and agonizing over his broken legs. John retrieved one of the heavy-duty deep cycle batteries along with some of the heavy copper wire so he could use it for electro-shock if Mike forced him to that point. John also found a first aid box with some wire splints and a scalpel. When he returned, John found Mike looking at Tran. John knew Mike had questions. He also knew Mike wouldn't ask any questions because Tran wouldn't answer them.

Mike watched as John laid out the tools he found in the crashed chopper, tools John was going to use for extracting information. Mike became very cooperative; he asked what he needed to know. Mike decided he would tell John everything he knew. After all, he owed Chow nothing. He did his job, and now Mike wanted to live. Mike had been moving money around, knowing he would get away from Chow sooner or later. Sitting in a forest ten miles from the border with Bhutan, both his legs broken. Mike wanted to be around to spend some of his money. Mike didn't really believe John when he told him if he was honest and told him everything, he would let him go. John told Mike he and the surviving Soldier would be picked up in a day or two. Mike was holding on to hope that, unlike himself, he thought John would stop short of outright murdering him. After all, Mike thought, he hadn't been all bad to John. Mike could remember he'd been nice to him a couple of times. Hell, he even bought John a beer after his first assignment, Mike remembered.

Mike planned to use some of his money to try and buy his life. If John let him go, he would go someplace quiet and live, just live. Mike sat and listened to his voice as he started to tell John the story of his life, then about the bank accounts Chow had around the world.

Chapter 47

JOHN SAT SHOCKED WHEN Mike gave him all of Chow's secret bank account numbers; he was writing the numbers down as Mike rattled them off. The real shock came when Mike told him the amount in each of the accounts. Each of the banks holding millions in funds was in a different country. John knew each of the countries listed refused to let the American government have access to their client's records. He was tempted to ask Mike how he got the account information. John knew Mike had lifted the info from Chow's personal computer, probably with the thought of drawing some money out of each of the accounts. When Mike gave up Chow's contact with the Chinese government, John almost fell over. Comrade So Yang, the third most powerful man in China. Mike looked sick when John asked his final question. Mike knew if he was going to make it out of this alive, he would have to answer this question very carefully.

"Who am I? I know my family was killed. You said I was given to you. Where did I come from?" John asked. What little color was left in Mike's face drained away, Mike tried to swallow, but his throat was too dry.

"Yes, you were given to me. You were a very young child, no more than three, maybe four years old, not any more than that. When your family was killed, your father was a journalist and your mother a lawyer. Your father came across a project called 'CRADLE,' a very deep, very dark operation run by a section of the C.I.A. The operation was so dark there were only a handful of people in the agency who knew about it. We knew someone who helped create the program must have talked to your father. Hell, only the Director and those working on the program knew about it. The Director and I, along with some physiatrists and behavior modification experts, came up with the idea of training men and women for black ops units from childhood." Jack could see Mike was sweating from the pain. John sat in front of Mike as the man went on.

"This was all off the record; the only one with knowledge of the program besides myself and the people involved in the training was the Director, hell he even hid it from the president, congress, everyone. Hollyford would give us names of people he thought posed a risk to the project, the agency, or the U.S. and her allies. Then the head of our unit would go around the country and kill the targets. If their children were of a suitable age for the training, the Director ordered us to keep them. If not, then the kid disappeared with Mom and Dad. We found through physical and physiological programming during their formidable years, children are better able to absorb the training. They, therefore, wouldn't be susceptible to the stresses of adults being trained as assassins." Mike explained. John smiled as he listened as Mike purposely left himself out of any role in the killing of the parents or the children. John knew Mike was the head of the unit. John also knew he would have been the one who would have gone and killed the parents. Mike would have been the one to place the kids in the cradle program.

"When your father came into contact with a former child psychologist, who helped develop the program, he ran with the story. We tried to stop him, then your mother became involved, and we knew the courts would become involved eventually. So the order was given to terminate while they were on vacation in British Columbia, Canada, then you came to the program." Mike said as he closed his eyes, the pain in his legs was threatening to make Mike sick, but after a few deep breaths, he went on.

"You were born in Canada. Your real name is Jack. Your father was a journalist for the National Post; that's all I know." As the word 'know' left Mike's lips, John shot him between his closed eyes. John watched as Mike's head snapped back from the impact of the nine milometer parabellum round. When Mike's head fell forward, John watched as a single drop of blood oozed out of the blackened hole where the bullet entered Mike's skull. It had been too easy, John thought before he turned to the Soldier.

"You can stay and be found in a day or two. You can tell them what happened here, or you can run." The Soldier smiled and looked at Tran, then back to John.

"I would rather go to a place where I can be free. I hate being in the Army. I have no one to go to, no home, I'm an orphan, I'll go to Bhutan then America to see lady statue in New York then." The Soldier shrugged his shoulders and smiled. Turning, he smiled and nodded to Tran, then started to walk into the forest. John watched as the former Soldier of the People's Army walked off into his future. Silently, he wished the man good luck. John and Tran hurried back to the van; as they stepped out of the forest, John found Scott holding a weapon guarding the van. The three men nodded to each other, and moments later, the van started and drove off.

Driving through the rain, Tran passed the Soldier who waved as they passed by. The older men sitting in the back of the van wanted to ask what had happened in the trees. They knew they heard a gunshot but thought it would be better if John and Tran told them when they were ready. An hour later, John, Tran, and the others were sitting on the side of a mountain looking into the country of Bhutan. John told the men they would have to leave the van where it was and cross the river on foot.

"I don't know how long it will be until we can find another vehicle, so we might have a long walk ahead of us; also, the food situation is getting serious. So far, we've been lucky in what we grabbed from the detention center lasted with what we could pick on our own. The storm has hit so hard that I don't think we'll have any luck finding any pickable fruit. From the wind and the driving rain, I think most of the hanging fruit would be on the ground and rotting, so we're going to have to ration food tighter and try to make up as much time as we can safely get away with.

"If we can get into Bhutan, I'll get the B.B.C. to wire us some money, and we can buy a car or something," Tomas told John.

"We won't need the B.B.C. to wire money, trust me," John said, smiling as he looked over at Tran.

Chapter 48

CHOW TRIED TO CALL Mike twice, but both times the call was redirected to a recording. All the recording said was the satellite phone he was trying to reach was out of the service area. The weather was affecting all communications in that area of Tibet. Still, it was a satellite phone, and its coverage area was everywhere. He would have to wait until the storm subsided before he found out if Mike had found John or if John had found Mike. If the answer was John had found Mike, he would leave Hong Kong within a week. If Mike had found John, Chow would stick to his six-month schedule. If Chow had been a religious man, he would have prayed for Mike to find and kill John. Chow had never been given what he considered the most incredible children's storybook in the world. For Chow, it didn't matter what religion a person followed; it was all bullshit to him.

Standing looking over the invisible line separating the invaded country of Tibet from the free land of Bhutan. The four men dreamed of being back in touch with their families. While their two rescuers, still holding their weapons, stood apart, knowing they could never have the comfort of a loved one. Both men had had a love of a mother and father stolen from them. Both John and Tran nodded towards the border and agreed the other men with them would get to hold their loved ones again.

John smiled as he watched the men who guarded the border between Tibet and Bhutan. He knew the rain would help with their border crossing. The Chinese guards, not wanting to get their uniforms wet and wrinkled, stayed inside their post and played mah-jong; it was the same all over the world. The better the men were treated, the harder they worked. The Chinese only treated their officers well, and the enlisted man was trash to these pampered officers. So the men would rather stay dry and warm instead of being out on their posts. While the border guards on the Bhutan side watched the Chinese side through the night, the ark vapor lights showed sliver through the rain. Tran led Tomas Jerry, William, and Scott, with John bringing up the rear a mile further west before crossing the river into the free country of Bhutan, the reputed happiest country of all Asia.

Once the six men made the crossing and hiked into the tree line, John took the lead position and then slowed their pace. He found a spot where the men could catch their breath. Standing at the edge of the trees, Tran smiled and said a silent goodbye to his homeland. Tran wondered where he was off to. Though Tran didn't know where he would end up. He knew he would return to this beautiful country to see the Chinese skulk back over the border, where they came from. Tran took up the tail position as John led the men off through the forest, it didn't take too long before William started to show signs of fatigue, and the older man began to fall behind. Tran lightened the older man's pack and stayed with William coxing the man along with words of encouragement. For William, it seemed they were trying to walk out of Asia. Then just as the eastern sky started to show the first sign of the dawn, John called a halt to look over an old barn just beyond the treeline.

"You see, William, you don't have far now; you are stronger than you think." Tran quietly said to the older man. Turning, William looked at Tran, he could see he was slowing them all down, but somehow he knew this man would never leave him behind.

"Oh, my lad, I hope we don't walk out of Asia." William laughed.

"If that is the plan, then you carry me." Tran's tone was so matter of fact for a moment, William thought the Tibetan was serious, then he saw Tran start to smile, and he nodded his gray head laughing. William's laughing caught the rest of the group's attention, and they turned to see what happened to cause the two men behind to laugh. Tran and William held up a hand and shook their heads in unison as if to say a private joke.

Jack couldn't see any house or any other structure that could be a house. Telling Tran to hold the others where they were, John made a circuit of the area before telling the others it was safe to go to the barn. The four journalists were wet, cold, and miserable. The rain pounded through their clothes as soon as they had left their old van in Tibet. Now they crouched on the edge of that forest in Bhutan. John and Tran made a complete circuit of the barn before they met back, where Tomas and the others waited and then led the men to the barn.

The men were happy to be out of the storm that raged at the walls of their shelter. Their first night in Bhutan was cold like any other night in Tibet, but for now, they were free. The barn held an old American deuce and a half in the main section with stalls for horses on each side. How the old army truck ever came to be in a barn in the mountains of Bhutan was something the men were discussing around a small fire John had made for them out of dry wood and twigs they found piled in the barn. Jerry was floating the idea the truck had probably been bought and sold until it had reached this farm. The men all watched as Tran climbed under the hood of the old truck. William looked at his friends, then at John, and said if anyone could get the old thing to run, it would be Tran. As if on cue, the old truck coughed to life, spewing black smoke through the barn. Turning, they looked at Tran, who smiled. He explained the battery was not dead, and the only thing wrong with the truck was the ignition switch was broken.

"So this truck might not be left here, and the owner might not be gone," Tomas said, looking through the barn doors.

"If he was here, he would have heard that thing start," Jerry said, joining his friend at the door.

"It might have broken down on someone who got it into the barn to keep it safe, then went to get the parts for it after he failed to get it going. We could take it and leave some money to pay for it. Hoping it will be enough for the man to buy himself a better one." William said, looking at the others. When the men grabbed their belongings from the detention center, Jerry grabbed their passports and wallets. Tomas emptied his wallet and stood waiting for the others to do the same. When the others had fished out what their wallets held, they held a total of two hundred dollars American. They hoped it would be enough for the truck owner to get another.

"He, whoever he is, probably only spent fifty dollars buying this one," Tran said. They tied the money in a small bundle with some orange twine Tran found in the truck's cab. Tomas took the small bundle of American money and hung it on a nail on the main support post in the middle of the barn.

"We should throw as much straw and hay in the back of the truck to try and soften it up so you men can get some shuteye. It won't be perfect, but it'll be better than sleeping on the hardwood." John said as he looked in the back of their new mode of transportation. John watched as Tran looked over the old truck's electrical system. John could tell his friend was worried.

"It gives enough of a charge to keep the battery charged and will keep the headlights working, but if I switch on the defroster for the windshield, the engine loses electrical power, and the batteries will not charge," Tran informed his scarred friend. For the rest of the night, as the men drove through the forest of Bhutan, John and Tran wiped the windshield clear with the sleeves of their sweaters. The six men listened to the stones ping off the undercarriage of the war-built truck as it rolled them to freedom. The journalists in the back, protected by the tarp and the rattling poles holding it up.

William broke the tension of the ride by clearing his throat and smiling said.

"Our old van back there, compared to this thing, was your Aston Martin." The older journalist said in his best Winston Churchill. The men laughed and slapped each other on the back. It was as if, with the joke, they realized they had made it out of Tibet alive. When they left London, Tomas remembered telling the head of the B.B.C. he wasn't coming back without proof the Chinese were committing genocide in Tibet. Now he had the evidence, it almost cost all of them their lives, but they had proof.

Chow tried again to reach Mike to no avail; he almost threw the phone in disgust when he heard the recording telling him the customer was out of the service area. Chow couldn't stall any longer; he had to go to a diplomatic lunch, and it would tie up his entire afternoon. Chow knew something had gone wrong. He couldn't allow paranoia to rule him, not now; there was too much riding on this.

Chapter 49

THE SIGN READ KULONG Chi Wildlife Sanctuary, and the men cheered as Tran drove through the open gate. The first time Tran was forced to leave his home was when he was conscripted into the People's liberation army. This was the second time Tran had left his home. Unlike the first time, this was his decision whether he would go or stay. Tran knew when he and John got the others to a safe place where their government could pick them up. Both he and John were returning to Hong Kong to kill one more man. Tran made his decision to go with John. The small group of escapes started to leave the storm behind, and for the first time, the satellite phone John had taken off Mike vibrated on the seat next to Tran. The sound it gave off when ringing sounded like the batteries were dying; John looked at the phone and then at Tran.

"I think it's for you," Tran said as the phone gave another warbling ring.

"I'm not at home." John laughed. Tran looked at his friend and was going to tell John he knew he was not home, then he thought John might have made a joke, though not a funny one. Tran stopped the truck on the side of the road so John could tell Tomas and William, along with Jerry and Scott, that he and Tran had found a satellite phone in the crashed helicopter. John told the men the phone was working now, and if they wanted to, they could call the B.B.C. and let them know what had happened. William said he would call the newsroom, then the embassy in Hong Kong. William turned and asked his friends if they wanted to say anything before he started the call. William walked around in a circle as he told the heads of the B.B.C. what he and the others had gone through in China. William told how the Colonel had taken their travel papers and burnt them. Then William told whoever was in on the call about the man seizing all the cameras and video they had shot. His arms started to wave around, and his face was turning a bright red when William told about the escape and how they had been and most likely were still being hunted about their run over the border into Bhutan.

"No, I don't think it's a good idea for me to give you my location right now. This phone could be tapped; it could compromise us." The older newsman explained. William listened and said he would tell the others, then pressed the end button. William told the others the Chinese government already gave a statement about their disappearance. The men stood dumbfounded as William told them what he had just learned. The embassy was informed, and they reported to their families.

"The Chinese told the embassy we had wandered into the mountains looking for what we called a better story', and being we're from the cities of Europe, we became disorientated and lost. However, after an exhaustive search by the People's Army search and rescue team, a search covering thousands of square miles, the bodies of the four men were recovered. Because of scavengers that fed on our remains, conventional identification of our bodies was out of the question. Therefore, the Chinese sent the fingerprints back to the embassy. Once it was confirmed the fingerprints were ours, the embassy wanted our bodies turned over for repatriation back to the U.K. What the Chinese turned over wasn't our bodies; instead, it was four urns of ashes. The Chinese said our bodies were too decomposed to travel. That cremation was safer and more sanitary." When William finished telling what he learned during the phone with the newsroom to his three co-workers. The three men stood struck silent by the revelation the Chinese had turned over urns of some stranger's ashes. Telling their government and their families it was the four men.

The B.B.C. was going to contact the home office and tell them their journalists had made contact with them. They knew the men had been taken captive after they unwittingly took still and video photos of a mass grave holding the bodies of Tibetan civilians.

Chow called, and the recording of the customer is out of the service area failed to enrage him. What was more worrisome than the recording was the lack of an answer when the phone rang and rang. Holding the handset of his phone away from his ear Chow looked at it; for the first time, he wanted Mike to answer. Hoping something had gone wrong with the phone during the storm. Chow called his tech support and told them to put a trace on all calls the phone made and to bring up the G.P.S. locator on it. The white telephone on his desk rang five minutes later, and one of the squints in the basement called to tell him the Satellite phone had just ended a call placed to the head office of the British Broadcasting Corporation. Chow's heart stopped. Mike wasn't calling the English. If not Mike, then who, "JOHN." Chow flinched when he said the name.

"Where the hell is that phone?" Chow asked.

"The phone is in the Kulong Chi wildlife sanctuary, sir." The man from technical support said.

"Where in the fuck is that? China, Africa, India WHERE!" shouted Chow.

"It's in, it's in Bhutan, sir, the phone is in Bhutan, and it's about three hundred kilometers over the border, sir." The tech finished in time to hear Chow swear and slam the phone down. Chow now knew why the phone hadn't been answered. John, it always came back to the monster that Mike had helped build.

Standing by the truck, John looked at the phone, trying to decide if he should call Chow. If he called Chow, it would give away his intentions. Chow must know John meant to come back and kill him. John knew he could always track Chow down and take him later when the bastard was relaxed. John would let Chow relax and think he and the rest of the world have forgotten about his crimes. Looking at the phone, John decided he would let Chow go. For now, he would go to the U.K. with Tran. From London, he could start to tear Chow's world apart.

As John made his mind up, his hunt for Chow could wait, and he would try to find out who he was first and if he had any family left in the world. The phone warbled and vibrated in his hand. John knew who the caller was. He knew it was Chow; John knew the man was starting his run for freedom. John knew Chow had a plan to get out and get away. John knew he was the only one who could ruin Chow's plans. As the others watched as John answered the incoming call, the four British journalists gasped when John spoke into the phone. "Hello Chow, if you're looking for Mike, I've sent him on vacation, a permanent vacation," John said calmly.

Chow hoped he had been wrong. He hoped Mike had followed John into Bhutan and was still on the hunt. However, when John answered, Chow felt something drop inside him; whatever dropped was heavy, very heavy.

"So what do we do now, John? Is it going to be man-to-man, or will I even know when it's coming?" Chow asked as he packed his laptop in a carrying case.

"Well, Chow, old chum, here's how I see things. If you leave me alone, I don't want anything to do with you. I know you've had an out planned for yourself. It was to include my death and a star on the wall at Langley, so if that happens, I'm dust in the wind. You won't hear from or see my handsome profile ever again. But if I think you or anyone else is looking, well, you can use your imagination. What Trang did to me will be a visit to the lighter side of things compared to what I'll do to you, do you understand." John finished and waited for Chow's answer.

"Ok, I'll list you as missing, presumed killed inside China. When you go, go far and deep, that account you have of mine, there's enough money to change your face, or before long, you'll be found." Chow didn't know if John heard anything he said. John hung up before Chow could finish his end of the conversation. Chow emptied his safe and placed all the papers and files from it into his attaché case, then threw his overcoat across his arm and left the office. Chow told his assistant he was taking two or three days to enjoy the sunshine. The smartly dressed raven-haired assistant told Chow it was about time he enjoyed himself a little. Chow smiled and agreed wholeheartedly. The smile was still on Chow's lips as he walked out into the sunshine. His next stop was to go to the apartment the agency kept for him. There he gathered up what he needed to disappear. Chow made sure to take nothing personal, nothing that could leave a clue to his destination.

Chapter 50

JOHN DROVE FOR THE first time since leaving the town of Ningchi. Tran drove the old van that saw the group of men through Tibet. Then when they found the duce and a half, he took the wheel of the truck, getting them into the country of Bhutan. The long hours behind the wheel had finely worn the sturdy Tibetan out. As John drove, he could hear his friends' regular breathing beside him in the dark cab. The four English men slept in the back of the truck as it bounced over the rutted gravel roads leading through the mountains of Bhutan. Stopping the truck at a sign, John got out and tried deciphering it. His skill with any of the Asian languages started and stopped with Cantonese; Tran looked at the sign and yawned.

"It is the name of a town; it says Trashi Yangtse, three hundred and sixty kilometers." Tran climbed back into the truck, balled his jacket up against his door, and went back to sleep.

Three suitcases were all that Chow had to pack for the start of his new life. From his apartment to the airport, Chow hailed a cab. He didn't want just any taxi. Chow wanted a cab that wouldn't record the fair. Chow waited until his gypsy cab turned the corner before he stepped out of the building. When he reached the airport, Chow chartered a private jet to take him to a small airport in South Korea where his own plane sat waiting for him to fly someplace, 'off the edge of any map,' as Chow called it.

When the Chinese official asked for a flight plan, he was given one for South Korea. When the official wanted more of a plan than Chow wished to provide, Chow showed his C.I.A. ID and told the man it was official diplomatic business. The official apologized and left the plane with a bow and a smile. The pilot was given permission to taxi and take off right away. Once in the air, the flight steward served a light meal of smoked salmon, which she said came from the natives of the Queen Charlotte Islands on the west coast of Canada.

Along with the salmon, she served asparagus in a light cream reduction and new baby potatoes with rosemary-baked baby carrots. Chow had a larger appetite than he would have thought after he had eaten his meal. He washed it down and toasted himself and his new life with a flute of champagne. When he had finished his champagne, he asked the flight attendant if. She could bring him a glass of forty-year-old Glenfiddich scotch with two ice cubes in the glass. Sipping his scotch, Chow closed his eyes and listened to the Gulf Stream as it carried him closer to the edge of the map.

The six men stood beside the truck and looked down at the small village below them. Jerry and Scott held two of the small digital cameras they had managed to grab when they had been rescued from the dentation center. The men were taking photos from different areas around the truck. John and Tran had to remind the men the truck was almost out of fuel. They should stop and see if anyone knew the owner of the truck. As the men stood on the hill overlooking the village, they could see in a village this size, there would be no way they would be able to draw any money from a bank. Most of the buildings looked to be homes looking around. John told the men he didn't even think they would be able to find a telephone. He also told the men the battery in the satellite phone was almost dead; looking over the village, both John and Tran hoped that there would be fuel at least.

The Gulf Stream landed. To Chow, it felt like it had barely touched the runway before the pilot started to reverse the thrust of the engines. Chow knew reversing the thrust didn't mean the engines ran backward; instead, it meant the forward thrust of the twin Pratt and Whitney engines was redirected out the bottom of the engine at a forward angle to help slow the plane. He thanked the flight attendant for her kindness on the flight from Hong Kong; a skycap placed his three suitcases on a cart and followed Chow to the office so he could file his own flight plan.

The flight plan Chow filed read like a man who had all the time in the world on his hands. The only thing of concern to him was the amount of fuel his plane held. His flight plan started in South Korea. His first stop was on the tiny island of Minamidaito-son, southeast of Okinawa, Japan. Where he would refuel and buy lunch. From the island of Minamidaito-son. Chow would fly south to the island of Palau for more fuel, then on to Bamaga, Australia. When Chow told the man who was entering his flight plan into the computer that he was going to the island nation of Papua New Guinea, he wanted to do some exploring, Chow told the man. Once Chow's flight plan had been entered into the computer. The man looked at Chow and said to him that he would never go to that place.

"I watched a program on the television once, and it said that the savages that live on that island still eat human flesh. Personally, I would rather spend the week at my mother in laws house." The man grimaced when he mentioned his mother-in-law. Chow laughed and bowed, thanking the man for his help, then left the office and walked out to his Stratus 714. It was fuelled sitting on the tarmac, waiting for him. The skycap placed the bags inside the cabin and then stood waiting for the tip he knew was coming. After placing a one hundred dollar American bill into the man's hand, Chow climbed into the plane and shut the door, then started his pre-flight check. Twenty minutes later, he smiled as the single Williams international FJ44-3AP jet engine came to life. After receiving permission to taxi to the only runway used for private flights at this airport. Chow was allowed to power his small jet up and leave the ground, smiling as he flew out over the ocean. Chow knew the man in the office where he filed his flight plan would remember the man who was going to the island of the savages. The skycap would remember the rich man who gave him one hundred dollars American. This was it, time to start his new life; not everything in his old life was over. Chow smiled as he thought about having his old boss killed. G.W. Hollyford, Chow decided he would send men to kill the old bastard and his son. Chow decided to wipe the whole family out of existence; he would tell his men to kill the old shit last.

Chapter 51

WHEN THEY RUMBLED TO a stop in what they thought was a village. John stepped out of the truck looking at the scattered huts and grazing cattle. Turning to Tomas, he shrugged his shoulders.

"I think we're right; we aren't going to find anything here in the way of a bank or phone." Tomas looked around and nodded in agreement. Tran walked to the door of one of the huts and knocked. He waited and then said something to someone on the other side. John couldn't understand what Tran was saying or what was being said to him, but the door opened, and an older man walked out. Tran and the man spoke for ten minutes, then bowed to each other, and Tran waved them over.

"This man agreed to sell the truck to us; this man tells me he became sick when he had to hike home. He was forced to leave the truck in the barn where we had found it. He was too sick to get back to fix it and is only starting to get around. His grandson will go to the barn and bring back the money. It is more than he wanted for the truck. Also, he is kind enough to give what fuel he has here. We will have enough for us to get to the next town, where we will be able to buy more." Tran translated for the older man. All the men thanked the old man by shaking his hand and bowing. Using a hand pump, John transfers fuel from a rusted forty-five-gallon drum to the truck's fuel tank. When John finished, he smiled and waved to the old man and a teenager standing beside his grandfather, then drove the truck out of the village. Holding a sheet of paper in his hand, Tran read the directions to the town of Tashigang.

"It will be easy. The old man said all we have to do is go south on this road; he said something else, odd." Tran told John.

"Odd, how odd, was it odd like it was out of place or odd like I'm crazy?" John asked.

"Odd, like it was out of place. The old man said that we should be careful on the turns the road takes. However, there is a bit of a difference in our two languages, so it might have been crazy." Tran said.

"That's not odd, the old guy just wanted us to be careful, and he was concerned about our safety, that's all," John said.

Chow's already good mood seemed to get better as he flew out over the East China Sea. Being a careful man, Chow ensured he stayed to his flight plan until he was out in international waters. Two hours into his flight, Chow would radio in a mayday, then dive below the radar. To air traffic control, it would seem Chow suffered some kind of malfunction, and he had crashed into the sea below. What Chow was going to do was to make a hard turn to the west and fly below radar into the Philippine Sea. He then would turn slightly north and fly to Laoag airport on the northern tip of the Philippines. There Chow would switch the transponder in his plane and fuel, then fly off.

The aircraft mechanic Chow paid to get a new transponder for him called. The man told Chow it was all set up, and he was waiting for him to land. Chow's mechanic told him it was a quiet day and that they would have no problem pulling off the switch. Flying at two hundred feet over the water, Chow knew he was using fuel faster than if he had been flying at thirty-eight thousand, but it had to be done. After he had a new transponder, he could worry about his fuel economy.

The first turn on the road from the village was more of a corner, a one-hundred-and-eighty-degree corner. John and Tran looked at each other as they finished the turn and then up the road at a second turn. The second corner was only a ninety-degree corner. They met another truck in the middle of the turn. Tran explained because John was empty, he had to back up and let the loaded truck go past.

"Now we know why the old guy told us to be careful on the turns," John said, thankful the old man's marbles were intact. The rest of the trip south to the town of Tashigang was slow going; the road in many places was single-track dirt ruts. They would have to give the right of way to loaded trucks they met. Because there was only one lane on the road south, it made the trip longer and harder. Just when Tomas, Jerry, Scott, and William thought they would never reach the town. Tran looked through the sliding window separating the cab from the cargo area.

"We can see the lights of the next town," Tran told the men. The four journalists whooped and clapped each other on their backs. Tran looked at John and smiled, knowing their run wasn't over just yet.

Chapter 52

THE LOW FUEL WARNING had been telling Chow he was running low on fuel for ten minutes. Thanks to budget cuts, the small airstrip in Laoag no longer had live air traffic controllers. This airport was a maintenance-only facility now, used mainly by private and regional carriers. So Chow had no air traffic controllers to worry about recording his landing or take off. The computer that would have recorded his transponder code had been turned off by his mechanic. Before anyone noticed, Chow's plane was in the hangar. The mechanic then turned the computer back on. The mechanic Chow had been paying switched the transponder out in twenty minutes. A flight plan had been filed with his new transponders flight code attached to it.

The official that filed Chow's new flight plan told him they didn't have any record of Chow landing at the airport in Laoag. Chow told the official he landed when they were having problems with the computer that recorded transponder codes. The man on the phone was upset, saying the people there should have called him with Chow's arrival time and transponder code. The official said it was a good thing Chow was filing a new flight plan. This flight plan reads like the first one. This one said that he was going to Australia also. The only one who knew what he was really doing was the mechanic, and the mechanic was expendable. It wasn't like Chow enjoyed killing the mechanic. Like many other people in his position, Chow used murder and threats of murder as security measures, as well as a way to save money in the future. The way Chow looked at it was dead men don't require hush money.

When the other mechanics came into work and changed into their overalls, they would find their friend and call the ambulance. The paramedics would say heart attack, and when the autopsy was finished, so would the coroner. However, what killed the mechanic was a fast-acting toxin the Chinese had perfected; this toxin was found in nature. The Chinese found a way to take this toxin and increase its lethality a hundred times. For it to work, Chow sprayed the poison into the face of the victim. Death came within seconds, then as fast as it killed, the toxin would break down to its non-lethal parts and be absorbed into the body's stored fat. Chow smiled as he walked out to his small jet, one loose end tied up in a nice, neat bow.

Chapter 53

THE TOWN OF TASHIGANG was larger than the village of Trashi Yangtse, but it might have been a stretch to call it anything but a large village. The one thing it did have was a phone, and all the men were allowed to make phone calls. Tomas and the other men from the B.B.C. called their homes and found out the B.B.C. had already contacted the families with the news the men were alive and had escaped the Chinese. Each of the men stood and patted the other on the shoulders as one of their friends spoke to loved ones back in England. When one was finished, another would take his place on the phone. When the men had finished, all were misty-eyed but elated at having made the calls.

Tran watched as the men smiled and told their families they loved them. He knew it wasn't right, but he felt anger and jealousy again. The anger was at the Chinese for taking what they had no right to, his home and his country. A country Tran wished he could get to know. He was envious of the men he helped, for the families waiting for them to come home to hold them. Tran, like John, had no one to hold him, to love him. Except for John, Tran was alone in the world.

John managed to get in contact with a bank in Switzerland that held Mike's account. He had all the funds transferred from Mike's account to his personal account. The person was dubious of doing this once John had recited the bank account number and the sixteen-digit password. The account assistant perked up and said the funds were being transferred as they spoke. Once the transfer was completed, the assistant asked if there was any other banking

John wished to do today. John told the assistant that he wanted to make another transfer of funds. This time John told the assistant he wished the funds to go to an account in the U.K. John gave the woman Tomas's account number and the branch of the bank he dealt with. When he had received the account transfer transaction number, John thanked the woman for her kind service and then hung up. Smiling, John turned and told the men they wouldn't have to worry about money for quite some time.

"There, you now have ten thousand pounds in your bank Tomas." John smiled.

"I can draw it out five thousand pounds at a time. My sister said because the B.B.C. didn't believe I or the others were dead, they never shut down my bank account, so we're in good shape." Tomas told John and the others. The men walked towards the local, national bank of Bhutan to withdraw some money. In this age of computers, where worldwide banking was done in a matter of minutes, it surprised Tomas to find out it would take one hour for the transfer to be completed. Once the money was in the bank, the manager told Tomas the exchange rates but explained traveler's checks would be better for them. American dollar traveler's checks would be accepted faster than the British pound sterling.

One hour later, Tomas walked out of the local branch of the Bank of Bhutan with five thousand dollars in traveler's checks in one hundred dollar increments. Tran filled the truck at the local fuel depot while Jerry and Scott bought food from a market for the trip to the capital city of Thimpu. Standing at the fuel depot, Tran watched John talk to the bank manager. The man pointed to the truck and nodded his head then another man walked up and joined the conversation. When Tran finished filling the truck's fuel tank, he walked over to where John was talking to the two men. It seemed the bank manager knew the old man who owned the truck, and the other man wanted to buy it. John had agreed to sell it to the man in the morning. The bank manager wanted to wait until then just so he could make sure it was all right for John to sell it to him.

The manager asked John if it would be alright to have his son go to the village where the old man lived and make sure John did indeed pay for the truck. The manager assured John his son would be back in the morning with the word. John looked at the men he and Tran brought out of China. They all agreed to stay in the local hotel for the night, then in the morning when the truck was sold. They would buy the car the bank manager had for sale. When the four journalists found out they were going to stay in hotel rooms for the night, they reminded John of little kids. The men hurried to the front desk, trying to be checked in before his friend.

Tomas hadn't realized how long it had been since their last shower. When he and the others stepped to the hotel's front desk, the poor girl working there frowned at the smell coming from the men. Though she was too polite to pinch her nose shut, the men wouldn't have blamed her if she had. Standing in the lobby, out of the breeze, John could start to smell himself. He began to smell the others as well and couldn't help but feel sorry for the girl. The hotel had three floors, and each floor had six rooms. She smiled as the men collected their keys and started for the stairs. Each man stopped before the stairs, then turned when Scott asked the question.

"Why rush to the rooms to take showers when they had no clean clothes to put on?" The men turned and looked at John, who turned and looked at Tran, who turned and walked back to the desk, where he asked the girl who had just checked them in where they might be able to buy some new clothes. To his delight, the girl covered her mouth when she giggled and told him of a clothing shop behind the hotel.

The clothing store clerk was sitting behind the shop's front counter when six of the worst-smelling men he had ever been around walked into the shop. All of them bought three pairs of trousers and undergarments as well as shirts and jackets, socks and hats. The four British men bought backpacks from the shop next door and boots. When the big American saw the boots, he bought the best pair he could find and hand-knitted wool socks. The clerk was happy to accept the American traveler's check to pay for all they bought. As far back as the clerk could remember, this was the single best day the shop ever had. With arms overflowing, the six men walked back to the hotel, ready for their long-desired and needed showers. The front desk clerk smiled at the men as they went to the stairs. Though too polite to say anything, she thought the hotel would run out of hot water before the men were clean.

Chapter 54

ONCE CHOW LEFT PHILIPPINE air space, he turned west toward the island nation of Malaysia. He wanted to fly to a small island called Samui. At the airport there, he would fuel for the longest leg of his trip. That leg would take him over the country of Myanmar. From there, he would fly north to Borjhar in Assam, then North West to the city of Paro in Bhutan. He would drive back east to the capital city of Bhutan, Thimphu. From here, Chow could keep up the appearance of a very wealthy man. He was a rich man who wanted to live the quiet life a happy country like Bhutan offered while keeping an eye on his investments. That's what the government of Bhutan believed; Bhutan was in the middle of Asia. He could live anywhere in the world and run his empire, but Chow wanted to be where he could reach out and kill anyone who was a threat. From Bhutan, he would look for John Smyth and run his empire. Chow would keep his business out of the country, so it never came back to soil his new identity. Running was too hard; it took time and money to set up his disappearance. Though Chow didn't mind killing himself in a plane crash, he liked the idea of being dead. Chow now had a new name and would soon have a new face, thanks to a plastic surgeon he was bringing over from Brazil. This was the same man who made his fortune changing the faces of very rich men and women. These people were being hunted by the world's premier law enforcement organizations. Chow never gave a second thought about his parents, he was getting what he wanted, and if he was asked, he could care less about his parents. As he Flew over the blue sea, Chow thought back to his mother and father. As far back as

Chow could remember, he only saw his parents getting in his way. They were an inconvenience at the best of times. Chow knew his death would break his mother's heart, but he could care less. Hell, he wondered if he should send flowers. Chow smiled and decided he would have a nice bouquet, something tactful for a tactless man. Chow knew his father was Chinese, he knew what his father did during the Korean War, and he also knew his father's real name.

Chapter 55

STANDING IN THE SHOWER, John had forgotten how much he enjoyed the feeling of hot water. He washed and rinsed his hair four times. During the escape from Tibet, John had forgotten about the damage to his face. He forgot how when the old man in the mountain found him, the old man wouldn't let John touch his own face. Now a heavy rope of scar tissue ran down the left side of his face. John could still remember the sadistic prick, smiling as he told John he was now so ugly little children would run away from him. He had been General Trang's assistant in some ways. The little man had been worse than the General. The general wanted something from him, and the little assistant tortured John out of sheer pleasure.

The six new friends met in the ground-floor restaurant attached to the hotel. There, they all ate their first real meal since Tran and John rescued them from the detention center in Ningchi. Drinking coffee and eating, the men told jokes and reminisced about when they were younger. Tran joined in, and for the first time in a long time, the Tibetan felt himself growing happy. Tran looked at his big scarred friend and knew John couldn't join in on the conversation. He also knew the man was too strong to ask for help or to show he longed to be able to recall his past or his family.

John was the only one who couldn't tell any stories about his childhood. When Tomas, William, and the others in their group were told about what John and Tran learned from Mike as the storm crashed around them. John had gotten information about his beginnings and where he was from. John told the men what Mike had told him.

John's parents had been killed when he was a little boy, and he had been raised in an orphanage run by a black-ops section of the central intelligence agency. There he was educated in the world's cultures, along with maths and the sciences. However, the bulk of his education was in the art of hunting and killing men. When he graduated from the orphanage, John was sent out to hunt and kill enemies of the U.S. At first, he pursued men guilty of terrorism, the indiscriminate killing of innocent men and women. John didn't see a problem with the eradication of these people. Later he was to be used to help stem the tide of North Korean aggression toward the world. After the North Korean action, he was involved in and accomplished a positive outcome. John found out he was being used to kill for the dirty section chief of the C.I.A. in Hong Kong. This man had taken over the Asian drug and weapons markets. Now the bastard was shipping his drugs all over Europe and North America and guns to the Middle East and African markets. John also told the four journalists his real father found out about the project. How at the time, the project was called 'CRADLE.' The director of the C.I.A. tried to scare him into dropping the story. John's father was trying to save the world in his own way; he wouldn't drop the story. Then John's mother, a lawyer specializing in corruption, became involved. The order came down to kill John's family. When the director of the C.I.A. found out John was the perfect age to go through the program, the decision was made to keep him and kill everyone else.

"Back then, there was no such a thing as the homeland security act, not that it would have mattered. Mike told me my parents Were Canadian, and I was born in Canada. So they killed my father and mother and placed me in the program. It was the directors' way of pissing on their memory. They washed any memories I had of my mother and father out of my head. Now the only memory I seem to have comes from reoccurring nightmares I have. I can see a woman, who I think is my mother, being shot in the head. A man is carrying off another young boy, a boy I can't remember." When John finished talking, Tomas looked at his co-workers and turned back to John.

"You said this; Mike Styles told you your real name. He told you it was Jack, though he couldn't tell you your last name. Well, 'Jack,' when I get back to London, I'm going to pick up where your father left off. I'm going to bring this dirty bit of business to light. When it's done, I'm going to give your father the byline." Tomas promised. The others sitting around the table nodded in agreement with Tomas. Then William stood, stuck out his hand, and introduced himself.

"Hello, Jack. It's nice to meet you." The older man said with a smile; when William sat down, Tomas then each man stood and introduced himself.

Chapter 56

THE SUNSET CHOW SET the automatic pilot to fly him over Myanmar. He called over the radio and received permission to enter the country's airspace. Leaning back, Chow closed his eyes and was soon droned to sleep by the sound of the engine powering the plane through the air at forty thousand feet. A chirp brought Chow back to reality from a dream of a tropical island. Sitting up, he checked his instruments and headed to see if he could find out what warning started to sound. The chirp came again this time. Chow knew what caused it; someone was trying to radio him. Placing the headphones on, Chow answered the voice calling out his transponder code.

"Ap one nine one tango over," Chow said. The voice over the headset ordered Chow to turn to a new heading and land for government inspection. Chow knew what was happening; he had heard of this in Myanmar. Chow couldn't understand; he paid off a government official, so this would not happen. The government inspection would find fault with the aircraft, and it would be deemed unsafe to fly. The owner of the plane would be ordered out of the country or arrested. The aircraft would then be turned over to the military leaders for repairs. Once it was in the hands of the military, it would become the government's property. Chow banked the plane to the left and pushed his throttle all the way to the stoppers. The Williams FJ44-3AP jet engine went from a relaxing drone to a fierce scream as Chow pushed the nose down into a dive as he finished his turn. His Stratos 714 pushed passed its advertised speed of four hundred and fifty knots as Chow dove to fifteen thousand feet and tried to get more speed out of the single-engine. The man on the radio ordered Chow to slow his craft down and turn to a new heading to land. Chow listened to the voice on the radio go from complacent to angry. When he refused to comply, the voice was now telling him if he did not comply, the army would be sent out to shoot him down. Chow told the man on the radio to "go fuck himself" as his Stratos screamed over the town of Switt and into the Bay of Bengal.

The military controller on the radio told Chow this would be his last warning to turn and land, or he would be shot down. Chow informed the man in five miles, he would be in international water. If anything happened out there, it would be another nail in the coffin of the military government of Myanmar. The controller told Chow it would make no difference where he was that the government of Myanmar would take his act as aggression. Chow told the controller what he thought of his family, taking time to tell the man how his mother became pregnant with him. As the man raged into an unintelligible screaming fit. Chow brought the nose of his plane up, climbing back to forty thousand feet to make himself clear of Indian radar, just in case Myanmar did try to shoot him down. As the man raged at him over the radio, Chow hoped having the man almost out of his head would distract him from scrambling the military.

Chapter 57

TRAN WAS STANDING IN the hall when John opened his door. The others started to call him Jack after they heard the story of how John came to be. Each man stood and reintroduced himself; Tran smiled and nodded his head. The man everyone called John until the day before now looked out at the morning and smiled. His friends started calling him Jack, and it felt right. The sun had been up for two hours now, and Tran was eager to get the others up and moving. Tran knew the others would want to sleep in. Tran had to explain he didn't think they should slow down too much right now. They were still too close to Tibet for his comfort.

"I heard the bank manager's son come back last night. He will know we did not steal the truck." John, who the others insisted on calling Jack, now said. Sitting around the table with William, Tomas, Jerry, and Scott, drinking his second coffee, John asked if he was going to be called Jack from now on. Though the others didn't know, John stood in front of the mirror in his room last night and called himself Jack for an hour, trying to see if it felt genuine. To his surprise, it felt not only authentic, but the name also felt right. It was as if by saying it over and over, he was casting aside the last shackle that bound him, that bound Jack.

"I think it will help you remember who you were, and it might bring back more memories of your mother and father. If you use the name, they gave you rather than the moniker those black-hearted pricks pinned on you." Tomas said. It was at the moment in the restaurant of a small hotel. In the town of Tashigang, in the small happy country of Bhutan in the center of Asia. John Smyth was left behind, and Jack started his climb back into life with the help of four B.B.C. journalists and a Tibetan man Jack called his friend. Jack knew John would always be part of him, but this wasn't such a bad thing.

A new beginning

Chapter 58

OVER THEIR MEAL, JACK told Tomas about Ben, who the monks took in and healed his wounds. He said the award-winning journalists of Ben Stills and of how General Trang had tortured him and when Trang thought Ben would die of the infection coursing through his body, had thrown Ben out into a mass grave behind the prison. Jack told the men when they reached the city of Thimphu, he and Tomas would have to contact the British authorities and inform them of Ben. The journalists sat talking about Ben, and the men discussed the different ways they could do an exposé of how the corrupt Chinese government treated foreigners. How they let them be grabbed and summarily tortured and murdered.

The smiling bank manager came into the restaurant. He told Jack and the others his son had talked to the old man, and the old man confirmed what Jack had told him the day before. The manager said the car was ready and he would have the papers prepared before they finished their meal. Tomas asked what was going on, looking at the others in confusion. Tran explained Jack bought a car so they all could be comfortable, one they didn't have to lay on a cold steal floor or in wet hay.

Chapter 59

CHOW CALLED OUT HIS call sign when he realized the controller had indeed sent a Burmese aircraft after him. Chow reached an air traffic controller in India and informed the controller he was in international waters and was in fear of being shot down by the Burmese military. After Chow had explained his fear to the Indian controller, another voice came on the radio because Chow's plane had a more sophisticated radio, as standard equipment. The Indian air traffic controller could hear the fighter pilot threaten to shoot Chow out of the sky if he didn't turn out of international waters. The Myanmar air force pilot stammered when he heard the Indian air traffic controller inform him this pilot was in contact with the Indian air force. If he fired on a civilian aircraft, he would not make it back to his own air space. The pilot informed Chow he would be a wanted man in Myanmar and that he was lucky the Indians were so close. The Indian controller told the fighter pilot he was encroaching into Indian airspace. If he did not turn, he would be fired upon. Chow had a perfect view of the two Indian fighters as they screamed past his Stratos 714. Each going past one on the left and one on the right, Chow wanted to turn his plane around and watch as they intimidated the pilot from Myanmar. He kept up the act of the scared civilian and never slowed his plane. The military jets pulled up on each side of him as Chow pulled his throttle back and slowed his plane. The military air controller asked if everything was all right and if Chow needed any further assistance.

"If you could point me in the direction of an airport where I could buy more fuel, running from the fighter has taken its toll on the tanks." The controller told Chow the jets would lead him to the airport beside the base. There he would be able to buy fuel and anything else he needed. Looking at the pilot on his left wing tip Chow snapped a salute to the pilot. The pilot smiled and saluted in return and eased his jet in front and above Chow. He made detailed plans, took in all the variables, and thought he had thought of everything. Chow would have never guessed about being double-crossed by the high-level General he had paid in the Myanmar military. Chow knew it was about money; Chow made himself a promise he would have the man and his entire family killed. Right down to the dog, the man himself would die last and very slowly.

Tomas looked at the used Toyota land cruiser over. It would seat the six men comfortably, and with its four-wheel drive, diesel engine, and four-speed manual gearbox, the sturdy suv could take them almost anywhere they wished. The bank manager explained the front of this truck and the rear axles worked all the time. Also, each side of the axle received equal power from the transmission. The smiling manager had taken the deuce and a half on trade. Then subtract the value he placed on the deuce and a half from the price of the land cruiser. After Jack paid the manager for the Toyota, the bank manager and mayor of the town handed over the title and two sets of keys, turning Jack gave one set to Tran.

"Partners," Jack said to Tran. The look that came over Tran's face surprised Jack.

"Um, I think being a friend is better than...." It was then Jack remembered what having a partner meant in Tibet. In Tibet, a partner was your wife. When Jack remembered, he laughed and held his hands up and said friends only. Though all the men could drive, Tran drove the first leg of the trip to the city of Thimphu; they planned to drive to the village of Mongar. From there, Tomas said he would drive to the next stop along the Trashigang-Semtokha highway, to another small town called Sengor. There they would stay for the night; that was the plan. It wasn't too long after the six escapes started their trip across the country of Bhutan the men realized it was going to take longer than they had planned.

While Chow filled out the paperwork required of him, a man from Indian customs inspected his passport. The passport was a fake, but it was made by a man who at one time had created fake identities for the C.I.A. Chow knew the man; he paid for his new identity himself so the C.I.A. would have no record of it, and the passport was as good as the real thing. Chow had a birth certificate, social security card, driver's license, pilot's license, and a whole array of credit cards. All of which had no limits on them, and all this backed up the passport. An immigration officer brought Chow back his passport and told him everything was in order. He watched as an officer with the Indian military walked into the room. The officer sat at the table where he was finishing his paperwork.

"We make it a point to never let any of our citizens fly into Myanmar air space; if the government sees something it wants, well then, like a pack of thieves, they steal it. They would have loved to get their hands on your little jet." The officer said.

Chow knew the man was right, even though he had paid not to be molested on his flight through.

"I thought I was going to be safe with a flight plan," Chow said in the role of Lee Mang, a very rich diamond merchant.

"Well, now you can go on with the rest of your trip, and you have learned about Myanmar." The officer said as he stood and collected the incident report from Chow.

"Is there any way I could thank the men who saved my life?" Chow asked.

"The two pilots are outside admiring your Stratos now." The officer said as he left the room. Walking out into the dazzling sunshine after being in a room lit by fluorescent lights, Chow was blinded; he realized he had left his sunglasses on the table where he had filled out his statement for the report. Squinting and using his hand to shade his eyes, Chow smiled and walked over to the pilots, introducing himself as Lee Mang. Each of the pilots shook Chow's hand.

When Chow, aka Lee, offered each of the men to climb into the Stratos, each man accepted and sat in the pilot and co-pilot seat, looking and commenting about the layout of the instruments. After the men asked all the technical questions and commented about the beautiful little jet. The air force pilots climbed out, and each man told Chow they were doing their duty when Chow thanked them again for saving him. While they walked back into the building to retrieve Chow's sunglasses. Chow knew it was men like these he would want for his own protection when he settled down, pros, professionals, no amateurs. Chow would have men who knew their jobs and their places. When he got settled down, he would hire men like these two.

Chapter 60

TOMAS WAS GLAD THAT this Toyota had been equipped for running in the mountains. When this truck was first bought fifteen years ago, the chrome bumper had been removed, and a heavy steal one was bolted and then welded to the frame. On the heavy steel bumper, a winch with a twenty thousand-pound load capacity was then bolted and welded on. Powerful halogen off-road lights were added on each side of the winch. With the headlights on bright and the off-road light blazing their way through the night, Tomas and his co-pilot Scott could see small deer and other nocturnal living creatures caught in the light. One of the small mountain deer moving in the night suddenly stopped in the middle of the road. Bracketed by the powerful off-road lights, the animal stood shivering in fear. Knowing the animal would stand there mesmerized by the lights, Tomas shut off the lights as he brought the truck to a stop. When he turned on the lights again, the deer had disappeared. Turning, Tomas waved his hands like a magician would and said 'Magic' to which the Scotsmen rolled his eyes. The second leg of the trip had taken longer than they thought it would; it was three in the morning when they reached the tiny village of Sengor. They all slept sitting up in the truck until the sun topped the mountains. The whole trip they thought would only take them three days, with the rain and the roads. They had managed to stretch it out into the fifth day before Jack and Tran, along with; Tomas, Jerry, Scott, and William, drove into the capital city of Thimphu.

William said he now knew what it must have felt like for the concurring heroes to return home in the days of old. All the men agreed; Tomas told everyone when he landed back in England, he was going to eat the biggest, rarest steak any of them ever saw. All the men were telling each other what would be the first thing they would do. Most of the men said they would hug and kiss loved ones, then came the other things like giving the Queen a high five. Scott had come up with that one, much to the amusement of all in the Toyota. Some of the things the men offered for suggestions were funny, but some were crazy. Jack liked it when Jerry suggested giving the Chinese ambassador a wedgie; it became funnier when Jerry had to explain to Tran what a wedgie was.

After checking most of the hotels in town, Jack went to one of the last on the list he had been given. Calling the hotel Draku, he was happy to discover they had six rooms open, and he reserved them right away. At fifty bucks a night compared to the almost three hundred a night of one of the other hotels, it was a deal. An hour later, Jack, Tran, and the others pulled into the hotel's parking lot. Jack and the other men checked in before they brought any of their baggage in. Jack and Tran still carried the weapons along with all the ammunition they took off the military police in Tibet. For the other men, the reason was much simpler; they wanted to have the bellhop to help them.

The AMR-2 Tran, found when he and Jack killed the two military police at the second roadblock, was disassembled and wrapped in towels. Jack carried the rifle in a large duffle bag, the ammunition for the weapon was in his backpack. One of the QCW-05s he had in his backpack, also with it, was the ammunition and the silencer. The type 64 automatic pistol Jack carried in his waistband at the small of his back. Tran was in the same boat as Jack when he unpacked his things from the duffle bag and backpack. Tran thought all the weapons and the ammo seemed to be over the top. However, on more than one occasion, Tran had heard Jack say, 'Better safe than sorry.' Jack could hear the footsteps in the hall;

before the knock came on the door, he knew it was Tran. Besides Tran and himself, none of the other men stepped to the side of a door before he knocked. Tran wanted to discuss what they should do with their weapons and the ammo, and they both agreed they needed to hold onto all of it.

"I was thinking about it as we drove through the mountains; I don't think the Chinese will let us go, just the opposite. We know they tried to recapture us back in Tibet. Now that we've slipped outside their borders and their control. I think they'll try and kill us now, capture is out of the question. Now you and I have an edge, our training will kick in and help us. I think Scott's training will come back from his time in the army. The others have no training to fall back on; they wouldn't stand a chance without us." Jack said. He looked at Tran and waited for his friend to say something.

"I think like you do. If we leave the others with their skill, it would be like we killed them; I cannot do that." Tran said. Sitting in the hotel in Bhutan, Jack and Tran discussed the possibility the Chinese wanted four men they had rescued killed. The men running China would wish for this to be done soon. The leaders of China would like the men dead before they made it back to England with the story of their abduction. As for the photos of the graves, the men had taken out of the detention center, they would never see the light of day.

"Ok, both you and I think the same way, and we both think the Chinese will want to silence William, Tomas, and the others. They would destroy the pictures to keep the rest of the world out of Tibet. We owe it to your family to bring the whole thing out into the light." Jack watched as Tran nodded his head.

Tomas's room was connected to Jack's by a common door; this was what most parents traveling with their older children wanted. It was a way to keep the kids safe and still have a bit of privacy. Nevertheless, it would serve Jack, too. Knocking on the door, Tomas answered in his best Churchill voice. Jack explained to Tomas what he and Tran planned,

"When housekeeping service comes through in the morning, Tran will bring his weapons into your room as housekeeping cleans his room. Then when they're done with his room, he'll take them back before the lady starts yours." Tomas nodded conspiratorially, then held up one finger.

"What if they have more than one girl working on this floor?" The balding Englishmen asked.

"Let's hope they don't. Now when the girl is done with your room, I bring the weapons over through this door, and she can clean my room. Then we put everything back until the next morning." Jack finished. Tomas held up his finger as if he was going to shoot Jack with it, then shook his head.

Chapter 61

CHOW COULD FEEL THE wings capture the air as his jet raced down the runway, lifting him free of mother earth and India. He was thankful for the rescue the Indian air force had given him. At the same time, he wanted to be on his way. Back at thirty-eight thousand feet, Chow felt free. In a few hours, he would be touching down at Paro international airport in Bhutan. From there, Chow would drive a new Land Rover to the capital of Thimphu. It was here Chow would stay until he found the island he wanted somewhere in the south pacific. If that was not possible, he would look elsewhere, like the South Atlantic. Maybe there would be something for him in the Mediterranean. To Chow, it didn't matter where it was so long as he could control it. Flying over the Indian cities, Chow could see the fog of bluish oil smoke from the countless two-stroke motors still in use here. From motorcycles to motorized three-wheeled rickshaws as well as some three-wheeled delivery trucks, all used the dirty two-stroke engine. Flying over this place, Chow was amazed anyone could breathe in the cities. The jungle seemed so green and clean as he approached a small city or large town. The visibility of the ground would diminish because of the bluish haze covering the area.

Chow smiled as he thought about Al Gore and his tree-hugging plaid-wearing hippies all crying for the polar bears. Four hours later, Chow checked in with the control tower at Paro Airport. The control tower gave him a heading and confirmed he was cleared to land on their one runway. The operator he spoke to sounded happy to hear from him, and to his surprise, Chow was pleased to be heard from. He would have saved a ton of money and time if he could have flown here straight from Hong Kong. This was impossible with mainland China on the way. His fake plane crash had to happen over open international water, so his body could never be recovered.

The landing was a breeze at the single-runway airport. As far as Chow could see, he was the only aircraft in the sky over the city. Chow stepped out of his Stratos 714 and was greeted by a smiling Bhutan customs and immigration official who led Chow into a reception area. There Chow was asked the standard questions, how long was he planning to stay if he was there on pleasure or business, as well as did he have anything in his luggage he should declare. Chow gave the correct answer; he told the woman he was retired and was taking a long overdue vacation. The customs official asked how long Chow planned to stay. Chow told the official he hadn't set a time limit on his stay. As for anything to declare, Chow said no and watched as the woman looked in the cases, then thanked Chow and wished him a grand vacation in Bhutan. Chow thanked the woman and bowed, then left the arrivals department, searching for his new Land Rover.

Chapter 62

THE FIRST NIGHT IN the city of Thimphu was spectacular. The sun set behind the mountains to the west, causing the snow-capped peaks to blaze with the faux heat of fiery oranges that bled into reds, then crimson. As the sun sank further behind the curtain of the world, the colors changed from those crying of the last battle of the day. As the day ended, the evening gave its whimper of surrender to the coming of night and its dark watch over the world. Jack sat alone on the patio, watching as the daylight faded to twilight. The orange so brightly coloring the snow of the mountains now slowly went through the subtle shades of red and crimson. Then the purple crier came with a royal proclamation and announced with all its majesty the night won again. Yet, another battle was soon to be turned over as the day would be back for its revenge. Another battle in the struggle between Solis and Luna. As the moon came over the hills to the east, the same snow cap held the colors of the end of day and the beginning of the night, now heralded the coming of the evening watcher. The rider of the sky through the night would keep all those secrets lovers whisper about over stolen moments. Jack wondered if he could share this time of day with anyone. Or was he going to watch the transformation of day to night by himself for however long he walked his path.

Chow stopped his Land Rover in a wide spot on the road from Paro to Thimphu for the first time; he wanted to see the sunset change the mountains. As Chow watched the sunset, he felt that the night and the next day could only get better. As Chow drove to his destination, he would pull over and let the loaded trucks go past when he met any. For this civil action, he would get a wave and a horn toot from the thankful driver. It was well past midnight before Chow checked into his hotel. He was happy to let the bellhop take his bags to his room, where he tipped the man and fell into bed. Chow had intended to take a shower before he fell asleep. The sun came over the mountains in the east, waking Chow from the best sleep he had had in years. Chow's first night of freedom, he only slept for six hours; he felt like he had slept for the whole day.

Jack and Tran's plan of moving the weapons from room to room worked like a charm. Though Tomas did receive a curious look from the housekeeper when he smiled and waved at her. After they had made sure their rooms were finished and locked, the three men joined their friends in the restaurant. There Jack informed Tomas when you're trying to sneak something past a person. Having a big grin on your face and waving like a kid isn't the best way to go about it. The rest of the group laughed. After the men finished eating, they sat and discussed what they had found out from the B.B.C. Their bosses contacted the foreign office of their government. William was telling them all what he had been told.

"Well, it seems we're not out of the woods yet. Some ass at the foreign office called the Chinese demanding to know where the Chinese got off sending bodies to them when they damn well knew we were alive. Now the Chinese want the four of us extradited back to Beijing to stand trial for interfering in a government investigation." When William finished, Tomas asked if he knew the name of this insufferable woolly-headed cock-up at the foreign office.

Leaning over to Jack, Tran whispered he didn't think that sounded very nice. Jack coughed and laughed at the same time, gaining the attention of the others at the table. William went on to tell the others that the British government was sending a plane and somebody from the embassy to bring the four of them home. If Jack and Tran wanted, they would be given sanctuary on British soil until they decided what they wanted to do. The two men looked at each other and nodded. With each thought, he would have to find out what the other was going to do before he made up his mind. Jack wanted this for Tran, but he was still undecided about what he wanted for himself. Jack knew he would have to go back and keep his word to Ben; this was unconditional.

Standing beside their Toyota, Jack and Tran talked about the offer the British government made to them. Jack knew Tran didn't have anyone waiting for him. He also knew Tran would never go to England without him. Jack wondered if he should go to England, finish healing, get all his strength back, then go and bring Ben home. Jack wanted to get Ben home before he started his hunt for Chow. Looking at the mountains that ringed the city, then at the blue sky seeming to hold the mountain birds still. Jack turned back to the hotel. Jack looked at the four men he and Tran brought out of Tibet. He could see them sitting by the restaurant windows.

"I think I'm going to take them up on their offer of moving to England," Jack said quietly. Jack watched as the small stout man gave the move more thought. Tran's answer was short and to the point. Tran nodded and then quietly spoke the words Jack hoped to hear.

"Me too." That's it, that's all. Jack shook Trans hand. Jack wanted to get back in the hotel restaurant before the four Englishmen started to try and out-drink each other. As he began to turn back into the hotel, Jack caught the sight of the brake lights of a new Land Rover. The driver stepped on the brake and then let off the pedal, only to reapply the brakes. Whoever drove the vehicle came to a dead stop in the middle of the street. Jack didn't know who was driving the suv, but the way it sat in the middle of the road, he knew the driver was looking into the hotel's parking area. Jack also knew they had just been found. Jack now knew they would have to run harder and faster than ever to get away again. He knew they were going to have to start running right now. Tran turned and watched the black Land Rover as it sat in the middle of the street in front of the hotel. Tran knew it was strange for a car to sit in the middle of the road. Turning, Tran looked at his friend, and the look on Jack's face told Tran his friend was worried about this car.

John Smyth, how, why, how could he be here in Bhutan? Chow sat stunned; it was impossible. He should have been gone, out of the country, by now. Why was he still here looking bigger and stronger than ever? After his flight through the mountains and his time at the hands of General Trang. The bastard shouldn't be in this kind of shape standing in Thimphu. He should be a shadow of his former self, not bigger and meaner looking. Chow realized he was drawing attention to himself by sitting in the middle of the street with his foot on the brake; he knew what he would do. When he got back to his hotel. He would call his contact in the Chinese government and let him know of the location of the four B.B.C. reporters, along with John and the other man. The Chinese would have them assassinated before the end of the week. For that length of time, he could stay in his hotel, enjoying the service and taking long naps. As Chow lifted his foot off the brake pedal, he knew he would see John dead before the week was out, and this time he would be there to see the lifeless corpse for himself. Then he could live without the worry of John Smyth returning to haunt him.

Chapter 63

JACK GATHERED THE MEN together he told them to meet him in his room. Jack didn't want the gathering to get too much attention, so he told the others to come one at a time. One by one, all the men gathered in Jack's room; as each man arrived, they realized the curtains were drawn closed. Leaving the room in a darkened state, standing in front of the drawn curtains, Jack looked at the men.

"We've been found," Jack stated. "I don't know who they were when Tran and I were standing in the parking lot, deciding whether we would go to England with you men or stay behind. A Land Rove drove past the hotel and then stopped in the middle of the street." Jack told the men. William interrupted.

"What would make you think he was looking at you or Tran?" William asked.

"I can't explain it; I just know if we stay here, then we're in trouble, and it won't take whoever is looking long to find us." Jack finished. The men discussed this new twist, and after five minutes, all agreed if Jack and Tran felt this way, they should pull out of the city. William used the telephone one more time to call the head of the B.B.C.

"Yes, Kent, I'm telling you the blasted Chinese found us. Now we have to haul out of here before they can overwhelm us and take us back, or worse." William told Kent Brown, the head of the B.B.C. The C.E.O. of the B.B.C. told William to tell him where they were going as soon as he could. So he could have hotel rooms waiting for them, and when they reached a place, they should get a satellite phone, so he could keep in touch. William said they would look for a satellite phone before they left Thimphu.

"Thank you, Kent. We are going to need all the luck we can get," William said before he hung up the phone. Once William told the men the B.B.C. was going to help with anything they might need, the men smiled. Jack and Tran looked at each other and then started to pack. As Jack finished gathering his things together, he knocked on the door, separating his room from Tomas. When Tomas answered his knock, Jack found Tran was helping Tomas pack the last of his things. Leaving their rooms, Jack returned all six of the room keys to the front desk.

Leaving the hotel, Tomas asked the desk clerk where he might be able to find a cell phone. The hotel clerk was most helpful and told William of a store one block east of the hotel; it sold phones of all kinds. Tomas thought it was funny when the clerk gave him directions. The man used the American vernacular of using city blocks in this eastern city. Then Tomas thought about the number of tourists who came to this place. Finding a satellite phone in the countryside of Bhutan would have been all but impossible. Here in this modern city cradled in the mountains of Asia, the group of escapees found acquiring the type of phone they required effortless. Setting it up on a prepaid account was more straightforward than any of the escapees could have hoped for.

The hotel manager was disappointed they were leaving; the man repeatedly asked if there was anything wrong with the rooms. Explaining something had come up back home that caused them to cut their vacation short. Jack explained to him that his companions wanted the rest of the money they paid for the rooms divided among the staff. It was their tips. Jack also said he and his friends would return to the hotel on their next trip. Relieved, the manager wished the men a safe trip, and he hoped to see them return soon. The men gathered at the Toyota, idling in the parking lot. Jack stood at the open driver's door, scanning the street for anything out of place. Tran watched his friend and then found himself watching the roofs of the building opposite the hotel; he was looking for signs of a sniper. The four journalists looked all over, trying to find what Jack and Tran were watching for. Two words from Jack brought the silence of the parking lot crashing in.

"We're leaving." Their big scared rescuer said, and without another word, the men piled into the Toyota. As they were leaving, the city of Thimphu Tran noticed Jack was driving around in no set pattern. When he asked about it, Jack said he thought they were being followed. Jack told Tran it was the same dark Land Rover that stopped in the street earlier. Whoever was driving the suv had done this sort of thing before. The black Land Rover always stayed far enough back to be hidden by the other traffic. Spotting the tail, Jack turned left at the next intersection and then watched as the black suv turned the same corner with other traffic. Whoever drove the Land Rover always kept two or three vehicles between his car and the group on the Toyota. Keeping his speed below the posted limit, it would seem to a police officer Jack, and his friends were tourists looking for a restaurant or something like that. However, Jack was trying to get the Land Rover into a narrow street where he could see who was driving it. Coming to a stop sign Jack turned right. He knew if he stayed on this narrow side street, it would lead him behind the hotel he and the others had just checked out of.

Chow watched as Jack turned right at the corner; now he knew for sure Jack had spotted him and knew he was being tailed. What Jack did not realize was Chow had agreed to watch the men in the Toyota for the Chinese. When he knew what the hell they were up to, he would call Beijing. Then Beijing would swoop in and kill all of them, ending his problem. Chow felt safe; there was no way John Smyth, who the journalists were now calling Jack, could know it was he who was the one tailing him.

Tran caught Jack rechecking the rearview mirror. Turning in his seat, Tran looked out the back window. Tran could see an old flatbed truck; he was going to turn back around and ask Jack what he was watching for when the old truck pulled over, and a black suv came into view. Tran did not have to look long before he knew it was the same one from the street in front of the hotel. As Tran turned and faced forward, he nodded to Jack. Now they both knew they were found, but for some reason, the idea of the Chinese finding them didn't bother Tran as much as he thought it would. Turning right at the intersection before the hotel, Jack found the alley that ran behind a warehouse of some kind. Jack accelerated, turning into the alley. Once in the alley, he pulled a hard U-turn and was at the alley's entrance when the black Land Rover turned the corner.

Chow turned the corner expecting the Toyota to be halfway down the block. What happened next was something he never expected nor wanted. The Toyota wasn't halfway down the block; instead, the damn thing was sitting at the entrance to an ally. Jack sat behind the wheel and watched as Chow was caught off guard and stared at him as he drove past. Chow could feel his breath catch in his throat when he looked into John Smyth's eyes. Besides Mike, John was the deadliest man Chow had ever known. Now Mike was lying dead in the forests' of Tibet, god only knew which one, and John was staring at him. Chow again felt something drop inside him. Whatever it was, it felt heavy and left an empty cold feeling behind.

Of all the people Jack had expected to see driving the black suv, Chow Yun was the last. As far as he knew, the man never got his hands dirty. Chow told Mike who needed to be killed, and Mike relayed the order to him, or Mike would do the job himself if the sick bastard thought he could get something out of the victim. Jack stumbled onto their real reasons for the termination orders. Then refused to kill a family man, and this bastard gave him over to General Trang. Jack would have loved to follow Chow, then kill him when the opportunity allowed, but he had other things to worry about. The four men from the B.B.C. and Tran came first; he had to get them to safety. Turning left out of the alley, Jack sped back to the main road that led them out of the city of Thimphu.

Back to Semtoka, Tomas read the map; he told Jack they needed to follow the Phuhentsholing-Thimphu highway south to the town of Phuhentsholing. There they would cross the border into India, and from there, they could go anywhere. The trick was getting them all across the border. Tomas and the other journalists had all their paperwork. Jack and Tran had none of the required documentation to cross international boundaries. Besides, with the amount and kind of weapons they had in the Toyota, the men would spend the rest of their lives in a Calcutta jail. After the prison where Jack had been held, a Calcutta Jail would be a step up in governmental accommodations. Watching the rearview mirror, both Jack and Tran knew about now; Chow was calling the Chinese. Both men knew he was telling them where their assassins would be able to find the escapees.

Chow still sat shaking behind the wheel of the black land rover when he called his contact in the Chinese government. He couldn't believe John had seen him. He had been so careful, but now Chow felt cold inside, his hands shook, and he felt as if he had fallen into an empty grave, his empty grave. When his contact in the Chinese government answered his private cellphone, Chow didn't go through the niceties of the modern age.

"It's John Smyth, yes, I'm sure. The bastard looked right at me as I drove past him and the Tibetan; he still has the four B.B.C. men with him." Chow listened as the man on the other end of the call conveyed a question asked by someone else in the room with him.

"No, I have checked. They have checked out of the hotel before they saw me. I think John only came to this place so he could buy some supplies and have the men contact the B.B.C. As for where they are now, I could not tell you, but they have a limited amount of routes out of Bhutan. The fastest way is aboard a plane, the other route. Well, the other is the Phuhentsholing-Thimphu highway which runs south into India." Chow finished and listened for a short time.

"No, I'm not going to get furthered involved." He told the man he was talking to, then listened with a smile growing on his lips.

"I don't work well with threats, especially when the men making them have been on my payroll for so long. Besides, as far as the Americans are concerned, my plane crashed in the sea, killing me and losing my body to the tides of time. Now I have helped you as much as I am going to, to the world I'm dead and gone. If I were you, people, I would not waste any more time. You know how they will leave this country and what they're driving; now it's up to you," Chow said. As soon as Chow finished telling the counsel where he could find Jack and the others, Chow drove back to his hotel and started to pack up his things. He packed the last suitcase and called the front desk asking the bellhop to come and take his cases to his suv. Standing in front of the desk, Chow told the manager he was going to drive around the countryside and see the sights. To complete his act as the tourist, Chow bought a Kodak d40 S.L.R. digital camera; he had the body of the camera hung around his neck with a strap and an aluminum camera case at his feet.

What couldn't be seen in the case was the array of lenses Chow had for the camera. He had lenses ranging from a standard 20mm to a large 200mm. Besides, the 200mm lens was a massive zoom lens and a lens for extreme wide-angle shots. Looking at all the lenses, one would think Mr. Lee Mang, who was Chow's alter ego now, was nothing more than an avid photographer of nature. All the lenses were for hiding the scope of one of the best-built sniper rifles in the world. Before Chow died in a plane crash at sea, he filed a request for a new lightweight and less conspicuous rifle for one John Smyth. The rifle arrived the day before Chow reported to the C.I.A. that John had been killed within China while working to find what faction had bought the new circuit boards; it was the new Walther WA2000.

Chapter 64

JACK WATCHED THE REARVIEW mirror waiting for the black Land Rover to appear behind them. Turn after turn, Jack and Tran waited to see the headlights of the land rover reappear behind their Toyota. When the lights failed to materialize in the mirrors of the Toyota, Jack feared Chow had called the police. Jack thought about it; he knew Chow shouldn't have been in Bhutan. Chow would never get clearance to come to Bhutan for anything. This was a clean neutral country, and Washington wanted it to stay that way.

"Let me see the phone," Jack said. Tran could tell by the look on his friend's face he was worried about what his former section chief was doing.

"What's going on, Jack?" William asked, looking to Tran for an answer as Jack dialed the phone. Sitting in the rumbling, four-wheel drive suv, the men listened as Jack spoke.

"I need to speak to Chow-Yun; what, I don't understand." The four journalists watched as a smile spread across Jack's lips.

"That is too bad; any sign of the plane. Still searching; no, it was a lunch date, that's all." The men all waited; from the smile on Jack's face, they could see whatever the call was about; it boded well for them.

"The man following us in Thimphu was my old section chief in Hong Kong. Now I would normally be pissed off to see the man. However, when I saw him, I thought a black ops wet work team would be nearby. As it turns out, my old boss crashed his plane into the West China Sea almost three days ago." Sitting back, Jack knew they still had the Chinese to deal with, but now he knew Chow couldn't contact the C.I.A. because Chow was as dead as he.

"So why did we leave Thimphu if he was no threat to us?" Scott asked.

"Because if he thinks Jack is a threat, then all of you are threats to whatever plan he had for his future. He might have called Beijing and given them your location." Tran said as he looked over at Jack, who was nodding his head.

"Trans, right? Just because Chow can't call the States doesn't mean he isn't above calling Beijing. Knowing this bastard as I do, I can guarantee he has already called Beijing." The four English men paled as they looked at each other and then silently urged Jack to drive faster.

Five men sat around a large polished black walnut table. The lights in this room hummed at a specific frequency. The frequency was precise; it was meant to render any electronic eves dropping equipment useless. This room was set in the basement of one of the most ornate buildings in Beijing. It was swept for electronic devices twice daily, never by the same people. If any devices were found, the team of four men who completed the previous sweep was taken to a secret location and shot. There the four bodies would be buried with the three other teams that failed to find the other electronic devices.

As the men discussed the fate of the four B.B.C. journalists, all agreed the world would believe the English men. The genocide of the Tibetans would come to light, as for John Smyth, he would have to die too. Just because he knew they held Foreign Service men and women, and against every international code, used torture to gain secrets. If the truth is told, for the most part, what they gained were lies, lies told in the hope the suffering would stop. The men who sat around this table knew torture seldom worked out. Often it got them no helpful information; for these men, it wasn't for the information. They tortured others for a sense of power. Each man in this room enjoyed the power he felt as they permitted a spy to be broken. They believed China was at war and they were going to win the war one body at a time.

Two women walked into the room, stopping just inside the door. The two female spies stood by the door neither one would admit to being uncomfortable in this room. One of the men at the table stood and walked through the fog of cigarette smoke. Like a natural fog, the smoke parted as his movement disturbed the air. The toxic smoke whirled and eddied until it knitted itself together and closed behind the man. The two women stood there as the General walked around them. He looked at each of the women as if he was inspecting a cow for slaughter. Each woman wanted to slap the old bastard, but he was a General, and they worked for his department.

Each of the women was supposed to be leaving for England at the end of the month. There they would attend Cambridge University, but something had changed; now they were being ordered to go to Bhutan and find a group of six men and kill all six. The door opened behind the two women, and two handsome young soldiers walked in and saluted the General. These men were soldiers and did not need to know all the particulars of the mission, said the General. They were there to help with the cover story of two friends getting married and going on their honeymoon together. The two soldiers would help with the killing of the six in Bhutan. The women were given the name of a man in the capital city of Thimphu. This man would be their contact for weapons and transportation, and because they were running behind, that man was going to meet them in the town of Paro. It would be up to them where in the town they would meet their contact. Suitcases were brought into the room, and it was explained they had been packed and a private jet was waiting for them. As the two spies walked ahead of their fake husbands, the plane impressed one of them. It was a Cessna citation x with twin rolls Royce AE3007C1 engines capable of pushing the citation x to a speed of 525 knots or 972 kilometers per hour. Jiao always wanted to be a fighter pilot, but in her country, the child became what the father wanted.

Jiao's father was a spy, so she became a spy. She wanted nothing more than to fly one of the fighters, not so she could kill; for Jiao, it was so she could escape for a short time. Jiao's partner was a girl she met during training; she often ate with Fen Fang and liked her. When the trainers saw the girls working well together, they started to train them as sisters. Now the girls thought that way of each other; Jiao told Fen once she dreamed of escaping China. Jiao told Fen of cities like Paris, Rome, Venice, and Florence, where the great artists lived and worked at one time. The girls made plans when they reached England to go to the English government and turn themselves in. Doing this, they would have a death sentence hanging on them for being traitors, but they didn't care as long as they were free.

The men, on the other hand, had never met before tonight. The taller of the two was to act as Jiao's new husband. He had introduced himself as Delun; the other Soldier had introduced himself as Aiguo. Delun stood when the seat belt sign was turned off and offered to get everyone a bottle of water. Standing in between seats, the men told the spies about themselves and what they liked to eat so when it came time to play their parts of loving partners. They could order food for each other in a restaurant or give the correct answers to a customs officer.

Chapter 66

ONCE AGAIN, THE DAY was surrendering to night. Tran and Jerry watched as the west side facing hills turned the colors of the setting sun. Jack turned on the headlights as the shadows claimed the landscape again. Night conspired to slow the getaway of the six men. Tomas and William were discussing which angle to tell the story of their finding the mass grave, then being held captive by the Chinese. It was the word 'captive' Tomas was arguing about; he wanted to say, hostage. William's point was a hostage was often traded for something. Williams said the Chinese were not going to trade them; they were going to kill them. The argument was settled when Jack interjected on William's side and said he was right; they were not going to be traded.

"You guys would have been tortured, beaten, used to test how sharp their knives were. Then one by one, buried behind the prison in the mass grave they keep opened because they have a steady stream of bodies." When Jack finished, it took some time for the conversation to pick back up again. Jack pointed to a sign that Tran translated for them.

"It states the border with India is only one hundred and forty-eight kilometers away." Jack was surprised by the distance they had covered.

"You sure can cover the countryside when you want to," Jerry said as Jack rounded another in the endless string of turns. Looking at the speedometer, William calculated the trip should take them just over two hours to make. Then the group would have to think of a way to get across the border into India. As the road took them closer to the Indian border, Jack was thinking, what would Chow and the Chinese be doing. What was their next move, Jack knew what he would've done if he was doing the hunting, but this time he and his friends were the hunted.

Chow had arrived at the airport in Paro, filing a flight plan. He explained he wished to fly around the mountains and take pictures. The woman smiled as she filed the plan. She thought to herself he would never get any good photographs flying. She was not paid to tell wealthy tourists how to take pictures. Walking out of the flight office, Chow noticed how the Stratos sat gleaming in the harsh and unflattering pools of sickly yellow light the ten mercury-vapour lights cast on the tarmac. The Stratos was white with a blue and gold stripe down the side; in the mercury vapor, it looked sickly. Even with the corrective phosphor coating, everything still looked off to Chow. The white wasn't white enough. It reminded him of someone with a touch of jaundice. In daylight, you might miss the yellowing, but under the harsh glare of manmade light, it became all too clear. For some reason, Chow thought this look held bad luck for him and his future. Chow shook his head and laughed at his minor bout with superstition. Chow remembered his grandparents held many superstitions. When he was younger, his mother had to explain to him what some of them meant. Even now, he could not grasp how old people could hold onto their superstitions in light of science and the marvels it brings to the world every year.

Standing beside the Toyota, Jack watched as Tran loosened the lug nuts. Jack had been driving and never saw the piece of jagged steel until it was too late. Now they were losing time; time was the one thing they couldn't spare. The six men unloaded the Toyota to get out one of the spare tires when the tire was changed. They lost more time because they had to load it all back in again. Tran and the other men would never have blamed Jack for the flat. They knew it would have happened to them if they had been behind the wheel.

Jack was the hardest on himself. He would never have said anything to any of his friends. He silently berated himself for being so careless. Jack knew the lives of these four men were in his hands. Jack cursed because the time they lost, changing tires allowed the Chinese and whoever else was chasing them to gain. If they were allowed to gain enough, it might come down to a fight before they could make it into India. Unlike movies where the hero always wins in a firefight, he couldn't be sure of saving everybody in his group. Jack looked at the four Englishmen, then at Tran. If he couldn't save all of them, would it come down to a choice of which one he would have to let die? Jack knew he wouldn't be able to leave one of these men behind, not after what he went through at the hands of General Trang.

Chapter 67

CHOW WAS GRATEFUL FOR the amount of engineering the makers of his Stratos put into every plane, from being one of the fastest private jets on the market. It could also be flown at a calm and somewhat enjoyable speed. Though it handled better at higher speeds. Chow flew over the road leading south, he divided his time from looking for the Toyota land cruiser Jack, and the others were in. Chow also had to keep a safe distance from the mountains he was trying to avoid crashing into. Flying at two hundred and fifty knots, Chow knew he had found Jack and the others sitting on the side of the road. He thought Toyota had broken down. Pulling out one of the impressive-looking lenses from the case, Chow attached it to something that looked like a small hand-held television. Turning it on, the night brightened, and he could see all the surrounding area in bright contrast. The technology for what is called a starlight scope has improved over the years, but with the latest model, even Chow was impressed. He could make out the men. Chow smiled as the four B.B.C. men looked up at his jet. Turning the Stratos one hundred and eighty degrees, Chow lined the nose up with the road and slowed his jet to eighty knots. He wasn't worried about stalling the little plane, its stall speed was sixty-four knots, and he would make sure to keep above its stall speed.

Most people look up when they hear a plane flying close to the ground they look up, and that's what the four men from the B.B.C. did again. The men looked up into the night sky as Chow flew overhead; only two didn't look up. Jack and Tran knew what it meant when they heard the plane turn and return at a slower speed.

Chow looked at the monitor and pushed a button on the side of the boxy camera. He didn't need to have all their faces; hell, he didn't need all their faces; all he really needed were the faces of the four British men. Just the four will do. Chow flew in a high orbit of the mountains, where he found the escapee. Chow flew around the mountains, trying to decide if he should call Beijing. Chow knew he could hire his own assassins; he could have his men kill everyone in the Toyota. Chow knew if he did this, the group in Beijing would never pay him back. With his mind made up, Chow picked up his Satellite phone and called the group in China. When Chow told the gathered men of the progress Jack and the journalists made, the group gasped. Once again, they tried to get Chow to do something, but he refused. Chow told the group in Beijing he would relay the men's progress to them as his fuel would allow.

Jiao acknowledged the transmission and repeated the new orders. She and the others were to go to India. There, they would wait for the Toyota land cruiser to come to them. When they encountered the targets, no time was to be wasted. They were to kill all the men in the vehicle and return home. Jiao relayed the new orders to the others on the plane as she took her seat. She looked at her friend and knew after they killed the six men, she and Fen would kill their fake lovers and escape. Both wanted to be free from the men that ran China. For the two of them, freedom was all that mattered in the end.

With the tire changed and everything packed back in their Toyota, Tran took the wheel. Both he and Jack worried about the little jet that flew over them as he was bolting on the spare tire. As he drove, Tran caught Jack looking out of the widows trying to get a glimpse of the plane. Now Tomas and the others were looking for the plane as well. Occasionally, when they came out of the dark forest lining the foot of the mountains, they were driving through. One of the men would say he could see the blinking lights on the wingtip of a plane. Jack explained the plane was in front of them when they could see the strobe lights. If the lights were not blinking, then the plane was coming at them. This way, the men wouldn't get excited if they saw a plane flying away from them. In addition, Jack tried to explain because they were closer to India, they might be seeing planes landing at airports in that country. Tran turned and looked at Jack, who shrugged his shoulders and smiled back. Tran knew Jack lied to the men in the back of the Toyota. Both men knew the plane they saw had to be looking for them, and both Tran and Jack knew it was the same plane. They knew the Chinese now knew where they were and the direction of travel.

Chapter 68

CHOW WATCHED AS THE men moved further south towards the border with India. Grabbing his satellite phone, Chow called the Indian information. He asked the voice on the other end if he could have the number for the immigration office at Jaigaon. After some clicking on the line, a man was on the phone. The Indian customs officer had a deep rumbling voice and less of an accent than the operator had. Chow told the customs officer he watched six men in a light-colored Toyota land cruiser coming to the border with drugs. They intended to sneak into his country. When the man asked for Chow's name and a return number where he could call him to verify his story Chow hung up without saying a word. Pissed off, Chow watched as the Toyota grew closer and closer to Phuhentsholing and the border. Chow knew the border immigration officer didn't believe a word he said. What angered Chow more than being thought of as a liar was before he killed himself; he could have had this shithead customs man killed along with his family. All he could do was swear about it, for now.

It was the middle of the night when Scott pulled over to the side of the road; he told the others the lights below were the town of Phunhentsholing. He pointed to a group of bright lights sending spikes into the firmament, searching for the floor of heaven. This, Scott told the others, must be the border with India. Scott asked what they wanted to do. Jack suggested they find a hotel and get some rest, then try to see if there was a way across. The hotel they had located was on the east side of the town. Scott and William, as well as Jerry and Tomas, shared the last two rooms available, leaving Tran and Jack to sleep in the land cruiser. The following day Tran spoke with some younger men sitting in the dinner across the street from the hotel. Thanking the men, Tran paid for their meals and returned to the hotel's parking lot. The men listened as Tran explained to his friends how well-guarded the border was.

"Those young men told me the Indians watched the gates closely. They are looking for drugs and guns; if you have the right paperwork, there are no problems." When Tran finished, William looked at the others in his group.

"Well, I don't know about the rest of my mates here, but I'm not about to leave any man behind over some silly little thing like a nonexistent line in the dirt," William said. Tran and Jack watched as the other men all nodded their heads.

Sitting in one of the internet cafés that dot the town, Scott and the others used one of the best search engines they could find to look at borders. Google Earth, Scott said it was the best tool to try to get across the borders in this part of the world, a real smugglers search engine. After looking at the border between the two countries of Bhutan and India, Jack decided a dry riverbed to the east of town would be the best spot to cross. They would have to do some surveillance around the area of the city where they wanted to cross. Jack knew, for the most part, the Indian military was good at their job. He hoped the Indian border protection with Bhutan did not show the same readiness as it does with other countries it shares a border with.

Because there was no airport in the region of southern Bhutan, Chow was forced to fly into India and try to rent a car. He desperately wanted to be there when the Chinese killed Jack, who he still called John Smyth. Though Chow didn't care about the journalists, he still wanted to see the six men in the Toyota killed. As Chow landed at the airport, he was trying to decide if he was going to kill the operatives his contact had sent. It would be suitable punishment for threatening to expose his death as fraud to the Americans. Did he really want the hassle of dealing with the Chinese after that? Chow didn't want to have to buy a car, just to dump it at the airport when he retrieved his plane after he watched the Chinese assassins kill the men in the Toyota.

The Indian government didn't seem too concerned about cross-border traffic with their neighbors, the Bhutanese. To Jack, they appeared to be more concerned with foreigners, though they did not give any too hard a time. After the customary paperwork check, most tourists would be sent on their way to continue their trips. Some of the unlucky ones, they would have to unpack their trucks and open their luggage. This usually only happened if one was unmannerly to the border guard and if you were cordial to the border guards. Then they were pleasant with you, and everyone was happy. In life, someone has to think they are important whether that person is wearing a uniform or not. The gate separating the two countries was out of the question. One, because Jack and Tran didn't have the proper paperwork, or any paperwork for that matter. The second reason, he didn't want to leave a trail of their route. Both Jack and Tran knew they were being followed. Not crossing the border created laps in the timing for whoever was following them. It was this timeline Jack wanted to throw into question if he and the others could mess with the timeline. Then they would be able to get behind the Chinese, which could make it almost impossible for any retribution the men in Beijing planned. Jack knew if you were trying to kill someone, the first task you needed to develop was your target's timeline. Without it, all you could go by was guesswork. Jack knew guessing never worked out for the best.

Chapter 69

CHOW LANDED AT THE airport in the town of Baghdogra. After passing through customs and immigration, he rented a newer Porsche Cayenne turbo s. Chow told the man at the rental desk he had owned one before, and he was very comfortable with its five-hundred-horse power engine. He also told the man he would like to rent it for an extended period. The clerk of the rental car agency was paid a modest salary, along with a commission on every rental. He was more than happy to have the most expensive car in their inventory rented for an extended time.

Delun felt the plane touch down and woke to find Jiao undoing her seatbelt before the plane stopped. He leaned over and whispered that she was breaking a rule.

"No fun in obeying all the rules; breaking the little ones makes you feel alive," Jaio whispered, then winked at him. Delun looked around and undid his before the seat belt sign turned off. The pilot came out of the cockpit to tell them they had landed in India at a town called Baghdogra. They told them it was in the north of the country, and they'd been cleared to rent a car and start to look for the journalists. The pilot stood in the doorway of the cockpit. The pilot knew what these four young people were here to do. The pilot wouldn't wish them luck; he didn't care if they were successful.

Fen and Jiao knew going through customs and immigration was part of traveling through another country. Fen told Aiguo and Delun to think of it as a checkpoint, nothing to worry about because all their paperwork was in order. Aiguo could not believe how easy it was to get into another country. He said if it was this easy, they must have spies all over the world. The others looked at Aiguo and smiled as if they had known the secret all along.

Jack wanted to sneak across the Indian border in the middle of the night. Tomas and William told Jack about a story they had collaborated on a few years before they had gone to Tibet. The story was about the border along the southwestern part of Texas and the southeastern part of New Mexico. The two men remembered the border patrol officers telling them they got busy when the sun went down. Jack had heard this before, so the men decided they would go during the evening mealtime. This way, it would minimize the chances of them running into an Indian border patrol. At six fifteen local times, Jack idled the land cruiser over the nonexistent line in the dirt, as William put it, between Bhutan and India. Jack decided to drive in the dry riverbed for half an hour. The only thing Jack worried about was the dust; the tires of the Toyota kicked up as he went into the riverbed. Jack turned out of the riverbed just before the town of Hasimara. Sitting at the edge of the paved road, Jack looked north and south. It seemed Jack was having a hard time making up his mind on which way to go. Then just as Tran was going to ask if everything was ok, Jack eased the clutch out and headed south.

Chow watched as the four Chinese agents rented a tiny Suzuki sidekick and then drove into town. He knew they would have to get weapons, and he knew the Chinese didn't have anyone in this area of India who could supply them. So that meant the Chinese would have to pay for the weapons. What they didn't know was they were buying the guns to kill the escapees from one of his men. Knowing he would profit from the killings and get what he wanted most of all made Chow laugh. After the lead female Chinese agent picked up the weapons and the ammunition. Chow followed the four would-be assassins to a small hotel, where they sat in the restaurant and ate lunch. One of the girls received a short phone call all at once the four young people stood to leave. Chow's phone rang, and when he looked at the caller id, Chow knew men in Beijing were calling. They wanted an update from him. They asked to make sure their people had gotten their weapons and started their hunt. Chow told the men the four young people received the guns and ammunition, and they had indeed started the hunt.

"Gentlemen, I'm going to be honest with you. I don't think these babies will do you much good." Chow said. The men sitting in the darkened, smoky room in Beijing all looked at each other.

"John Smyth is going to see these four kids coming, and before they know what is going on, he will kill them," Chow told the group.

"How can you be so sure of the outcome?" One of the group asked.

"John was trained to spot people like himself, then to dispatch them with no more effort than he puts into putting on his pants. Unlike your people, John was trained to do this starting at a very young age; it's in his nature now. Deep down in his soul, John is a predator, and like most true predators, he lives for the hunt." Chow said as he watched the four would-be Chinese assassins driving ahead of him, knowing he was looking at four dead people. Chow waited for the group to say something. He could hear the nervous unsettled shifting of men in their seats.

"Can you monitor the situation and report if they fail?" one of the men asked.

"For old friends, I can do that," Chow answered, then ended his call.

Jiao answered her phone; one of the generals was calling with an update.

"Your targets are driving a cream color Toyota land cruiser. It has been modified for off-road use, and you are looking for five white men and one Tibetan. When you find them kill all of them, then dispose of the bodies. You are being watched by a friend of the counsels; you must not fail." Then the phone went dead, and Jiao relayed the message to the others in the sidekick. They were told the targets crossed the border during the night. Delun drove east to find their targets, whom they presumed were moving west, to try and get into Nepal.

The sun started to shine into the windshield of the sidekick Delun was beginning to wish he had some money so he could've bought a pair of sunglasses. The four assassins had been driving for about two hours when Delun cried out there was a light-colored Toyota land cruiser coming at them. As the big four-wheel drive passed them, Jiao could see it had been heavily customized for off-road use. Fen said she counted at least six in the truck. Delun slowed without using the brakes. He pulled off to the side of the road letting the traffic pass before he tried to pull a U-turn.

Jack came to the "T" intersection of the road he had followed from Hasimara. Now he sat looking east then west on the highway N.H. 31C, just before Tran could ask if everything was all right again, Jack released the clutch and turned east on N.H. 31C. Tomas and William soon gave into a sleep induced by the constant humming of the heavy off-road tires the land cruiser was outfitted with. Hours later, Jack woke Tran and asked if he would take over the driving. The men decided it would be a good time to relieve their bladders on the side of the road as the sun rose to the east. After the call of nature had been answered, Tran took over the driving. Soon after he had taken the wheel of the Toyota, Tran decided the posted speed limits in this part of India were too slow. As he and Jack did not have a passport, he kept it to the limit, though to show his displeasure at it, he would sigh and shake his head. To Tran, it was a crime with good roads. Everyone had to travel so slowly, but before he could go on any further, a little sidekick passed.

The woman in the back seat and the one on the passenger side of the front seat took a lot of interest in their Toyota. Trying to watch the road in front of them and at the same time trying to watch the sidekick as it slowed, Tran failed to notice the Porsche go past. He called out to Jack and told him of the sidekick and the two Asian girls in it of how they seemed overly excited about their land cruiser.

"Ok, you guys in the back watch for that sidekick, Scottie; you keep an eye out for any other cars that seem out of place," Jack said as he watched to see if the Suzuki turned to follow.

Chapter 70

DELUN WAITED FOR THE dark suv to pass before he made his 'U-turn, then sped after the targets. Of course, with a sidekick and its 1.5-liter engine, there wasn't much speeding involved, he thought. However, Delun did his best and was now behind a small car.

William watched for the sidekick to come back into view, but after five minutes, he thought they were in the clear. With Jack and Tran checking the rearview mirrors, the other men started to relax. William was surprised when a large truck behind their Toyota turned off, revealing the sidekick behind a small Opel cadet. The little car was belching bluish oil smoke from its rusted tailpipe. The smoke wasn't enough to hide the black sidekick. Caught by surprise, William cried out the sidekick was behind them. Tran pressed on the fuel peddle of the Toyota's diesel and listened as the turbo spooled up, increasing the torque as the rpm needle slowly climbed. The engine in this model was a turbo direct injected diesel, with a heavy sound it growled out of the exhaust. It sounded like it had more than its slim one hundred and twenty horsepower when it was new. Now after twenty-five years on the planet, how many of the horses were left was a guess that no one wanted to make. With a steady stream of black smoke, Tran tried to make their getaway.

Climbing over the seats, Jack started to toss the bags onto the other men in the land cruiser. While he was trying to get at his bag, the little Opel cadet turned off, leaving nothing between the back of the land cruiser and the front of the sidekick. As Jack looked into the face of the driver of the sidekick, he knew the Chinese had found them and were following them. Jack watched as the sidekick closed the gap Tran tried to open. The diesel of their Toyota was no match for the speed of the gas engine powering the newer sidekick, not on the road. Tran shouted he would have to slow down to leave the blacktop, and Jack called back not to slow down.

"If we slow, then they can pull alongside and strafe us through the side windows." As Jack told Tran what he thought the killers behind them would try, a ricochet whined off the steel rack on the roof of the Toyota. Rummaging through his bags, Jack found what he wanted. He could see the girl in the passenger side seat of the sidekick trying to line up a shot through the back window of the Toyota. Jack shouted for the men to get down on the floor. Jack almost laughed out loud when he heard two heads knock together, then Jerry cursing in an oh-so-British way. Jack could not believe he was smiling as he screwed in the silencer to the type 64 automatic pistol he'd been looking for. Sitting up, Jack took aim, fired one shot, and watched as the girl dropped her weapon. Jack fired one more shot as the driver of the sidekick slammed his foot onto the brake pedal. The second bullet sparked off the edge of the roof above the windshield over the driver's side. Jack didn't think he hit the girl. He was sure she dropped her gun because the driver of the sidekick slammed his foot onto the brake peddle and slid to the side of the road, trying to avoid Jack's return fire. Sitting facing backward, Jack watched as the black sidekick disappeared in a cloud of dust created when Delun left the paved road and slid to a stop in a dusty parking lot.

Jiao was angry with herself, she had underestimated her target, and then when Delun swerved to save her life, she dropped her weapon. She couldn't believe she had to hold up the chase and retrieve the pistol. Walking back to their car Jiao berated herself for being so careless. Delun stood by the door of the car, waiting for Fen to sit in the back with Aiguo. They all wanted to get after the targets, but they knew Jiao was angry with herself and needed time to get it out of her system. Chow watched as the female walked back to get the gun she had dropped.

"God-damn amateurs, where did they find this one." Chow cursed as he drove past the sidekick. He should call the group in Beijing and tell them of the first fuck up their professionals managed. Hell, he could have done a better job. After this, he should hire some mercenaries and let them finish John and the others off.

Jack checked the map and looked up in time to see a sign for hwy 12A Jack wanted to stay on this road, but now the Chinese had found them; he knew things had changed, and it was time to adapt.

"Take this turn-off; it will take us to a town called Jalpenguri, there we can get food for the road and see if we can find out who the hell that was back there," Jack said. State hwy 12A was smaller and more cramped with local traffic. Nevertheless, Jack thought it was off the main hwy, and if the sidekick showed up again, the people in it would be less inclined to start a firefight. Jack hoped with so many witnesses around, it would give him time to turn the fight around. Jack and Tran's biggest fear was the men back in China wanted William, Tomas, and the others, along with Jack and himself, dead. The killers would be under orders no matter what they were to kill the men.

Tran did his best to pass the locals with their ox-carts being pulled by every kind of tractor and animal, including the lowly donkeys and oxen. Dodging the wagons and whatever drew them, Tran managed to make good time. Before Jack realized where they were, Tran passed a sign announcing the town of Jalpaiguri. The business district seemed to have been built on the state highway. Tran pulled up to the gas pump marked diesel at a tidy fuelling station. Stepping out of the Toyota, Tran asked a teenage boy if he could fill the tank and if he knew of any place where they could buy some jerry cans. An older man walked out of the little service station into the bright Indian sun.

"Everything you need is here, good sir." The man stated.

"I have extra jerry cans if you need them. My good wife sells fruit grown in our own orchard. If there is anything else you require, my son can give you directions." Tran gave a slight bow of thanks to the boy's father. Tomas walked over to the side of the building and smiled at a woman setting the fruit out on a large stand with an impressive striped awning. Tomas was going to ask if she was open when a young girl ran out from behind the stand letting out a yelp of surprise. The little girl turned and ran back behind the stand, grabbing her mother's skirt.

"She reminds me of my granddaughter," Tomas told the woman.

"She has always been fearful of strangers." The woman said. Tomas thought it was a beautiful singsong voice. He remembered when he was a boy and lived in India with his mother and father. Tomas always loved India; he loved the countryside of India. The cities were too crowded, traffic was chaotic, and the noise was all-encompassing.

"Maybe that's not so bad in the world we live in now," Tomas said as he looked at the bananas.

"Do you think living in fear is better than going out into the world, happy and free?" She asked Tomas as her daughter clung to her skirts. The question caught Tomas off guard, and he thought about it for a moment before he shook his head as he looked at the one large brown eye of the girl as she peeked out from behind her mother.

"Your right. Living in fear is no way to live." Tomas said. The woman smiled, handing Tomas a bag with the bananas in it. She added peaches and pomegranates to the bag.

"To be free also means to be free of fear. Your heart must be able to beat freely throughout the world." The Indian lady said as the little girl peeked out again from behind her mom and smiled at Tomas. Jack bought five five-gallon jerry cans from the service station. Then got directions to the Indian State Bank, and the teenage boy told him it would not be hard to find.

"Go to the intersection, and it will be on the North West corner." The boy said. Jack thanked the boy and gave him a tip for the help filling the cans and then lifting them up to Tran. Scott, Jerry, and William each thanked the young man for his help, then climbed back into the Toyota. At the state bank of India, Jack decided neither he nor Tran could go in and try to draw out money. If the teller asked for identification and they couldn't produce it, then he or she might call the local police.

"I can go in and draw out some money and have it put into traveler's checks, I have ID, and it wouldn't look like anything more than a tourist pulling out more funds," William told Jack.

"Okay, but ask for the funds to be in cash; no American currency, ask for Euros. You being English will make more sense to them, and it might keep the Chinese off our trail for a while longer." Jack told William before he walked away. Jack didn't know how, but Jack was sure Chow had something to do with the Chinese finding them. It was the one rule Mike taught him; there are no coincidences. It was then, standing in the Indian sun outside a bank Jack had made up his mind. As long as Chow was walking free in the world, none of them would be safe or free.

Standing beside the Toyota, Jack, Tran, and the other men were eating the fruit. Tomas bought at the stand beside the service station when a jeep stopped beside them. Looking over. Tomas said something in Indian to the two police officers, who smiled and nodded, then pulled away when their turn came at the four-way stop.

"You speak Indian?" Jerry asked, looking at Tomas, shocked.

"When I was a young lad, my father was stationed here for twelve years with the embassy. I went to school here, and most of my friends could speak it, so I learned." Tomas said. Jack smiled and chuckled.

He wondered what the hell else these two old men knew. William came out of the bank he walked over to the jeep.

"I couldn't get any Euros; I did get traveler's checks drawn on the pound." He looked a little sheepish, like he had made a mistake and was waiting for a scolding.

"That'll work," Jack said as he gave the older man a pat on the back. Leaving town, the six friends headed away from the sun and for Nepal. Jack was driving while Tran lay in the cargo area of the Toyota. While they were stopped at the service station, Tran, Jerry, and Scott unloaded the baggage and the spare tires. They then loaded all the gear onto the roof rack. The only bags left in the Toyota were Tran's, and Jack's bags remained in the cargo area. With the baggage and tires out of the back, Tran could lie down. He could also get at the weapons and shoot facing backward if the black sidekick showed up again.

Jiao was sullen; she had never dropped a gun before, and even during the most challenging parts of the training, she had never dropped a weapon. Now she was in the field on an actual assignment, and she failed. Jaio knew if she did this again, she knew Fen, and she would never make it out of the grasp of the men in China. Delun drove as fast as the little sidekick and traffic would allow. Soon they would have to face the fact they had lost the targets. Aiguo sat behind Delun; he stared out the window of his door, hoping to catch a glimpse of the Toyota. Looking at Delun in the rearview mirror, Aiguo asked a question that caught the others off guard.

"If it were us being hunted, would we stay on the area's main road?" Aiguo asked. Fen looked at her pretend husband.

"No, training tells us to get off main roads, get into a town or crowd, to disappear into the crowd." Jiao looked at Delun and nodded. Delun remembered a road turned off the one they were on; it was called State hwy 12A. Once again, Delun pulled a 'U-turn and raced back the way he had just come.

Chow watched as the little sidekick made another 'U-turn and drove eastbound in his rearview mirror. Pulling to the side of the road, he waited for the traffic to pass, then turned and shoved the accelerator to the floor. The Porsche's five hundred horsepower turbocharged engine responded instantly. Once the Pirelli tires hit the blacktop, the speed of the big suv increased. The evidence of the ferocious power Porsche built into this model lined the ground. Two black tire marks and the bluish haze of smoke were the evidence the traction control had difficulty reigning in the powerful engine. Chow had to be careful he didn't catch the sidekick too fast. The Porsche was almost six times more powerful, and as far as Chow was concerned, it was a hundred times the car the little Suzuki would ever be.

Delun pulled into the first service station he was in the town of Jalpaiguri. A teenage boy hurried out to fill their fuel tank and wash the windshield. Delun and Jiao walked to the service station. They asked the owner if a light-colored Toyota land cruiser had come to his station this morning.

"Oh yes, six men all traveling together. I think with all their supplies and gear, they must work for some news channel. They bought all my extra jerry cans and some food from my wife." The Indian man said. Jiao thanked the man and went to the fruit stand beside the service station. Jiao walked over to the fruit stand and bought a bag from the lady. She smiled at the young girl hiding behind her mother. Looking around, Jiao walked back to the others and looked along the dusty street before getting back in the sidekick. Leaving the service station, Fen told Jiao that when the teenager told her, he gave the men directions to the local state bank of India. Fen also told Jiao the boy had told her of a large strange, looking cell phone the men had on the front seat of their truck. Jiao knew by the description of the phone it had to be a satellite phone; the men could call for help from anywhere in Asia.

"They would have drawn out money, which means someone would have to place money in an account for them." She didn't have to say anymore. They all knew the men had contacted the BBC; Jiao called the group of generals in Beijing.

"The targets have been getting help from the BBC. They stopped in a town in India and withdrew some money, plus the money they had to buy supplies. A boy at a service station described what sounded like a satellite phone." When she had finished giving her update, a rough voice could be heard in the background.

"Keep up the chase; if anyone interferes, kill them too, we will handle the BBC." Snapping the phone shut, Jiao stared straight ahead. She did not really want to kill these men. She wanted to be free from the men on the phone and her father; she hated all of them. Looking back at Fen, Jiao shook her head. It was their way of telling each other soon they would be free.

Chow watched as one of the female assassins talked to a young teenage boy as he pumped gas. The other female went into the service station and then to the stand beside the station. Once their vehicle was full of gas, they left, heading west. Chow pulled the Porsche into the service station and asked the boy to fill the tank and wash his windshield. The boy commented on how beautiful his car was. Chow told the boy if he did well in school and worked hard, he could have anything he could think of, but if he were lazy, nothing would ever come. Chow didn't believe any of what he considered bullshit he told the young boy. It made him look good in his father's eyes. Chow knew the father was standing behind him when he gave the boy the advice. Now he looked like a nice man who cared about his son's future. The father told Chow a Toyota had been here this morning, and the men headed west.

"Good, I can catch them," Chow said. When the father asked what it was all about. Chow said they had forgotten one of their telephoto lenses for extremely long rang photo shots. He thanked the man and his son, then drove west through town.

Jack could see the sign for the town of Siliguri. When they came to the city center, Tomas said he would like to go into the supermarket and buy water and other supplies. Jack thought about it for a moment, then nodded his head thinking if the extra supplies were purchased now, he wouldn't have to worry about it later. When they finally found a large market, Tran and Jack were surprised to see that, along with the usual Indian foodstuff, it also advertised military food rations. Tran and Jerry stood at the back of the Toyota and watched the road running through the town. One of India's major highways ran through this town, and they could hear large trucks rumbling to a stop. Then changing gears as the drivers fought to get the trucks and their loads back up to speed.

Walking up and down the aisles of the market seemed surreal to Jack; everything he wanted was here. Turning around, he found a petite elderly lady looking at the top shelf. Jack pointed to an item; she smiled her toothless grin and nodded. Jack smiled back as he handed the older lady a box of noodles. The old lady patted Jack on the hand to thank him and shuffled off down the aisle. Jack came out of the market with a shopping cart full of things, including six twenty-four bottle cases of water, three cases of energy drinks, and four first aid kits. Tomas came behind Jack with a cart full of dried fruits and meats. Scottie found the market had, as advertised, bought cases of m.r.e. He knew the military rations lasted a very long time in their vacuum-sealed packaging. So when he came out of the market, he proudly carried his basket with a week's worth of the sliver vacuumed sealed military rations. Tran was on top of the Toyota, strapping down some water and energy drinks. The dried fruits and meats, as well as the rations the men bought, fit into the duffel bags and backpacks.

One of the tires was now strapped to the hood of the Toyota, while the other was strapped to the roof along with their bags, water, and food. Tran was about to climb off the top of the Toyota when he looked up and watched a black Suzuki sidekick drive up the main street. Jumping off the roof, Tran pulled Jack down and put his finger to his lips. Without asking, Jack knew Tran saw something. The other men ducked down instinctually. Tran grabbed Jack because he was the tallest and stood out the greatest. Jack crabbed walked his way to the front of the Toyota and watched as the sidekick slowed and then pulled to the side of the road in front of the market. The detour had only worked for a short time, but it had worked long enough.

"Shit, okay, guys, that black sidekick has stopped in front of the market. I don't know if they've seen us. I'm going on the assumption they have, so everybody in the car, Tran, you're in the back. I'll drive." Jack was surprised to find that the others had already gotten in the Toyota. Everyone liked the Toyota except when Jack started it in the parking lot of the market; the diesel made a horrible sound when it started. It did not gracefully start like a gas engine. Instead, the diesel coughed and rattled itself into being. The sound seemed incredibly loud to Jack and the others in the Toyota. Jack could have sworn all the other noise in the town had suddenly stopped when he turned the ignition of the Toyota.

Aiguo heard the sound of a diesel engine starting. He turned towards the sound and saw a light-colored Toyota land cruiser pulling out of a parking stall. He whistled to Fen; when she turned, Fen could see him pointing across the parking lot to a large cream-colored suv. It was the Toyota they were hunting. She watched as the bigger four-wheel drive lurched its way out of the parking stall and across the parking lot. Jiao could see the Toyota start out of the parking lot and turn right as Fen and Aiguo ran back to their car. It was the Toyota, and she could see all six men in it.

Chow watched as the Toyota pulled out of the parking lot, belching black diesel smoke. Jack revved the engine of the Toyota to its red line before shifting gears, seeking more speed out of the workhorse. Two of the would-be assassins ran through the parking lot back to the Suzuki parked on the side of the road. At least they had done that right, Chow thought, parking on the side of the road. They stood less of a chance of getting boxed in, letting their targets getaway. Still, Chow couldn't believe the group from Beijing would send this quartet of amateurs to kill the men from the BBC.

Jack watched the sidekick pull out into traffic after them. He was about to tell the others when Tran spoke.

"I have seen the same vehicle. It is always behind the sidekick, and it, too, is black. Do you think it is with the others?" Jack looked back, and all he could see was the sidekick as they drove through town.

"Can you describe it?" Jack shouted back to Tran. Tran thought about the best way to describe the second car, but the best he could come up with was.

"Strange looking." Tran said as he watched for the 'strange looking' car.

Once they left the town of Siliguri, Jack managed to get the Toyota up to seventy miles an hour. With the big off-road tires and the off-road lift kit, he could feel how unstable the Toyota was and decided seventy would be all the speed they could handle. Jack shouted back to Tran that the border with Nepal was only fifty kilometers ahead. Tran was going to answer when a bullet smashed the back window of the Toyota. It passed through the cabin without hitting any of the men. It punched a neat round hole in the front windshield, traveling off into the Indian countryside. The four journalists stared out the small hole in the windscreen. Scott was the first to utter anything.

"Well, I don't think they want us back now." He said and watched as the others nodded in agreement.

Tran lifted the type 64 automatic pistol with the silencer still attached to the barrel. Squeezing the trigger, he fired one shot and saw a neat round hole appear in the windshield of the sidekick. The pursuing Suzuki dropped back, and Tran could see the woman in the front seat waving her arms. She was ordering the male driver to speed back up so she could continue to fire at them. Before the Suzuki caught up to Toyota, Tran flipped the selector switch from single shot to fully automatic fire on the 64 and took aim on the front of the sidekick. Slowly taking up the trigger slack, Tran sighted through the dot scope and fired when the sidekick filled his vision.

Jiao watched as the Tibetan in the back of the Toyota rested the barrel of his weapon on the edge of the tailgate. She was expecting another single shot when a stream of holes appeared in the windshield in front of Delun. Jiao knew the Tibetan had a fully automatic type 64 military police-issue weapon. Everything slowed down; the first round came from the man in the back of the Toyota and hit the windshield above the first hole. The next four marched closer to Delun. Jaio heard a garbled scream from the back seat as she ducked. Jiao could see one of the bullets hit Aiguo in the maxilla. It crushed the hard palate and smashed its way through the front of the man's face, slamming into the back of his throat. The single punched through the soft tissue exiting between the first and second cervical vertebrae. Jiao banged her head on something as she ducked; it was now digging into the side of her face. Delun pulled the wheel to the left, leaving the road. When he felt the wheels of the sidekick drop off the pavement, he slammed his foot into the break peddle.

Tran watched as the Suzuki pulled off the road and stopped in a cloud of dust.

"There's one less in that car." He shouted from the back of the Toyota. Jack knew Tran wasn't bragging about killing the person. It was such a precise count of their enemies could be kept. Three left.

Chow watched as the sidekick took a full clip from an automatic full in the windshield. He knew one, maybe more of the young assassins would be dead. Chow liked how the driver hauled off the road at speed and brought the car to a stop in a cloud of dust. If the driver had been hit, he would have flipped the narrow sidekick pulling a stunt like that; Chow knew the driver was okay, at least.

Delun took his weight off Jaio and let her up to survey the damage. Aiguo was dead; Fen was covered in his blood but not hurt. They knew the men they hunted had superior weapons to theirs and were not afraid to use them. That should have been something the group included in their briefing, what the group told Jiao and Fen was four of the men worked for the BBC as newsmen, so they had no training. Of the other two, the Americans trained the large white man. She thought he would be fat and lazy; after all, this is what they were taught in China. All the pictures she had ever seen of Americans had shown fat people eating fattening foods. The American wasn't fat, he was tall, and by the way, he moved, she could tell he was in shape. The generals left out the American kept himself in condition. She also knew the men that ran China forced Tibetan boys into the army. This Tibetan was smaller than the other men; he looked right at her and fired.

There was no second thought; the Tibtan knew he was going to kill. He was not a coward, as the generals told her all Tibetans were. Driving into the forest, Delun stopped behind a large bush. He first checked to make sure Jiao and Fen were alright. He pulled Aiguo's body out of the back seat and rolled it under the brush. The vermin would eat it before it was discovered. Fen and Jiao went behind another bush so they could wash Aiguos blood off and change into clean clothes. The two young women discussed whether they should kill Delun or tell him of their plans to run away. Fen told Jiao she was scared; she said she did not want to kill anyone.

"I know; I also do not want to kill anyone, but to be free of the men in Beijing, we must. As for Delun, we will wait and see." Jiao said, and Fen smiled, knowing her friend would make the right decision.

Delun walked through the thick stand of trees and found they had almost driven into another village. Standing at the edge of the small town, he could see a man working on an older Mercedes Benzes. Walking up to the man, Delun asked if the man spoke English. When the man smiled and said he did, Delun asked him if he knew where he could buy a car. Smiling broader, the man said his car was for sale. He was just changing the oil, so he could take it to the market.

"Won't your wife be angry if you sell the car?" Delun asked the man.

"HA, my wife died and left me alone, so I buy and sell cars to live now." Before the words finished coming out of the old man's mouth, Delun stabbed the man in the chest with his service knife. Doing as he was trained, Delun held the old man close. Delun smiled as he felt the life leave the old man; he liked to kill with his knife. The General pulled him aside before he went on this mission. Delun's orders were to kill Jiao and Fen once the task was complete. When Delun had asked if Aiguo was to come back, the General just shrugged his shoulders; he couldn't wait for the end of the mission. First, he would kill Jiao fast; he would stab her in the base of the skull. It would be over in a second. She was dangerous. Once he was done killing Jaio, Delun knew he could take his time with Fen. He fantasized about the rape and torture he would use on Fen. Once Fen had broken, when she wouldn't respond to the pain anymore, he would take his knife and gut her slowly, keeping her alive for as long as possible.

Jiao could hear the car coming through the bush. She had changed and was waiting for Fen, who was topless and was still trying to wash the last of Aiguo's blood from her Breasts. Jiao had started to think Delun had deserted her and Fen; if he had, she was beginning to think it would be for the best. Jaio knew if they were alone, she and Fen could start to run now and not have to kill the English men. They could just run away; that would be for the best.

Delun was surprised to see Jiao smile at him when he drove the big Mercedes Benzes through the bushes to where he had parked the sidekick. Delun almost hit the bullet-riddled sidekick when he drove to the spot Jiao stood. He was distracted by Fen splashing water over her breast, trying to wipe the blood from them. Stopping the car with it facing away from the bush Fen was attempting to use for privacy, Delun smiled as he thought of the time he would enjoy with Fen.

"I thought we should have a new car, seeing our first is full of bullet holes and there's blood all over the inside," Delun explained. Jiao told Delun he was right to find a new car for them. Fen smiled as she pulled a T-shirt over her head; with no bra, the T-shirt accentuated the fullness of her breast. The cold water tightened her nipples so they stood erect. Delun held the door for Jiao to enter the front seat. Jiao knew Delun looked at her breasts. He seemed to be more interested in Fen. Jiao knew it was because her friend's breasts were more prominent and swayed when she moved, smiling as she turned and looked at Fen.

"I think he likes your breasts," Jiao said.

"He's a man; he likes all breasts. Do you think he can drive with you and me not wearing a bra?" Fen asked.

"I hope so," Jiao said as Delun opened the driver's door. Jiao knew they should have felt bad for Aiguo. They didn't know him, so his loss wasn't felt. Both women knew before long they might have to kill Delun. What the two unsuspecting women didn't know were the orders Delun had once their mission was finished. They also didn't realize the demented type of training Delun suffered through and what that training did to his young and fragile mind.

Chow was waiting for the sidekick to come out of the forest and head west. He knew that they had gone into the woods to dump the dead body, where it would be eaten by the vermin. This was the standard operating procedure. While he waited, he still wanted to call the group in Beijing. Chow knew they would ask him to intercede on their behalf again. He wanted nothing to do with this other than to see John killed. Chow almost missed the older Mercedes Benzes drive out of the forest, then turned west on Highway 31C. Chow smiled as he followed the three in the German car.

Chapter 71

TRAN WATCHED FOR THE black sidekick. Jack told him he had probably hit the radiator and that the car was no good now.

"That will only slow them down," Tran said as he turned to face forward.

"Yeah, I know; when they get a new set of wheels, we won't know what to look for until they make their next move," Jack said. Watching the road, Jack knew what his move would be. He hoped that these people weren't as well trained in hunting men as he was.

"Well, I don't know about the rest of the lads, but as far as I'm concerned, I owe you two another bottle of forty-year-old Glenfiddich scotch," William said as the other journalists chimed up with, here here's all around.

"Thanks, boys, but let's save the drinks until we're back in golly old' England." The men all agreed that was for the best.

"How do you plan to get into Nepal, Jack?" Tomas asked.

Jack knew it was a good question, but no matter how hard he thought, he couldn't come up with an answer for it. They couldn't afford the time it would take them to watch the border and look for a weak point, but they couldn't afford to. If they spent the time to do it right, the Chinese would be on them, and they would have to fight their way out of a trap. Jack was still thinking when he saw a sign for state highway 63 South. Turning on the road, Jack hoped what he was planning would lead them out of danger, not further into it. Tran was sitting in the cargo bay of the land cruiser; he never saw the sign for the highway or the direction of it.

"Where are we going now, Jack?" Tran asked, not caring about the answer. He spent the afternoon watching their escape from the vantage of what had just passed.

"Change of plans, boys, instead of trying to get across another border into Nepal and getting screwed at it. I think we should head to Delhi. I remember something about an airport or an airbase there." When Jack had finished, Scott told them there was an airbase and an airport. Looking in the mirror, Jack smiled a new plan formed.

Chapter 72

THE MERCEDES WAS MUCH older and bigger than the sidekick. It was also much faster than the sidekick had been. It was this speed that allowed Fen to see the Toyota heading south on state highway 63 if they had been ten seconds later. None of them would have ever seen the suv through the trees. Delun turned south and followed. The sun was well past its highest point, and the shadows were growing long on the ground when Jiao told them what she planned for tonight. She told them her plan would wait until the men stopped for the night; before she could go on, Delun cleared his throat and pointed out they had six men to drive the Toyota. They would probably only stop to switch drivers and fuel and keep going through the night. Jaio swore she knew her make-believe husband was right; they wouldn't stop. They will have to change drivers and fuel and answer the call of nature; her plan would be simple.

"When they stop to switch drivers or fuel, Delun will pull alongside. We act like we want to help them, then we open fire, catching them in the open and unprotected. Once we confirm they are all dead, we will drive to the next largest city and call in." When Jaio was finished, Fen looked sick; she wanted to be free. Both Fen and Jaio didn't want to murder anyone. Delun smiled. Soon he thought, soon Fen would be his toy, and Jaio would be out of his way.

Chow watched as the three killers turned south onto Highway 63. He wasn't in time to see Jack and the others turn and head down this road; Chow followed the Chinese operatives. He was starting to wonder what the hell they were doing when he realized the escapees must have taken this route, opting to stay inside India. Chow knew if

Jack and the others were staying inside India, they had found another way out. Then it hit him; they were going to fly. They had planned to fly out of India and back to England.

Jack drove as fast as the traffic and the law of the area allowed. Signs for a city called Purina came and went; some of the signs were in English and Indian. Those he could read told him he was one hundred and seventy-five kilometers from the city. Two hours later, he could see the glow of the city reflected off the bottoms of the clouds gathered in the night sky. Tran was sleeping in the back of the Toyota, and all the journalists but Tomas slept. He sat in the front seat, watching Jack to ensure he wasn't becoming fatigued. Tomas recounted the time his father tried to drive from their home in London to his grandparent's home in Scotland. Tomas never realized he and his mother had fallen asleep until the sound of the family car leaving the road and crashing through a farmer's fence woke him. He could remember his father apologizing to the farmer and paying for the damage to the fence. Tomas told Jack his father also had to pay for the damage to the family car. After that, Tomas's mother would make his father stop and get a room for the night; no more trips into fields, she would say.

Delun loved to drive, but he knew he had reached his limit. He was going to tell Jaio either she or Fen would have to take over. Just before Delun was going to wake Jaio, the brake lights of the Toyota came on. This was it, he thought; they would pull to the side and stop, then he would pull up alongside, offering to help, then Jiao and Fen would shoot all of them. Delun smiled at his reflection in the rearview mirror.

"They are stopping," Delun said loud enough to wake Jaio and Fen. The two young female operatives woke instantly and watched the back of the Toyota.

"You all right, Jack? You're starting to wander a little." Tomas could tell Jack had reached his limit and needed to be spelled at the wheel.

"I think it's about time you took over Tomas," Jack said. "I've just about had it."

Chow couldn't understand why the traffic was slowing down. He watched as the big Benzes slowed and started to turn off the road. Then

Chow saw the distinctive small round tail lights of the Toyota. Chow thought this was it. In mere minutes John Smyth is going to be dead, then he could start his new life without having to look over his shoulder every five minutes.

Jack had pulled into a wide spot on the shoulder when he and Tomas got out of the front to switch sides. The others climbed out to stretch their legs. Scott was standing at the back of the Toyota when he saw a Mercedes pull into the wide spot behind them.

"Now, what do you think they want?" The big red-headed Scotsmen started to ask when the first bullet hit the edge of the Toyota. The bullet broke into two pieces; the first piece ricocheted straight up into the night sky, screaming into the stared firmament. The second piece cut a long deep, ragged furrow along Scott's right cheek ending at his ear. Screaming, the Scotsman went down, scrambling to get around the corner of the Toyota and out of the line of fire. His training kicked in. Scott hadn't stood flat-footed to get shot again; he had found cover.

Jaio turned her attention to the Tibetan in the back of the Toyota. If she had to kill him, she would for her own freedom. She didn't care about avenging Aiguo; Jaio didn't hate the Tibetan; she didn't hate anyone of these men. She only hated the men in Beijing and her father. She now knew for sure everything she was taught had been a lie. Her and Fen's freedom was at stake, and she needed to be free. She was about to reacquire Tran in her sights when she saw him lift the boxy shape of the QCW-05 into view and fire on fully automatic. Oh god, she thought she was going to fail. She was failing herself and Fen; they were going to be killed here.

The first five rounds out of the barrel of Tran's rifle hit the door, and walked up. The bullets sounded like someone was outside the door, battering the door with an enormous hammer. The next four rounds found their way into the car. Jaio couldn't get over the sound of the bullets buzzing through the interior of the vehicle. The shots reminded her of giant angry hornets. The first round split the door trim and drove a piece of it into Jaio's right breast. The second round, to find its way into the car, hit the steering wheel with the core of the steering wheel being a round piece of quarter-inch steel stock. The bullet was redirected into the back seat of the car, hitting Fen in the chest and knocking her back onto the seat. The third round hit the door post behind Jaios head, cut a gouge out of the headrest, and then hit Delun.

The bullet cut through Deluns Levator's scapulae muscle and the upper part of the sternocleidomastoid muscle of his neck. When the bullet came to a stop in Delun, it had severed the spinal cord and the nerves controlling the autonomic functions of the body. He sat and listened as his heart slowly stopped beating. Part of Delun was screaming it wasn't fair he hadn't gotten his prize of Fen Fang. Delun knew he had been cheated, then the side of him the trainers hadn't corrupted washed over him, he couldn't see Fen, but he was happy she would live. Delun was thankful there was no pain; it just grew darker and darker until there was nothing, not even the sound of his heart. The fourth round to enter the car's interior came through the side window of the back seat. When Fen started to sit up, she was holding her right breast where the ricochet from the steering wheel hit her. As she sat up, the fourth and final round to enter the car hit her in the right side of her already wounded chest. The bullet punched a round hole in her left hand, then impacted her chest. It passed through the fatty tissue of her breast between the rigid protections of her ribs. Her lung offered little resistance to the subsonic projectile traveling through her and collapsed when punctured. When the bullet was finely brought to a stop, it rested at what was left of the torn pulmonary vein.

Fen Fang slammed back onto the seat; she knew she had been hit again harder this time. First, there was nothing, no pain, just a great numbing in her chest. Then the pain came. She could only take small gasps of air, then she would cough, and foamy blood would fly out of her mouth. From her training, Fen knew she was hit in the lung; she could also feel the cold start to set in. The young would-be spy knew she was dying; Fen knew the cold meant shock and blood loss. Reaching up, she touched Jaio's shoulder. Fen tried to force a smile for Jiao, and she tried to reach up and touch Jaios hair for the last time, but she was too weak. All Fen could do was sit back and watch as the world went from the dark of night to the black of death.

Chow watched as the big German car was rocked by the automatic gunfire delivered from the back of the land cruiser by the little Tibetan man. He wanted to stay and see what happened next. Chow knew the men in the Toyota would be on alert for any strange cars around them. He slowed momentarily, then looked straight ahead and drove off into the night, knowing the Chinese had failed. Just as he predicted they would, god damn it, he told those fucks in Beijing these kids wouldn't get the job done, he screamed at the steering wheel.

Tran and Jack held their weapons up at eye level, knowing that if anyone in the car moved or looked at them, they would kill them. Both knew where the other was going, but each man stayed out of the other's line of fire. Tran ran to the driver's side of the Benzes. One look and he knew the driver was dead. The female on the passenger's side of the car was alive. Jack stuck his weapon through the broken back passenger side window. When Jiao felt the muzzle of the military police-issued type 64 press against the back of her head. She thought she was going to die right there. At least she would be free of her father and the others in Beijing. Instead, the man holding the gun to her head opened the door, grabbed her by her hair, and pulled her out. Jack was so fast she couldn't get her feet under her, and she fell to the gravel, tearing the skin off her knees and hands. The Tibetan went to one of the backpacks in the back of their vehicle and came back with rope. As the Tibetan tied her hands, Jiao looked into Jack's eyes. Jaio was scared of Jack because of the scare that lined his jaw; his eyes held no light in them, and to her, he seemed to have no soul. Then the men loaded her into the back seat of the Toyota, and her thoughts turned to rape.

Jiao had never been with a man before. Her instructors told her of the American male, of how he uses rape to brutalize women. One of the older English men looked at her chest and then told her he wasn't going to hurt her, but he needed to patch her up. Jiao knew this was a trick; this is how they would start, show her some kindness then they would begin to hurt her. At least, this is what her training told her would happen. Jiao knew her instructors lied, that they manipulated the truth. Was this another manipulation, or was she in real danger? The lies of her own government confused her?

Jack loosely held his pistol where Jiao could see it. He watched as William made the hole in Jaio's shirt bigger. William hoped the part of the door trim that stabbed her hadn't remained in the wound. When he could see the trim had been pulled out whole, William disinfected the wound and applied a pressure bandage. Jiao was confused; she had been told if she or Fen Fang, if either of them were caught, they would be abused by their captures. This old man had just given her first aid, and he had hardly touched her. When he had to move the hole in her T-shirt to see the whole wound, he only moved it as far as needed, and the older man blushed at that. She thought they must be toying with her, building her hopes up, so she would drop her guard then they would start.

Chow picked up his phone; he was going to call the group in Beijing, but then he changed his mind. When the four assassins failed to check in, the Chinese General's paranoia would kick in, and they would assume the worst. In this case, they would be right. The only thing Chow needed to decide was whether to fly back to Bhutan, or he should stay with the Toyota and see what happened.

Because Jack could speak Cantonese, he asked the girl her name. She only glared at him and refused to answer. When William asked her in English, she turned and looked at him because he asked politely.

"Jiao, my name is Jiao; I cannot tell you more than that." Tran was surprised to see her speak English.

"They sent you to kill the newsmen?" Jack asked. He had set his gun on the front seat where Jiao could not see it.

"Well, should we keep her?" Jack asked when Jiao refused to answer more questions. He smiled as Jiao glared at him. Part of her was seething at Jack for the killing of her only friend in the world. She knew Tran killed Fen defending his friends and himself. "Or should we take her to Delhi and let her off on a street corner." Jack finished

Chow decided he would follow Jack and the others. He didn't care about the men in Beijing. As far as he was concerned, they had fucked him by sending these useless kids to do a job that should have been given to seasoned professional killers.

Chapter 73

CHOW STAYED WELL BEHIND the Toyota as they drove around the city of Purina and headed west on NH107. Chow knew they were heading to the city of Patna, then from there, god only knew where to. All Chow knew was he would have to stop soon, or he would fall asleep behind the wheel. Cursing when Chow thought about losing Jack when he stopped, Chow could feel his eyes trying to close as he started to pass hotel signs. Pulling over in a service station, he watched as the Toyotas tail lights faded into the night; Chow reclined the seat in the Porsche and closed his eyes. The sun was starting to come up when a smiling boy lightly knocked on Chow's window, waking him.

"Good morning, sir. We are open and have coffee and food for your morning if you wish." The boy said brightly. Pulling to the gas pump, Chow asked the boy to fill the Porsche as he went in to get a large coffee and something to eat. Watching the young boy fill the Porch up with fuel, Chow thought of how he hated John Smyth; he never really liked the man. His hatred now bordered on the psychotic on the pathological.

With the city of Purnia behind them, Tran drove west, following the signs for another city. Jack told him to head for the city of Patna. He had a route all planned out in his head for now.

"From Patna, we'll head for Lucknow," Jack told them.

"Hey now, I like the sounds of that town, Lucknow. Hopefully, we'll start having some luck now," Jerry joked. Everyone in the Toyota groaned and rolled their eyes at the attempted humor Jerry tried to slide into the conversation. The only one who didn't complain was Jiao; turning to her, Jerry asked her.

"Was my joke that bad, miss? Really, you can tell me you can be honest with me. After hanging out with this lot for as long as I have, my sensibilities have been armored." Jiao looked at Jerry, Jack, and the rest of the men she was stuck with. Jaio was struggling with the situation; she didn't know if they were toying with her. If they were really going to set her loose on a street corner, not knowing made her angry.

"What is wrong with you, people? I have been sent to kill you; I shot you in the face!" She shouted, indicating Scott. "And forced you to kill my best and only friend in the world!" Tran continued looking at Jiao in the rearview mirror. "And now you sit here making jokes and asking me if you are funny!" She finished looking at Jerry. The men were silent for a moment before Jerry spoke.

"So, not funny, huh?" Jerry asked. The other men in the car burst out laughing. Jiao knew the men weren't laughing at her. The men laughed because the tension of the situation was relieved. Despite her assumed predicament, Jiao turned, looked out the window, and smiled. Maybe just maybe, could her freedom be at hand? Jaio started to weep for her dear friend Fen Fang. Jiao wondered if she had found the freedom she and Fen had sought for so long. The freedom they were willing to kill these men for. Looking out the window of the Toyota as it drove through the Indian night, Jaio knew she was free of her father and the others in Beijing.

The drive from the city of Purnia to the city of Patna took five hours. They entered the ring road around the bustling Indian city before lunch hour. William talked to Jiao for the whole trip, though often he went without an answer to his questions. Her silence didn't bother William. When faced with it, he would shrug his shoulders and act as if it didn't happen. Once they stopped to refuel, William helped her out of the suv.

Jack stood and watched as Jiao walked around with William and Tran. Both the men were telling her what China was doing in Tibet was wrong. Tran told Jiao about his sister and of his mother and father and how they had been murdered at the hands of the twisted Colonel. Of how he and other boys had been forced into the PLA, he even told her of a time he and his unit went to the desert to kill a village that wasn't even in Tibet; they had orders to wipe out anyone in the desert for a new base. Jiao wanted to hate this Tibetan and the others, but she couldn't do it. She couldn't hate people who were fighting for their own freedom.

Chow stopped at one of the road signs; he tried to think of which way the Toyota would have gone. When the name came to him, Chow smiled and knew he was correct; the bastard was going to Delhi. That big bastard was taking the journalists to Delhi. Chow knew from Delhi the escapees could go anywhere in the world. Just then, his satellite phone buzzed and vibrated with the notification of an incoming call, looking at the caller display. Chow smiled, so the old bastards were calling him again. He thought about letting their call go to voice mail then he thought there might be more money to be made by talking to the men in Beijing. Chow answered with a statement that made the men in the room go silent.

"Your assassins have failed you, gentlemen," Chow said. Each man of the group looked to another before all eyes stopped on the one General who sat at the head of the table.

"What can you do for us?" General Bok asked, looking around the room from his position at the head of the table.

"I know of some men in this part of the world, you will have to pay for their service, and it won't be cheap," Chow said. General Bok looked at the nodding heads of his fellow Generals.

"We can do that. How long until we know you have secured their services?" He asked.

"I'll get in contact with them and call you back, let's say, one hour." Chow heard a click on the other line and knew the General had ended the call. The men he knew were American, Australian, and two British brothers. Both had been part of the British SAS at one time. These men had been charged with unlawful killings during desert shield in the early nineties. The four men met while serving time in military prison, then escaped, and now sold their expertise to the highest bidder. When Chow called, he found they had hired an answering service. Laughing, Chow left the name the men knew him as and his number, then hung up. Twenty minutes later, his phone rang, and he heard the unmistakable Californian in the voice of Ticker.

"Dude, long time no speak; you got something needing work on." Chris was the name this individual's mother gave him at birth. However, this man's mother only kept him for about two weeks before she realized her love of partying and drugs was greater than her love of her son and his hungry crying. So she abandoned Chris at a local Catholic church and never looked back. The nuns had called him Christopher for as long as he could remember. The judge had called him Mr. Harry when he told Chris he had a choice, either join the military or go to prison. So into the army, Chris went. It turned out he liked the army. They trained him to blow things up and how to kill. After basic training, he received the nickname Ticker; now, he only answers to Ticker.

"Yeah, Ticker, something like a cream-colored Toyota land cruiser, six men inside," Chow told the California-born and bred killer. He could hear Ticker speaking to someone in the room with him. Gunner, the Australian, took the phone. This man loved what he did; to say Gunner was happiest when he was killing would be an understatement. Gunner found he liked to kill things when he was a boy living on his dad's farm in the northern territory of Australia.

"Hey mate, six, you say, when and where." That was Gunner just give him a place and a time, and he would kill anything that was there, no questions asked. Unlike Ticker, Gunner had come from a good home, a safe home. His mother was a stay-at-home mom who home-schooled her three kids along with children from the next farm. Gunner's father worked the cattle and taught Gunner how to hunt and live off the land; it was the hunting Gunner liked the most.

"All I can tell you is that they're driving a cream-colored Toyota land cruiser, and they'll be heading for Delhi from Patna." Informed Chow.

"Shortest route or roundabout way?" Gunner asked.

"There running, trying to get out of the country, two protectors and four journalists; the contract will be for all six men." Chow knew Gunner would love to kill news media, especially ones from the BBC. It had been a war correspondent who had taken photos of Gunner torturing and killing Iraqi royal guards. Gunner was ordered to get information, but his officers didn't care how he got the information. Well, they didn't care until the video of Gunner cutting the hands off Iraqi Soldiers aired on the BBC news, then Gunner was left out in the cold.

"Reporters, you say, though I would like to do if for free a man and his mates need to eat," Gunner said. Five minutes later, Gunner and Chow agreed on a price. Chow thought it was steep, but after all, it wasn't his money, and if Gunner and the crew pulled it off, it would be worth the money. He could always offer them a more permanent job strictly working for him. Calling the group back in Beijing, Chow told the group he had the right men for the job. He also explained how these men worked.

"Because of the lack of time, they have to prepare, and it's for six people, their charging one million Euros, gentlemen." Chow could hear shouts of outrage over the price; he waited for the men to calm down. Chow knew these men believed only they should become wealthy from the death of others. After a moment, the group agreed to pay the amount on completion of the task and only on confirmation of a positive outcome. Chow called Gunner and Ticker back and told them the deal; it was the same deal everyone they worked for had. Gunner added if they tried to stiff them, he and Ticker would kill each man's family slowly before ending the call. Chow knew of one person who had hired Gunner and the others. This person tried to break the deal after the job had been completed. He remembered what had happened to the man's family. Gunner had the man's wife and teenage daughter raped to death, then he castrated the man's poor son while he was forced to watch the boy bleed out on the floor. When the boy died, Gunner killed the man by skinning him alive. Chow knew this had been the only time any contractor ever went after a client before. This made Gunner and his crew a last resort for anyone needing wet work to be done.

Chapter 74

WILLIAM ASKED JACK if he could untie Jiao's hands; Jack looked at her and then nodded to William. Once she was free of the knotted ropes, Tomas offered a bottle of water to her; Jiao looked at the bottle with suspicion.

"We haven't poisoned the water with anything." William offered. He undid the cap of the bottle and took a sip to prove the water was safe, then offered it to Jiao.

"But now you have drank from it," Jiao stated, looking at the bottle. Jack chuckled as he turned and tossed a new bottle from the front seat.

Jack watched as Scottie rubbed at the bandage on the side of his face.

"You'll get it bleeding again if you don't leave it alone," Jack said to which Scott complained about itching.

"I have more iodine if you want me to wash it out again." William offered.

"NO! Christ, no, I think I'd rather have the cheek rot and fall off!" The big Scotsman exclaimed. Jiao looked back at Scottie; she could see the bruising and swelling, trying to hide how handsome Scott's freckled face was. The impact of the bullet piece blackened his right eye and ripped a long deep, ragged cut along the lower right jaw line. The fragment cut part of Scottie's masseter muscle. Even this injury couldn't hide his handsome features, Jiao thought; when Scottie tried to smile at her, he winced from the pain. She even liked how he sounded with his Scottish accent; these men treated her nicely. They hadn't touched her other than to help her, and now she wasn't even tied. Was anything she had been taught right or not?

Jack looked back and could see from the wrinkle in her brow that Jiao was trying to puzzle together what had happened.

"If you have questions to ask, just ask; we hide nothing. In this car, there are no secrets." Jiao thought about what the man the others called Jack said. She wanted her first question to be a good one. All Jiao could think about was the torture they were supposed to do. The whole time she had been in training, her instructors had told Jiao and the others that if caught, they would be tortured; they were told to be prepared.

"How come you don't torture? How come you don't ask questions?" Jaio asked. Jack turned sideways in the front seat, so he was looking at her.

"I don't torture because I am a victim of torture at the hands of General Trang. Because of his methods, I will suffer for the rest of my life." Jiao had heard of this Trang. It was said he raped little boys; even his grandsons were not safe from this monster.

"I know how it feels to be helpless, not know when your next breath will be your last. I also know what it's like to pray this breath will be your last." When Jack finished, Jiao looked at him and then back at the wounded Scott.

"Why did you not kill me at the ambush. I shoot your friend, but you don't kill me?" Jack looked at her and then back to Tran.

"These men you sit with, they came to Tibet to try and stop the killing. We only kill when it is a last resort for our lives and freedom." Jack said. Jiao looked at the men nodding; even Scott was nodding.

"I was trained as an operative for my country. I was to be sent to England as a student. I was going to defect once I was there. I only did this so I could go to England and be free." Jaio told Jack. When she finished her explanation, a tear rolled down her cheek. She held still as Scott reached with his right hand and wiped the tear away. She explained because her father worked for the secret service, she had no choice; when she turned fourteen, she was thrown into training.

"If you want, you can come back to London with us." William offered, he didn't know, but he was sure that the BBC would love to interview a former spy for the Chinese.

"I don't know; if I go, how long will I have to spend in jail for shooting at you." She asked, and for the first time, Jack could see the little girl in her; William looked shocked at her question.

"I don't think you'll spend any time in jail. The foreign office might want to talk to you about your training, but that's all." Before William had told her about the foreign office. Jiao had made up her mind that she would defect with the English reporters. Jiao wanted to go to England and live, and now she didn't have to worry about her government calling her home or trying to. She was going to be free; she was going to be free. Scott placed one of his big hands on her shoulder to try to comfort her. When Jiao looked at it, she could see it had red hair and freckles. Before she could stop herself, Jiao wondered if Scott had freckles all over his body. Though Jiao hadn't said anything aloud, Jiao blushed at her boldness. Jack looked at Jiao and wondered why she was blushing. He thought it might be from the heat inside the suv.

Gunner drove their converted Humvee to highway NH24 east of the town of Bareilly and sat by a service station waiting for a cream color Toyota land cruiser to pass with six men in it. Ticker was sitting in the jump seat. For the first time, it was just the two of them; the British brothers weren't to be found. What Gunner and Ticker failed to tell Chow or anyone, was one of the brothers was killed when he turned and tripped over a bomb Ticker had planted; the blast killed him instantly. Enraged by his brother's death, the other brother was going to shoot Ticker. Gunner entered and shot the second brother in the head. Even though Gunner lived with these two brothers, he felt no more remorse about killing one of the brothers than he would have for killing a rabbit dog back on his dad's farm. When Gunner and Ticker finished that job, he told Ticker he never really liked the limy bastards anyway.

Now the two men split everything fifty-fifty, straight down the middle. Chow knew calling these two men he called two born killers. One was born and bred by the foster system in America. The other wasn't made; he was born with the need to kill. Chow was well past to city of Patna, on highway NH 28, as the sun traveled through the sky. Chow felt this would be the day all his troubles were put behind him. Gunner and the boys would kill John and the others. He would be free to disappear; hell, he was even thinking about retiring to a small island somewhere as he dialed the number Gunner had given him.

"Hey mate, what's-up?" The Australian asked.

"Just need an update if you don't mind, sir." Chow joked. He knew Gunner hated to be called sir.

"Oh, sorry mate, you want to talk to a sir? I'll give you to Ticker." Gunner laughed. In the background, Chow could hear Ticker telling Gunner to 'bite me.' Coming back on the line, Gunner informed Chow he and Ticker were parked on hwy NH24 in Uttar Pradesh. Chow said he would be looking for them, then hung up.

Chapter 75

THE FIVE MEN AND ONE Chinese girl standing by the side of the road made for a funny sight to those who passed. Most of the truck drivers going past assumed the two Orientals were married or at least dating. What they were was waiting for William to appear out of the bushes, where he was forced to run to relieve himself. Complaining about the damn rations, Jerry had bought at the market. Tran retrieved a bottle of water from the roof of the Toyota. With the sun beating on it all morning, the water was quite warm. With a small bar of soap he had taken from the hotel, William was able to wash his hands. Standing beside Jiao, Tran was caught by surprise when she asked him how he had come to be with Jack. For a moment, Jiao didn't think Tran was going to speak, then he smiled up at the sky and started.

"I think god willed it." When Jiao and William looked at him, he waited and then told his story again. "I was conscripted into the people's army. For five years, I played the part of the good soldier. Little did I know my father, mother, and little sister had been butchered. They were killed by the commanding officer of the region of Tibet where we lived...All because my little sister fought back when he tried to rape her; she disgraced him. The Colonel had my family killed that night when he heard about the honors the village had shown my family. The monster came back and wiped out every living person left in the village." Tran told her.

Jerry took over driving, and he watched the road as the others in the Toyota listened to Tran tell how his family died.

"I found out about my family when I returned home. I swore to kill the man who did this to them and my village. Jack was found by an old man and taken to the monks who still live in the mountains. They healed him and gave him what he needed to get away. Together we found his torturer and the killer of my family and ended their existence. We knew these men were being held. They were going to be sent back to the prison where Jack had been held. We thought that they should leave with us." When Tran finished, Jiao looked at him and Jack.

"You weren't sent in to rescue them; the British government never sent you in?" Jaio asked Tran.

"No, happened to be at the right place at the right time," Jack said. The men were all surprised when Jiao covered her mouth and giggled. Jack was frightened at how Jiao giggling made her look like a little girl. Jiao reminded Tran so much of his little sister his heart broke, and he had to look away.

"The Generals thought the borders had been breached. They thought they had a traitor in their midst." Jaio said. Then laughed into her hand again. "The men with power started looking at each other, wondering who they could blame for this." Jiao giggled into her hand again. Jerry called out as they passed a sign stating they were entering the city of Lucknow.

"Take the ring road. It's called NH24 A. It'll take us around the city's traffic." William said to Jerry.

"Who wants to have a hot shower and get into some clean clothes?" Jack asked to a chorus of Here Here's from the men. Traveling through the city, Jack told Jerry to pull into a hotel called the Deep Palace. Getting out of the Toyota, Tran looked at the ornate building; William went inside to see if they could have rooms for the night. Returning like a concurring hero, William held up room keys for the men and Jiao. She looked at the key William gave her. Jiao thought they would tie her up and leave her covered in the Toyota for the night.

Sitting on the bed in the room William rented for her. Jiao looked at the deep red curtains of the television, at the light reflected off the bathroom mirror. Jaio started to cry again. She missed Fen; she didn't blame Tran for shooting her friend. Jiao blamed Fen's death on the men in Beijing. Standing Jiao wanted to be around the others who escaped from China. When Jiao went to Scott's, she wanted to make sure his bandages hadn't gotten wet. Jiao found all the men were sharing rooms. Because she was a woman, they gave her the room with the biggest bed.

Another thing her teachers lied about, men from the West did not treat women like animals. Jiao always hated liars and the lies they used for their own gain. It went deeper than that. Now she actually wondered if there were any honest men in the government of China.

Scott sat on the edge of the bed and let Jiao remove the bandage that William had placed on his wound. When she saw the laceration left by the bullet fragment. Scott tried to smile to show it looked worse than it really was, but he winced instead of smiling. Gathering up some rubbing alcohol and gauze, Jiao gently cleaned the dried blood; she had never shot anybody before. Jiao's instructors told her it would be like shooting a cow. Jiao passed all her range tests, and she said all the right things when she had to take any of the personality tests. The one time her father came to see her, he told Jiao her instructors told him she was going to be a great spy. Jiao's father told her he was proud of her, then left, and she never saw her father again. Now the tears rolled down Jiao's cheeks as she cleaned this handsome Scotsman's wound, a wound she had inflicted. When Scott saw Jiao start to silently weep as she ministered to his face. Scott reached up, took both her hands in one of his big freckled ones, and looked at a tear as it hung on her delicate jaw.

"I'll live, and I'll be all right; you don't need to cry for this little scratch. I forgive you; it wasn't you who did this. It was the lies you've been fed for so many years," Scott said. Jiao buried her face in her hands, wept out loud, and leaned against him. Standing, Scott made her sit on the bed. He watched as Jiao curled up into the fetal position. Scott started to rub her back because he couldn't think of anything else to do. Scott listened as Jiao wept until she was asleep; pulling the comforter off the second bed in the room, he covered her and left the room. Stopping at the door, Scott turned and looked at Jiao curled up under the blanket. He did forgive her for his wound; as far as he was concerned, she wasn't to blame. The blame laid squarely on the shoulders of the Generals hiding in Beijing. The rest of the men had gathered in Jack and Tran's room. When Scott told the others about the episode in his and Jerry's room with Jiao. William spoke up and told them of a story he did about brainwashing and what happens when the victim becomes aware of it.

"From what I learned, the victims often break down and weep. Some never come to terms with the damage they've inflicted because of the lies forced on them. Some can go into a type of catatonic state for extended periods. This is usually if the brainwashing is done quickly and using drugs. With Jiao, for the most part, she was subjected to the lies of a group that, over the years, has tried to instill fear of the West into her and their people. For whatever reason, Jiao had a better grounding in the truth than some of her countrymen. So when she hurts someone trying to act on her plans of escape, the reality is that she has lied all these years. Well, you could imagine what we would feel like, knowing your whole life is a lie." William said as Tran sat beside him on the bed.

"I can empathize with her," Jack said, shaking his head. He knew just exactly what their latest escapee from China felt like. Tomas hung up the phone and smiled.

"Well, lads, they'll have a plane waiting in New Delhi and are going to fly us out on a royal jet under diplomatic cover." Tomas looked at William and the others.

Chapter 76

"WHEN WE GET TO NEW Delhi, I'll put you four and Tran, as well as Jiao, on the plane, but I won't be going this time." Tran knew why Jack was going to stay behind. The four journalists tried to argue, saying Jack would be foolish to stay in India.

"I can't go. I gave my word to a man who was saved by the same monks that saved me. His name is Ben Stills; I need to get him out of there." When Jack explained why he could not go back with the others, Tomas turned and left the room.

"I know that man, William said. He worked for the embassy in Hong Kong. The embassy reported him missing three or four years ago. There were rumors he had defected and that the Chinese were keeping him concealed. But it didn't make any sense; he was a low-level analyst and didn't have anything the Chinese would want. Because of this and his low-level security level, his section chief didn't think he or the others in his department needed a security detail. When Mr. Stills went missing, everybody had round-the-clock security. When we got word from the Chinese that Ben defected, everybody knew he had been snatched," William finished.

"He was sold out by the C.I.A. station chief in Hong Kong. The same Fucker who gave me to the Chinese. A man named Chow Yun, I found out Chow reopened the Silk Road and used C.I.A. black ops to take out the competition. This Chow, it was his right-hand man who helped start the 'CRADLE' project. Chow and Mike Styles used me to kill, so Chow's profits would climb higher and higher." Jack told the others. Tomas walked back into the room, holding a cordless phone from his room. Jack wondered what Tomas was up to and who was on the other end of the line.

"Could you give coordinates to the mountain and the cave Ben is being helped at?" He asked of Jack.

"No, not really, but I could lead a team there," Jack said. Tran stood up and looked at Tomas.

"I can give them the exact mountain, the side the cave is on, and at what altitude they will find the opening," Tomas spoke into the phone. He told whoever was on the other end what Tran had said, then hung up.

"The English ambassador to India has been on the phone with London. Downing Street, to be exact. We have all been ordered to get on that plane and come home, all of us. With Tran's expertise, the government is going to send in a small five-man team to rescue Mr. Stills and bring him home." Jack was going to argue, then realized Tomas told them the British government wanted all of them to come home. It was the word 'home' that hit Jack home. Could this be the chance Jack was looking for?

Chow passed a black Humvee parked behind a service station. Pulling to the side of the road, he stopped and watched as the high-powered lights on the roof rack flashed on and off twice. Turning around, he wondered if Gunner had found the Toyota and killed everyone in it, and was waiting for him.

"What do you mean they never came past?" Chow knew he was behind the Toyota. He couldn't have passed them; he would have seen them and called Gunner back. Chow walked to the edge of the highway and looked east, then west. That fucking John Smyth had gotten off the road somewhere. Where was he and the reporters, where, turning Chow looked at Gunner and Ticker.

"What is the one thing you can count on from a reporter?" Chow asked.

"For the fuckers to stick their noses in something that don't concern them," Gunner answered.

"No, they're like actors; they can't stand any hardship. Can you imagine four B.B.C. journalists driving around in the heat and humidity of India in a big un-air-conditioned noisy land cruiser," Chow said and watched the realization wash over first Gunner's face, then Tickers.

"The whining fucks stopped at a hotel!" Gunner exclaimed. Chow made a gun with his thumb, and index finger, then made it like he shot Gunner.

"Bingo, the only city they could have stopped at would have been Lucknow." Picking up his phone, Chow dialed information in Lucknow and asked for hotels and their numbers. Chow called each of the hotels, starting with the most expensive and working his way down. He knew John wouldn't use his name, so he used the reporters, and when he called the hotel Deep Palace, his perseverance paid off.

"There in Lucknow, at a hotel called the Deep Palace," Chow told Gunner and Ticker.

"Sounds like a spot for queers," Ticker said as he wondered what they were going to do.

"You think they'll spend the night?" Gunner asked. Chow wanted to turn back and drive to the hotel and be done with it, but something was telling him to sit and wait.

"I guarantee you the reporters will want a night with some hot food and a soft bed. This is what we'll do; there's a roadside motel down the road. We'll get some sleep and be back here at sun up waiting for them to pass. When we do, we'll work on getting them off the main road and kill the bunch; sound good." Both the men agreed and followed Chow to the motel.

Jiao woke and was confused. She wasn't in the room the others rented for her. Jiao remembered she started to cry when she tried to help Scott. Now she was in his bed with all her clothes on, and he was gone. For a moment, she thought Scott and the others had left her behind. Just before Jiao placed her feet on the floor, she heard a key in the doorknob. She watched as Scott peeked into the room and saw her sitting on the bed.

"Good, you're awake. The others and I are in the other room, and we have some news you need to hear." Scott told her. Then he gently took Jiao's hand and led her from the room. Jiao looked down and was amazed at how small her hand looked in Scott's hand; she liked this big Scotsman, and she felt safe.

Jack smiled when Jiao entered his and Tran's room. Jiao noticed whenever Jack smiled, the smile only touched his lips. It went no further than that. Jack's eyes held no merriment in them; when the smile lingered on his lips, it made his eyes seem like great pools of despair. His face held no laugh lines, and his mouth had a downturn cast to it from too many years of being sad. Jiao thought the scar lining the left side of Jack's face added to the air of great sadness and loss that held Jack in its embrace. Jiao knew if she had stayed in the service of her country in time, she would look like this. Alive and able to breathe and function but dead or dying inside. William stood and offered her the chair he'd been sitting in; when she had sat down, Tomas spoke.

"I have been in touch with London, and you have been offered asylum in our country. All they ask is you tell them about China's espionage training." The men all smiled at her and nodded their heads. Jiao knew they weren't trying to tell her what to do; this was more of a hopeful gesture. She only had one question.

"Will I be free, not in prison?" Jiao asked.

"As free as a bird," Tomas said, smiling and holding both her hands.

"In parts of China, birds are caged." She reminded them. Scott stepped to her side.

"You'll be as free as you could ever want." The big Scotsman said.

"Ok, now that we know, we're all going on the plane. We're going to have to be extra vigilant. The head of the C.I.A. in Hong Kong is out there somewhere, and I don't think him seeing us in Thimpu, and the Chinese sending Jiao to us is a coincidence." Jack reminded them.

"No, you are right. The group that runs China was talking to someone following you. He told the generals where you were to be found." Jiao confirmed what Jack suspected all along. Tran had noticed that Jack hadn't said 'to kill us' when he talked about Jiao. Tran watched the girl, and she lowered her head. Tran lost all he had known, but he thought all she had ever known was a lie, and now she has lost even that. Jack was asking a question,

"Which route do we take? Should we stay on NH24 and take it into New Delhi? Or should we take the southern route up the NH91 and come closer to the airport?" Tomas and William looked at the others and nodded to Jack.

"You've brought us this far; you're the leader of our little band of brothers and sisters. As far as we're concerned, it's up to you." Tomas said; Jerry and Scott seconded and third Tomas and William's sentiment.

"Well, Tran, what do you think?" Jack asked. Tran looked at the map spread out over the desk.

"If I wanted to wait for somebody, I would want a place that offered traffic but not too many locals," Tran said as he looked over the routes he had to choose from.

"NH24 has large stretches with no towns, farm traffic will be slight, this would be a good spot to attack." The Tibetan said. Jack watched as Tran's finger traced the route of the highway through Uttar Pradesh.

"That's what I was thinking, 91 has more towns on it, and it would offer more security." Jack offered. Tran didn't answer. He just placed his finger on Highway 91 and nodded. Jack looked at Jiao, and she nodded in agreement with Tran.

Chapter 77

FRESHLY SHOWERED AND with a fresh change of clothes, Chow banged on the wall separating the two rooms. He told the two mercenaries to come to his room. Chow was telling the Gunner and Ticker about the rifle he ordered for one of the men they were hunting.

"This was supposed to be for John Smyth; he was my go-to man for issues that come up with the competition in my business." The two mercenaries knew Chow as a very wealthy man. He had hinted at the fact he owned many companies. Chow never told the men why he was doing this job personally, and as long as the check cleared, they didn't care.

"It's the most beautiful fucking thing I've ever seen after we're done here. I'm going to buy one and have it hung in a frame." The big Aussie said as he rubbed the Walther WA2000.

"Listen, what do you guys think about Highway 91," Chow said as he taped his map with the manicured nail on his right index finger. Tinker looked at the map and then turned to Gunner.

"I've traveled that road a few times. It's packed full of local farmers with their wagons and tourist traffic, a real pain in the ass." Tinker offered, and Gunner nodded his head in agreement.

"If you're worried about it, there are roads connecting these two highways," Ticker said as he pointed to one that wasn't far from their motel.

"With that buggy of yours, you could scoot down and keep an eye out. If you see the fuckers then you call, and we kill." Chow looked at the map and looked out the window into the Indian night.

Jack explained he and Tran would get up at three am and have everything packed in the Toyota. Then they would get all the other men and Jiao up. Jack planned to be out of the hotel and on the road by three thirty am. He explained to the men they should be ready for a running fight if it came to that.

Jack went to the lobby of the hotel and, using their computer, found out that from Lucknow to New Delhi was almost five hundred kilometers. The trip would take seven and a half hours. If all went well, that was a big if they should be off the ground and on their way to England before lunch the next day...if all went well. Those four little words worried Jack 'If all went well' in his experience, when in the hell did it all go well. In his experience, 'it went all to hell' before 'it went well.'

Both Jack and Tran slept in twenty-minute stretches. These short naps were called combat naps. Some spec opp soldiers learned how to sleep this way. It helps to fight off fatigue while keeping the mind alert. Being trained to do this when he was young, Jack knew with lack of sleep, the risk of missing something that could mean life or death grew by the hour. It was the numbing of the mind, which Jack and Tran were worried about. Jack looked over at Tran and found his friend lying in the moonlit room, staring at the ceiling.

"We have four hours until we wake up; I'm going to go down to the lobby and read a newspaper. You grab two hours' sleep, and then I'll come up and go to bed while you keep watch in the lobby." Tran nodded to Jack. Leaving the room, Jack noticed Tran had rolled on his side and had slid his right hand under his pillow. Jack knew Tran's hand was beside the type 64 pistol he had hidden under it earlier. Tran was always ready; it didn't matter if it was a flat tire or a firefight, he was always prepared. Two hours of reading an American newspaper convinced Jack the world was just a mass of corrupt politicians and dirty cops. He tried to find one good news story, and even though he'd gone through the paper three times, he ended up folding it for the next person to be disappointed.

Tran rattled the doorknob twice, then opened the door. He found Jack sitting on the edge of the bed, rubbing the sleep from his face. Neither man said anything as they picked up the bags and backpacks from the small hall in the room and walked to the elevators after packing the gear on the roof of the Toyota and the duffle bags in the cargo space. Jack went back into the hotel to wake the others. Tran checked the oil level and the coolant level in the radiator. When the others walked out of the hotel, they could hear the rattling of the Toyota's diesel engine. Jack nodded to Tran, who stood by the back corner of the suv. Tran shook his head to indicate he hadn't seen anything out of the ordinary. The two men stood by the running Toyota, slowly looking around the hotel's parking lot.

Satisfied, Tran climbed behind the wheel while Jack closed the passenger side door. It took forty minutes to go around the city of Lucknow and then down a secondary road before reaching the highway NH91. Tran drove the first shift; he had been awake and drank three cups of coffee while reading an English newspaper in the lobby of the hotel.

The coffee had been particularly strong as it was an Indian blend, and the night clerk said it would keep the dead from falling down; the man wasn't lying. Jack smiled when he heard Williams light snoring. He knew leaving this early in the morning was hard on the men. Especially after the week they had suffered, it was almost over, and soon they would be safe. The men would be back in England with their loved ones. They knew the world press would be hounding them for their story, each station wanting an exclusive. The men would get the account of their ordeal out to the people.

It took Chow forty-five minutes to cover the one hundred and thirty kilometers from NH24 down State Highway 33 to NH91. Sitting in a small service station with a coffee shop attached to one end. He had left Gunner and Ticker at two thirty in the morning and arrived at this coffee shop at three fifteen. Watching the sun come over the horizon, Chow sipped his third cup of hot coffee. Gunner was going to check in at five and every hour on the hour until he spotted the Toyota. Sitting here, Chow thought of where in the world he would go when this was over. Bhutan was blown, and now he could never return to that country. It may be time to look at an island in the south pacific. Chow thought it was a little cliché for a man like him to want his own island, but he could see the advantage in it. The first advantage he could see was not having to worry about the law or politicians. The second was he could come and go as he pleased, and the third was that his private army would be unknown, and he could deploy them as he saw fit. Chow smiled as he thought about his own personal killers hunting down the heads of the B.B.C. for helping Jack and the others get out of China, then Bhutan.

Tran was amazed at how the road went from empty to crowded in less than an hour. Men with tractors and wagons stayed on the dirt shoulder of the highway, wanting to avoid being run over by the larger and much faster trucks. The traffic was thick but traveled well, only slowing to let a large truck off or too slow when one came on the road. Tran thought it was like breathing; it felt natural. Jack was starting to become unsettled and, for a moment, considered the Chinese and Chow might have given up. But he knew Chow and the thought of him or the Chinese giving up didn't feel right.

"What are you looking for?" Tomas asked.

"Something that doesn't belong," Jack answered.

"Like that sesame street game," Scott added from the back seat.

"Like what game?" Jack asked, looking over his shoulder.

"You've never heard of sesame street. Those men that had you are evil, like the emperor in star wars evil." Jerry told Jack.

"What the hell is a Star Wars, and who the hell is the emperor?" Jack asked as he looked out the windshield again.

"Oh my chum, the first thing we do when we get to London is to rent a video of star wars and make some popcorn," Scott said as he nodded to the others. Looking out the windshield, Jack was surprised to see a Porsche suv sitting in the dusty dirt parking lot of an all-night coffee shop and service station. A large truck, its driver tired of waiting for a break in the traffic, eased his truck onto the highway. This forced Tran to break hard to miss rear-ending the truck, and the men and Jiao were forced to brace themselves to keep from crashing into the seat backs in front of them. Jack no longer looked at the black Porsche; instead, he was surveying the interior of the café. Chow sat holding a cup to his lips, staring at the Toyota. The look of shock almost made Jack laugh; at the same time, Jack fought the urge to get out of the Toyota and open fire on Chow through the dinner's large front windows. Jack wanted to, but he needed to think of the men, along with Tran and Jiao. Then there was all with the innocent men and women in the dinner.

Chapter 78

THE BLARE OF A HORN and the sound of tortured breaks made Chow look up and straight at a cream color Toyota land cruiser. When Chow saw the suv, he was about to say got-ya, then he saw the face of the man sitting in the jump seat. Chow felt like he had been the one who had been gotten. Standing, Chow left the coffee shop and ran to his car. Dialing his phone, he told Gunner the Toyota and the men had taken NH91, and they had spotted him. Before Chow had hung up the phone, he heard the Humvee starting. The sound of the engine made him feel better. Chow smiled; he would have his way; John Smyth would be dead, and he could stop all this running around. He would stand over the body of Smyth and laugh.

"Chow, that bastard." Jack hissed through clenched teeth. Tran looked back through the rear-view mirror and saw a man running to the black suv.

"Bad news?" Tomas asked.

"Yeah, see that black Porsche pulling out of the service station; well, the man driving it was my station chief in Hong Kong. I think he's relaying our location to some people who want to stop us. I say stop us in the most permanent sense of the word, and the people are in Beijing." Jack said. Tomas and the rest of the men turned to watch the suv pull out onto the road. Jack was about to climb over the seats to get into the cargo space in the back of their vehicle. A heavy chuff came from behind the men. Looking into the back, he found Jiao holding one of the QCW-05s with the silencer on it. Jaio smiled and pointed to the Porsche as steam started to billow from under the hood. Turning, she rubbed Scott's hand.

"I am free; I will not go back." The petite Chinese woman said with determination. Tomas, William, Jerry, and Scott cheered Jiao for shooting the pursuing suv in the radiator. Jack watched as the former Chinese spy and assassin removed the clip from the weapon and ejected the round from the breach. He looked at her and then gave her a thumbs-up for her quick action.

Chow had seen the woman in the back of the Toyota. He saw her lift something, then he heard the heavy impact of the bullet; he knew what it was. Chow knew she had shot at his vehicle; steam belched from under the hood covering the windshield and obscuring Chow's vision. He never saw the second truck pull out of the cafe in front of him. Chow drove his Porsche into the rear end of the large vehicle. The impact wasn't at any great speed, but it was hard enough to deploy the airbags leaving Chow with a red face and a broken pair of sunglasses. Sitting in stunned silence, Chow could hear people trying to open the door of his car. Steam still whistled out from under the hood of the Porch. Chow reached up and hit the unlock button on the door and was helped from the car into the Indian morning.

After the local police finished the accident report, and asked Chow for the third time if Chow needed to go to the hospital. The two officers offered him a ride to the nearest car rental agency. The only car at the agency available was an older Alfa Romeo. When the woman asked what had happened to the other vehicle Chow had rented before, he told her of the truck, leaving out the part about being shot at. Chow agreed with the woman when she said the drivers of the trucks drove on the roads like they owned them. She told Chow her husband and son had been run off the road by a truck once. Chow played the part of the angry traveler; he agreed that the drivers were a hazard.

New Delhi was a madhouse. It was as if the whole city was on this one road. Tran drove in the middle lane of the highway, he wanted to drive on the outside lane, but every time he tried to move over, another car raced past.

"The Safdarjung airport is in the southeast part of the city, so you might as well stay in this lane," William told Tran. Tran looked as if he was afraid to take his hands off the wheel.

"Stay on 91 until you come to where 91 and 24 meet, then get on 24 until you come to the national highway. Get off and go west to fly over, then go north, and you'll see the airport on the left." William said. Tran and Jack tried to read the sign, which was impossible. If you slowed to read the signs, cars behind started blowing horns. If Tran didn't read the signs, he was afraid he would miss his turn. Tran was about to voice his belief the people who lived in this city were furious when they drove, and they should try meditation to see if it would calm them. At the very second Tran was about to start speaking, William shouted from the back seat to take the ramp to the right.

Chow called Gunner and told him the targets had indeed taken Highway 91 and were past him. When he explained what had happened, Gunner laughed and told Chow he and Ticker would race back to New Delhi and get the targets before they made it to the airport. Chow told them he would tell them what airport they needed to be at. It took over an hour, but at last. Chow found the only British diplomatic flight leaving New Delhi was flying out of the smaller Safdarjung airport. Chow called Gunner back and told him which airport to be at. Chow also told Gunner the flight was going to take off at one pm.

Tran accomplished the maneuver from Highway 91 to Highway 24 without killing anyone in the Toyota. He was very doubtful the big suv had been designed to make the kind of sudden lane change he made when William had shouted.

"TURN HERE!" Jiao must have thought it was funny because she giggled through the next kilometer. When Tran had pulled the steering wheel hard to the right to make the exit ramp from 91, Scott had been sitting beside Jiao. When the big Toyota leaned into the turn, she was forced to put her hand on Scott's thigh to keep from falling face-first into his lap. She giggled because she heard William tell Scott that he was a lucky bugger. The transition from 24 to the road called the national highway was smoother. Though Tran still was forced to cut off a taxi, Jerry told Tran not to worry about it. The taxi driver deserved it for the number of times he had cut others off.

Chapter 79

JACK KNEW WHATEVER Chow was up to wasn't going to stop just because Jiao put a bullet in his car. The closer they got to the airport and freedom, the more he worried about what Chow could be up to. William was telling Tran to take the next exit and go north to reach the airport. William was slammed forward into the back of the front seat, a fine mist of blood coating the windscreen. Jack heard the sound of bullets hitting the body of the Toyota, and out of nowhere came a black Humvee. Tran slammed his foot on the brakes and swerved to the right leaving the road and heading in the direction the Humvee had appeared from. Tran didn't want to travel with the black Humvee, so he cut behind the larger vehicle and away. Jiao watched as the big black Humvee completed a sliding turn and started after them. She opened the duffle bag and found the QCW-05 she used to shoot the other suv earlier. Slamming the clip back into the well, she racked back the bolt, chambered the first round, and set the weapon aside. Jiao found another one and handed it to Scott along with the clips, which he handed over to Jack's waiting hands. Jiao was proud of Scott. He placed himself on top of William, using his body to shield his friend and adding pressure to the wound to help stop the blood flow.

Gunner saw the Toyota and smiled when he saw one of the men in the suv crash into the seat in front of him, pushed there from the impact of his bullet. Ticker was going to ram the side of the Toyota, hoping to flip it over, but he missed when Tran swerved to the right, then cut behind them and out into a dirt soccer pitch.

When Jack looked into the back seat, he could see Scott taking his shirt off and pressing it over William's wound. Scott also had Tomas and Jerry on the floor of the Toyota and was using his body to cover William. As Tran fought to bring the Toyota back on the road, he drove through a shallow swale launching the heavy Toyota into the air. Another heavy landing and the ride became smooth again; both Tran and Jack could hear a new and heavy noise coming from under the suv. Jack couldn't worry about the noises coming from under their truck. He was watching Jiao as she looked at the Humvee grill. She was worried about the men in the Humvee, the men Chow hired to kill them, the men who were gaining on them again.

"I think it's the transfer case; it sounds like it's coming apart." Jerry was telling Jack. He was going to ask the producer if he wanted to get out and check the oil, then remembered these men were never in this situation before.

"When Tran swerved back there and left the road, we might have bottomed out and cracked it, then getting back on the road, well, that might have finished it," Jerry said. Jack never said a word; he just watched as the Humvee gained ground on them.

Jiao could see the man in the passenger side seat of the Humvee smiling at her as the heavy truck pulled up behind her. His smile turned to a look of shock when she raised the type 05 and opened fire on fully automatic. Jiao wasn't trying to kill them; Jiao thought she could shoot out the radiator like she had on the first car. The Humvee had an armored radiator, and when she realized this, Jiao knew what she had to do to protect the men that were going to save her. She wanted to go with Scott and the others to England. She had to save these men. The next four rounds hit the windshield on the driver's side of the Humvee. The bullets caused the glass to crack and distort, but none of the deadly sub-sonic rounds made it through the protective glass. Jiao could see the men in the Humvee laugh at her. Looking through the other duffle bag, Jiao came across the bullets

for the AMR-2 anti-materiel sniper rifle. Jiao knew what she needed
to do as she looked at the missile-like rounds for the rifle.

"Now, what the fuck do you think she's playing with there?"
Ticker asked Gunner as the two of them watched Jiao lift the big
duffel bag and start taking things out of it.

"Beats the hell out of me, but if you get a shot, take it. We'll
figure it out after this lot is dead." Gunner said as he aimed out the
window on his side of the Humvee. Gunner didn't care how most of
his victims died, just as long as he got paid to do the killing. In this
case, he wanted to kill Jack and the others for the million dollars and
a new rifle. That was all the motivation he needed.

Jack turned around so his back was against the dash of the
Toyota, sitting on the door facing backward; Jack took aim at the
side of the Humvee and fired when he saw the hand come out with
an Uzi in its grasp, unlike Jiao, who could use both hands and control
her weapon when she fired. Jack could only use his right hand to
hold onto the roof rack of the land cruiser, so when Jack saw the Uzi
fall amid a spray of blood, he was a little more than pleased with his
shot. Turning, Jack sat back in his seat and turned to find Jiao loading
the clip of the AMR-2.

"Give us some warning before you fire that thing, ok?" Jack said.
Jiao turned and smiled as she slapped the clip into the rifle well. "You
men the concussion of that rifle when she fires, it will feel like you've
been knocked out or just about in this confined space. You all must
keep your mouth open so the concussion wave can travel through
you more easily." When Jack had finished, he looked at each man to
make sure they understood.

"Holy fuck, mate, my arms busted. That fucker, he put a bullet
through my best tattoo." Gunner howled as he wrapped a pressure
bandage around the wound in his bicep muscle. Ticker was about to
tell Gunner he liked that tattoo when the round from the A.M.R.
rifle imploded the driver-side windshield of the Humvee. The round

and most of the windshield hit Ticker on the left side of his head. The impact of the bullet, along with pieces of the windshield, caused Ticker's head to explode, spraying the interior with blood, skull fragments, and chunks of brain matter. Gunner couldn't move for a second. The shock of losing the only friend he ever had in the world stunned him. It was in that brief second of indecision his life became forfeit. Gunner never heard the shot or saw the incredible muzzle flash, which indicated Jiao had fired the rifle for the second time.

Jiao knew when she gently squeezed the trigger for the second time her aim was true. She'd killed the driver, and Jiao wasn't proud or pleased she'd been able to use the rifle. Jiao knew for the men and her own safety, she did what needed to be done. Now she watched as the 12.7x108mm round exploded the head of the man in the jump seat. The two headless men wanted to kill her and her friends now they were safe, she hoped.

The Humvee started to gain ground on the wounded Toyota. Jack watched as the heavy black truck started to speed up. He was sure it was going to plow into the back of the Toyota. Just before the impact, the Humvee slowed and slowly turned to the right. It turned off the side of the road and into an empty dirt soccer pitch, where it drove in circles. Knowing the driver was dead, Jack knew his foot had forced the throttle to the floor and then slipped off the pedal. Second, if he had been driving with both hands, the way the American army taught, then one of his hands might have fallen off the wheel and caused the turn.

The men inside the land cruiser were shocked and deafened by the report of the heavy rifle. Jiao was dizzy and couldn't lift her head for a moment. When she could, she was amazed Tran still had them on the road, and he didn't seem to have slowed. Jiao knew Tran was tough, but she had more respect for him now. To be able to take the abuse of the report from the anti-material rifle in an enclosed space like the Toyota and keep going as if nothing had happened was incredible.

Tran could see the first sign for the airport, his head buzzed, and he thought he'd been deafened by Jiao firing the rifle inside the Toyota. Turning, Tran told Jack the airport was on the left. Jack turned to look back over his right shoulder. Tran tapped him on the shoulder to get his attention. Tran shouted about the airport, and Jack smiled and gave a thumbs-up. William was now lying across the laps of his friends; he tried to tell Tran to go to the last gate, which was for the chartered flights. Scott heard William through his ringing ears and relayed the message to Tran, who was looking at the airport fence, waiting for the gates to start. Tran nodded to Scott to show he heard him and drove on. Tran hoped the buzzing in his head would go away; it made it hard to concentrate on his driving.

Chapter 80

AN ARMED GUARD AND a fat man stood at the gate and waved the rattling, smoking, battered Toyota through. Tran drove right to a set of stairs positioned at the waiting plane. An Airbus A330-200F was converted, so it housed a small airborne surgical suite and diplomatic offices. As the group of escapees grabbed the equipment from the inside of the Toyota and ran for the cover the plane provided, Tran turned and patted their Toyota, thanking it for being so tough. Once inside the Airbus, introductions were made all around. Richard was the man waiting at the gate with the armed guard.

"This plane." Richard, the chosen representative of the British government, boasted. "Has better anti-war deterrents than the American air force one. If you were to fire a missile at it, the computers would trigger a change in the skin while firing chaff and flares from a rear compartment if the missile cleared the debris in the air. The plane would hold a different signature, and to the computer in the missile, it would be the wrong target. In this plane, there is also a computer that can counterman the weapons orders and return them to the point of origin, in the words of Elvis' return to sender." Richard finished. Jack knew it was all to make them feel better and safer.

"I like your plane, and we feel safe on it, but do you think we can get this show on the road," Jack said, looking out the window. Without saying a word, Richard picked up a phone and told whoever was on the other end to take off as soon as possible. Two royal medics had taken William back to the surgery. A royal air force surgeon waited with a portable X-ray machine and a surgical contingent. About a half hour later, one of the medics stood and spoke in whispers to Richard.

"I have good news; your friend William will make a full recovery, his injury while bad is being taken care of as we speak. The surgeon had x-rays and will be able to get the bullet. Also, he has sent word while your friend has sustained major trauma, he will be his old self in time. What will be the worst for him at his age is the broken shoulder and the clavicle. I can tell you from personal experience that bloody well hurts." Richard told everyone. Jack could see from the smiles on everyone's faces a great weight had been lifted off them.

"I think that deserves a toast," Scott said as he spied a stocked bar. Even the rotund Richard gave a 'here here.' Sitting in one of the plush chairs equipped on this plane, Jack was wondering why they hadn't started to taxi yet when the sound of the idling engines changed. Looking out the window on his side of the plane, Jack started to laugh when he saw a security guard standing beside the open driver's door of the Toyota, scratching his head. Behind him, Jack could hear what sounded like keys being jingled on a key ring. Turning, Jack Found Tran holding up his set of keys for the Toyota; reaching into his pocket, Jack found his set.

"Didn't want it to be stolen," Tran said, and both the men started to laugh.

"In a way, I'm going to miss her. I think I'll try to find one like it in England." Jack said as he looked at the battered Toyota.

Chow passed a crowd on a soccer pitch; he thought it was just another game starting until the police cars converged from all directions. When the group stepped back, Gunners and Ticker's black Humvee was reviled. From the amount of red Chow could see on the windows, he knew the men were dead. The Alfa couldn't get Chow to the chartered gate fast enough. Chow found the gate locked, and he was forced to watch from the outside of the gate the plane he hoped the escapees would never catch take off.

Chow knew he was really fucked now, Mike was dead, and John had gotten away. Standing there watching the plane gain speed and then lift its nose into the air, Chow knew he would have to give up on his plans of staying in Bhutan. Moreover, he would have to move way off the edge of the map, or he would never feel safe.

Standing in the growing heat of the day, Chow cursed out loud. John, he had ruined everything. John's sense of right and wrong has fucked it all up. Now, the bastard was out of reach.

Chapter 81

JACK WATCHED THE TOYOTA, and then something caught his eye. Someone was standing at the gate to the chartered area. Jack knew he could never make out the face of the man standing by the gate; in his heart, Jack knew it had to be Chow at the entrance. The bastard never quit trying to kill him and his friends. Jack knew killing Chow wasn't the answer. Chow wouldn't suffer doing that. Instead, Jack knew what would hurt Chow most was taking his wealth. Jack smiled and knew exactly what he was going to do. Jack looked around for Richard.

"Is there a place where I can get some privacy and a computer with banking access?" Jack asked Richard. Richard being a true gentleman, led Jack to his personal office. After the door was closed, Jack started with the computer. An hour after he sat down, Jack opened the door to find Richard sitting in a chair across the hall.

"Did you get to finish what you started?" Richard asked, smiling.

"Yes, yes, I did. When we land in London, how about I take you and the others out for a great meal in the best restaurant in the city." Jack offered. Richard sat looking at him. Richard wanted to ask Jack how he could afford to be so kind. Richard knew it would be right or proper to ask about a man's finances.

"I know a place. They seat the Queen and the Duke." Richard offered. Jack just nodded and went back to see his friends. He wouldn't ask the man about his finances; a gentleman wouldn't. The spy in Richard wasn't above snooping, and besides, he was an incurable busybody. Richard knew it, and he smiled as he sat at the computer in his office. He tried to recall the history. All Richard could find were bank names. Jack took the time to expunge the numbers from memory. Richard smiled. Whoever was chasing Jack and the others through Asia had just lost more than they knew. Richard wished he could be a fly on the wall when whoever had been chasing Jack, and the others found out what they had lost. Richard looked at the monitor on the wall of the office. It showed the cabin of the plane. He smiled when he saw Jack look up at the camera and wink at him.

"Cheeky bugger," Richard said as he laughed.

Chow didn't want to drive back to the town of Baghdogra. Walking into the charter office of the Safdarjung airport, Chow found a small company going to fly to the city. With his ticket in hand, Chow watched the Indian countryside pass below the wing. He started to get a hunted feeling, how this could have happened, John Smyth goddamn the day that bastard walked into his life. This was Mike's fault. He found John and trained him; Mike did this. He could see his Stratos sitting in the bright sunlight; he smiled when he thought about flying to some remote island in the south pacific or maybe to South America. First, he would have to go back to Bhutan and collect the rest of his things.

Chow stopped and thought for a second, then he smiled; he could always buy new things. He had all he needed. All the rest of it was dead weight right now. Before Chow left the ground in India, he called one of the banks where he had an account and thought he would explode. When he reached this bank, a computer handled his call. It was a service Chow chose so his voice couldn't be remembered. Now, this service told him he had withdrawn everything from the account and closed it. Sitting in stunned silence, Chow looked at his cell phone. The computer thanked him for his business and disconnected the call. This account once held two hundred and fifty-five million Euros, and it was gone. Who could have done it? He was the only one who knew the account number and the passwords to get into it. Chow felt like he was being held underwater and drowning. Chow dreaded what he was going to find out. Looking at his cell phone, Chow pressed the icon and called another bank. Chow knew what he would find before he started, as if, by foresight, Chow was rewarded with the answers he expected. One by one, Chow called banks all over the world, and one by one, he found his accounts had been drained and closed. The computers would thank him for his business and disconnect. While the banks still had real people answer their phones, Chow would try to tell them there had to be a mistake. However, like the computers, his indignation would fall on deaf ears. By the time Chow had hung up on the last bank, he had decided it would be better if he left the rest of the clothes he had in Bhutan there. It was almost as if he was a non-person, he didn't have a country, and now all he had was the cash he had stashed in the interior of his plane. Chow knew he had enough money to get set up where ever he would end up. Once he had everything set up, he would start to hunt down John and the rest of the men with their families just for pissing him off and stealing from him. Also, Chow thought this was the perfect time to reorganize his operation and make it more streamlined.

Chapter 82

JIAO LOOKED OUT THE window and could see a blue sea below; on the sea, she could make out specks. As she looked closer, Jiao could tell the specks were the white sails of large yachts plying for the wind over the water.

"What is that water down there?" Jiao asked Richard as he was walking past.

"That, my dear, is the romantic Caspian sea, home of the rough and romantic," Richard said as he pretended to have a sword. The others watched as Richard stopped and spoke in hushed tones with Jack. Jack explained to Richard about Ben what Ben told him about finding out about a C.I.A. official in Hong Kong.

"I think that official was Chow. I can't prove it, but I'd put money on the fact he sold me out to Trang, and I bet he sold out Ben too." Jack finished.

"I'll tell MI-6 they should tell the Americans about their breach. When we contacted them earlier, they said this Chow is presumed killed in a plane crash in the East China Sea." Richard said. Jack could tell by the look on Richards's face he didn't buy their story.

"I have one more question," Jack said. "How long did it take to find the body, and how bad was it torn up?" Jack asked. When he finished, Jack could tell the answer before Richard even started to speak.

"I couldn't tell you; a body hasn't been recovered. Do you want to know something strange? No aircraft pieces have floated to the surface, no evidence of fuel on the water, nothing." Richard finished.

"Sounds like the cleanest plane crash in history; sounds like Chow is always neat and tidy." Jack finished.

"Quite," Richard said.

Chow took a heading south and east after he took off from the airport. He knew where he wanted to go. A small group of islands in the south pacific, the biggest being Fiji. He loved Fiji, and with the money he had stuffed in the panels of his Stratos and his fake identity, he could live like a king. Chow decided he could run his empire from Fiji and regain his fortunes. Then he would have an army hunt down John Smyth. He would have him brought back to Fiji and skinned alive for stealing from him. Southeast to Fiji, making sure to avoid Burma.

"What's that ocean called?" Jiao asked Tomas as she looked out the window. Tomas looked out the window and could see the water.

"I think that's the Black Sea, yes it the Black Sea," Tomas confirmed his thought when he saw the Sea of Azov to the north.

"When we see the land again, we should be over Romania, then it's straight across Europe to London. Of course, it will be dark for most of the trip over Europe, some of the cities, you'll be able to see their lights. Paris looks like a gem glowing under its lights, and the Eiffel Tower with its lights pointed straight up." Jiao watched as the water passed far below the plane. She wished Scott were sitting with her. She liked the man, he was big, taller than Jack, and she felt like Scott liked her even though she hurt him. The doctor came and took him to tend to his wound. Jiao wanted to go, but the doctor told her he was safe and would be back in no time. Jiao was worried, Scott had gone with the surgeon an hour ago, and she was scared something had gone wrong. Just when Jiao decided she was going to go and look for Scott, she watched him walk through the door and smile at her. Jiao could tell the doctor had fixed the damage she had inflicted on his face. Before she could stop herself, Jiao felt tears running down her cheeks again.

Richard stood in front of them and gave them a basic itinerary.

"When we land, the press will be waiting for William, Tomas, Jerry, and you, Scott. Now William will have to be carried off the plane; that should work in our favor. Now as for questions, answer only simple ones like how you're feeling and stuff like that until you've been debriefed. Now, as for Jack, Tran, and Jiao, I hate to do this to you, but the three of us will have to wait until the press gets tired and leaves. Once the press leaves the area, then and only then will you three be able to leave. We don't want the Chinese or the Americans to know you're with us immediately. We would like them to think you stayed behind in India. Jiao, we don't know if China knows you're alive or if they think you're dead." When Richard finished, he looked at the group, then turned and sat down.

Scott sat with Jiao; she held onto his arm as she finally fell asleep. The others looked at Scott and Jaio; all the men smiled, hoping something good was coming out of something so bad.

Scott touched Jiao's arm when the lights of Paris came into view. As she woke, Scott pointed out the window, smiling. Jiao was amazed she could see the lights of the city the world dubbed the city of love. Jiao hoped they might even be able to see the L'Arc de Triomphe, she doubted it, but she could hope. When Jiao was a little girl, her mother showed her pictures of the Arch. Jiao would draw pictures of it, and her mother would hang them in their small apartment. Jiao remembered her father would tear up the drawings when he came home. After her mother had died, Jiao's father came home and packed her things. He turned Jiao over to the military for training. The bastard gave her away, but she had gotten out, despite everything she had gotten out. Jiao couldn't believe how someone with red hair and freckles could be so hansom. The doctor looked at Scott's face. He told Scott the laceration in his Masseter muscle needed to be fixed before he used a skin glue to close the wound. Jiao was looking at him when he leaned forward and kissed her. With the help of his medic, the doctor repaired the damage to his face, and Jiao thought he was even more handsome than before her bullet had hurt him. She found the tears flowing down her cheeks again as she remembered trying to kill these good men. When Jiao was a little girl, she wanted to draw all the great things in the world. They had taken her mother away from her and tried to turn her into a killer, like her father. Scott brushed her tears away and kissed her for the second time. Jiao knew she was falling in love with him.

Richard announced they would be landing in twenty minutes and that they should put anything away they had taken out. The lights of London seemed to be brighter in the gloom of the English morning. Jack and Tran watched the English coast appear as if by magic out of the channel. Jiao watched with Scott beside her as the ground started to rise to greet them. Twenty minutes on the nose, the plane touched down on the number one runway at London's Gatwick Airport. As Richard had promised, the press was there.

Not only the English press was there. Press from around the world, also the leading American daily news program, had its London office broadcasting life from the terminal, as well as the Canadian, the French, and the German. These stations didn't have the deep pockets of the Americans but made up for what they lacked in quantity with quality. Richard could see the Japanese press behind them. The official Chinese embassy delegation standing off to the side, waiting to call the men from the B.B.C. liars. The official line when Jack did not come out of the plane would be that this was a pack of lies. Thought up by the B.B.C. to increase world anger about China being in Tibet.

When the plane came to a stop at the terminal, William was the first to be wheeled off it on the surgical gurney at the sight of the older man with his chest wrapped in bandages, lying pale under the blue institutional blankets. The press started shouting questions as William and the two medics were forced to squint amide the blitz of flashes from the photo gallery. To make a good show of it, William weakly raised his hand and waved to the press before the medics rushed him to a waiting ambulance.

Tomas, Scott, and Jerry stood and answered some easy questions from their international colleagues. Richard was standing beside the men watching the crowd. The reporters had been told the men couldn't answer any questions about being held captive in a Chinese detention center. Only when the four of them had been debriefed would all the answers come out? This didn't stop some reporters from shouting questions asking which detention center and where they had been held. At these questions, the Chinese delegation tried to push through the crowd of reporters and disrupt the arrival of the returned men. This action brought a dozen heavily armed security men into the shoving match. The Chinese quickly realized they couldn't win. When the shoving settled down, the Chinese were, in front of every news agency in the world, ordered to leave the airport grounds. While William had been whisked away in an ambulance. Tomas, Jerry, and Scott walked out and stood blinded in the epileptic-inducing flashes of the press gallery. MI-5 had brought limousines' to take the men to where they would be staying. Richard told them their families were brought there earlier in the day and briefed on what to expect in the coming days.

"What about Jack, Tran, and Jiao? Where will they be taken?" Scott asked. Richard looked at him and smiled, knowing his biggest concern was Jiao. He could see something was growing between the two young people.

"They will be coming as soon as the press is out of the way. We have to debrief them a little differently than you men. Just because they are military and involved in the fighting, they would tend to see things differently." Richard explained.

"I can tell you they did see things differently," Scott said. "When the bullets started to fly, the four of us started to look for a place to hide." When Scott finished as he and his two friends laughed.

Jiao stood at one of the plane's windows and watched as the last of the news vans started and drove out of the parking lot. She motioned to Jack as a large man entered the plane.

"I think that's the last of them; if you want, we should leave now. I can get you to the designated housing arrangement in time for the morning tea service." When you listened to the man speaks, he sounded like he was raised with money. Never had to work a day in his life, however. When you looked at him, a different picture came to mind, this man was tough, but not in a boastful way. He knew what he could do and was comfortable with his abilities.

"Can you tell us where we're going?" Tran asked.

"No sir, I am under orders. What I can tell you is it's not military." Tran nodded and led them down the steps and out to a waiting car. The driver of the car seemed intent on seeing if he could break every speed limit ever posted in London. Jack wanted to ask the driver of the car if he was trying to set a new record from the airport to wherever it was they were going, but he managed to restrain himself. Tran, on the other hand, had asked to sit in the front, and their armed escort allowed it. Now Tran was holding to the dash and smiling ear to ear. The broader Trans smiled, the faster the driver seemed to try to go. At one point, when the driver turned left onto the A3212 and Parliament Street, Jack thought the tires would break loose off the blacktop, and they would spin out of control into the parked cars. The driver smiled and nodded to Tran as he brought the car to a stop in front of the hotel. The world-famous Dorchester Hotel, Jiao looked at the front of the famous building. The front of the walk was covered in red and white roses; Jack opened the door and held it for her. Richard met them in the lobby and handed each of them the keys to their room.

"Each of you will be debriefed in his or her rooms; we will do this in two-hour sessions, so you don't become exhausted. I hate to tell you this, but we will have to sequester you three in the hotel. We are worried that Chow Yang might leak your photos to the press. So while you are here, we will do anything we can to get you everything you may need or want." Richard finished. He gestured to the man who had brought them from the airport. Jack started to follow one of the escorts assigned to keep Tran, Jiao, and himself from falling into the hands of the ratings-hungry press.

Jack knew with the indigent cry of 'the people have the right to know!' then the inaudible. 'Whatever we think they will gorge themselves on the longest.' The glory hounds from any of the three-letter acronyms, once the bastions of government security agencies, would happily broadcast their whereabouts to the world. Then when one or all of them ended up dead, they would hold their hands in the air and feign sorrow and outrage at the lack of government security. While on the evening news, some talking head would, for about the required ten seconds, look sadly into the camera and claim sorrow for the loss, then onto the weather.

Jack has never been in front of the press or the cameras. One time in Japan, he used an American reporter to find his target. The woman sat at a table in a quaint little Americanised restaurant. She ranted about how this and all the governments would someday realize what the press wanted they get. Nodding his head, Jack remembered saying.

"The people have a right to know." Though he said it, he did not believe it.

"The people don't know shit; they hear what we tell them. They believe what we think they should. The people are like cattle marching along chewing their cud, happily stupid. We say turn, and they turn with no questions. When something bites us in the ass, well, we say it came from a government source, and like magic, it's all fixed." When the reporter finished telling Jack how dumb the general public was. Jack told her of some new information he had on a guy, how this prick was being let off with human trafficking in Japan for his testimony on a federal organized crime back in the good old U.S. of A. Once the prick finished, the government was going to put him in the witness relocation program. When Jack told the reporter the U.S. government traded some hacker for the piece of shit, she was almost frothing at the mouth for the story. Jack watched as the reporter grabbed her cell phone and almost ran out the door. Jack followed the reporter to the safe house the embassy set up to protect his target. Jack didn't know how the reporter knew where the safe house was, and he didn't care. Jack remembered the small man who told him this reporter bragged about knowing where all the safe houses were around Tokyo.

After the reporter was drug off by the F.B.I. Jack waited and watched as they started to move their witness; they were sloppy. The human trafficker looked like the agents drug him out of bed by his hair. The man was scared and stumbling; one of the agents stood the prick by the car door while he fished out the keys. One shot, and it was all over; when Jack remembered this operation, he knew this one made a difference. The man he killed was responsible for the kidnapping and wholesale of little girls on black markets throughout the Middle East and Asia. Once caught, the bastard ratted out others, so he wouldn't have to go to prison. As for the reporter, Jack went back to see her. She was shocked when the man who had given her a great story showed up at her door. Jack remembered knocking her out and giving her heroin. While unconscious, he placed the reporter in a tub of hot water and held her head underwater. The reporter's autopsy read drugs and accidental drowning. He remembered the reporter. Jack knew her family buried her thinking their daughter had fallen into drugs. They would never know the truth.

Chapter 83

FIJI, CHOW COULD SEE the islands that make up the archipelago of the small country. Chow landed at Nausori on the island of Fiji; he was going to be calling Suva home from now on. This tropical paradise would serve him well; here, Chow was unknown, and he would keep it that way. While circling the island, Chow contacted the people holding key positions in his organization. When these men heard where Chow's new base of operations was, he could tell they thought this was odd. These men couldn't understand why Chow would want to live so far from his empire. Chow explained it was safer for him to be removed from his empire. Chow listened as one man stood out from the rest. Li, as the rest said they understood Li said nothing. He looked at the others sitting around the table. He noted most of the men smiled at each other, scheming.

Chow trusted none of the people working for him. He knew all of them and hand-picked each one. Out of all of them, Li had the best returns on his product. He would personally cut the hand off anyone he caught stealing. If Li caught one of his sellers using the product, he killed that seller and gave another a chance to make money. Chow heard Li had two hundred young men and women waiting for the opportunity to sell for him. Chow liked Li mainly because the man didn't look like a drug dealer; also, Li had no criminal record, so he could travel. Thanks to some friends Chow made in the governments around the world, he was able to gain a waiver on his visa. This waiver allowed him to stay in the country of Fiji indefinitely. The waiver also allowed him to come and go as he pleased, so long as he upheld the laws of the government and nation of Fiji. Chow decided to make one last call before he landed in Fiji.

"Li, I want you to come to Fiji, but before you do, I want you to gather all the family together. I'll teleconference again, but I'll give you the time to do so." Chow ordered. Li agreed to the time and place he told Chow he would have the heads of the family ready. After Chow landed and cleared customs, he met his real estate agent, who drove Chow to the new house he bought on Queen Elizabeth Drive in the capital of Suva. When Chow stood in the driveway of the large home overlooking the Pacific Ocean, he smiled. He could smell the salt air and the tropical flowers; Chow placed both hands on his hips. This was going to be where he ran his empire and hunted down John Smyth; he would kill everyone who stood in his way.

The next day Li and the other men Chow picked to run different aspects of his empire sat around a table waiting for their boss to call over a secured teleconference line. At twelve on the dot, Chow's face appeared on the monitor in the middle of the oversized teak table.

"I know some of you have been wondering what I am doing moving to Fiji," Chow said as he looked at the men on the high-definition television in his living room on the island of Suva.

"Well, I have decided I needed a break away from work and Hong Kong. I'm still close enough to get things done, as well as hearing things. I am far enough away that I am kept apart from it in the eyes of the law." Chow stopped and looked at each man around the room.

"I have heard some of you men here are not happy with the way the allotments have been handed out in the past? I want everyone to be happy, so I have sent Li out to get a hat. The allotments will be drawn out of that, fair?" Chow asked. The men around the table all smiled at the thought of getting more drugs and guns to sell. The men watched as Li returned with a large cowboy hat for the draw. Some laughed, and a few of the others rubbed their hands together. Chow looked at the greedy men; all were smiling. The smiles dropped from their faces when Li dropped the hat revealing a Heckler and Koch 9mm sub-machine gun with a fat silencer attached to the barrel. The first man at the table never heard the working of the bolt as the automatic weapon cycled, spitting 9mm bullets through his head. Before the thirty-round clip was empty, all the men at the table were lying on the floor, dead or dying. Those trying to hitch their way across the floor like a broken insects, Li finished with a bullet to the back of their heads.

"You have your men in place?" Chow asked as Li used a rag to wipe the blood from the monitor.

"Yes, they will take over all the operations before sunset. The ones who change with us will find a home in your new, more streamlined organization, those who don't." Li never finished his sentence. He looked down at the floor and shot a man who was not dead yet. Li reaffirmed he would be in contact with Chow at nine am sharp with news of how the night went. Chow thanked him for his loyalty and disconnected the call. Chow smiled; part one complete of his plan was completed.

Chapter 84

JACK KNEW THE DEBRIEFING started with Tran; he knew he would be next. Jiao, he thought they would save for last, her being a Chinese-trained spy. She was happy to be here and explained she only took the orders to kill them. Hoping she might get a chance at freedom. Hell, Jack couldn't blame her; he had done a lot worse for a lot less. Jack was sitting on his bed, trying to remember some of the people he had killed. The ones he knew who were actual targets, terrorists, or like the man in Japan. People were so evil they needed killing when a polite knock came on the door. When Jack answered it, he found a room service attendant pushing a lunch cart covered with a variety of light sandwiches and pastries, then a second cart with beverages. The portly Richard followed along with another man and a third who carried a laptop computer and a large briefcase.

"I hope everything is to your satisfaction Jack," Richard asked. He looked around the room, noting the bed was sharply made. Richard could tell Jack had been sitting on the bed; he hardly disturbed the covers. Richard had also noted housekeeping had yet to make it to Jack's room.

"Things are fine, thank you, Richard," Jack said. Richard made introductions around then Jack offered the men a seat at a table that had been set up.

"Jack, I don't like it, but MI-6. The people who run it want all the people to be hooked to a polygraph machine. Now if you refuse, they can't force it, but they will turn you out in the cold; you would be persona non grata." Richard said as the man with the polygraph machine set up. Richard and Jack talked in the corner of the room,

Jack could tell Richard felt awkward about the polygraph, so he changed the subject of their conversation.

"How is Tran doing?" Jack asked.

"Oh, he's doing well, we got him one of those video game consoles, and he's having a time of it." Richard chuckled. "You know he made us wait until he finished a race," Richard told Jack. The MI-6 man with the polygraph machine cleared his throat to signify he was ready. Jack and Richard went to the table, and the MI6 technician placed the sensors on Jack. Once satisfied with his readings, Richard started to ask questions.

"Is your name John Smyth?" Richard asked.

"No," Jack answered, and the man with the polygraph nodded.

"No? Well, could you tell me your name, please?" Richard asked.

"Jack." Was his answer.

"Jack, Jack, what?" Richard asked.

"Just Jack for now. When I find out more, I'll let you know." Richard smiled. He was starting to like this man's personality, short straight, and to the point. Behind it, there was a dry sense of humor.

"What was your job in Hong Kong, and who did you work for?" Richard asked.

"I would kill any supposed threat to the security of the U.S. and her allies. I was attached to the C.I.A., and my section chief was Chow Yang." Jack answered as he stared at the floor.

"Who captured you, and where did they take you?" Richard asked.

"I was grabbed by General Trang of the P.L.A., as for where they took me. I still don't know the name of the place; all I know was that it was by a large river." Jack answered as he recalled the bush he hid under. Then he remembered the face of the soldier who found him under the bush. He knew it had been Tran who let him go. Richard asked his questions, the nameless man with the polygraph kept nodding, and the other man stood by the door. Two hours later, and good to his word, Richard announced they would pick up the debriefing in the morning.

Tran and Jack wanted to watch a movie. Both men were tired of fighting and killing, and Tran and Jack decided they wanted to see a comedy. Richard apologized. He was afraid of Chow out in the world someplace. Along with the world news, hounds looking for him and the others. There would be no way he could guarantee their safety. Feeling bad for the escapees, Richard brought in a stack of movies, all classic comedies. The three men sat watching movies until after midnight. The next morning was a repeat of the day before.

"After you and Tran joined up together, what was your first target?" Richard asked.

"General Trang, for me, for Tran, it was the Colonel that had killed his family," Jack answered. The way the questions came and went, Jack, felt they were just filling time until Richard asked the real question. The one the power people wanted the answer to.

"Why did you help the journalists when you were hurt and didn't know if you could get them out?" Richard asked.

"After being in the hands of the Chinese army and their brand of questioning, well, I couldn't let others go through that, hurt or not, I had to try," Jack replied.

"You killed two men at the first roadblock. Was it then you realized you needed to get out of the country. If so, why didn't you try and find a radio and call for help?" Richard asked as he cleaned his glasses.

"I knew long before we killed those two at the roadblock we needed to get out of Tibet, as for calling for help. The Chinese military would have found us before the good guys." Jack said.

"How did you get into Bhutan?" When Richard asks Jack, the man from MI6 looks up from his computer. Jack looked at the man from MI6, then at the guard who stood stoically with his back to the door.

"Because the Chinese don't care for their men like other countries, the men don't care to suffer any more discomfort than is necessary. So when the storm hit, I knew it would be a good time to cross the river at night." Jack answered. The rest of the morning, Jack responded to questions about Bhutan and how he came to choose their path through the small country. How he came to own the Toyota, if they had left any evidence behind that could lead the Chinese to England.

"No, I don't think so; hell, I still have the keys to the Toyota," Jack said. He pulled his set of keys from his pocket with a chuckle.

Li couldn't believe there was a place on earth like Fiji. He'd seen the national geographic programs on television. This was far better than watching any program on television. He couldn't smell the ocean salt air, or the tropical flowers on T.V. Li watched as the main road along the ocean curved to the right. The azure sea, with its white-capped waves, rolled to the island. Li thought of a worshipper bowing to its goddess. Chow stood on the veranda of the home he bought, standing in cotton slacks and a white oversized cotton shirt. Chow let the onshore wind whip his hair around his head. Chow greeted Li and offered him a chair; Li bowed and sat in the offered chair.

"Everything is as you wanted; the others are dead and gone, and now the only people you want are running your empire," Li reported.

"Also, new bank accounts have been set up," Li told Chow as he handed over all the account information. "The first deposit was made this morning. You were right to suspect some of the others were stealing from you." Li said as he handed over their bank account information. Chow stood and walked to the edge of the veranda; he looked over the water.

"Li, I am going to promote you to the second spot. Mike Styles was my right hand; now it is you. I will pay you what I paid Mr. Styles. For this post, you must give up your ring to someone you trust, only to the person you trust the most." Chow told Li. When he turned, Chow found Li on his knees with his head bowed. Going over to the man. Chow sat down in front of the man and held his chin, forcing Li to look at him.

"All the rings of the family are your responsibility, and you're in charge. You answer only to me, but all answer to you." Chow said. Then Li stood and walked down to the water's edge.

"Like the accounts before, you must set up a tax differed bank account and a corporation with a preferred charity. I know some accountants who work wonders in the U.S. and other countries. We have a lot of work to do; with your hard work and diligence, it will pay off." Chow finished as the men stood, letting the waves lap at their feet. "This world will be ours once we have regained all stolen from us. Only then will we go after the people responsible and kill them and all they hold dear." Chow stated with Li smiling at his side.

Chapter 85

Truth

ON THE THIRD AND FINAL day of the debriefing, the questions came and went. The only time the rhythm of the questions and answers stalled was when Jack answered why he hadn't just killed Jiao.

"I thought I saw something vulnerable when I looked at her. I knew she had been sent to kill us. When I had her at the end of my weapon as I was starting to take up the trigger slack, I could see something else in her. She looked like a child, one told to do something, something she knew was wrong." Jack said. He looked out the window into the courtyard at the back of the Dorchester.

"Did you know she came up with the plan to ambush you?" Richard asked.

"Oh, I have no doubt, especially when she told us after we brought her along," Jack said to Richard's amazement.

"However, the thing we can't understand is why you would help a woman sent to kill you. To stop you from escaping the grasp of the county so desperate to secure your deaths, they were willing to breach the sovereignty of another country?" Richard asked.

"It was just our way of thumbing our noses at the bastards," Jack said as he smiled. Richard nodded to the man with the polygraph and smiled. Jack watched as the MI6 technician started to pack his computers up.

"Well, that should just about do it," Richard said to Jack

Jack had a sneaking suspicion that was the only question that really meant anything to Richard and those he answered to.

"How is Jiao? Will we be seeing her soon?" Jack asked.

"Jiao is happy, and she has already given us so much insight into the training and deployment of the Chinese espionage unit. Though her insight is limited to personal knowledge and training. When she is through, she is offered a job with the government. Nothing involves a security clearance, but it pays well, and she can have a good life. You needn't worry about her; Scott won't let her out of his sight." Richard told Jack.

"Good, that's good; I hope she does well for herself," Jack said. He noticed the polygraph operator had left the room, but the guard still stood at the door. Richard stood by the cart, choosing sandwiches for himself. When he had what he wanted, the portly man turned and looked at the guard.

"It's really a lovely lunch cart; help yourself, young man." Being a true professional, the young guard at the door thanked Richard and never moved a muscle toward the cart.

"Jack, I come from this country, and I love my homeland and all it stands for. Now, my family has money and the name to back it up. My family is the house of Windsor." Jack saw the young guard's face tighten at the news that Richards's last name was Windsor.

"While I was called to help bring you here to England, I don't work for the English government; I work for and head a branch of the United Nations. This branch is separate from the sitting counsel in New York; it was convened in secret shortly after the creation of the U.N. Four of the founding Nations knew when the politicians were brought together. The work needing to be done around the world would be left for discussion and disruptions." Richard said as he sat down.

"We are funded by these founding countries and manned by those same countries. This branch has secret locations around the world; these locations are in areas we have needed to intercede in over the years." Richard said. Jack noticed this revelation didn't have the same effect on the guard as Richard, a member of the House of Windsor, did.

"So, why tell me?" Jack asked.

"I know you must be disillusioned at how the C.I.A. used you and destroyed your past, but I think I can help you. We have the best regressive hypnosis therapist in the world working with us." Richard said as he looked into the teapot.

"So you want me to let you get in my head and see if there's anything left of my past," Jack stated. Richard sipped his coffee and looked at Jack, nodding.

Chapter 86

CHOW'S BANK ACCOUNTS started to grow, but he had a long way to go before he would be back to the billions of dollars he had lost. When he told Li about how he was betrayed and how he knew his enemy was hunting for him. Li said, for now, they should concentrate on growing. In the future, they could exact revenge when least expected, hunt down the man who dared to go against him. Chow knew Li wasn't any more intelligent than Mike had been.

Unlike Mike, Li was patient, which was worth more in the end. Fiji was good for Chow. He had two women come clean his house and cook his meals. He found an Australian woman who lived in Fiji. She stayed after the spat between her native country and the Fijian government in 08. She stayed to help the school system, for the kids, as she put it. They sat and talked on Chow's veranda; she would tell him about growing up in Melbourne. He would tell her about being an air force brat and not staying in one place long enough to make friends. This lie served two purposes, one, she wouldn't ask about his past so much; two, it negated the need to remember a bunch of lies that could trip him up later. As for his money, he told her he had made it big in the dot com boom of the eighties. Then before the bottom fell out of it, he had a dream, and the next day he sold out and reinvested everything in a small diamond outfit.

The small company then found one of the most extensive diamond deposits in Canada's North West Territories. To finish up his story, Chow told her when he wanted to retire, people he didn't even know tormented him day and night. Each one wanted money for this venture or that venture, each scam worse than the one before.

Therefore, with his money and contacts, he could pull some strings and move to Fiji. Now his banker flew to him once a quarter and filled him in on his investments. This lie covered everything Chow thought, the money, his being here, and it allowed him to donate money to the education system in Fiji. It wasn't that Chow cared about the kids; hell, he could care less if the little beggars could read or not, but it made him look good. Chow smiled as he thought about the money; with his money, he funded the building of a school and greeted some of the island's highest-ranking natives and politicians. Chow always told them of the beggars he left behind in the United States, and this is why he asked no pictures be taken of him, with the kind of money and how he was helping the children. The elders and politicians were happy to oblige him, and no pictures of Chow were taken.

Jack relaxed in the oversized plush chair; Richard brought him to this office and told him little of the man he was going to see. Richard said this doctor was the best man in the world at reaching back into the past and letting the person remember what had happened. Richard said doing this would let Jack start to heal. Jack looked at the television, then he turned and looked at the stack of paperback books in the center of a small table. It wasn't that Jack didn't like T.V.; it was he couldn't stand what some asshole termed a reality show infesting the cable networks. Jack refused to watch something so far from reality that one would have to suffer from the worst kind of delusions to think it was close to reality; he usually opted for a good book.

Jack found he had an affinity for Louis L'Amour and the tremendous Western panoramas his stories painted. His favorite of all the stories Mr. L'Amour inked was those of the Sackett family. It was something about the triumph of a family's love for each other over the lust for wealth that drew Jack to these stories. Jack was just going to start to thumb through a book when a smaller man walked through the door of the office and sat across from Jack in an identical chair. Jack hated to be the one to open any conversation, so he waited for this newcomer to start.

"Your name is Jack." The man said. It hadn't sounded like a question, so Jack didn't answer. "My name is Phillip Peters, and I'm here to try and help you remember who you were." The man said.

"You said to try and help. Aren't you going to help?" Jack said, looking at Phillip.

"It's up to you and how much damage has been done to your noodle." He stated, pointing at Jack's head.

"Damage, what do you mean damage?" For the first time, Jack wondered if this man knew something he didn't. Phillip stopped writing in his folder and looked at Jack; he uncrossed his legs and sat forward in his chair.

"They haven't told you anything?" Phillip asked. Jack sat looking at the man and shook his head.

"Ok, think of your brain as the safety deposit box. Besides your safety box is a large file cabinet; these two things store all information for your life. When you start life, your safety deposit box stores things you need when you're a baby, like the smell of your mother. Especially if you were breastfed, the sounds of her voice, and your father's voice if he played a part in your care. As you grow older, those memories are taken out of that box and filed away. These memories never really go away; they just get filed away. The older you get, the more files are made. From when you started school to your first love, it's all in there." Philip said as he pointed to Jack's head.

"Most of those files can be retrieved in the form of remembering or reminiscing. Most people know this as déjà vu; when they were younger, they were brought to a spot, and later on, in life, they come to the same spot and have a flash of a distant memory." Phillip told Jack.

"But in your case, your safety deposit box was broken into, and they locked your file cabinet. I don't know what kind of technique was used to try and erase those early memories. Later when you became a whole person, and by that, I mean your personality. I mean your likes and dislikes and also your moral compass. This would be instilled by your parents, which would also depend on what age the bastards grabbed you at. I will be finding out what kind of behavioral modification they employed on you. So as we go along, I'll be learning as much as you." When Phillip finished, Jack asked.

"Well, why don't you just hypnotize me and see what comes out?" Jack said, not knowing the subtleties of the process. Jack thought being hypnotized would be like what he had read about. There would be some guy sitting in a chair and another with a large gold pocket watch. It turned out it wasn't like that at all; as Phillip sat on the edge of his chair, he started to speak to Jack in a soft, even tone. The soft and even tone came naturally to Phillip. Though he was a smaller man than Jack, he had a voice that would have commanded the respect of the legions of Rome. It reminded Jack of the famous actor James Earl Jones and the baritone voice he cultivated throughout Hollywood. He thought like the actor. Phillip held the same striking looks, and along with his voice, it made a first impression that people liked.

All at once, Jack was in the chair. He could feel the rage in him. It blanketed him, burned through him. The urge to rend, to rip and tear, to kill seemed to fill him. His fingers clawed open the leather arms of the chair. His throat was burning, his mouth hung open, and he could still hear the scream of rage cut off when Phillip ordered him out of the trance he had induced.

"How do you feel, Jack?" Phillip was asking when the door to the office burst open, and Richard stormed in with an armed guard in tow.

"I heard a scream. Is everything?" Richard was going to ask when Phillip interrupted him.

"Everything is fine. I told you that these sessions might get quite involved, and some might even come to the point where I might have to restrain Jack." Richard stood looking at Jack, then at Phillip, then back to Jack.

"Yes, yes you did; sorry about all this." Richard apologized as he backed out the door, closing it as he left.

"What the hell happened, one minute, I'm in this chair, and the next, I'm back? I know that it's later in the afternoon, and my hands and forearms feel like I was trying to tear cement blocks apart." As Jack spoke, he watched as Phillip nodded, then came around to sit in his chair again.

"When Richard first approached me about you, he told me what happened to you. He told me you think you saw your mother and father killed." As Phillip recounted his and Richard's first meeting. Jack sat and nodded over the points he knew of.

"When you found this Mike Styles in the crashed helicopter, you say he told you the boy with you was your cousin, not your brother?" Phillip recounted. Jack looked at his hands and nodded to this question, afraid of where it might lead him. Jack still felt the heat of the rage built in him while he was under hypnosis. Jack looked at Philip as the man sat forward on his chair; Philip told Jack to relax. Then he started to reveal what had taken place so long ago. After Philip finished telling Jack what he had learned in their first session, both men sat silent for quite some time. Philip sat waiting for a reaction, and Jack sat stunned into silence. Silently Jack stood and left the office; he nodded as he walked past Richard.

"Can you help him?" Richard asked Phillip.

"Well, I can take him back to the point where he was taken to the orphanage. He remembers the head of the program, and he shouldn't, good lord, he shouldn't. His mind has found a way around some of the more minor blocks they have installed in him, but the major ones still remain strong." Richard sipped his tea as Phillip continued.

"It's these blocks that concern me, that unaccounted burst of rage you heard this afternoon; that was my first attempt at dropping a minor block, so you could have a name to go after," Phillip said. Richard looked at him, then at the ceiling.

"Do you think it's worth the effort? Can he be made a whole person again?" Richard asked.

"Well, he is a whole person now. When whoever did this to Jack not only tried to erase his moral coding, they tried to reinvent his personality. They did the right thing by grabbing him early, but they weren't early enough. His parents had taught him well in his formidable years. He knew the difference between right and wrong." Phillip told Richard. Then what was revealed in his first session with Jack?

"The act that solidified their hold on Jack was his cousin. They brought his cousin out and concocted a scene where Jack was forced to kill his cousin. He had to do this to save a woman who was with Jack from the moment he arrived at the center. This, and I use the term loosely, the lady helped in the torture that allowed the others to reinvent his mind." Richards's cup of tea hovered between the table and his lips.

"The unconscionable bastards to do that to a child; it's no wonder the man has rage!" Richard said angrily. Phillip nodded his head in agreement. He watched Richard's hand holding his tea start to shake from his own rage over the act just described to him.

"It gets worse after Jack kills his cousin; the bastards lock Jack in the room with the boys' corps, for the night, with no source of light. This single act allowed them to tear down his moral code and install their own. They essentially shattered his young mind."

"What happens if we are successful? What becomes of Jack?" Richard asked, looking out the grand window of the Dorchester.

"That's the part I need to talk to you about. If I can break through all the walls they have installed in Jack, and I mean 'if.' There is a very good possibility Jack will be so damaged by the past and his recollection of it. Well, he might have to be put in a home, he could slip into a catatonic state, and we may never be able to pull him back. I think we need to discuss this with him." Phillip said. Richard watched as a breeze caressed the nodding heads of the Dorchester's white roses.

Chapter 87

WHEN THE NEW SCHOOL opened, Chow smiled and thanked the students for inviting him to the opening on the monitor he had bought for the school. It was a Cisco smart board; Chow explained he couldn't go because he had a meeting he couldn't miss. Chow asked Liz if she would go for him and take pictures of the ribbon being cut by the village elders. Chow smiled at pictures of her standing beside an old man with long braids hanging down his side. When he joked about using the scissors to give one of the elders a haircut. Liz laughed and kissed him on top of his head. Chow watched as Liz walked past him, she was a beautiful woman, and she worked hard to keep her body fit and limber. As Liz passed, he reached out and rubbed her ass. She smiled at him, stopped at the door, and winked at Chow. With her index finger made the come to my gesture. They spent the rest of the afternoon making love in the master suite. When evening came, they showered. Though he didn't think it was possible, Liz managed to arouse him again and offered him a quickie under the shower's hot water.

Li came every three months and met Liz once; Chow was impressed by Li's dress. He always came clean-shaven with a freshly cut head of hair. The cut was always business-like, parted on the left and razor cut on the back and sides. He wore tailored three-piece suits. When Li spoke using English during the last meeting. Chow stood and walked over to Li and placed both hands on Li's shoulders like a proud father. Chow thought this man was even better than Mike could ever hope to be. Li was willing to change and grow, whereas Mike thought he was finished and could get no better. As for Mike, Chow didn't miss the man at all Chow thought about Mike lying dead somewhere in Tibet. With the insects cleaning his bones, Chow thought it was fitting Mike be lost forever; it was his fault John Smyth came to Hong Kong. When he was looking for someone to do the dirty work, Mike devised a plan to use John. The man would be perfect, Mike said, and look what had happened; Mike deserved what he got.

"What do you mean I might have to live in a home?" Jack asked. Astonished at this turn of the conversation, he looked at the two men sitting across from him. John was going to tell them if it came to that, then he would have to stop. It wasn't that he was afraid of the outcome; he had taken responsibility for Jiao and Tran, and he didn't feel that being locked in a home was helping them.

"If we keep going and break down the walls in your mind, it might be too much for you to grasp. I'm afraid you'll shut down." Phillip told Jack. Richard was sitting, nodding his agreement in the second chair.

"Can we do it a little at a time, so I have time to adjust?" Jack asked. Time was vital, he thought.

"Yes, I can do that, but you must understand. If I break through one wall, then doing so might cause the others to fall. It's called the domino effect." Phillip said. In his mind's eye, Jack could see the dominions falling in a line.

"Then that's what I want; I need to know who I was meant to be. Who my mother and father were, where I come from, I still have to be in my right mind for Jiao and Tran." Jack told the two men. Richard understood and admired Jack for his bravery and looked at Jack in a new light. The man could lose his mind, Richard thought, but he still worried about his friends first.

"Now, if you'll excuse me, gentlemen, I need to go and let the Americans know that we have this disgusting cradle operation." As

Richard said the word of the secret C.I.A. operation, he looked like he had bitten into a lemon.

Chapter 88

CRADLE, HOLY SHIT, he thought that futile experiment was long behind him. Now some limy bastard found it and went to the top of the food chain in Washington with it.

"Who the fuck told him about cradle!" Hollyford shouted into the phone. On the other end of the long-distance call was the current Director of the C.I.A. Neither man liked the other. To be honest, one wouldn't waste his time pissing on the other's head if his hair was on fire.

"I don't know how the fuck he got it or who gave it to him but understand this, you stupid old son of a bitch, I'll not let your fuck ups hurt this agency anymore. If it lands on my doorstep, I'll hang it around your fucking neck, right in front of Congress and the President!" The current Director shouted back before slamming down the receiver on his phone. The disgraced former Director of the C.I.A. knew his bid to become the next senator, for his home state of Montana was over. If he was lucky enough to stay out of prison for signing off on the project in the first place would be a miracle, he would never be able to show his face in public again.

After the current Director had slammed the phone down in the ear of his predecessor. He turned to look at the vice chairmen of the Joint Chiefs and the current vice president of the United States. Attached to the phone was a machine used to measure stress in the voice of the person on the other end of the call. A young man sat behind a laptop, watching the readings as they rolled across his screen. The technician looked at the Director and nodded to an unasked question.

"Yes, sir, when you said the word 'cradle,' his stress level went through the roof, then when you told him the English had it. Well, sir, I can hear the handset of his phone creaking from him, squeezing it so tightly. As you were chewing him out, I could hear him grinding his teeth." The Director thanked the young man, who nodded and left the office after dismantling the equipment. The rest of the men sat in silence until the soundproof door to the office silently closed.

"Call Richard, and see what it's going to take to keep this quiet, then get back to me, and I'll tell the President. He's going to have a stroke when he finds out about this." The vice-president said as he stood to leave. Both the Director and the vice-chairmen stood and watched as the vice president walked out the door. Both men knew how the President felt about the exploitation of children, and now to find out, your country's spy agency was involved in the murder and kidnapping of families. Then the torture of young kids just to serve the twisted whims of a man protected by his family's money his whole life, the roof will be lifted off the white house tonight.

"Well, holy shit, what the fuck went on around here before you took over?" Asked the vice-chair; he was a big man when in uniform, his chest dripped with medals earned in Vietnam and many other areas around the world. His name was Wyatt Whistler. The men who served with him called him 'the whisper' for a good reason. The Director looked at his old friend and shook his head.

"I don't know, but every two or three months, something that idiot ok'd jumps up and tries to bite me in the dick. I'm telling you, I'm getting tired of it." The Director told his friend. "Now there's some scuttlebutt floating around that a section chief from Hong Kong didn't die in a plane crash like we thought. Rumour has it the man faked his plane crash." The Director informed 'The Whisper.'

"I know I don't fly, but how the hell can you fake a plane crash?" The Whisper asked. The current Director of the C.I.A. had been a pilot for the American Marines. He met Wyatt in Vietnam when he was shot down and taken as a P.O.W. The Whisper and his unit of expeditionary first-strike marines watched him go down and later found and killed all the North Vietnam soldiers. They freed the Director and ten army rangers who were captured, and both men remained friends over the years.

"How in the name of Christ was this man left in this office for so long?" The General asked.

"A very rich and a very powerful family helped. That fucker's family held controlling interest in most of the oil wells from northern Texas to Montana. He was kept from going to Vietnam by his daddy. Then given this job after the old man died, sort of a way to pay the old man back for all the oil he'd given to the strategic oil reserves." The Director said.

"Well, in the words of my granddaddy, 'this won't do at all' It's time your predecessor comes to account for his decisions while he sat in that chair," The General stated. The smile on the General's face told C. Stephen Willson what his old friend was thinking.

Richard sat in front of the oversized liquid plasma screen watching the current Director of the C.I.A. and the vice-chair of the America Joint Chiefs of Staff as they tried to explain what they were thinking to do with the former Director of the C.I.A.

"Do you folks still have that little bank. The one on that little island off the coast in Northern Scotland?" The Director asked Richard.

"Yes, if you're talking about Oddsta Island, in the Shetland Islands, we still have one or two active accounts open there." Richard smiled as he finished.

"Well, could we make a deposit there? We would pay for the upkeep of the deposit, of course. As with all deposits we make, this one would be a lifetime account." The Whisper said as he shuffled some papers; Richard loved all this cloak and dagger stuff.

"I'll have the paperwork on your account ready upon your arrival. Director, General." With that, Richard signed off.

"Now, what about the dead section chief from Hong Kong?" The Whisper asked, looking at his friend.

"That's easy. We find this Chow and make his plane crash a reality." Said the C.I.A. Director, "Or do you think we might use the cells for him as well? After all, what he's done amounts to treason?" Both men looked at the plasma screen and decided to call Richard back.

Chow and Li celebrated their goal of taking over the drug trade from Asia to Europe and the U.S. The Russians tried to stop them, but with better weapons and the willingness to go into their homes and kill their entire families. Including, in one case, an infant child. The Russians backed down and now worked for Chow, though they didn't know it. With the last of the families in Europe falling under his control, Chow now had ninety percent of the drug market tied up. Li came to him with a plan to get Muslim teens to sell their drugs for them, saying they could target Christens and Jews. Li told these kids they would be doing great work. Most of the kids tried to keep the money when they came up short. Li would tell their ring boss to cut off a hand. If the kid went to the police or told anyone at their temple, he would have their family killed before he killed the kid.

Li informed Chow they made so much money he had to store it in warehouses. He had staff putting the cash into ten million dollar bundles, then stacking it on pallets. Li thought Chow would bust when he told Chow he had a sea container full to overflowing with pallets of cash. The money was coming in faster than they could move it, Li finished. Chow sat and thought; in all his life, he didn't think this would be a problem he would ever have to address. But here it was, and the thought of it made him laugh, making money faster than he could ship it. Truckloads of money, hell if this kept up, he could afford to buy Fiji. Sitting on the veranda, Chow thought for a moment, then smiled.

"Ok, I want you to go Korea; I will have bought a small container ship and will have it sailed to the docks. You are going to load the container on the ship and have it sailed out into international waters. Then whenever you have another container loaded, we'll bring the ship in for the container. As we wait for each container, we will have to try and launder the money. This means our legal business will have to become more involved." Li was nodding his head as Chow finished.

Chapter 88

RICHARD INFORMED JACK the man who ordered his mother and father killed when he was a child was going to be dropped into a secret prison. This prison had been built for this reason; it was for men and women who held enormous power and influence. These men or women used their power for their own gain through illegal and immoral ways, often with monstrous results. Richard explained this prison was built and maintained by the section of the U.N. that he ran.

"Once a person is sentenced to this place, there is no escape, no parole. Every person living in a cell on that island is going to die there; they don't even leave the island when they are dead." Richard told Jack. Jack nodded, then gave Richard a look that chilled him.

"I want to be there. I have to be there when the bastard is brought into this prison. I want to tell him it was me; I put him there. This is the kindest punishment for him, rather than me finding him at his home, alone." Jack said.

"I think that will do you some good, a bit of closure and all that," Richard said as Phillip nodded his agreement.

"Then I'm going to hunt down that bastard Chow." Richard held up his hand to stop Jack.

"The Americans are looking for him now, and I think I know how we can help them, but not until we are all face to face," Richard said.

Jack couldn't believe how hard the northern winter winds bit into the flesh of his face. He and Tran, along with the four journalists, escaped from Tibet and made their run through Bhutan and India. They did it in late spring and early summer. Now tiny specks of ice slashed at his cheeks as the wind sought to leave its teeth marks in his flesh. Jack read a book once where the writer expounded how vicious the wolves of the winter winds were. At the time, Jack thought the writer sought to gain the reader's sympathy about his struggles in the North.

Jack wasn't sure if the writer wanted sympathy or if he was trying to instill fear of the winter winds. Richard brought him here to witness the imprisonment of a man who ordered the killing of men and women he thought opposed him. This man didn't care if the opposition was real or imagined. If their children were suitable, they were forced into the 'cradle' program. If not, then the kids disappeared with their parents. Jack wondered how many were out there like him, being used, killed, dead, or dying. Jack asked Richard if there was any way they could find out and try to help the others. The program records were destroyed when Hollyford was forced to shut down CRADLE. Unfortunately, like their families, most of the others will be lost to time.

Jack couldn't hear anything over the constant rage of the wind. It was accompanied by a grating undertone as the ice pellets skittered across the frozen landscape. Jack turned and looked at the only entrance or exit to the ultra-secret and beyond ultra-secure facility built under the flat stone plain of this island. The opening was built into the only stone outcropping that rose from the flat table of the island. The whole island was so dark grey that it looked black most of the winter. The portal into this island's secret could only be seen from one direction. The only thing in that direction was the cold deep grey of the North Sea with its fierce winds and brooding temperament.

Jack looked at the door; he knew it couldn't be seen from a boat or plane because of the way the door was built and then painted with a non-reflective coating. The entrance looked like the rocks surrounding it; Jack could hardly see it from thirty feet away. From under the sound of the winter storm, Jack heard the beating rotors of a helicopter. Jack tried to discern which direction the chopper was coming in from. He could only wait until the pilot turned on his powerful landing lights.

The American pave hawk military chopper landed fifty feet from the door. Nothing was on the island that would've told the pilot there was anything here other than Jack. Even then, Jack was wearing a black winter Gore-Tex survival suit. Before the pilot powered down the heavy pave hawk, the left side door slid back, and a large man wearing a heavy parka jumped to the ground. Jack watched as the man lifted a hooded man to the ground. A third parka-clad man jumped to the ground, then both men grabbed the hooded man by the elbows and escorted him to where Jack stood.

Without saying a word, Jack nodded and led the trio to the door on the island. Jack held the door against the wind as the others marched into the four-man elevator waiting for them. Once in the elevator, Jack could see the men better; both men were in their late fifties or early sixties. The taller of the two had a heavy Texas drawl to his speech, while the other sounded like he hailed from the Boston area. The Texan stood ramrod straight while his friend had a slight stoop to him. To Jack, it looked like the man had sustained a back injury at some time. None of the men in the elevator made a sound; he could hear the man in the hood breathing heavily.

Fear will do that. It causes the heart rate to speed up, which is part of the fight or flight response. Jack remembered one of his instructors told him it was a natural primitive response. The instructor taught him how to use it and not to give in to it. This man was giving into the fear; his fear had him; he didn't have his fear. Jack looked at the hooded figure as they stood, waiting for the doors to open. All his hate and fear stood two feet away. He could just reach out and snap this man's neck, quick and painless, to the east. Way too easy, Jack thought.

The doors opened with a hiss of air actuators, and there was no 'ding' to announce the floor. This prison only had one floor; it was Fifty feet below the island's surface. One floor, only one way in and one way out, no daylight. Air was exchanged through the elevator. Everything came and went by elevator, air, food, the living, and the dead. Jack was told if any group tried to break into the prison, explosives planted in the shaft would be detonated and seal the shaft. The same would occur if a breakout was ever attempted. This would seal the prison until the unit could get in. When Jack asked about his people in this secret prison, Richard smiled. He told Jack the living quarters for the guards were separated from the cells, and the staff could live for over a month. While the prisoners would die after a week of no food or water. Jack watched as the door to the elevator hissed open.

"General, Director." Richard was there to greet them. When the hooded man heard the term director, he brought his head up.

"Not talking to you, cretin." The General said as he gave the hooded man a shake. Richard smiled as he turned and walked past two heavily armed guards. The procession started down a long hallway.

"You can take the hood off now, Jack," Richard said. The former Director of the C.I.A. stood in the middle of a hallway looking for a way out. Hollyford knew his replacement; he was there when they had taken him from the Langley after Chow set him up. Hollyford was thrown so far out of the government he could not even touch the section chief of Hong Kong. The second man in the room also knew General Whistler. The new Director was also there when he was grabbed right out of his house. It was the General who made him watch as a corps had been placed in his bed then the house had been set on fire. Bad wiring, the General had joked; his home was custom built, and it was in the foothills overlooking the Ruby Valley. The other two, he had no idea who they were. The fat one was English, and the younger one must be American. The younger one, the one they call Jack, scared the former Director. This man just stood staring at the former Director. Then he spoke.

"Do you know who I am?" Jack asked.

Looking around to make sure he was the one the question had been directed to.

"I don't know you or what this is all about." Hollyford wanted to sit down.

"You ordered my mother and father killed," Jack said to the sweating former Director of the C.I.A.

"Oh, you have got it wrong; I haven't been the Director for almost a year. This is the man you want." Hollyford said. The former Director said as he pointed a thumb at his replacement.

"DO I LOOK LIKE I'M TEN FUCKING YEARS OLD!!!" Jack roared so loudly that all the men in the room except for the General jumped. Jack could feel the rage that swept over him with Philip on their first session start to rise in him again. It must have been apparent on his face. When he turned away from Hollyford, Jack caught Richards's eye and saw the look of concern from his friend.

The former Director had started to sweat profusely. Jack could see tears of fear straining on his bottom eyelids. He could smell the older man sweating; Hollyfords fear was coming through his pores. The man was starting to smell, making the General look down at the man with disgust. Jack looked at Richard; he was fighting to calm himself. Richard nodded so slightly most people would have missed it; Richard knew what Jack wanted him to do.

"When you were the Director of the C.I.A., you ordered the deaths of people who opposed you. Whether the opposition was real or imagined, of those people, most had children. If the poor child was of a suitable age, he or she was turned over to a program called 'cradle'; if not, they were killed and buried with their parents." Richard stated as if giving testimony in front of a courtroom. Richard watched as the former Director of the C.I.A. started to think of a way out. All he could think of was deny it, all of it.

"Cradle, it never existed; I don't know what you're talking about," Hollyford said shakily.

"Well, I think you might want to rethink that line of rebuttal. You see, this man standing in front of you is a product of your program, and he can remember his parents." Richard said as he patted Jack's shoulder.

"Bullshit, I was told that...." Hollyford stopped speaking before he could say anymore. Jack turned, staring at the older man; he was holding his rage in check, not winning but not giving into it either.

"All we want is the names of the sick bastards who invented the program," Richard said, then continued.

"If you give up the people who thought up the conditioning, then you will live a happy life. If you insist on being stubborn, I'll let Jack at you, and you will talk. Afterward, you will be changing your colostomy bags, I promise." Richard said. To prove his point, Jack drove his knee into the former Director's groin so hard the blow lifted the man off the floor two feet before dropping him to the cement. Hollyford couldn't breathe; the pain in his groin was all-encompassing. The hall was spinning away into the distance. He was going to pass out, Hollyford thought when a viscous slap brought him rocketing back from the edge of unconsciousness. He looked up into Jack's face, and for the first time, Hollyford knew what absolute terror felt like.

"At this point, I want you to keep your fucking mouth shut, please," Jack said through clenched teeth. Jack held Hollyford on the floor, one of his large fists clenching the older man's shirt together at his throat.

Before he could stop himself, G.W. Hollyford was giving names of some of the most highly respected men and women in the field of psychology. Once the names started to flow out, he was powerless to stop them; it was as if a damn had burst in him. Some men and women the former Director named were tenured professors at Ivy League schools, schools like Harvard, Yale and, Stanford, Berkeley. Richard was shocked when the name of a man who was a professor at Oxbridge came from Hollyfords mouth. Two of the people he named still did consulting work for the U.S. federal government. Their work centered on many of the soldiers that suffered from post-traumatic shock.

"You're not going to hurt me again, are you?" Hollyford whimpered from the floor. The three men looked down on the quivering man; General Whistler wanted to stand the man up and slap him for being so much the coward. Richard and the new Director of the C.I.A. were disgusted by the man's show of spinelessness, and Jack just wanted to be away from him. His rage was gone now; Jack stood and looked down on the broken Hollyford. Jack could feel himself wanting to be sick.

A tear slid down Hollyford's face as he was led down a corridor. Every thirty feet, a large bullet-resistant window made of polycarbonate allowed a view of large cells. Though these cells are larger than the typical prison cell, the prisoners here will never see the outside again, not even after they die.

"This facility can house one hundred of the world's worst. Right now, we have only thirty here. This is where you will spend the rest of your natural life." Richard said as the door to one of the cells rolled open.

"But I told you everything you wanted to know. I know my rights. Everything I did, I did while in the office of the Director of the C.I.A. The only person who can hold me to account is the President." The former Director argued.

"You're not in the U.S. anymore, so as far as your rights go, you left them behind when you crossed into international waters, as for your second argument about who can and cannot hold you to account. The current President had to sign for your incarceration here when we told him about your little experiment with young kids and how you murdered their parents. The President was all too happy to place his name on the paper that brought you here. You should know once he is out of office, the paperwork showing you're here is destroyed." The current Director of the C.I.A. said as he pushed the older man into the cell.

"You can't do this to me; I have friends, they will wonder ..." G.W. Hollyford started to say. Then the former Director of the C.I.A. was forced to watch as the heavy concrete and steel door with the polycarbonate widow rolled closed. The concrete door rolled shut with a bang; it proved the finality of his position, and Hollyford's rebuttal was cut off. Hollyford watched as his replacement reached for something on the wall, then his voice came through a shielded speaker above the door to the cell.

"Remember, your dead, the victim of a tragic house fire." C. Steven Wilson, the current Director of the C.I.A., said. Hollyford listened to the final lock click into place, rendering the door unmovable. Hollyford turned and looked at his new home, a bed jutted out from the wall on one side of the twenty by twenty-cell. There was a bathroom that afforded him no absolute privacy; it had a flush, a stand-up shower, and a sink. A small table and that was all, no television, no window, nothing else.

When Hollyford turned back to the Lexan window, he found the four men who brought him to this cell had stepped back. Another man had stepped to the window. This new man had a look of finality. Hollyford knew this would be the man in charge of this place; he wondered if he could somehow convince this man that he shouldn't be there. A second look at the man told Hollyford his pleas would fall on deaf ears.

"Mr. Hollyford, in this facility, I am the law; all the guards work under me. I am what you would call the Warden. If you have a problem with how you are treated, I could care less. This is not going to be some cozzie camp. You are here because your own country is ashamed of your existence." The Warden said in a heavy Scottish inflection.

"You will have no contact with the outside world. If you want to read, we have a library; it never changes. In this facility, we housed men who had read the entire library three times before they died. You will not live that long. You will not be permitted to know the date, nor if it is day or night. Your meals will come three times a day; the days and the meals never change, so you will not need a menu. You will shower daily and change your clothing daily. If you refuse to follow this rule, you will be washed with the aid of a fire hose. You can see there is neither radio nor television nor will you ever be allowed a newspaper." The Warden stated.

"If you try to talk to a guard or ask the date or time, and if you fail to keep your cell to my standards, then you will be punished. Most men here are only punished once, only once." The Warden repeated as he watched tears stream down G.W. Hollyford's face. This man had seen the world's worst; this was the first time he had had one cry. The Warden liked the man less now than when he heard why he was coming to this facility. This man was married, and he and his wife tried for years to have children to no avail. When the Warden heard that this monster had ordered the murder and kidnapping of young kids, he was too happy to have him brought here.

"This is now your home, and in it, you'll stay until the day you die. When that glorious day happens, your body will be removed and incinerated. Your ashes will then be taken to a small landfill on the lea side of the island and disposed of." The Warden watched as the man sat on a chair and cried unabashedly.

"You have murdered innocent husbands, wives, and children; families have been lost to the tides of time. You have ripped the memories from childhood and used those lost children for your own sick and twisted ends. Now that someone has decided you must pay for these actions, you dare sit and cry." Torquil, the Scottish Warden of this prison that did not exist, said to the weeping figure of G.W. Hollyford.

"You'll not find the pity you crave at this moment, and for crying as you are, the next forty-eight hours will be spent in darkness." When the Warden finished speaking, a dark liquid started to fill a space between the two sheets of Lexan that made up his only widow. Then the lights went out, and the ex-director of the C.I.A., a man who thought he could do no wrong, started to scream. The last face he saw was Jacks, smiling at him as the window filled with the black liquid.

"They usually scream themselves horse, then once they realize we can't hear them, they smarten up." The Warden said. Jack smiled as he imagined Hollyford screaming as the lights slowly dimmed to nothing in Hollyfords subterranean prison. The man was responsible for an unknown number of murders and the kidnapping of children. Jack thought he would like to stay and see what the man looked like after his first week in here. Richard and Jack left with the American Director of the C.I.A. and the General. The winds still screamed across the flat stone plain of the island; for some reason, it didn't seem as cold to Jack.

"How is it going?" Tran asked as he walked into the living room of the house he and Jack shared.

"Still looking for Chow; in time, I'll find him," Jack said.

Chapter 89

CHOW HEARD THE KNOCK on the door; he still lived alone though Liz would spend the nights with him. When she traveled back to Australia, he would start to miss her warm body beside him. Chow thought about Liz; he smiled as he felt he was becoming domesticated. Walking over to the front door Chow opened it to find an official census taker for the Fijian government smiling at him.

"Good morning, sir; I am part of a group from the government taking the official census for Fiji. Could I please have a moment of your time?" The smiling twenty-something said as he held his clipboard in front of his chest.

Chow smiled. "Sure, how may I help you," Chow said, trying to be friendly.

"Can you tell me how many people live here with you?" the young man asked.

"I live alone," Chow answered. With his smile, Chow was alert to anyone who seemed out of place. Chow knew a man in his position made enemies of everyone he crossed, and he betrayed them all. The young man didn't see the Glock 19 Chow held behind the door in his right hand.

"Really, such a big and lovely home. The others and I thought it would be a large family." The young man said as he looked over his shoulder. Chow could see the young man motioning toward two other young people. These young people were walking down the road with clipboards in hand. Relaxing, Chow smiled and waved to the other census takers as they walked past his drive. After the questions were asked and answered, Chow was handed the clipboard and signed where he was told. Thanking him, the young man turned and walked back to the road, presumably to another house down the way.

One kilometer off the coast of Fiji, a large tandem-hulled yacht lay anchored in a shallow cove off a small volcanic islet. On the topmost part of the yacht, a single man looked through a telescope. When the young man with the clipboard turns and motions over his shoulder at two other people, the watcher catches his movement. Focussing on the man being interviewed, the watcher pushes an innocuous little button on the side of the telescope. A faint click could be heard from the telescope, and the watcher twirled a little knob on the tripod. The man watched as the view changed to another young man with a clipboard. Chow's image is then sent via fiber optics to a computer in the central part of the yacht. From the computer via a satellite link to another computer in a room in the basement of the C.I.A. in Langley. This is where an information technician looked astounded at his monitor.

"Holy shit, that's Chow. The fucker isn't dead." A technician blurted out as the photo of Chow materialized on his computer screen.

"What fucker's not dead?" A rough Texas voice asked.

"This man was thought to be dead, some kind of plane crash, sir." The tech added, sir. He knew the man who asked the question was General Wyatt Whistler.

"Give me that picture and all the information of the location he was sighted in." The General ordered. Once the tech handed a picture over along with the global longitudes and latitudes. The technician knew there would be orders, so he stood and waited for the general to tell him what he wanted.

"Now go back and make sure all this disappears. I don't ever want to see this again. I will have the very best we have to try and find it, so you better do a good job, and son, I mean an outstanding job, do you understand?" The General said. The technician being a civilian, stood and nodded. The technicians in this room had grown used to seeing the General on a daily bases. So they knew when the old man said he would check that he would check and soon. Good to his word, the General had checked, and the technician had indeed made all the information disappear. Then the General, along with the Director of the C.I.A., called Richard.

"Fiji, what do you mean, you think he's on Fiji?" Richard asked. Jack walked through the door of his and Tran's rented house on the beautiful island of St Martins. The island sat on the most southerly tip of the British Isles,

"Who's in Fiji?" Jack asked Tran, who was sitting in the room looking at his new fishing rod.

"Richard and the C.I.A. might have found your Chow, but they need to confirm it," Tran stated. He spooled fishing line on the heavy deep-sea reel Jack had given him as a gift.

"Before you get all set to, go and kill this man. We are going to wait for confirmation of his identity." Richard said as he held up his hand, fearing Jack would run out the door and fly off to the south pacific.

"I don't think I want to go flying around the world right now; Tran and I are going out fishing," Jack said. He couldn't believe finding Chow didn't bring the old anger and the rage out of him. Jack knew the sessions with Phillip were working instead of wanting to find and kill Chow. Jack looked forward to the fishing trip he and Tran planned. Jack was surprised when he didn't have to fake being indifferent about Chow. Jack really just wanted to go fishing. One of the local fishing charter operators offered to take Jack and Tran out into some of the best fishing waters around the islands for the whole day. Jack and Tran are not too keen on spending the day with other tourists. Rented the boat and his services, and they paid enough to make it well worth his time to take only them out. Laughing as he and Tran reached the docks, Jack thanked the captain of the charter and tipped the man and his son. He and Tran had great luck catching fish while out off some of the small islets doting the waters off the south coast of England.

The boat owner and captain gave Jack his wife's recipe for the batter; he told Jack if he cooked the cod fish as soon as he got back to his house. It would make the best fish and chips he's ever eaten. Richard took the fish when Jack and Tran reached the house. After the meal, Tran announced that this meal was his first fish and chips. However, he added that it was not his last. For the rest of the night, the three men sat and enjoyed a bottle of scotch. Richard listened as Tran told stories of the trip. Not once was Chow brought up, or what would happen to the man when he was captured. The next day found the men sitting at the breakfast table, sipping hot coffee and eating breakfast. Once Richard sat down, the conversation turned to Chow and what would have to be done with the man.

"I know you want to go down and kill this man, and who could blame you after what he's done. However, let's go about this using our heads. I want to get this man too, but I would also like to get whoever is helping him." Richard said. Tran watched his friend as Jack stood and started to pace.

"I know it's hard to wait; we are getting more information from the Americans along with the Canadians. It looks like he might be tied in with a new and very powerful, very violent, and ultra-secretive criminal organization." Richard said. Both he and Tran watched as Jack stopped pacing. He looked out the window at the blue waters of the English Channel.

"How long?" Jack asked.

"It could take days to confirm; it's hard to say. All we know is Chow is living on the island of Fiji under the assumed name of Lee Mang. This Lee Mang was to have made his money in Canada, in the country's North, in diamonds. He has become romantic with an

Aussie woman. She flies back and forth, trying to raise money for the education system in Fiji. This Mr. Mang has built a school for a remote village and sponsored other building projects." Richard said as he read a report. Tran watched Jack as he heard of Chow's new life. Tran picked up the phone when it rang. Tran thanked whoever was on the line and then hung up.

"We have company," Tran stated. Then turned and walked out of the room. Richard, Tran, and Jack were standing on the porch as C.I.A. director C. Steven Wilson and General W. Whistler walked up the path from the narrow road. The five men shook hands and then entered the house.

"It is confirmed; the fingerprints make it one hundred percent positive Chow is living on the island of Fiji." Director Wilson stated.

"Now, about the rest of it, Chow isn't tied in with the new and powerful organization. The bastard is the head of it. He used C.I.A. funds and our black ops operators to find, then hunt down and kill his competition." With a sigh, the Director finished by shaking his head. They knew Chow was dirty from Jack's debriefing, but how dirty astounded even the C.I.A. and its new Director.

"Another thing we know is Chow's second in command is a man named Li, now this Li, well, he's loyal like your best old hound dog." The General told them.

"He flies from their new base. They bought some docks in Seoul, South Korea; this Li flies to Fiji every three months. Once we found Chow, we found Li. Now we know they have been at this for quite some time; we haven't found the money yet." The General said, looking at Richard and Jack.

"You can go down to Fiji and kill this man, Jack, and no one here would blame you. Not after what the prick did, but we talked this over with Richard, and from what we found, Chow has killed or ordered the killing of children. Hell, he even had the infant granddaughter of a Russian drug boss killed in her crib. I mean to say this bastard needs killing like a rabid dog. We think this would be too quick and easy for him. We would like to stick him in the same prison as Hollyford; what do you think?" The Director asked, looking at Jack.

"This might sound like a ghoulish thing to say, but the billions he's made from human suffering would go a long way in funding our operations throughout the world," Richard added. The men watched as Jack stood and walked out of the room. Tran and Richard, along with the Director and the General, watched as Jack slowly made his way to the dock. Jack walked to the end of the dock and stood looking out to sea. Tran watched his friend stand on the dock in front of the house. He knew the torment his friend went through; Tran could hear it in the nightmares Jack suffered every night; Tran felt the wind on his face as he walked to the dock, slowly heading to where Jack stood now with his head bowed, his black hair being blown around his head.

"This is something you will have to live with; I still live with the face of the Colonel every night. Can you do that with your Chow?" Tran asked as he and Jack stood and watched as the wind blew in from the south whipping a spray from the tops of the waves. In time, Tran heard Jack take a deep breath and blow it out; this was a signal his friend had reached a decision.

"If it were you, Tran, and you had to do it all over again, how would you do it?" Jack asked; it was a question Tran asked himself many times, and he would always come to the same answer, always the same.

"I asked myself this many times, and I would do it the same; I think when we were in Tibet, we did the right thing. Now we are not in Tibet; the right thing to do has changed." Tran said. Standing looking out over the water, Jack nodded his head and then turned to walk back to the house with Tran beside him.

"I know Chow should be punished, so let's get him and send him to Oddsta Island," Jack said. Richard and the other men smiled. "I want to be there again, to see the look and his face. Chow has to know we did this." Jack added, nodding to Tran.

Chapter 90

LI SAT ON THE CHARTERED private jet as it flew over the Philippian Sea at almost the speed of sound. The meal he'd eaten was one of the best Li could remember. Li couldn't remember the name of the lobster in a cream sauce with pasta. He also had four shots of scotch with it. The steward came over and gave him a pillow, along with a blanket, as a feeling of complete peace washed over him. The warm, peaceful feeling sparked panic, a sense of being trapped. The next time Li woke, he was trapped. Somehow he was strapped to a surgical table in a cell.

"What is going on here?" Li tried to ask a man who was sitting outside of the cell. As soon as he spoke, Li knew he was in trouble. The guard nodded to someone he couldn't see, then got up and walked out of the room.

"Well, my little friend, you're in some shit now." An American said. The man had a southern drawl to his speech. Li had never been to the U.S. He had watched enough of their television programming he placed the drawl of this man around Louisiana.

"I want a lawyer; I have rights," Li said. He tried to look around the room. The American stood and walked out to where Li could see him. The man looked like he could eat Li, his beard covering most of his face and dark wraparound sunglasses covering the rest. When the man walked over to the table Li was strapped to, he smiled down at him, Li could feel his bowels loosen.

"Why yes, you do have rights; I don't want you to think we're going to infringe on those rights." The American said. Li thought they were looking for answers, and soon he'd be set free. After all, they can't do anything to get answers if he doesn't want to talk. Li thought he was going to thank the weak American justice system. His smile faded as another man rolled a surgical cart into view; on the cart was an array of needles filled with different colored fluids. The American smiled at him as the first needle was inserted into a intervenes line taped to his left arm. Li could feel a warm feeling wash over him as whatever drug they were using started to course through him. Li knew he was drugged; Li knew it was only a matter of time before he told them all they wanted to know. This wasn't the way it was supposed to happen. In the movies, the bad guy always walks out of the police station with a fancy lawyer beside him. The dumb cops left to watch him walk away. The last thing Li heard before the world faded away into a drug-fuelled haze was the American telling the medic to 'make sure to catheterize him so he doesn't piss all over the place when the second round takes effect.' Li was lying flat on his back. He was still strapped to the table when he opened his eyes. Li was staring into a bright light. The American was still there, standing beside the bed.

"Why hello sunshine, how you doing? You know, you were a good boy, answered all the questions we asked, and turned over all the numbers we needed. I just wanted to thank you for being such a good guy." The American said as he brushed wet hair from Li's forehead. At any other time, it would seem a gesture of affection, but when this man did it and smiled, Li could feel his bowels' loosen a bit more. Another man walked into view and helped remove the straps holding Li to the table. Each man had Li under his arms and brought him out on the deck of a large white yacht.

The sun felt good on his shoulders, and the breeze helped dry the perspiration from his skin. He knew they drugged him to get the location of the money ship and the amount the vessel was carrying. Li also knew they had gotten all the accounts and the amount in them. Li could remember some of the questions and the answers he'd given. The ship's name and the container count and the amount in each container, even where the warehouse was and how many people would be guarding it, he gave them everything.

"I still have rights, and you have violated them. I will never go to jail." Li said. He could hear his voice, and how slurred it was; still, he felt a smile touch his lips.

"You're a pretty smart little fucker ain't ya." The second American holding him said.

"It's too bad you didn't put your brains to work at law school; you might've lived longer." The big American said. As the two men held Li over the railing of the yacht, he could see the patrolling great white sharks attracted by men throwing chum into the water.

"Now me, I'm a bit of an environmentalist," The bearded American stated. "And I was concerned about the drugs we used on you. You know, will the drugs have an adverse effect on a shark if he ate you." The American said. Li stared, horrified, as the sleek grey forms slid under the surface of the blue South Pacific.

"As it turns out, none of the people we talked to knew, so you're going to help advance the knowledge of shark anatomy," The American said. Li felt the knives slice through his thigh muscles just before the big American and the bearded man threw him over the railing. The last thing Li heard was his scream being cut off by the water.

Opening his eyes in time to see the first great white charge out of the deep blue of the ocean brought by the smell of his blood. The sun sparkled off the spray of water as Li broke the surface of the Pacific. His left leg was in the shark's mouth all the way to the thigh, where the femoral artery sprayed blood across the nose of his attacker. Again, Li heard his own incoherent screams as he entered the water. Again Li opened his eyes in time to see a dark arrow-like shape solidify into a shark. The last thing to register in Li's oxygen and blood-starved brain was this second shark coming for his face.

Li never heard the sound of his head being wrenched free from his body or the sounds of his legs being ripped off with the coming of the second shark. His weakened heart gave out a massive coronary, stilling him at the vital last second. Nobody stayed after the first shark attacked Li. The men on the yacht knew what the outcome would be, one less drug dealer in the world.

A call was made to a small house on a small island in the English Channel. Richard answered the call, then said in his quite British way, 'Very good, thank you, good day.' This always made Jack smile.

"So, was it good news, or did the stock markets crash?" Jack asked.

"No, the markets are fine. We have found Chow's money ship, and our unit has taken it over and is now sailing it to the American naval base in Guam. We have emptied all of the accounts we learned about, along with his warehouse in Seoul, South Korea. You're not going to believe it. They found five fifty-three-foot sea containers full to their roofs with pallets of cash waiting for the ship to come and pick them up. The warehouse held currency from all over the world ." Richard told Jack.

"Have you counted what was found at the docks yet?" Jack asked.

"No, not yet; the accounts totaled nine hundred and ten million euros," Richard said.

"As for the hard cash on the docks and on the ship, I've been told it could take as long as two months with a team and machines counting." When Richard finished, the three men sat in the living room of the small blue house, amazed at how much money was made from the suffering of millions of people.

Chapter 91

SITTING UP IN BED, Chow thought he heard something. Sitting in the dark room listening to the night, nothing seemed out of the ordinary. The tropical birds chirped and twittered as they and bats flew through the night, catching insects. Chow convinced himself he'd heard the sound in his sleep while dreaming. Laying down again, Chow never heard the sound of the dart gun being fired. He certainly felt the bite of the dart as it sank deep into his thigh. The name Smyth screamed through his mind as the drug took effect, and Chow blacked out.

Chow could hear muffled voices in the darkness; he didn't know how long he'd been unconscious. When Chow became conscious, he found a medic checking his blood pressure.

"What are you doing? Where am I?" Chow asked. He heard someone behind him. Turning, Chow found himself looking at a fat English man.

"The medic is checking you out for your trip; we wouldn't want you to become ill." The English man stated. Chow knew whatever trip he talked about couldn't be good for him. How could this have happened? He covered his tracks. No one knew who he was, not even Liz. This was the Russians doing this or one of the tirade families. His mind raced in circles looking for an answer, and Chow stopped. He knew who this was; what he didn't know was what would happen next.

"I don't know what's going on. My name is Lee Mang. I have money if that's what you want." Chow said. He hoped this was nothing more than a kidnapping. Turning, Richard looked at the man and chuckled.

"Not anymore; we have found and emptied all your bank accounts and warehouse along with your nice ship. What was yours and made through your criminal activities around the world. Well, we have taken that money to fund our operations around the world. Operations that save lives, not waste them." Richard said. Chow sat stunned by what he heard. Richard sat and watched the shocked expression on Chow's face. A slight tap came from the door. C.I.A. director Wilson opened the door and looked at the once-dead Chow.

"Is he good to go?" The Director asked the medic. Turning, the medic nodded and left the room as a high-pitched whine started. Shutting the door behind them, the two men left Chow sitting on a small cot, wondering what had happened.

Jack and Tran sat playing Texas hold'em porker; the stakes were high. Pretzels were worth ten bucks, Oreo cookies worth fifty dollars, and Reese's pieces worth one hundred.

"I don't know how you're doing it; you must have another deck hidden someplace," Jack said as Tran again beat his two pairs with a straight.

"I win because the gods like me better than you." Tran returned as he bit into one of the peanut butter cups. The air force steward came to tell them to buckle up and to stow everything for take-off. They were seated in the first class section of a converted Boeing 747 jumbo jet. Under them, an extended cargo hold housed one prefabricated ten-foot by ten-foot room. In this room, Chow sat on the edge of the bed and tried to think of what had gone wrong. He was one of the wealthiest men in the world and the head of the most powerful criminal syndicates to ever exist; how could this happen to him.

Jack watched on a monitor as Chow was given another shot and quickly fell asleep. Reaching up, Jack turned off the monitor. He frowned as Tran won another hand, taking his last three pretzels. Smiling, he watched as Richard walked past and ate the three pretzels. The men sat and talked as the plane took off. Twenty-four hours later, Jack watched as the drugged Chow was wheeled off the 747 and into a hanger where their next ride sat, waiting for them. Chow hadn't woken from his last shot until they were in the EH-101 Merlin helicopter. Before Chow could fully regain consciousness, a black hood was placed over his head. Just like Hollyford, Chow wouldn't know where he was going. Sitting between Richard and a guard, Chow kept pleading for them to listen to him.

"You have made a terrible mistake; I haven't done anything wrong; I'm Lee Mang; check my papers." Chow pleaded. The only thing that shut him up was when Richard nodded to the guard sitting on the other side of Chow. The nod brought an elbow to Chow's diaphragm knocking the air from his lungs and leaving him gasping and straining against his harness.

The big Merlin helicopter touched the stone plain on Oddsta, the pilot powered down the big aircraft and gave a thumbs-up to Jack. One of the flight crew opened the helicopter door and Jumped to the ground. At first, Jack didn't think it was possible. He was sure the wind screaming across the stone plain of the island was blowing harder this time. Unlike the last time, the air wasn't filled with ice specks. This night the island greeted him with wind-driven rain. The rain was driven so hard by a never-ending wind it stung Jack's cheek. For Jack, it seemed like the island was protesting his standing on its stone-armored surface. Jack, Richard, and Tran walked to the lone door hidden from view by the familiar upwelling of rock. Two guards half dragged Chow by his handcuffed arms. When they reached the door, Jack stood holding it open. The guards pushed Chow into the elevator, nodding to Jack. Both men turned and walked back to the helicopter. The men looked as if they touched something that would stain their gloves.

Chow knew they were going down; he also knew three men were with him in the elevator. There wasn't any ding or beep to signal they reached a floor, the lift slowly hissed to a stop, and the doors opened.

Jack knew when the doors opened on the elevator, and they stepped out, the doors would close. Jack was going to pull the hood of the man who betrayed his country and him. As Jack reached up to grasp the hood, Richard touched his arm and shook his head. He wanted him to wait a little longer. Jack was surprised to see the Director of the C.I.A. and General Whistler of the Joint Chiefs. Once again, the men shook hands, and all the men were silent. Then Jack smiled, looked at Chow, and turned to Steven Willson, the Director of the C.I.A.

"Paying Hollyford a visit?" Jack asked with a smile. He knew how the General and the Director felt about the man; he knew the answer before they gave it. When Chow had heard the name of Hollyford, he raised his head. He thought he knew the voice of the man who mentioned the name; Chow couldn't be sure. Oh god, he thought, not him, please. Chow's mind screamed at him. It couldn't be true, not John, not John.

Chapter 92

THE HARSH FLUORESCENT lights blinded Chow as one of the men ripped the hood from his head. Chow could see three men standing in front of him; the fat English man was there along with one of the Joint Chiefs. The other man he recognized but for some reason couldn't place him.

"What do...?" Chow had started to speak when the General, some called 'The Whisper,' barked, causing Chow to twitch.

"Shut your mouth; here you do not speak." General Wyatt Whistler barked.

Jack shoved Chow from behind to get him walking. Chow tried to turn to see who was behind him. Tran grabbed him by the left elbow and jerked him forward. The message was clear. He was to walk. Chow understood he was to look forward at all times.

"Chow Yun, you have been found guilty of treason against the United States of America and her allies. You have also been found guilty of dereliction of duty, along with being complacent in the kidnap and torture of your own people. Also, those of the United Kingdom and Canada," Richard stated. Chow knew he was responsible for everything the English man said.

"Along with these many charges, you have also been found guilty of crimes against humanity. These crimes are for the murders of children and their families in your quest for power and wealth in the world's drug and weapons trade." Richard said.

Every time the English man said the words 'found guilty,' Chow felt like he was falling further down the rabbit hole. He thought about telling them they had grabbed the wrong man but gave up.

The large cells stood on the right side of a long corridor. Chow was escorted past fifteen; ten of the cells had men sitting at tables reading or staring at him as he was marched past. Chow recognized four of the men. They were from a watch list; three had been reported as being killed in bombing raids on Al Qaeda headquarters in Afghanistan. While the last cell held the most wanted man in the world. Chow hardly recognized the Saudi-born terrorist. With his hair cut and his long beard shaved, this man was sitting lotus on the floor in deep Buddhist meditation. Chow knew his terrorist followers would kill him if they knew what really happened to their martyr. Once Osama was placed in his cell, it took less than a year for him to convert to Buddhism. The men stopped for a second unable to grasp the image presenting itself to them.

A heavy-set man with a red handlebar mustache stood by a large opening in the wall; the man smiled as Chow was escorted to him. Just as Chow reached the waiting man, a hand grabbed his shoulder and spun him around. It happened so fast that Chow almost lost his balance. When he recovered, Chow knew he would either die right on the spot or wish for it. At over six feet tall, Chow was forced to look up into the eyes of the man he dreaded to see.

"J. Jo, John, let me...." Chow started. Quicker than anyone could imagine. Jack grabbed Chow by the collar snatching the terrified man off his feet. Jack slammed Chow into the wall so hard that Chow pissed his pants.

Only inches separated Chow from the man he most feared in the world. Now he was forced to look into the eyes of the man he gave to General Trang. Then when Jack escaped with Tran and the journalists, he helped the Chinese hunt them throughout Bhutan and India. Chow knew what the people he ordered killed must have felt before they died.

"My name isn't John Smyth; that's the name you fuckers hung on me. My name is Jack; did you really think I would leave you alone with the money, you. The piece of shit who sold me to the Chinese? Don't fuck'n answer; know this it was us, all of us, everyone in this place hunted for you. Every corner of this planet was searched; did you really think we would let you go?" Jack asked. Before Chow could try and beg for mercy, Jack threw him bodily into the cell. Chow scrambled to his feet as a large door started to roll closed. He stared out at the four men he knew and one Asian he had seen on the run with Jack almost two years ago. The men stood and watched as the door banged shut. The man they locked in this tomb walked up to the Lexan window as a tear rolled down his cheek. The man with the big red handlebar mustache stood in front of the cell and pressed a button.

"Chow Yun, you are here because of your actions and the shame they have brought to your country. Unlike the other men you have seen as you were brought to this, your final home. You murdered and turned your back on your country and fellow man for nothing more than wealth and power; no god rules you, only greed." Torquil said as he watched Chow stand at the Lexan window.

"So, for these reasons, you are here. You are also here for the death and destruction of children and families your drugs bring to the populist of the world every year. This cell is your final home; in it, you will remain until you are dead. When that bright day dawns, your body will be removed and cremated. Your ashes will be taken to a landfill and disposed of. You have wasted so many young lives with your drugs. Now you will be treated as waste." The Warden told Chow.

"You will be brought three meals a day; the meals will be the same every week. You will shower and change your clothing every day if you do not. You will be cleaned with the aid of a fire hose, and your cell will be maintained to my satisfaction." The Warden kept speaking. "There is a library, and it never changes; it is a large library. We have men here who have read it twice, and some have made it to a third reading of our library. I doubt you will last that long. You are not permitted to talk to any guard or to ask for the date or time. If you are caught trying to make a calendar or anything to help you keep the time, you will be punished." The large Scottish Warden said.

"You will never again see the sun, moon, or stars; you will eat what you are given and dress in what we say. Welcome to the rest of your life." When the Warden finished, he pushed the button again and stepped back from the Lexan. The men all stood and watched Chow as he stood shaking at the glass.

Chow watched as the four men who brought him to the cell turned and walked away. He tried to yell and quickly realized he couldn't be heard through the thick door. As they started to leave, he ran to the polycarbonate window and tried to punch it, only to be knocked back and stunned by an electrical charge. Laying on the floor, Chow realized at some point he had pissed his pants, then he heard the voice of the red-haired man again.

"Oh, by the way, the window is protected by a thirty thousand-volt stunner. It won't kill you, but it will knock you down. Now, so you don't do that again, you will be punished for two days, forty-eight hours of total darkness, along with a week of bread and broth." The Warden said. As Chow watched, a dark liquid started to fill in the gap between the Lexan windows. Thirty seconds later, Chow was locked in total darkness and had to crawl on his hands and knees to the bed he had seen when he was thrown in there.

Jack would have never thought that this place could have such a glorious office the Warden led them into. Richard sat down in a beautiful French colonial chair; Jack was amazed it didn't break under the strain of supporting the man's almost four hundred pounds. A guard came in and told the Warden Hollyford was at it again.

"That old fool, ok, I'll be along in a moment. Until then, stun him and make sure he goes down." The guard nodded and left smiling.

"Has he been much trouble for you, Torquil?" Richard asked.

"Ey, he has been a right pain in the ass. I think he's trying to kill himself by running at the window and getting stunned." Jack and Tran followed the others as the Warden led them to Hollyford's cell. As Jack watched, two big guards picked the stunned body of G.W. Hollyford off the floor and dumped him on the bed. A medic checked the man over and stood shaking his head.

"Yeah, he'll live; I think we should pad the walls." The medic said. Jack noticed the medic had an Australian accent. The Warden walked into the cell and looked the man over, then walked back out into the corridor and ordered the door closed. Looking at a guard, Torquil told him to put Hollyford on bread and broth for three days and keep his cell lit for forty-eight hours.

"Every time he looks like he nods off, blast him with sound, keep him awake for the whole time." The Warden ordered. Jack looked at the man who killed his mother and father, and all he could do was shake his head at what he saw. At the office, Richard and the Warden, along with the General and the Director, discussed the facility's future. They came to an agreement. The state the world was in now showed the need for this and another facility like it was growing.

"I dread to think the world might require another of these prisons; what does that tell you of the world?" Torquil asked. He walked Jack and the others to the elevator that would take them back into the world above. They all shook hands and watched as Jack walked down the hall to the cell of G.W. Hollyford. He placed both his hands on the lexan and closed his eyes. Leaning so close to the barrier separating him from Hollyford, Jack whispered.

"You took from me all I could have been. Now I take what's left of you." Jack whispered. Only Tran heard Jack; Tran knew what it meant. He had whispered it in the ear of the Colonel in Ningchi. The man that had taken his family and village from him.

The chopper lifted off before the sun rose over the horizon. This was the one thing Richard had stressed. The only times they could go to or leave the island was at night. If there was a storm with a heavy wind, that would be better. No landing lights or strobe lights, nothing, less chance of being seen on a night where only fools would be out, was the way Richard had put it.

Chapter 93

A new beginning

"I KNOW YOU HAVE A LONG way to go before you have it all back," Richard said. Jack and Richard were enjoying breakfast sitting on the deck of the house on the island of St Martin. Both men watched as Tran stood on the small dock and reeled in another fish.

"You know what I'm the head of, and I want to ask you to come and help me," Richard asked. Jack sipped his coffee and watched the sea birds dive for fish. Richard never asked Jack to join him in 'the unit.' He always thought he would know the answer if asked.

"I don't know, Richard; I know you're trying to bring around peace and stop the madness. I don't know who I am, and with what I do know of my past, would I be the best choice for what you want?" Jack asked as he looked into his black coffee. Tran stepped up onto the veranda, then turned and looked out into the distance like he could see the past; when he turned back to Jack, he smiled.

"I know who you are; you are the man who helped me avenge my family and called me a friend when I had nothing in this world. You have given me something new to look forward to." Tran said as his gaze turned to the prayer flags he tied to the railing of the veranda. Jack looked at the wind chimes Tran had hung on the porch. On the bottom of the chimes was a set of keys; these keys were to the Toyota they had used to escape the Chinese through Bhutan and India; Jack smiled.

"You gave me something too old, buddy. Richard, if Tran is going to help you, then I'm in. I want to keep working to find out who

I am." Jack said as he tapped his temple. Tran looked from Jack to Richard then he smiled.

"I will go with Richard, but we pick and choose targets and missions. Only bad men, if we think a mission is not for us, we turn it down no problem." Tran said. Richard looked at the two men and smiled. He knew with these two on board, the madness was in for a fight.

"You run your missions your way, no problem, as long as the job gets done and no collateral damage." Richard finished. The rest of the morning was spent on details Tran thought would be essential, like how to buy the house he and Jack now called home.

A week later, Jack walked into the office assigned to Philip Peters.

"Hello, Jack; ready to try again?" Philip asked as Jack sat down.

"Yeah, I want to remember, but I can't come back every week, doc." Jack started to say.

"I know; Richard called me and told me I was to be stationed with you." Jack wanted to thank the man. Instead, he turned and nodded his head.

"Jack, I want you to understand one thing," Philip said as Jack turned to look at him.

"When we start to tear down the barriers they have built-in you, that's when it will become the hardest for you. Right now, it's like you are standing at the foot of Mount Everest, and you must reach the top." Phillip said as he looked at his big scared patient.

"But when you do finely reach the summit, you are only halfway there. Do you understand?" Philip asked.

"I think so; if you climb up, then you have to climb down, right," Jack answered.

"Yes, but you are making this climb blind without any gear and no sense of touch. This mountain has waited for you ever since Hollyford and the others took you and killed your parents. This climb will be the hardest and most brutal thing you'll ever do in your life. It's going to make running from the Chinese look like a day in the park...Can you do it?" Philip asked.

Jack looked at the floor between his feet, then at his scared callused knuckles.

"I have to; I have to do this climb. I have to remember, not only for myself but for the family I was forced to forget...they deserve to be remembered."

THE END©

WRITTEN BY:

Todd LeRoux

Don't miss out!

Visit the website below and you can sign up to receive emails whenever Todd LeRoux publishes a new book. There's no charge and no obligation.

https://books2read.com/r/B-A-MMEEB-MRBYC

BOOKS 2 READ

Connecting independent readers to independent writers.

Did you love *The Cradle Operation*? Then you should read *The Beginning*[1] by Todd LeRoux!

[2]

As a young boy, Rene watched as his mother was murdered by two men paid by a wealthy man who had raped her. This man knew his father would disown him if he found out a girl his son raped had given birth to a bastard son. Rene was raised by an old man who seemed never to age. Joseph had told Rene of his son, his first son, and how this son was killed by men who feared losing power. Rene watched as Joseph taught him to work with his hands and listened when Joseph spoke of the bible and his first son. Rene would become angry when Joseph said of his mother. Rene knew Joseph was right when he told him how she had loved him. When Rene was seventeen, Joseph told him he was dying and that a man was

---

1. https://books2read.com/u/49aq8W

2. https://books2read.com/u/49aq8W

coming to take him to see his brothers. Rene looked at the door when someone knocked on it; slowly, Rene opened it to a giant of a man. Josephus stood in the rain looking down at Rene; he stepped into the tiny house and went to kneel at Joseph's side.

"You will go with Josephus. He is your brother. He will finish training you for what is to come." Joseph said before he died. That night, Rene started his new life with a man he didn't know, a man bearing terrible pain and hiding a horrid curse.

Read more at https://www.toddleroux.com/.

About the Author

Todd lives on the banks of the Miramichi river. After years of working away, he now enjoys his time at home with family and friends.

Read more at https://www.toddleroux.com/.